BABOUSHKA

Criminals whisper her name in fear!

BABOUSHKA

The enigmatic heiress to a noble Russian line
— socialite by day, assassin by night!

BABOUSHKA

Blackmailed by the US government to carry out
dirty jobs even the CIA can't sanction!

BABOUSHKA

You might think she's a hero.
That would be a mistake.

image

★ MISSION BRIEFING ★
ANTONY JOHNSTON

★ HIDDEN CAMERAS ★
SHARI CHANKHAMMA

★ TRANSCRIPT ★
SIMON BOWLAND

★ EXTERNAL STAGING ★
SHARI CHANKHAMMA

★ CONTINGENCIES ★
TULA LOTAY
LEILA DEL DUCA
ANNIE WU
TESS FOWLER
KATE LETH

IMAGE COMICS, INC.
Robert Kirkman – Chief Operating Officer
Erik Larsen – Chief Financial Officer
Todd McFarlane – President
Marc Silvestri – Chief Executive Officer
Jim Valentino – Vice-President

Eric Stephenson – Publisher
Corey Murphy – Director of Sales
Jeff Boison – Director of Publishing Planning & Book Trade Sales
Jeremy Sullivan – Director of Digital Sales
Kat Salazar – Director of PR & Marketing
Emily Miller – Director of Operations
Branwyn Bigglestone – Senior Accounts Manager
Sarah Mello – Accounts Manager
Drew Gill – Art Director
Jonathan Chan – Production Manager
Meredith Wallace – Print Manager
Briah Skelly – Publicity Assistant
Sasha Head – Sales & Marketing Production Designer
Randy Okamura – Digital Production Designer
David Brothers – Branding Manager
Ally Power – Content Manager
Addison Duke – Production Artist
Vincent Kukua – Production Artist
Tricia Ramos – Production Artist
Jeff Stang – Direct Market Sales Representative
Emilio Bautista – Digital Sales Associate
Leanna Caunter – Accounting Assistant
Chloe Ramos-Peterson – Administrative Assistant
IMAGECOMICS.COM

CODENAME BABOUSHKA, VOL 1. FIRST PRINTING. MAY 2016.

Published by Image Comics, Inc. Office of publication: 2001 Center Street, 6th Floor, Berkeley, CA 94704.

ISBN: 978-1-63215-678-5. Contains material originally published in magazine form as CODENAME BABOUSHKA #1-5.

Copyright © 2016 Antony Johnston & Shari Chankhamma. All rights reserved. CODENAME BABOUSHKA (including all prominent characters featured herein), its logo and all character likenesses are trademarks of Antony Johnston & Shari Chankhamma, unless otherwise noted. Image Comics® and its logos are registered trademarks and copyrights of Image Comics, Inc. All rights reserved.

No part of this publication may be reproduced or transmitted, in any form or by any means (except for short excerpts for review purposes) without the express written permission of Image Comics, Inc. All names, characters, events and locales in this publication are entirely fictional. Any resemblance to actual persons (living or dead), events or places, without satiric intent, is coincidental. Printed in the U.S.A. For information regarding the CPSIA on this printed material call: 203-595-3636 and provide reference # RICH-676541.

For international rights, contact: foreignlicensing@imagecomics.com

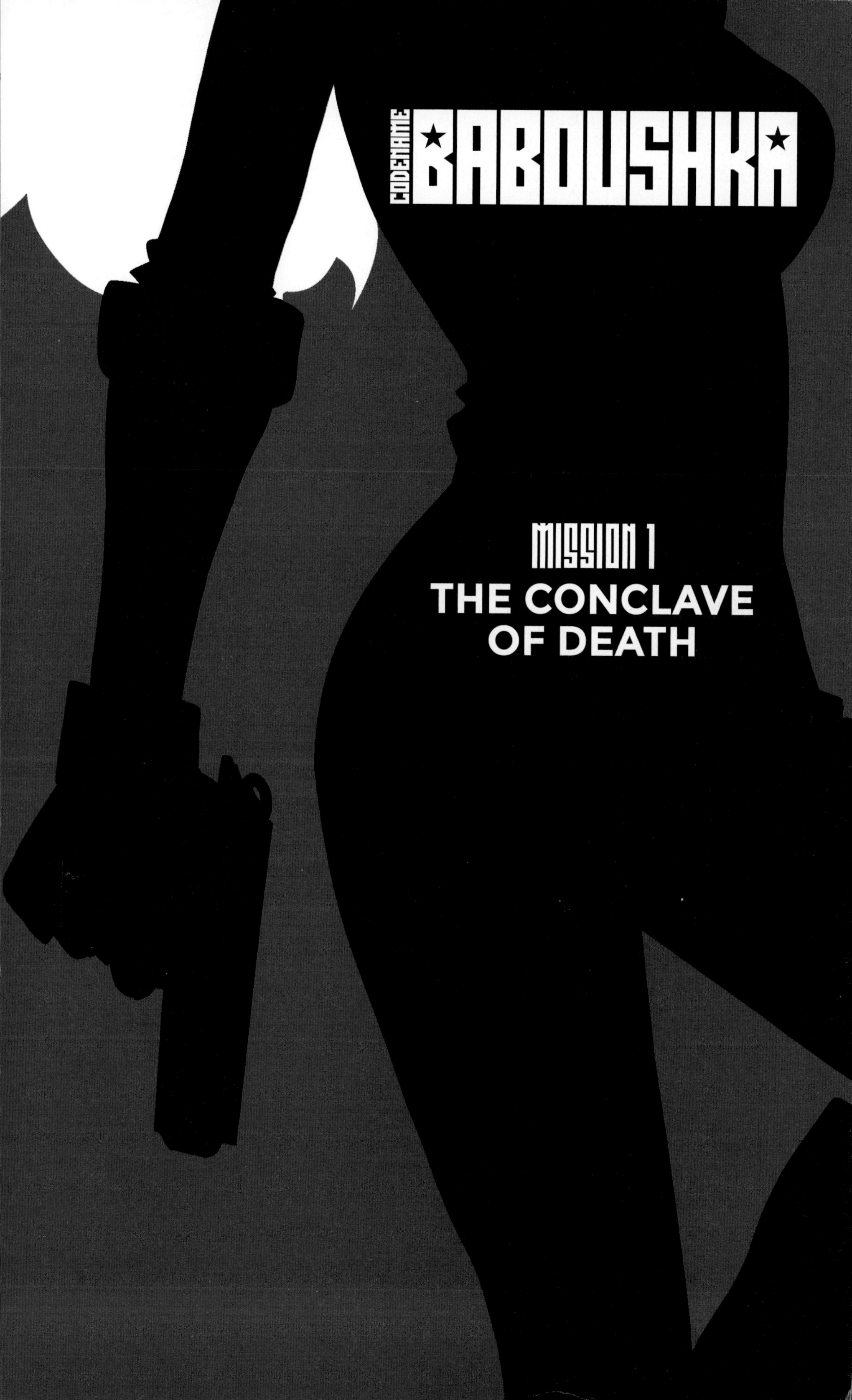
CODENAME
★ BABOUSHKA ★
MISSION 1
THE CONCLAVE OF DEATH

PART 1

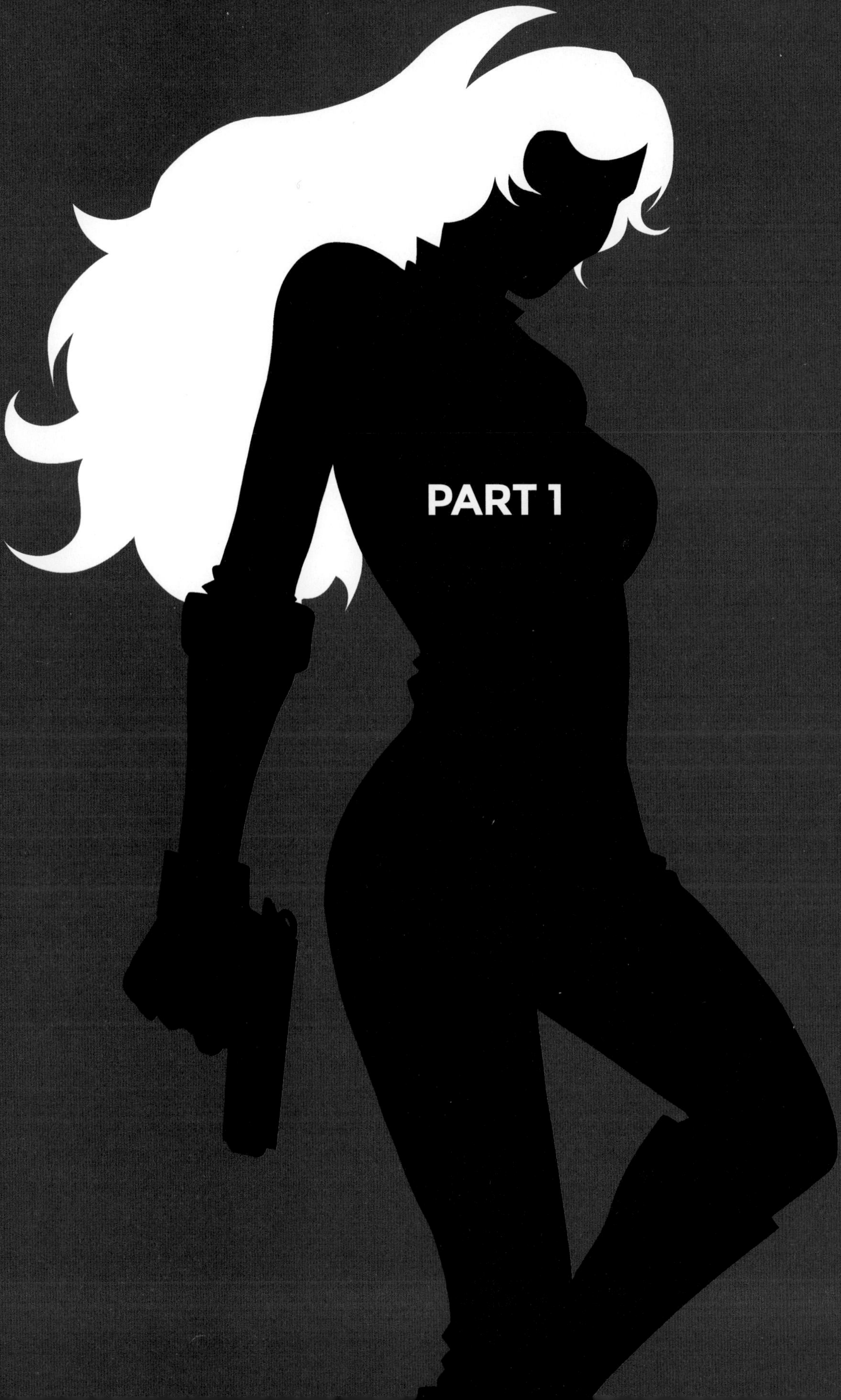

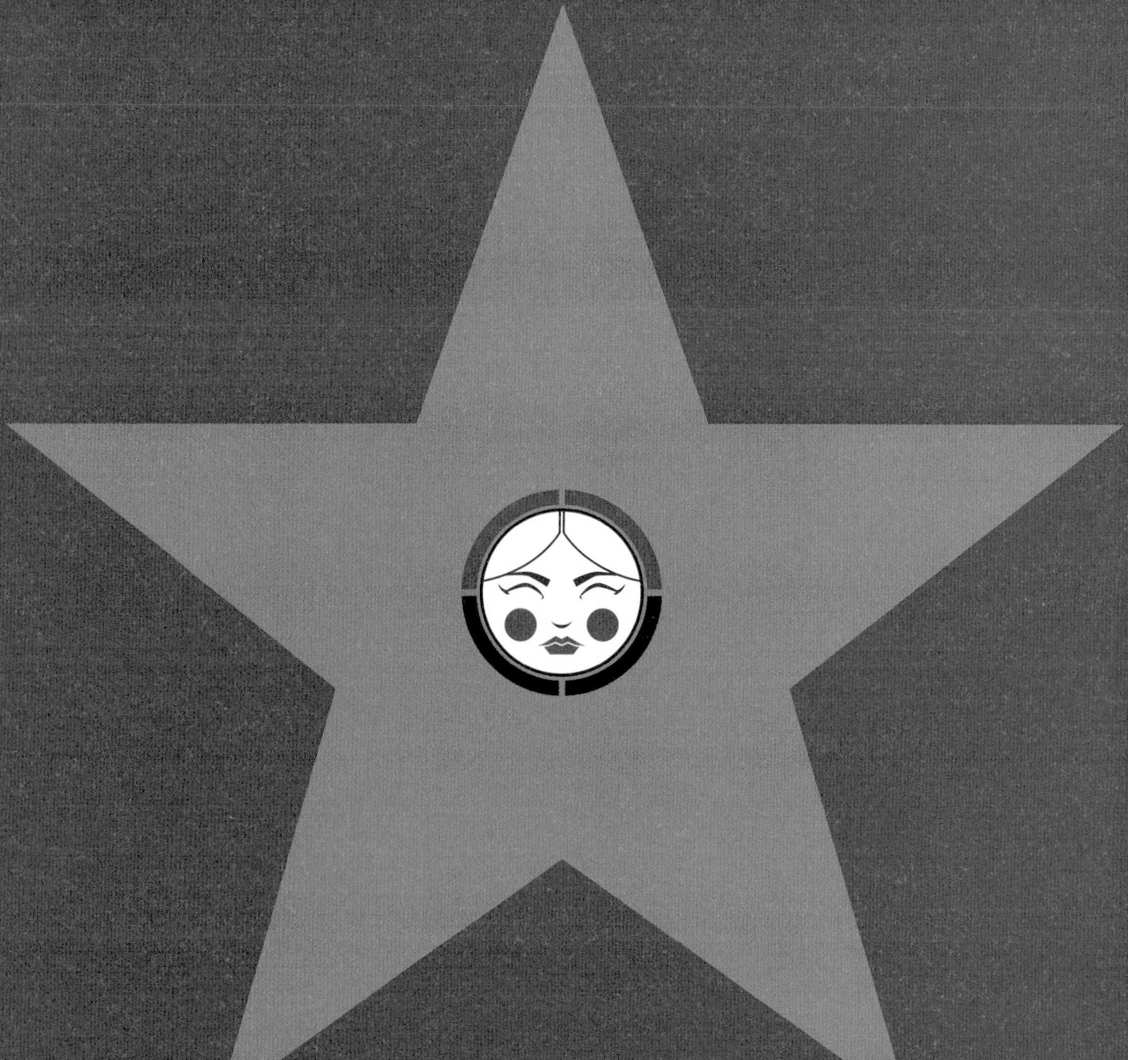

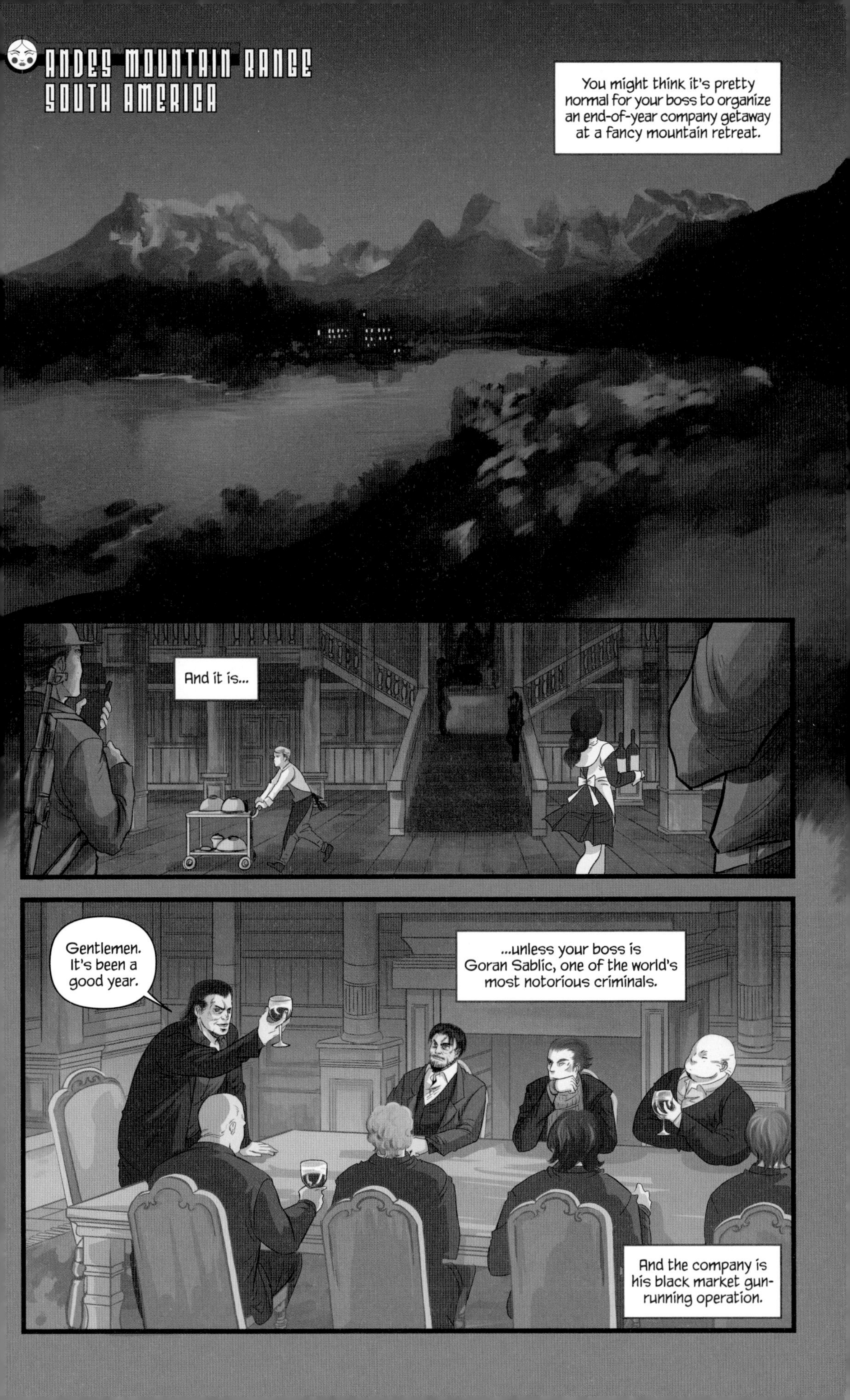
ANDES MOUNTAIN RANGE
SOUTH AMERICA
You might think it's pretty normal for your boss to organize an end-of-year company getaway at a fancy mountain retreat.
And it is...
Gentlemen. It's been a good year.
...unless your boss is Goran Sablic, one of the world's most notorious criminals.
And the company is his black market gun-running operation.

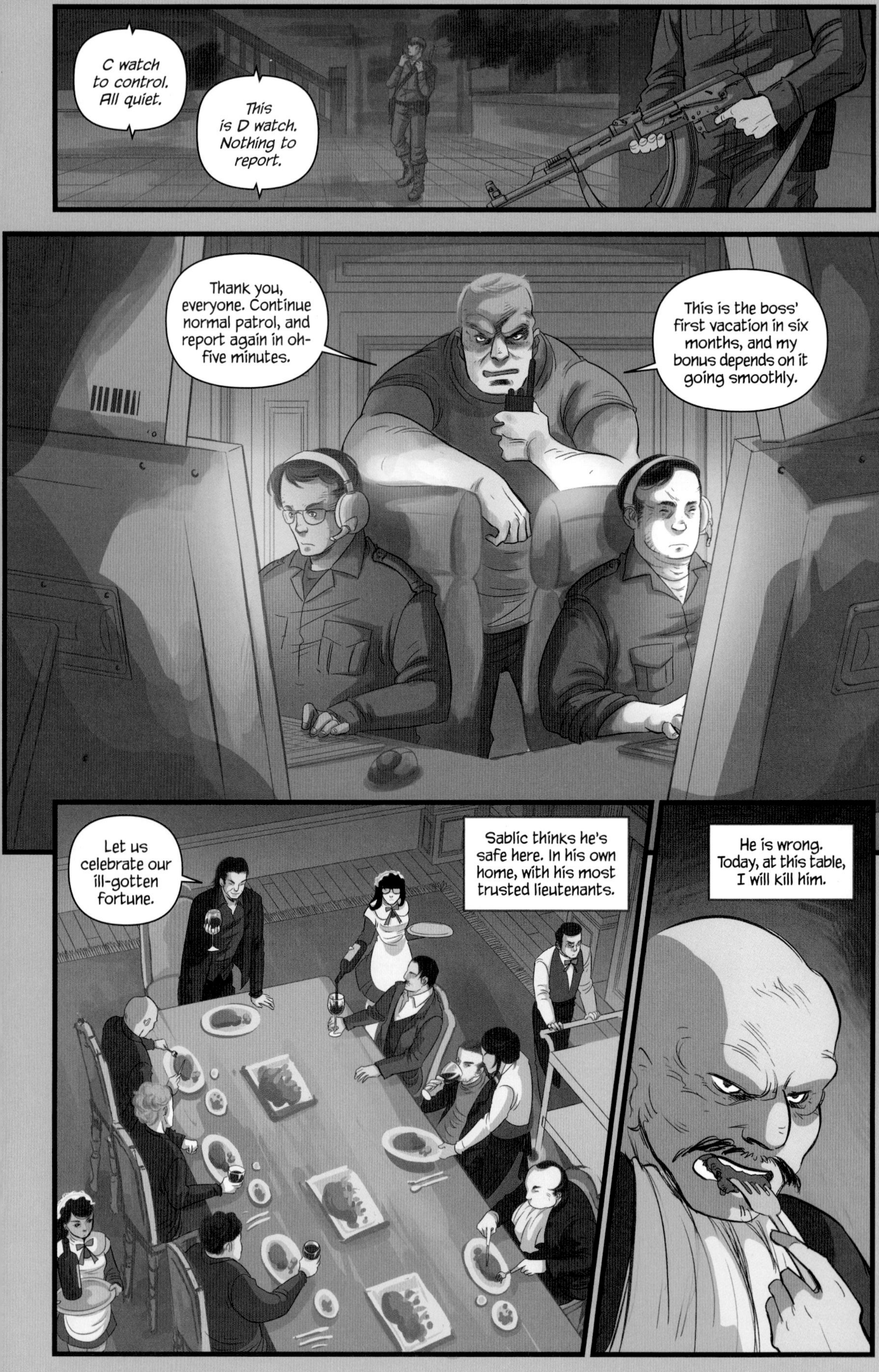
C watch to control. All quiet.
This is D watch. Nothing to report.
Thank you, everyone. Continue normal patrol, and report again in oh-five minutes.
This is the boss' first vacation in six months, and my bonus depends on it going smoothly.
Let us celebrate our ill-gotten fortune.
Sablic thinks he's safe here. In his own home, with his most trusted lieutenants.
He is wrong. Today, at this table, I will kill him.

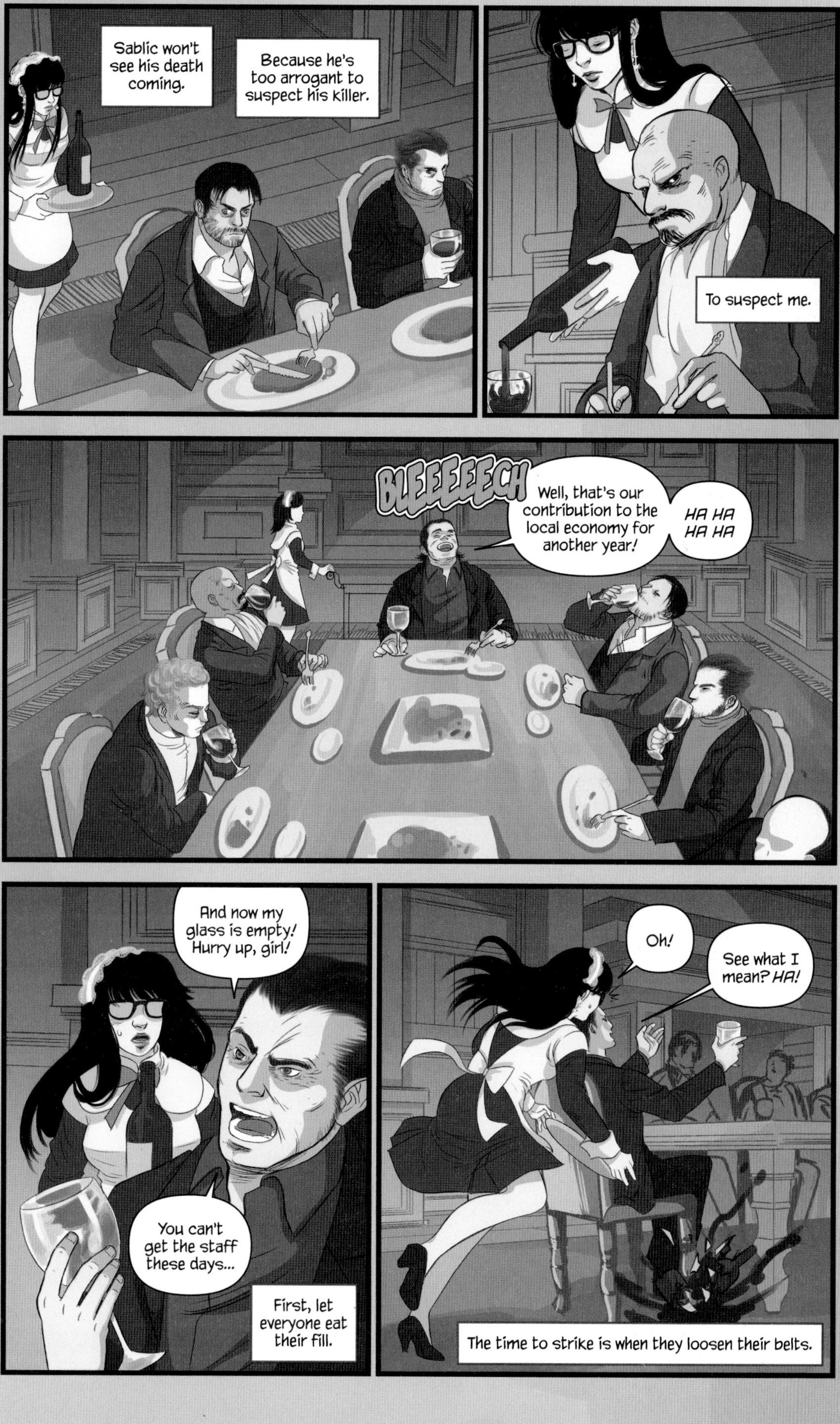
Sablic won't see his death coming.
Because he's too arrogant to suspect his killer.
To suspect me.
BLEEEEECH
Well, that's our contribution to the local economy for another year!
HA HA HA HA
And now my glass is empty! Hurry up, girl!
You can't get the staff these days...
First, let everyone eat their fill.
Oh!
See what I mean? HA!
The time to strike is when they loosen their belts.

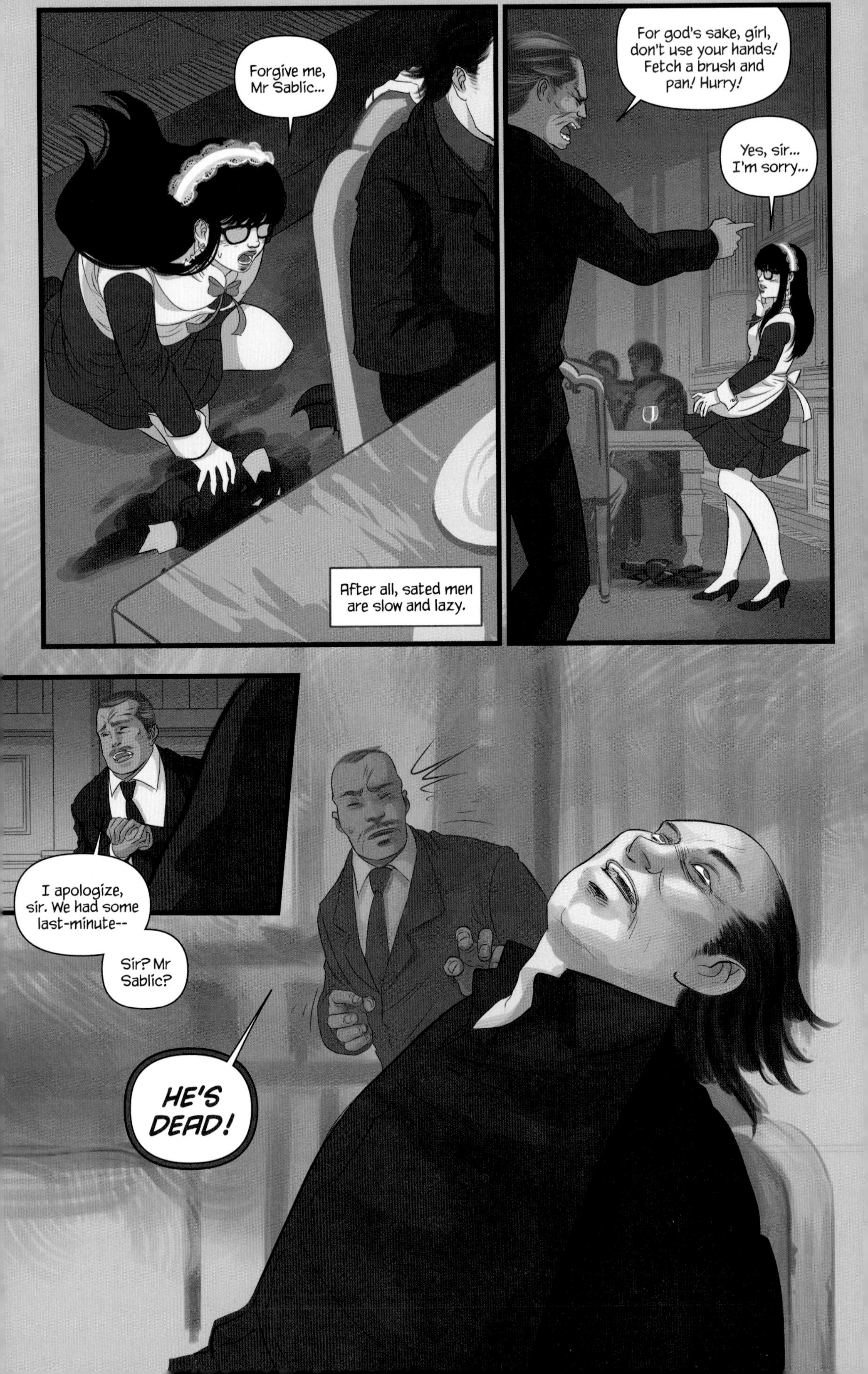
Forgive me, Mr Sablic...
After all, sated men are slow and lazy.
For god's sake, girl, don't use your hands! Fetch a brush and pan! Hurry!
Yes, sir... I'm sorry...
I apologize, sir. We had some last-minute--
Sir? Mr Sablic?
HE'S DEAD!

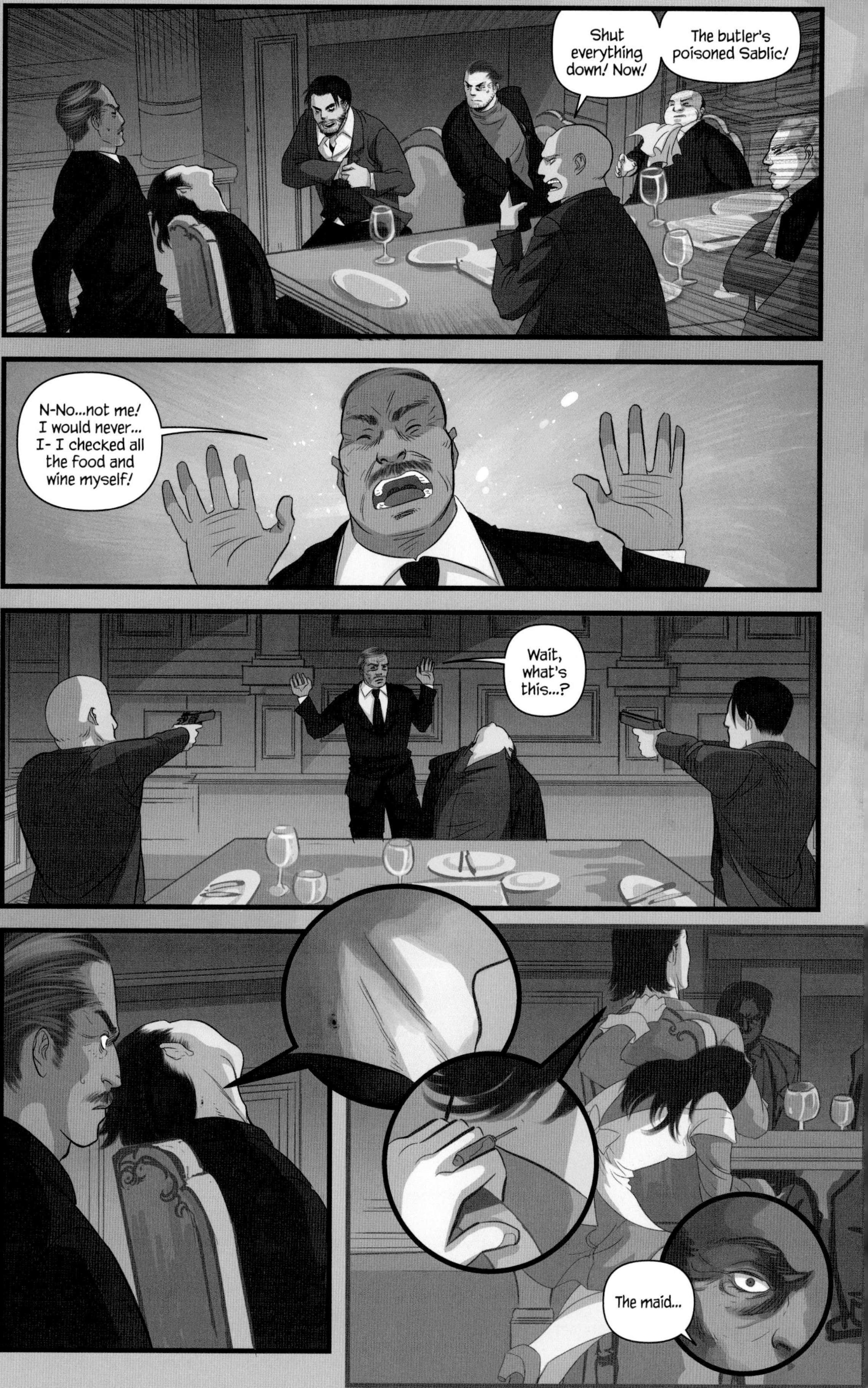
Shut everything down! Now!
The butler's poisoned Sablic!
N-No...not me! I would never... I- I checked all the food and wine myself!
Wait, what's this...?
The maid...

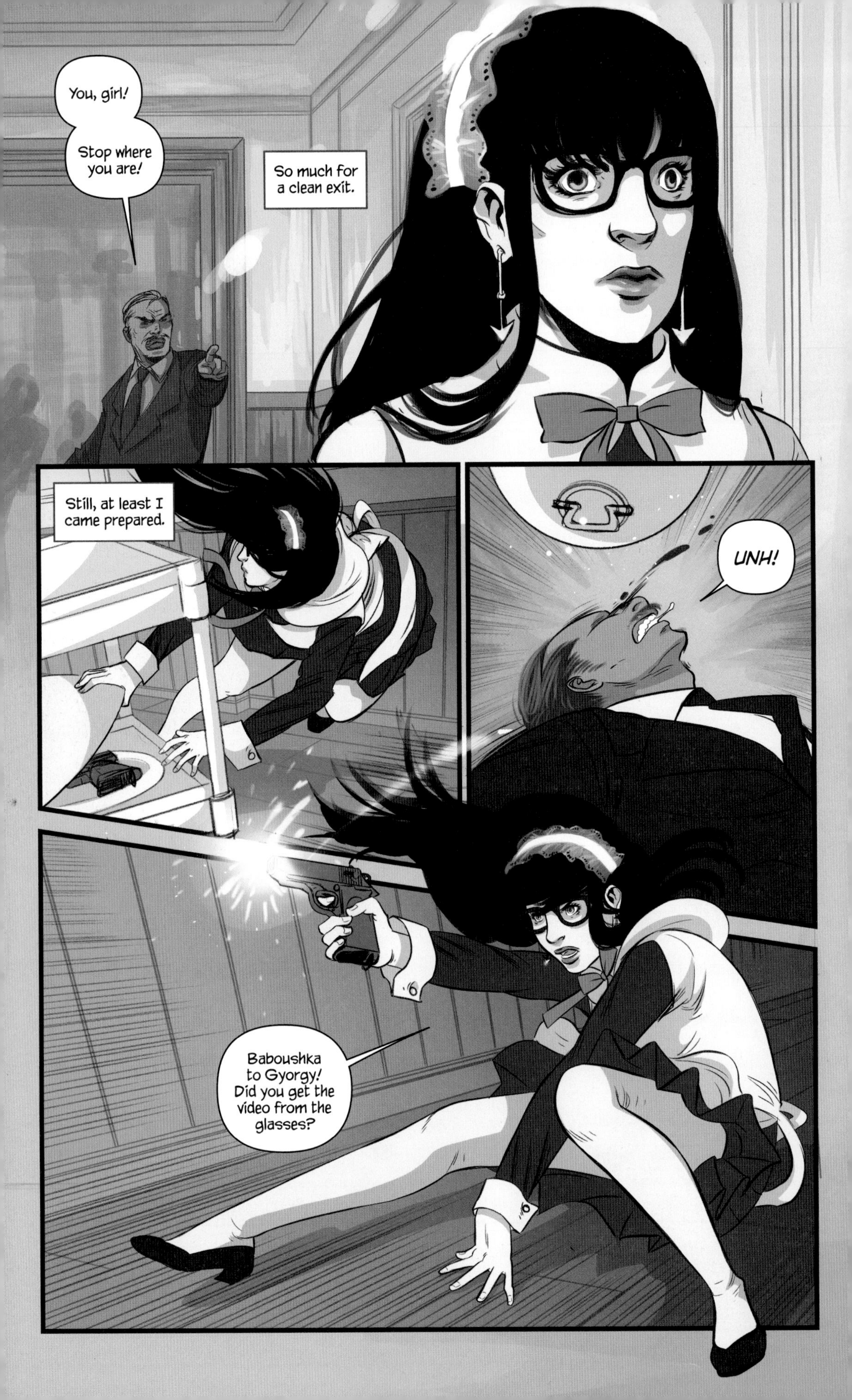
You, girl!
Stop where you are!
So much for a clean exit.
Still, at least I came prepared.
UNH!
Baboushka to Gyorgy! Did you get the video from the glasses?

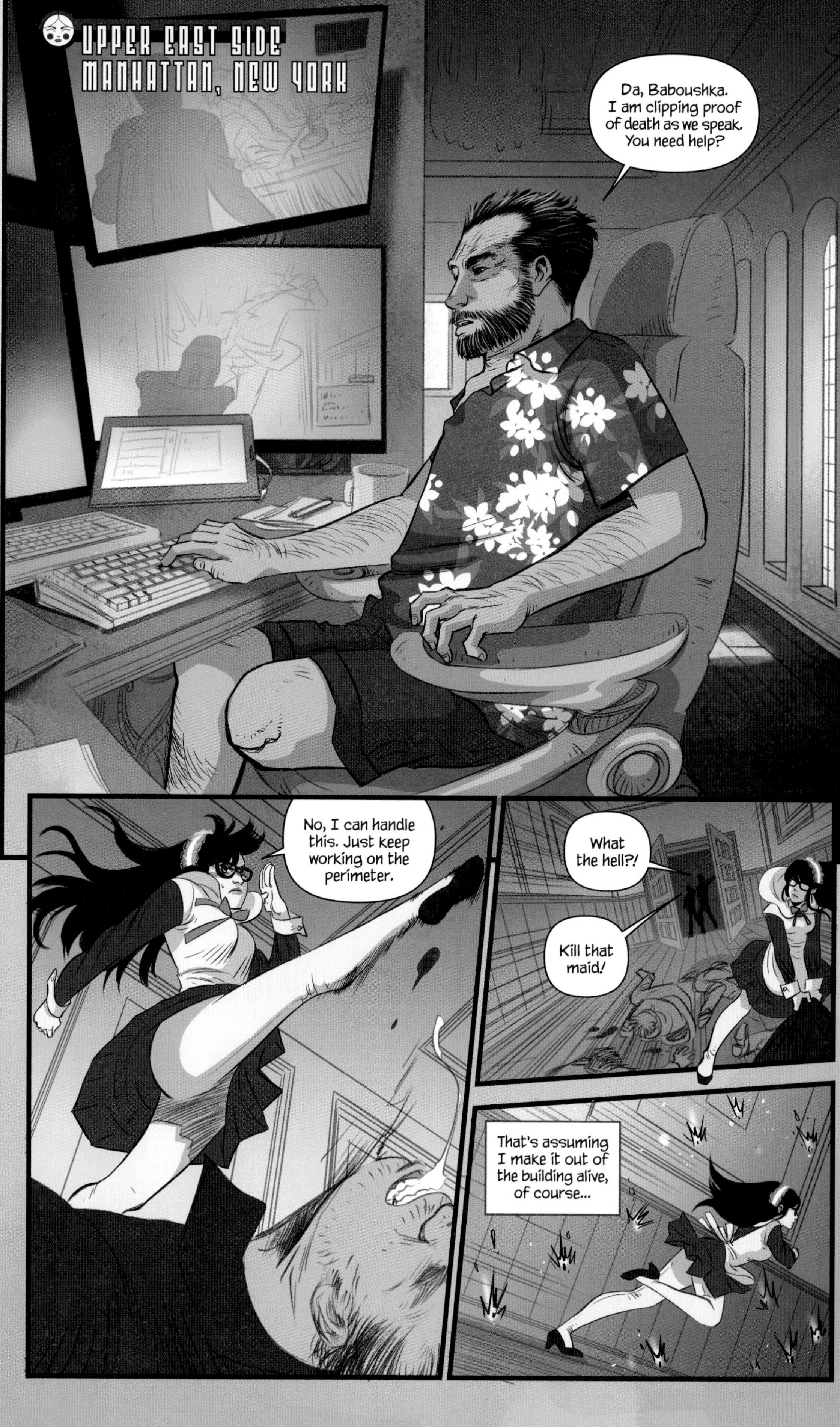
UPPER EAST SIDE
MANHATTAN, NEW YORK
Da, Baboushka. I am clipping proof of death as we speak. You need help?
No, I can handle this. Just keep working on the perimeter.
What the hell?!
Kill that maid!
That's assuming I make it out of the building alive, of course...

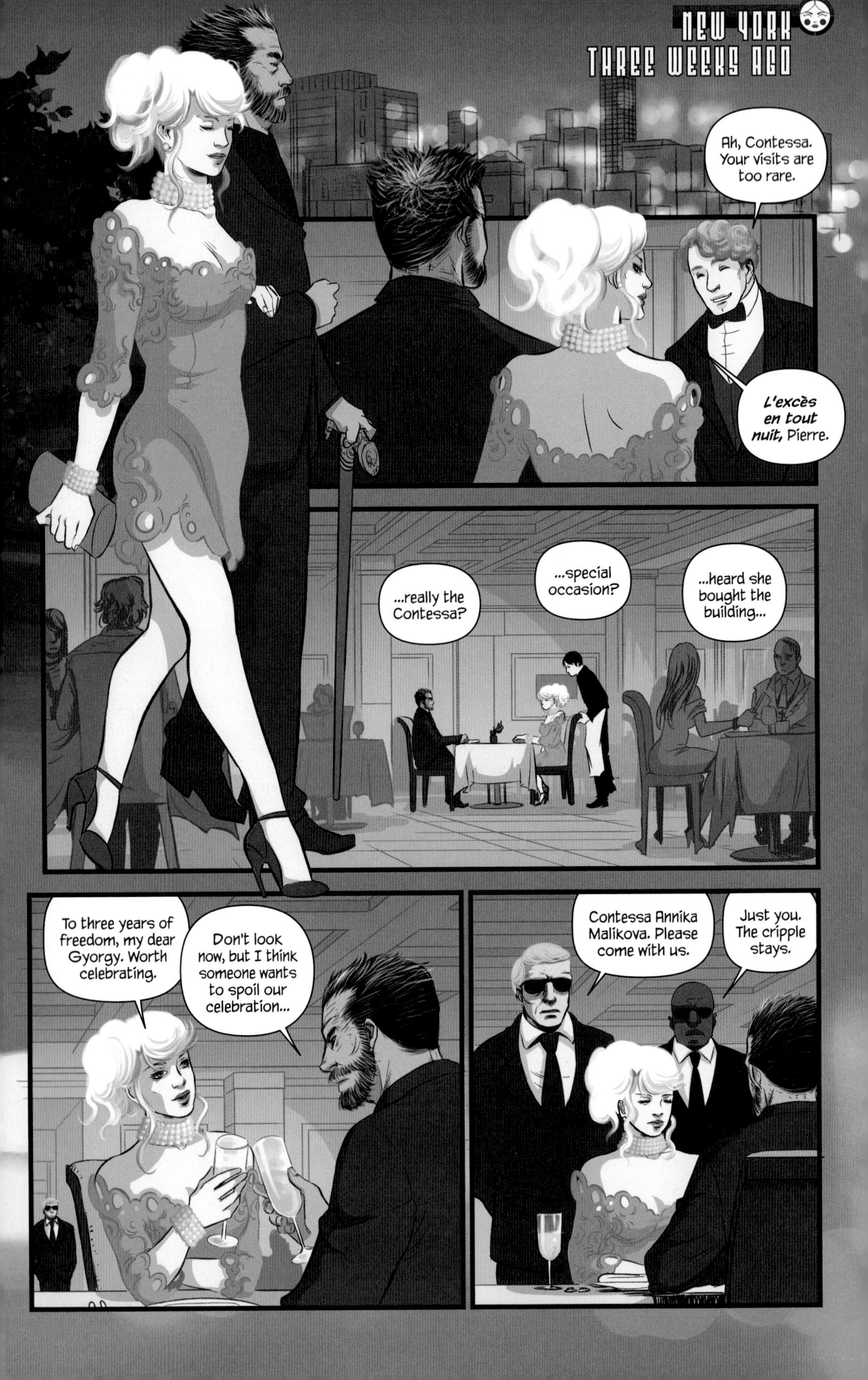
NEW YORK
THREE WEEKS AGO
Ah, Contessa. Your visits are too rare.
L'excès en tout nuit, Pierre.
...really the Contessa?
...special occasion?
...heard she bought the building...
To three years of freedom, my dear Gyorgy. Worth celebrating.
Don't look now, but I think someone wants to spoil our celebration...
Contessa Annika Malikova. Please come with us.
Just you. The cripple stays.

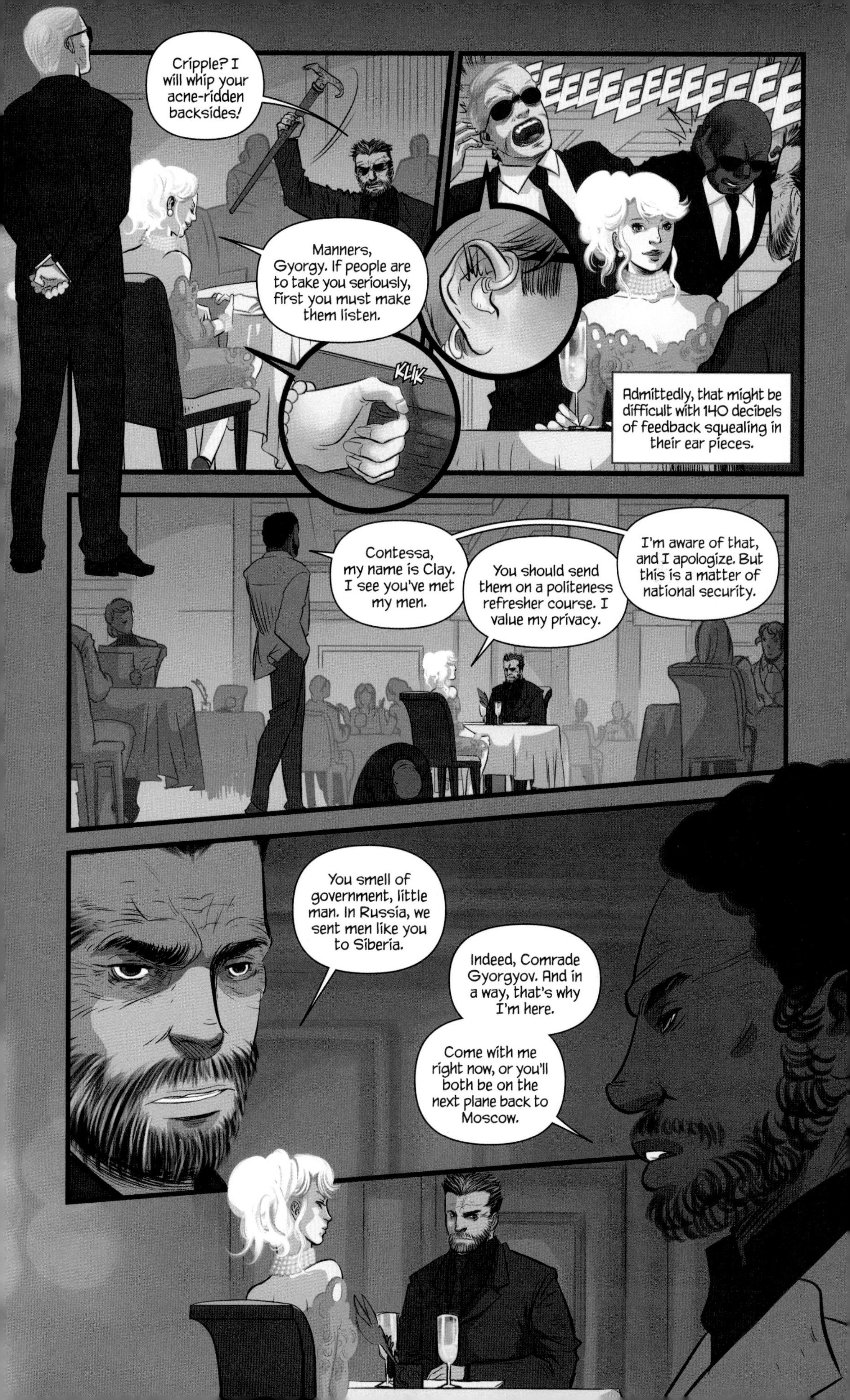
Cripple? I will whip your acne-ridden backsides!
EEEEEEEEEEEEEE
Manners, Gyorgy. If people are to take you seriously, first you must make them listen.
KLIK
Admittedly, that might be difficult with 140 decibels of feedback squealing in their ear pieces.
Contessa, my name is Clay. I see you've met my men.
You should send them on a politeness refresher course. I value my privacy.
I'm aware of that, and I apologize. But this is a matter of national security.
You smell of government, little man. In Russia, we sent men like you to Siberia.
Indeed, Comrade Gyorgyov. And in a way, that's why I'm here.
Come with me right now, or you'll both be on the next plane back to Moscow.

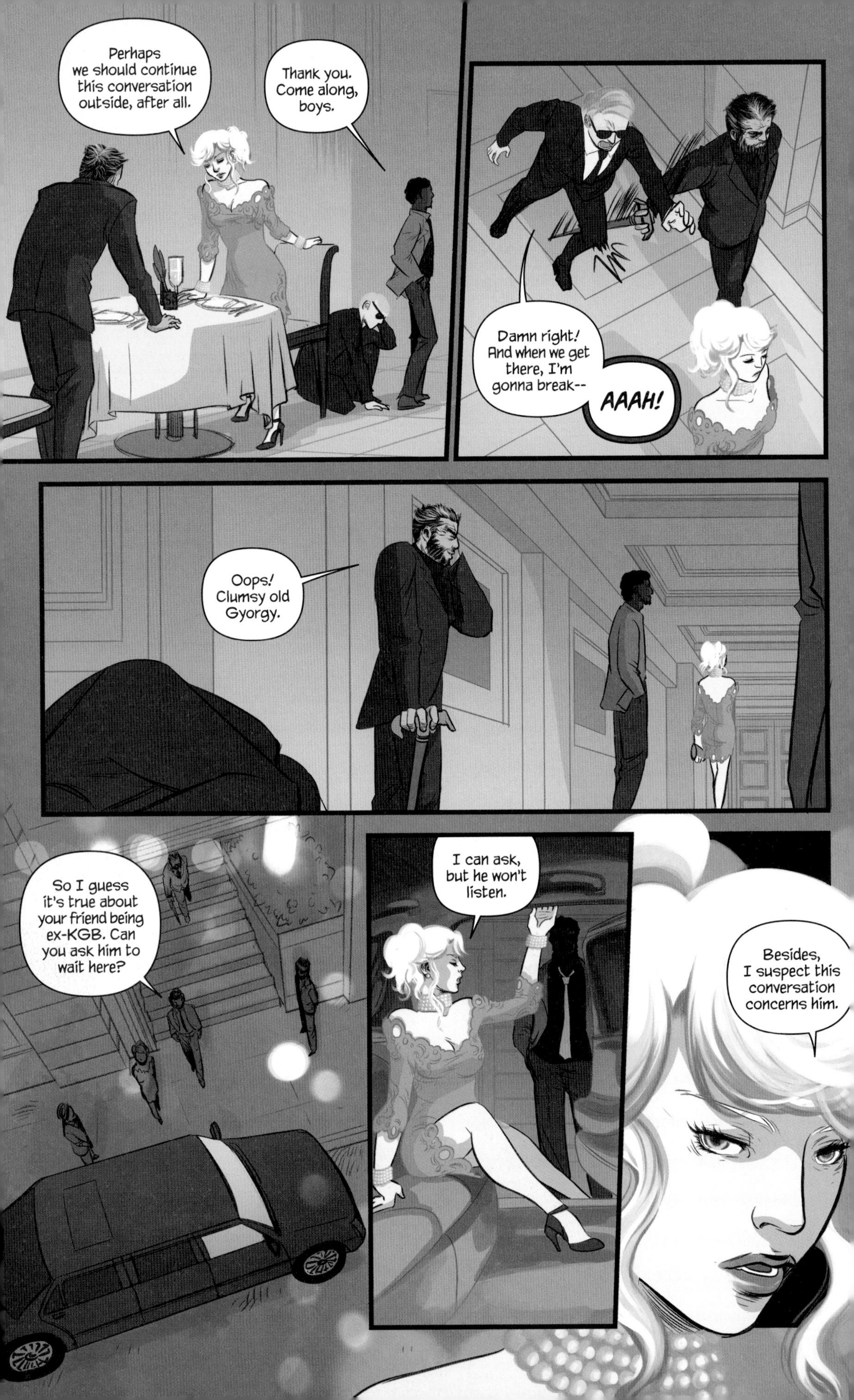
Perhaps we should continue this conversation outside, after all.
Thank you. Come along, boys.
Damn right! And when we get there, I'm gonna break--
AAAH!
Oops! Clumsy old Gyorgy.
So I guess it's true about your friend being ex-KGB. Can you ask him to wait here?
I can ask, but he won't listen.
Besides, I suspect this conversation concerns him.

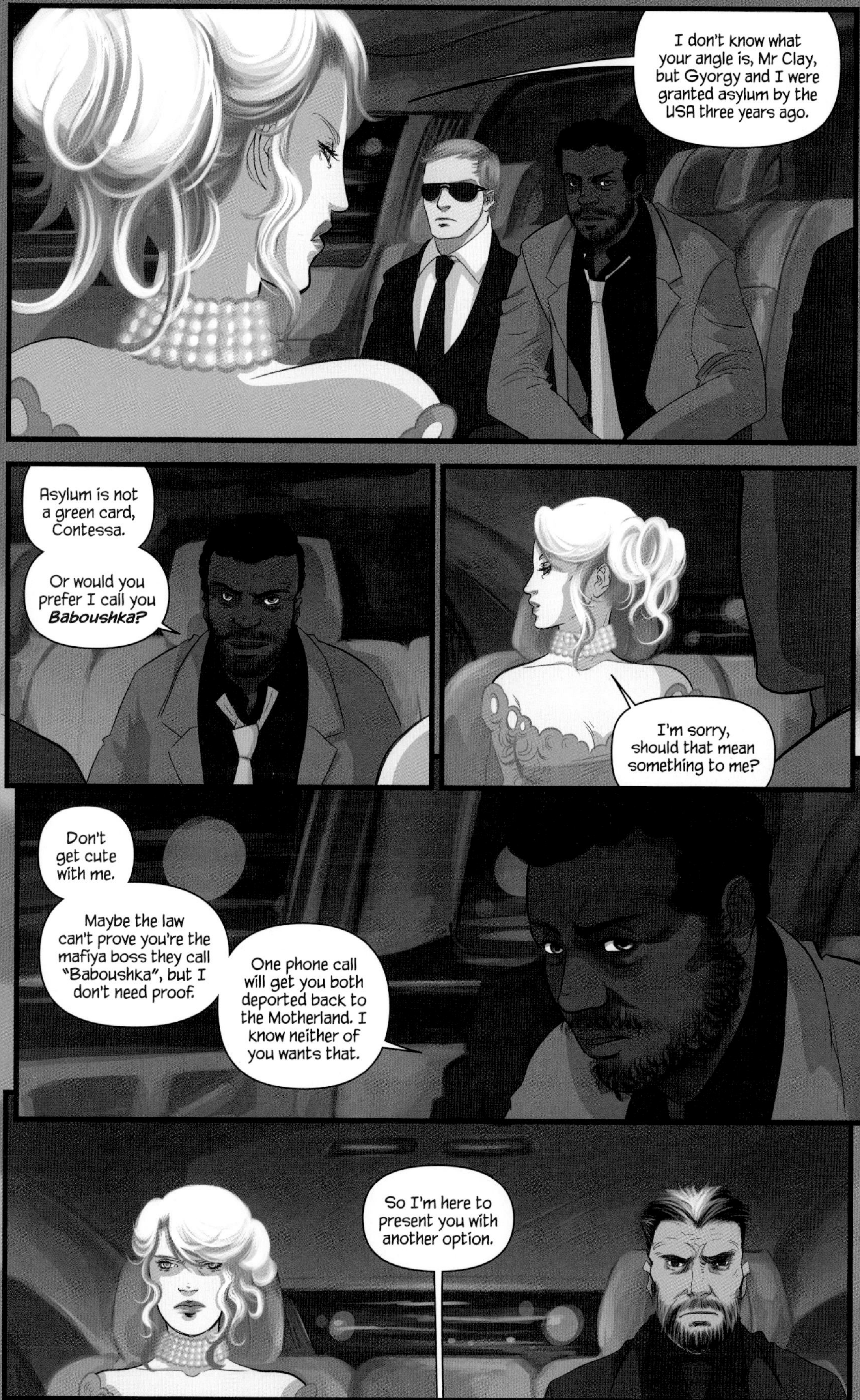
I don't know what your angle is, Mr Clay, but Gyorgy and I were granted asylum by the USA three years ago.
Asylum is not a green card, Contessa.
Or would you prefer I call you *Baboushka?*
I'm sorry, should that mean something to me?
Don't get cute with me.
Maybe the law can't prove you're the mafiya boss they call "Baboushka", but I don't need proof.
One phone call will get you both deported back to the Motherland. I know neither of you wants that.
So I'm here to present you with another option.

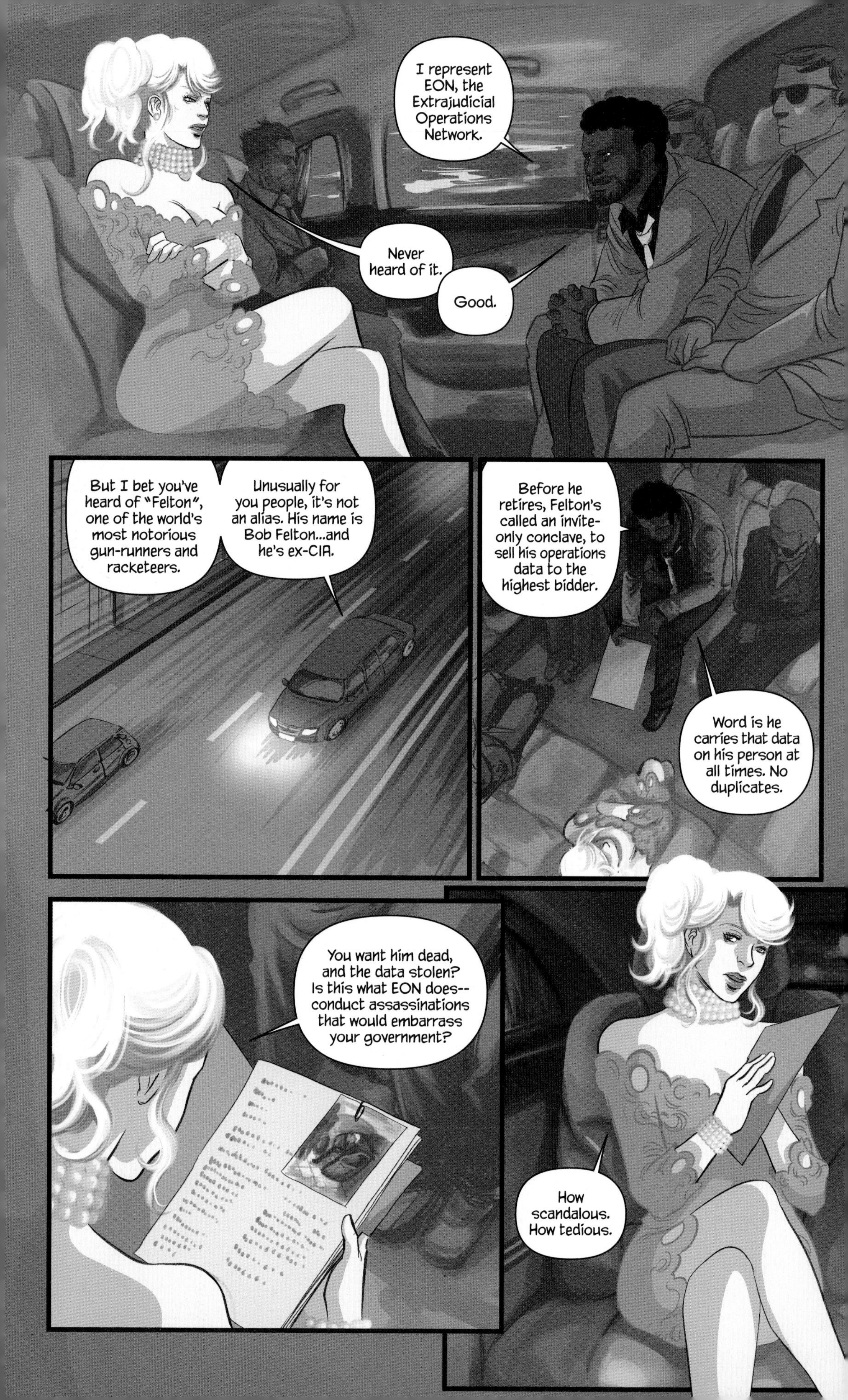
I represent EON, the Extrajudicial Operations Network.
Never heard of it.
Good.
But I bet you've heard of "Felton", one of the world's most notorious gun-runners and racketeers.
Unusually for you people, it's not an alias. His name is Bob Felton...and he's ex-CIA.
Before he retires, Felton's called an invite-only conclave, to sell his operations data to the highest bidder.
Word is he carries that data on his person at all times. No duplicates.
You want him dead, and the data stolen? Is this what EON does--conduct assassinations that would embarrass your government?
How scandalous. How tedious.

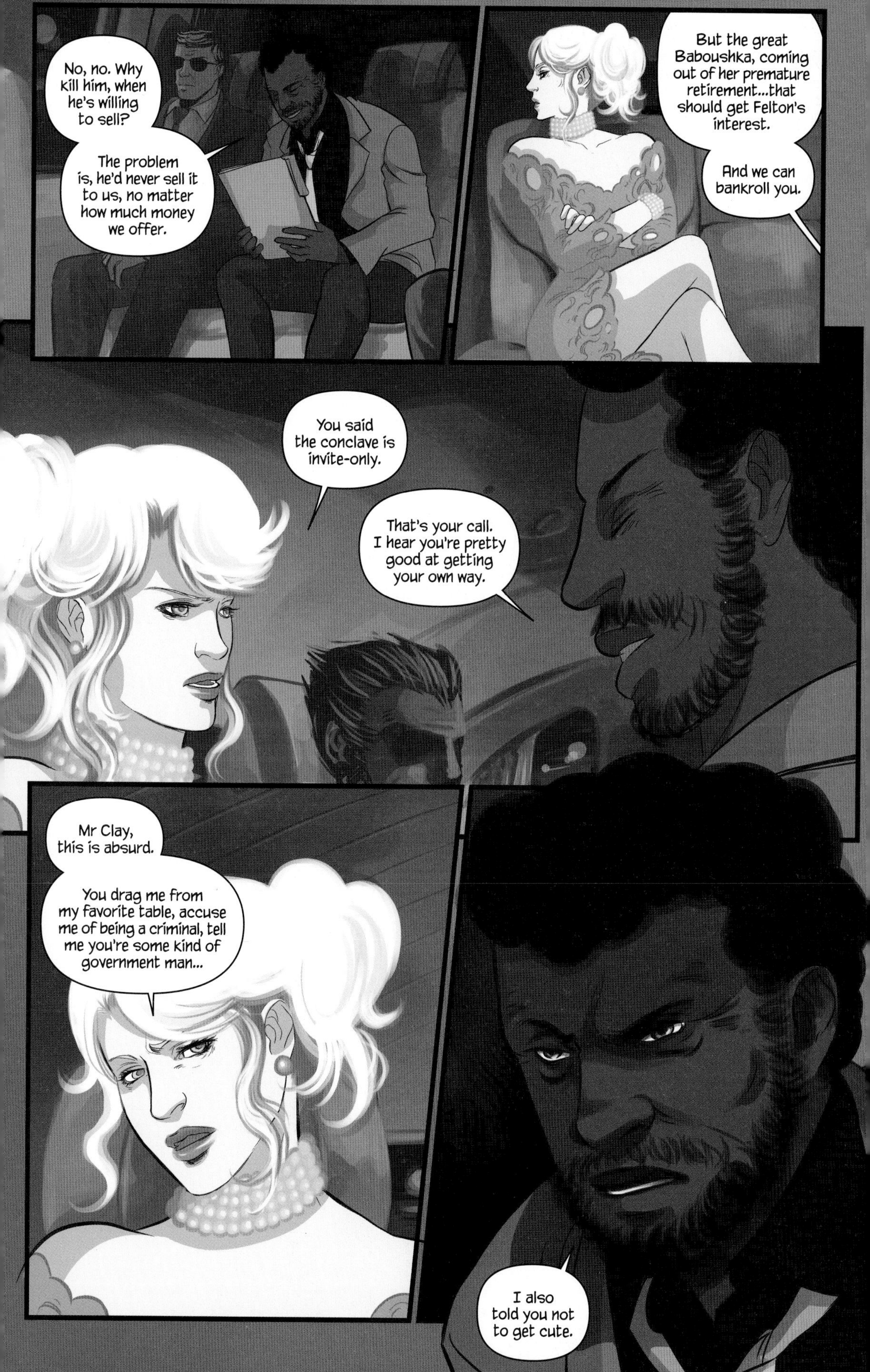

No, no. Why kill him, when he's willing to sell?
The problem is, he'd never sell it to us, no matter how much money we offer.
But the great Baboushka, coming out of her premature retirement...that should get Felton's interest.
And we can bankroll you.
You said the conclave is invite-only.
That's your call. I hear you're pretty good at getting your own way.
Mr Clay, this is absurd.
You drag me from my favorite table, accuse me of being a criminal, tell me you're some kind of government man...
I also told you not to get cute.

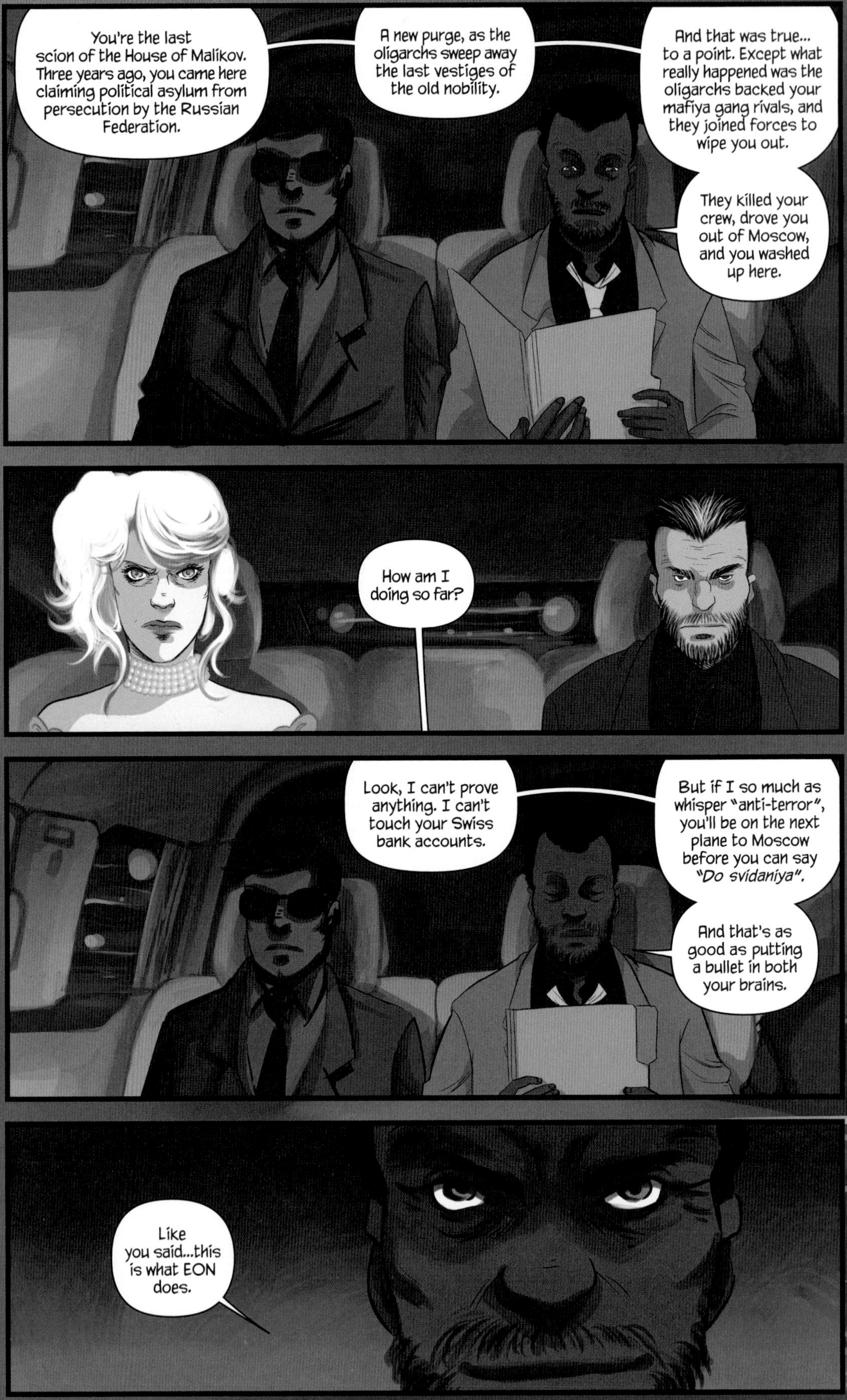
You're the last scion of the House of Malikov. Three years ago, you came here claiming political asylum from persecution by the Russian Federation.
A new purge, as the oligarchs sweep away the last vestiges of the old nobility.
And that was true... to a point. Except what really happened was the oligarchs backed your mafiya gang rivals, and they joined forces to wipe you out.
They killed your crew, drove you out of Moscow, and you washed up here.
How am I doing so far?
Look, I can't prove anything. I can't touch your Swiss bank accounts.
But if I so much as whisper "anti-terror", you'll be on the next plane to Moscow before you can say *"Do svidaniya"*.
And that's as good as putting a bullet in both your brains.
Like you said...this is what EON does.

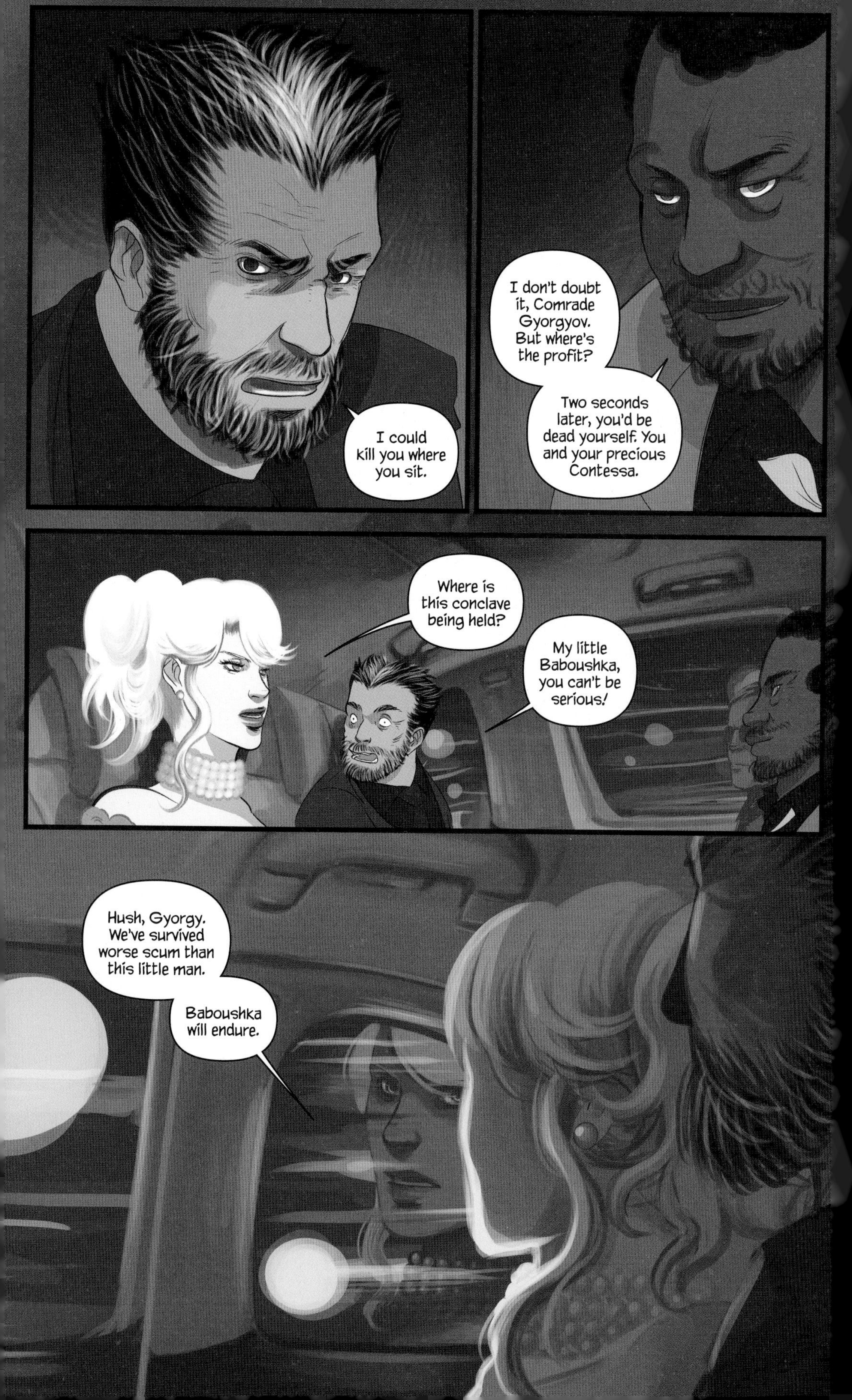
I could kill you where you sit.
I don't doubt it, Comrade Gyorgyov. But where's the profit?
Two seconds later, you'd be dead yourself. You and your precious Contessa.
Where is this conclave being held?
My little Baboushka, you can't be serious!
Hush, Gyorgy. We've survived worse scum than this little man.
Baboushka will endure.

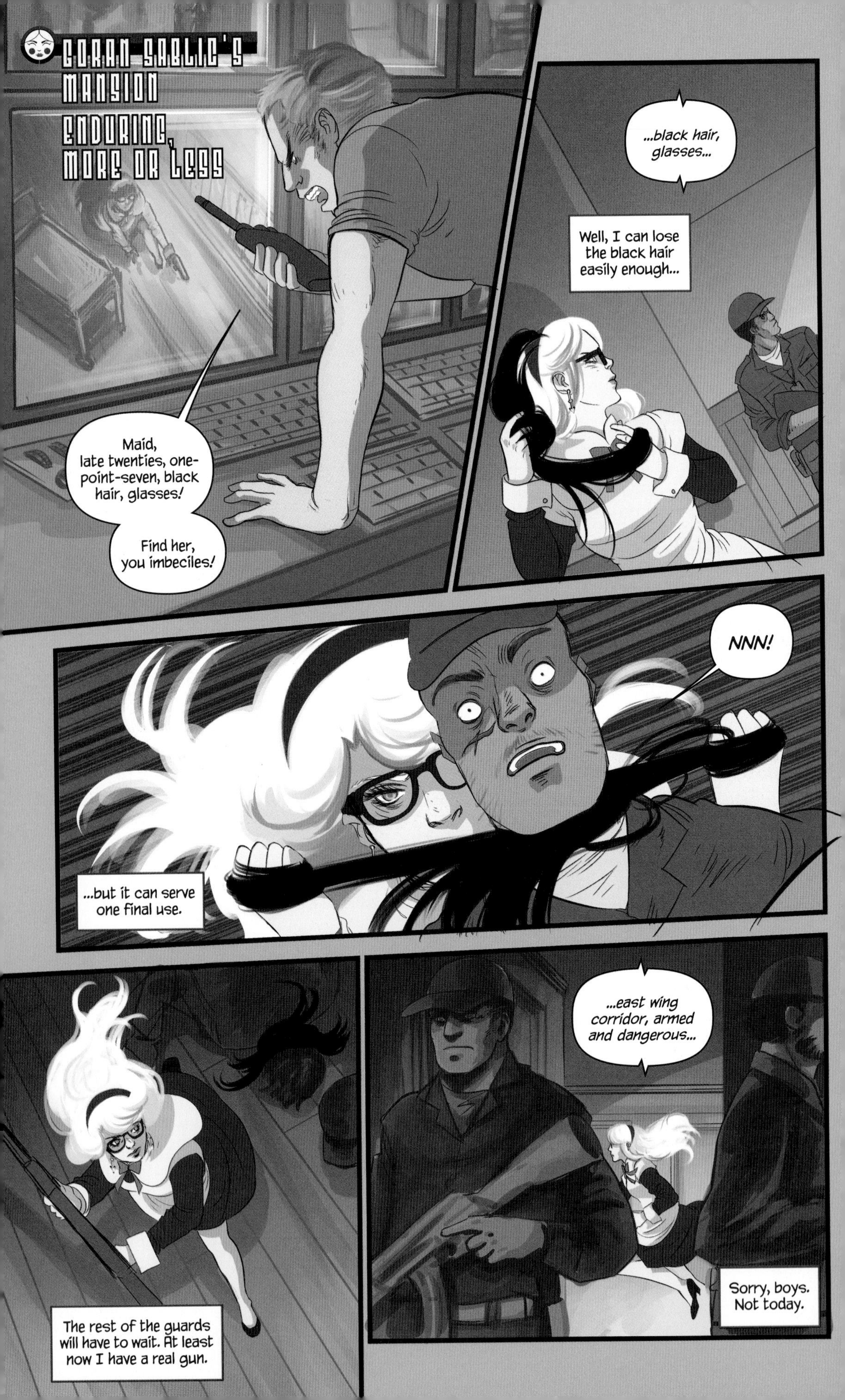
GORAN SABLIC'S MANSION
ENDURING, MORE OR LESS
Maid, late twenties, one-point-seven, black hair, glasses!
Find her, you imbeciles!
...black hair, glasses...
Well, I can lose the black hair easily enough...
NNN!
...but it can serve one final use.
The rest of the guards will have to wait. At least now I have a real gun.
...east wing corridor, armed and dangerous...
Sorry, boys. Not today.

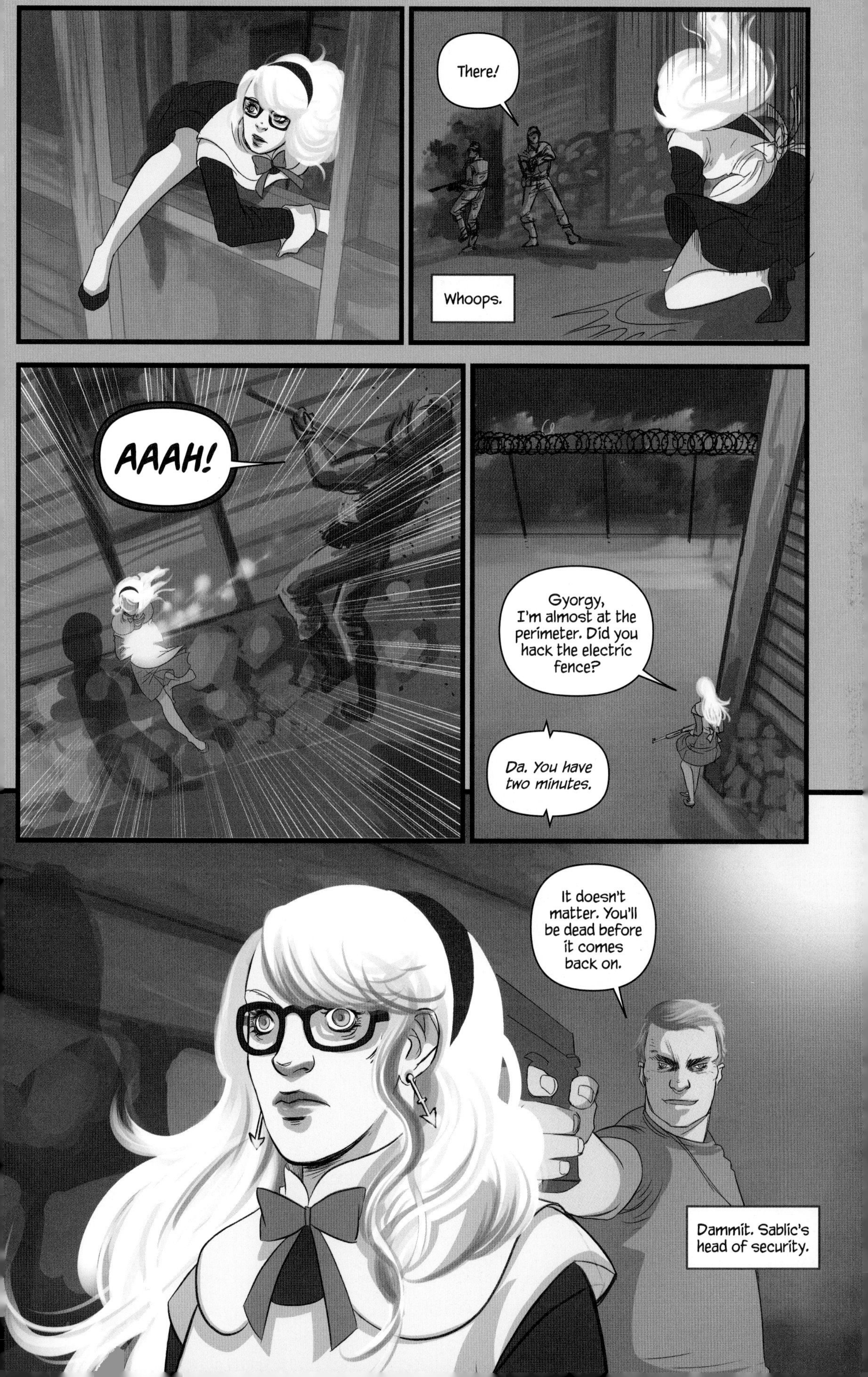
There!
Whoops.
AAAH!
Gyorgy, I'm almost at the perimeter. Did you hack the electric fence?
Da. You have two minutes.
It doesn't matter. You'll be dead before it comes back on.
Dammit. Sablic's head of security.

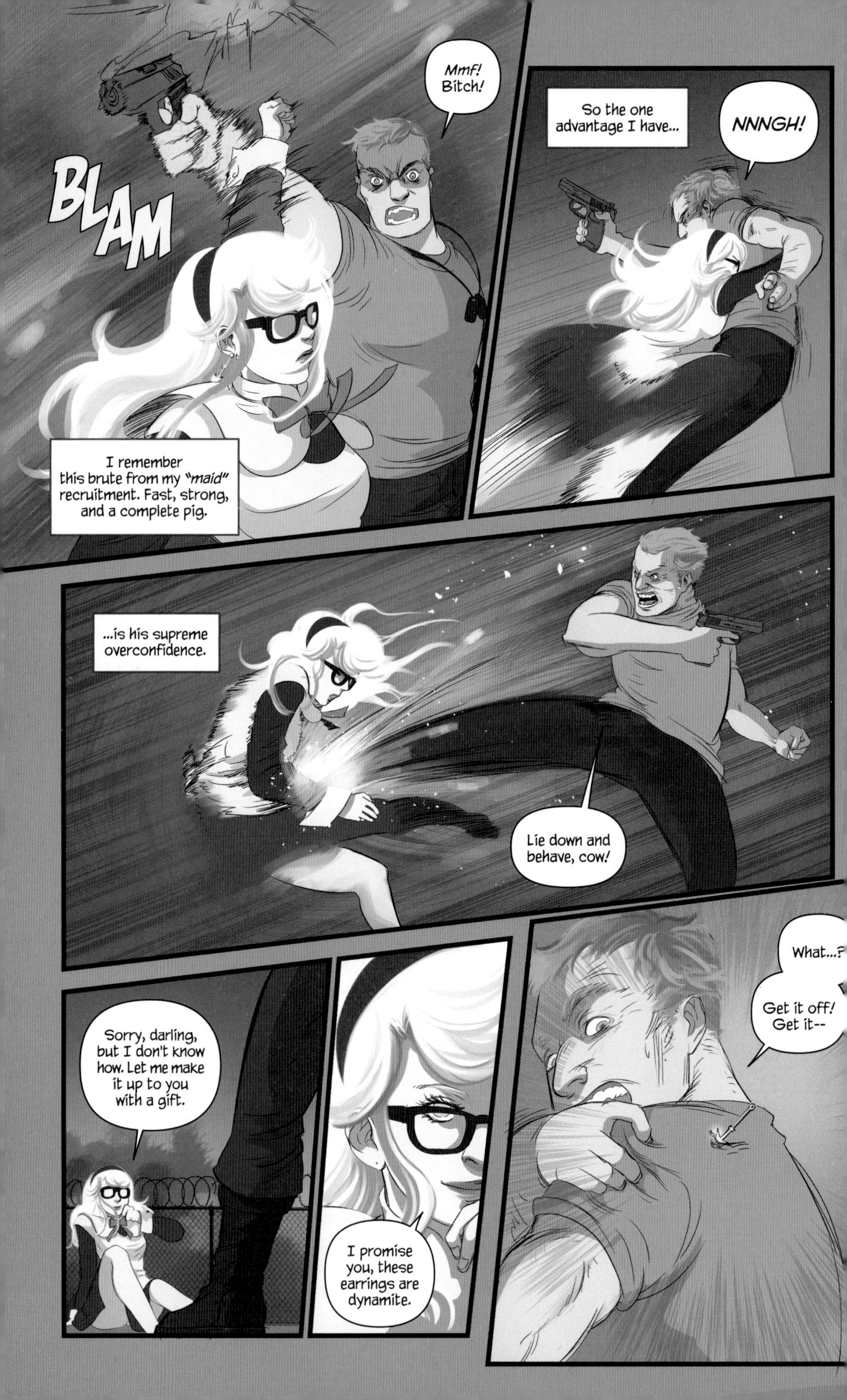

Mmf! Bitch!
BLAM
I remember this brute from my "maid" recruitment. Fast, strong, and a complete pig.
So the one advantage I have...
NNNGH!
...is his supreme overconfidence.
Lie down and behave, cow!
Sorry, darling, but I don't know how. Let me make it up to you with a gift.
I promise you, these earrings are dynamite.
What...?
Get it off! Get it--

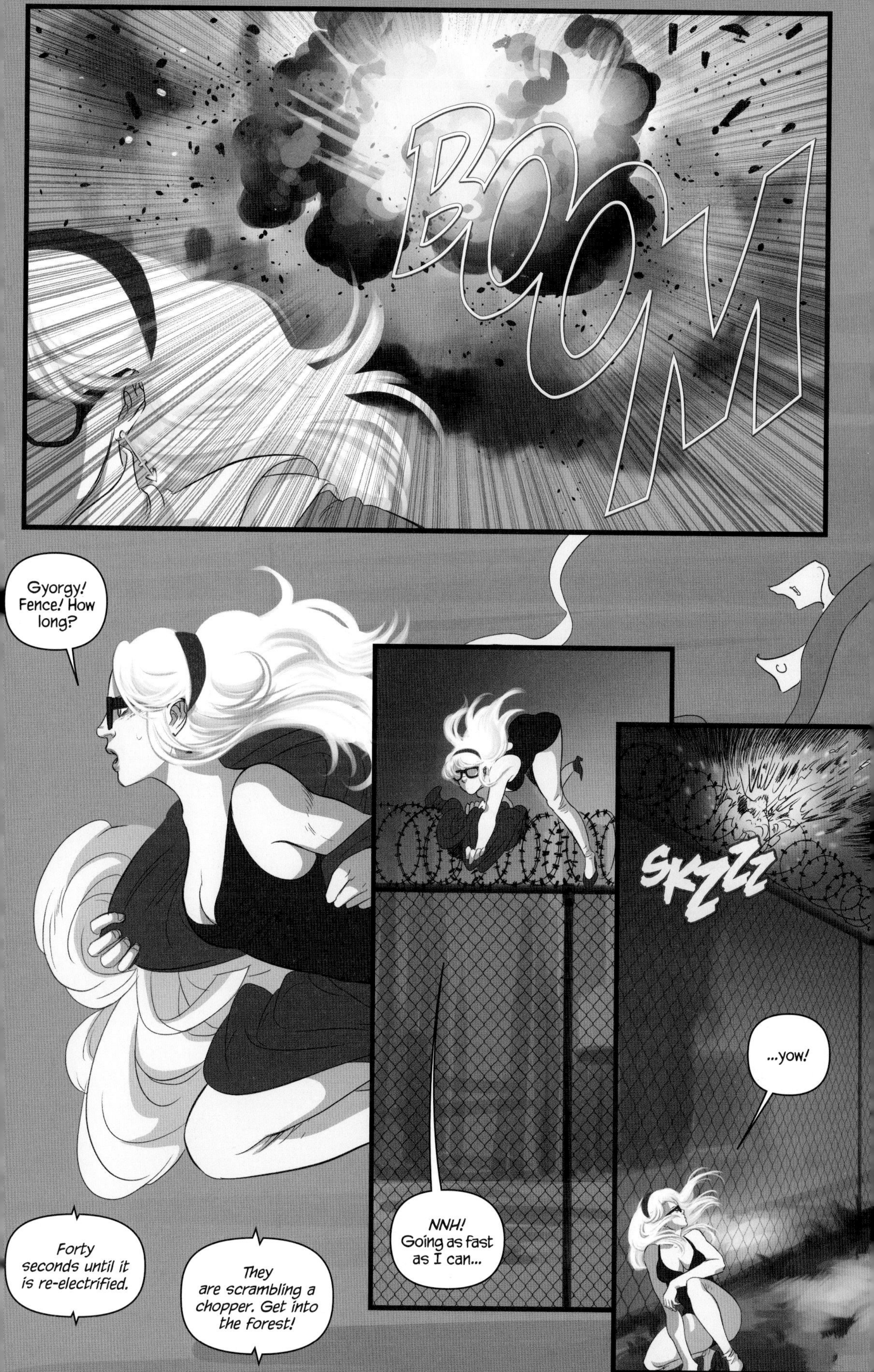
BOOM
Gyorgy! Fence! How long?
Forty seconds until it is re-electrified.
They are scrambling a chopper. Get into the forest!
NNH! Going as fast as I can...
SKZZZ
...yow!

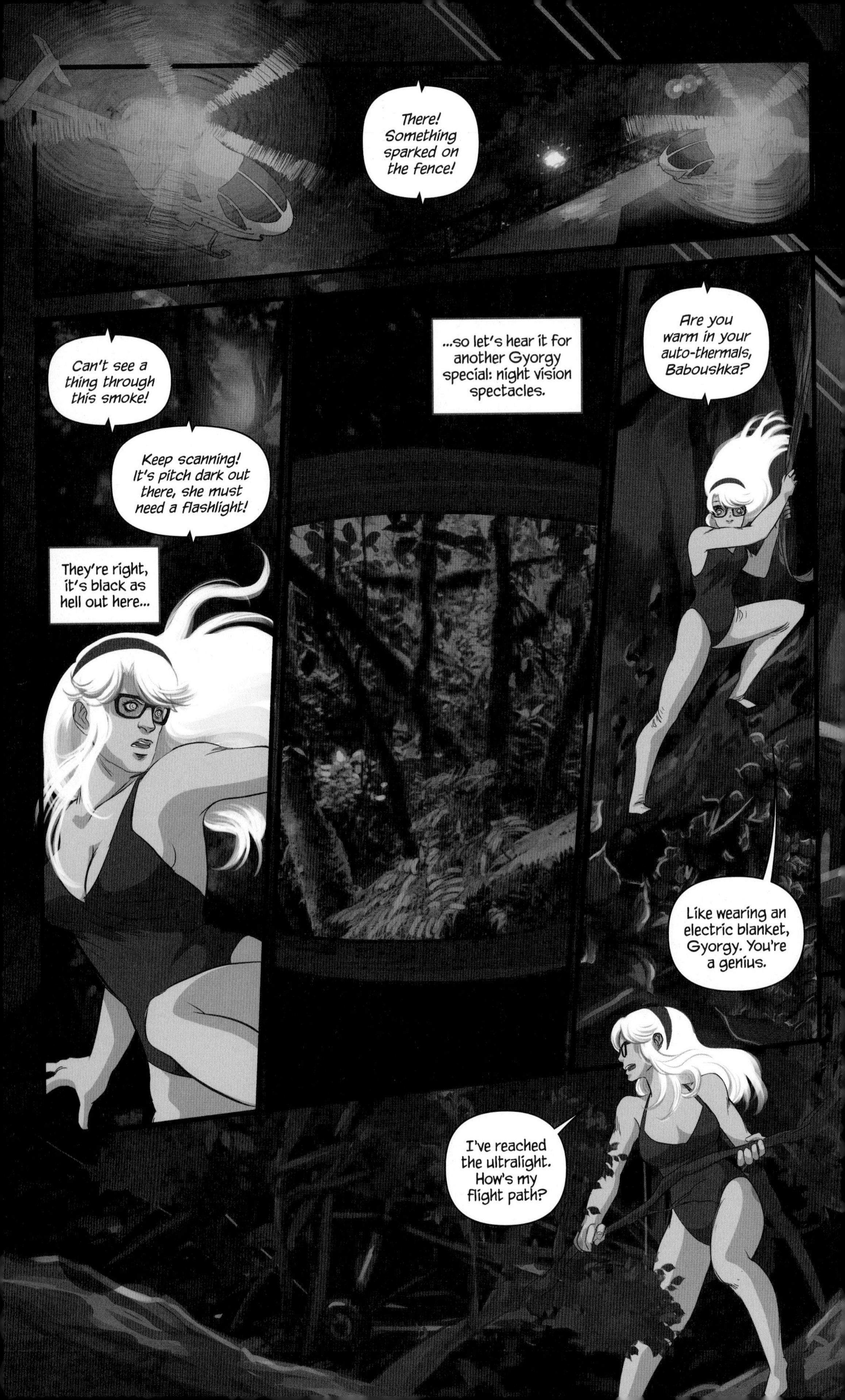
There! Something sparked on the fence!
Can't see a thing through this smoke!
Keep scanning! It's pitch dark out there, she must need a flashlight!
They're right, it's black as hell out here...
...so let's hear it for another Gyorgy special: night vision spectacles.
Are you warm in your auto-thermals, Baboushka?
Like wearing an electric blanket, Gyorgy. You're a genius.
I've reached the ultralight. How's my flight path?

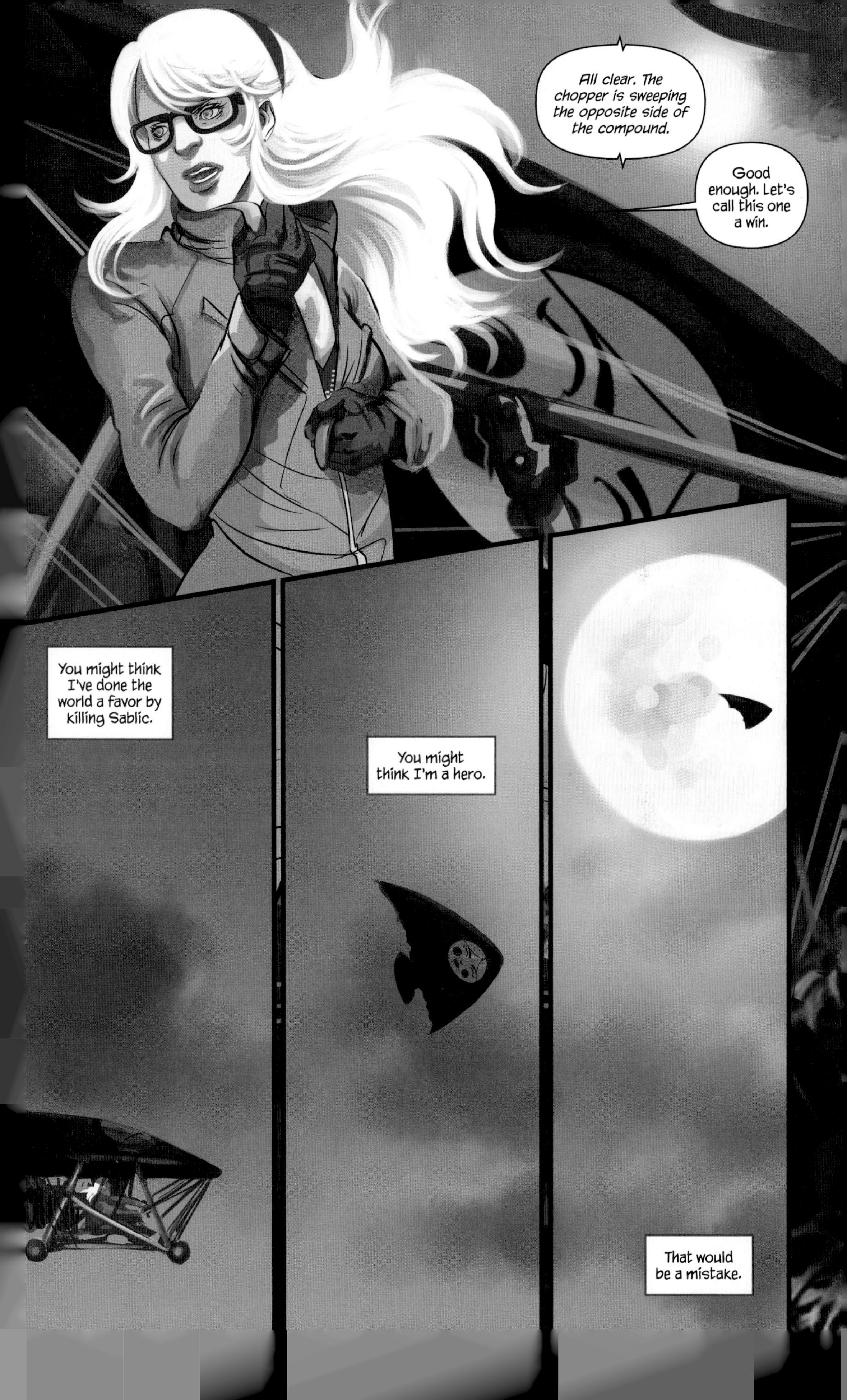
All clear. The chopper is sweeping the opposite side of the compound.
Good enough. Let's call this one a win.
You might think I've done the world a favor by killing Sablic.
You might think I'm a hero.
That would be a mistake.

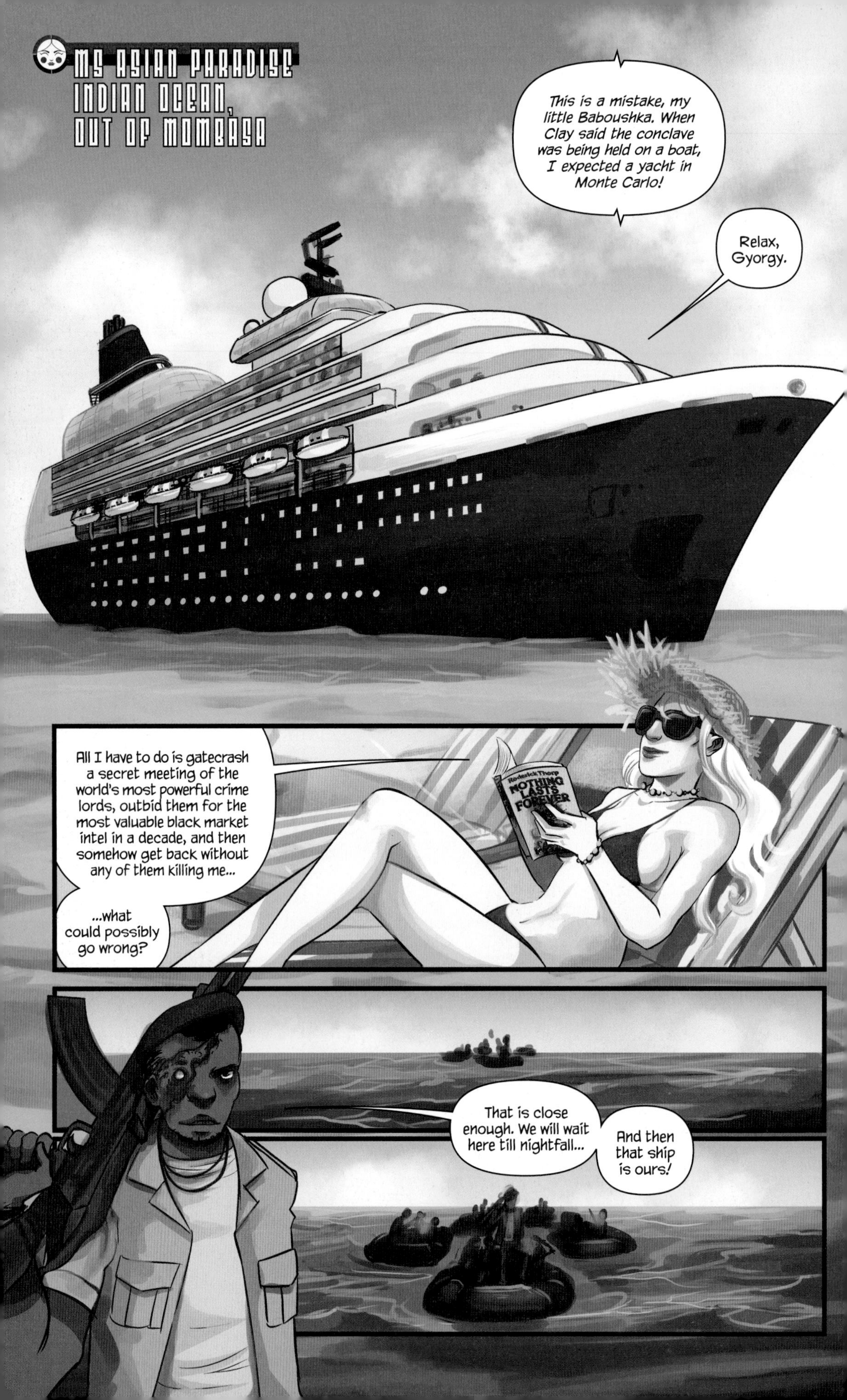
MS ASIAN PARADISE
INDIAN OCEAN,
OUT OF MOMBASA
This is a mistake, my little Baboushka. When Clay said the conclave was being held on a boat, I expected a yacht in Monte Carlo!
Relax, Gyorgy.
All I have to do is gatecrash a secret meeting of the world's most powerful crime lords, outbid them for the most valuable black market intel in a decade, and then somehow get back without any of them killing me...
...what could possibly go wrong?
Roderick Thorp
NOTHING LASTS FOREVER
That is close enough. We will wait here till nightfall...
And then that ship is ours!

PART 2

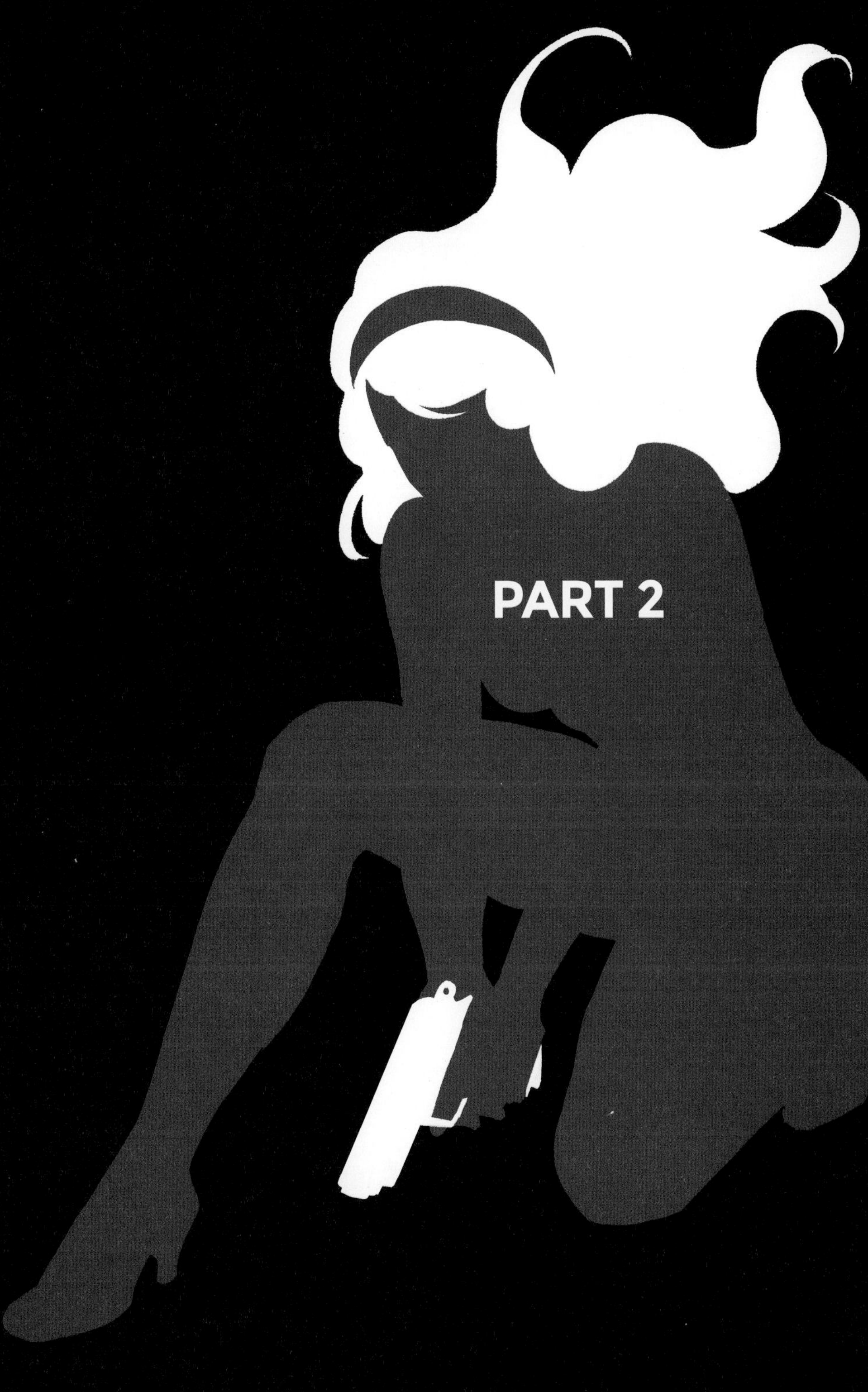

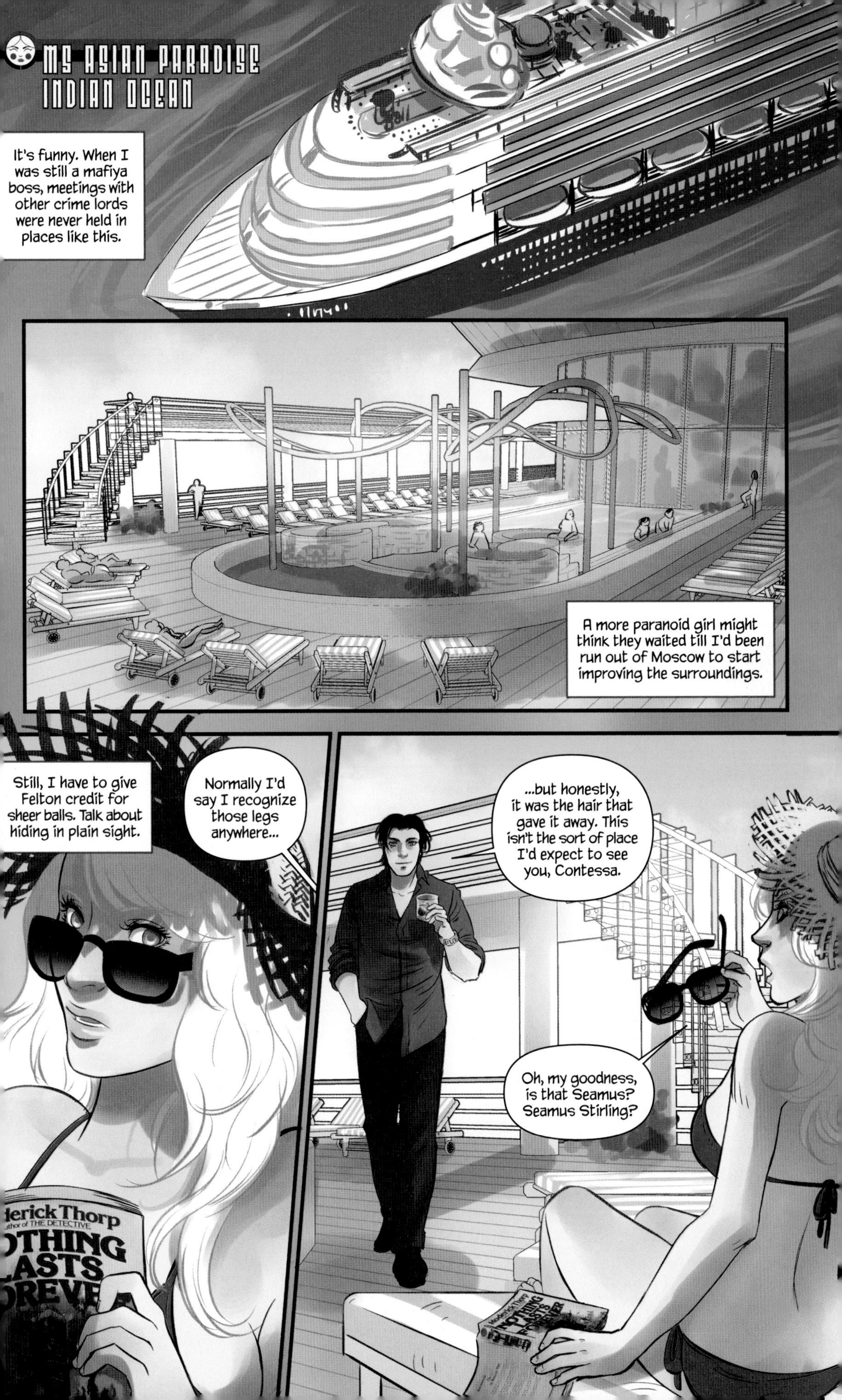
MS ASIAN PARADISE
INDIAN OCEAN
It's funny. When I was still a mafiya boss, meetings with other crime lords were never held in places like this.
A more paranoid girl might think they waited till I'd been run out of Moscow to start improving the surroundings.
Still, I have to give Felton credit for sheer balls. Talk about hiding in plain sight.
Normally I'd say I recognize those legs anywhere...
...but honestly, it was the hair that gave it away. This isn't the sort of place I'd expect to see you, Contessa.
Oh, my goodness, is that Seamus? Seamus Stirling?
THE DETECTIVE

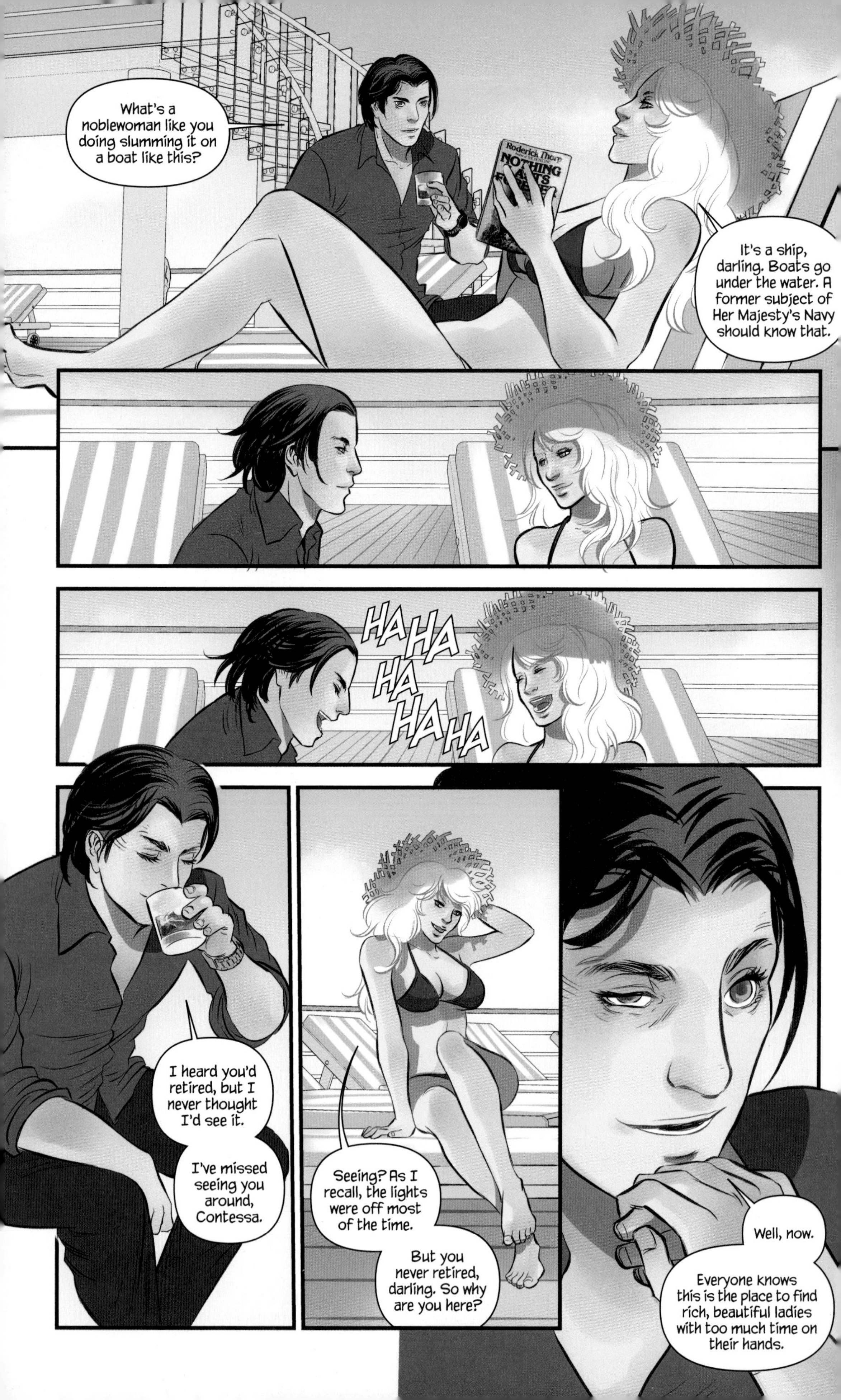
What's a noblewoman like you doing slumming it on a boat like this?
Roderick Thorp
It's a ship, darling. Boats go under the water. A former subject of Her Majesty's Navy should know that.
HAHA HA HAHAHA
I heard you'd retired, but I never thought I'd see it.
I've missed seeing you around, Contessa.
Seeing? As I recall, the lights were off most of the time.
But you never retired, darling. So why are you here?
Well, now.
Everyone knows this is the place to find rich, beautiful ladies with too much time on their hands.

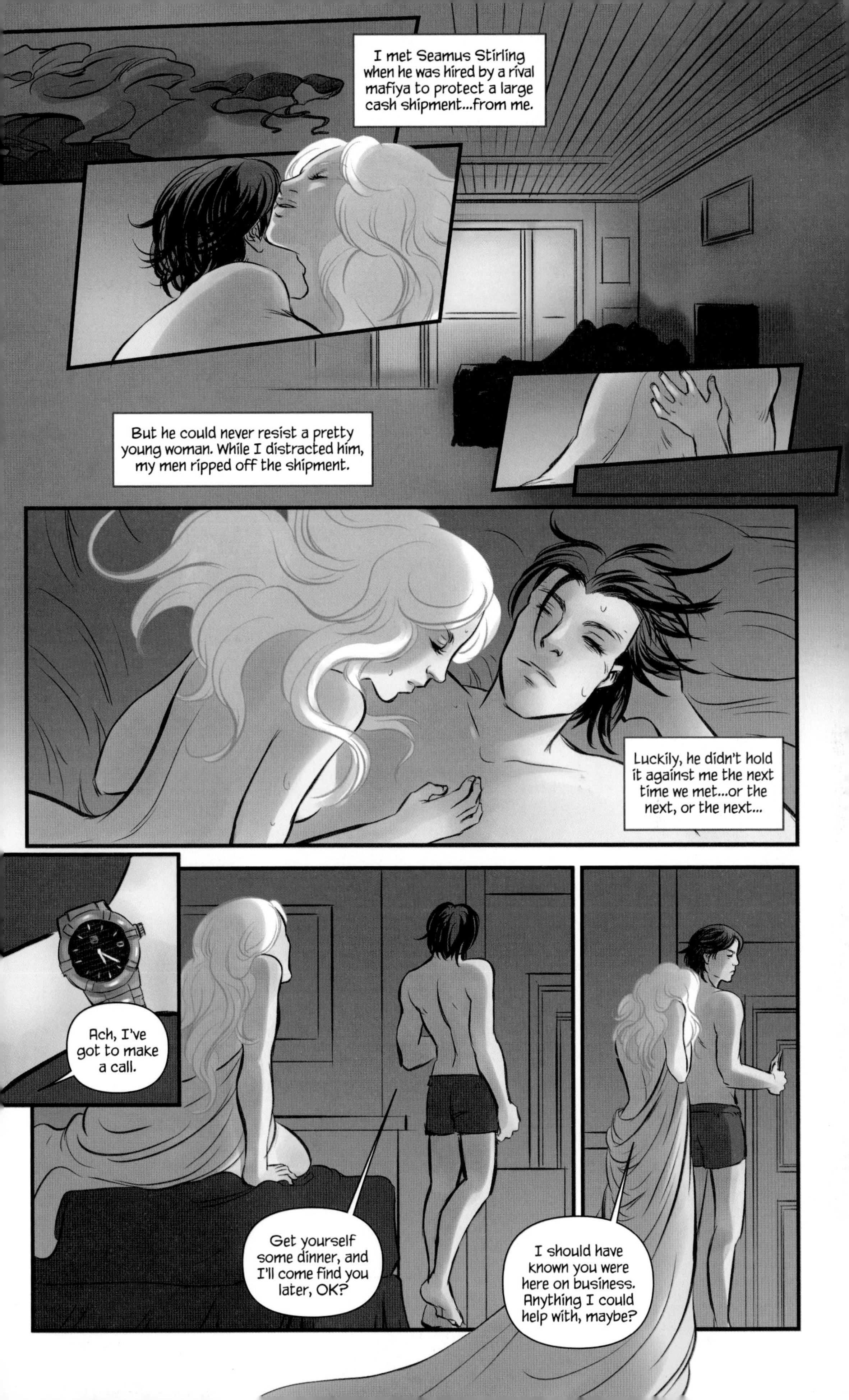
I met Seamus Stirling when he was hired by a rival mafiya to protect a large cash shipment...from me.
But he could never resist a pretty young woman. While I distracted him, my men ripped off the shipment.
Luckily, he didn't hold it against me the next time we met...or the next, or the next...
Ach, I've got to make a call.
Get yourself some dinner, and I'll come find you later, OK?
I should have known you were here on business. Anything I could help with, maybe?

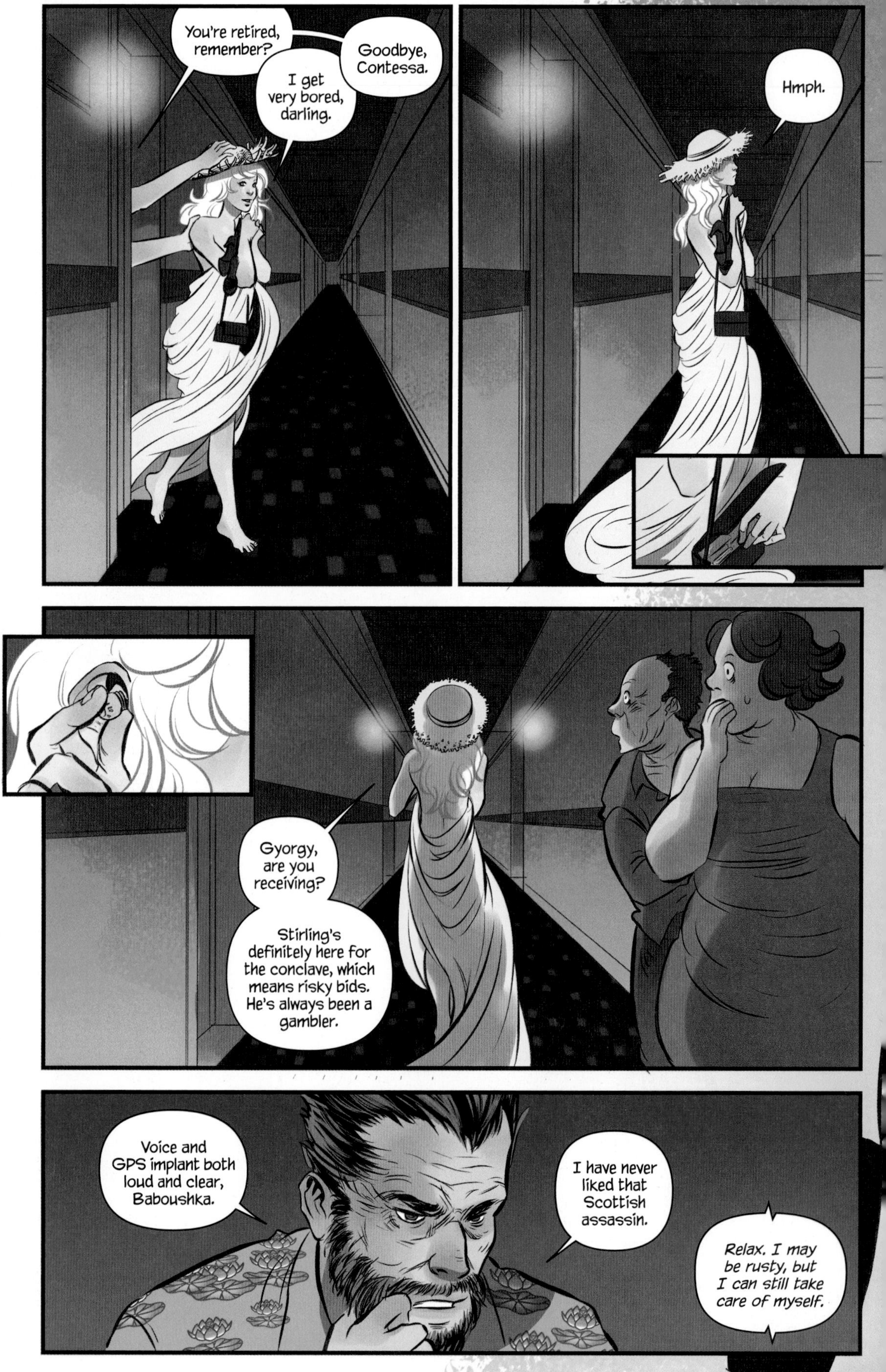
You're retired, remember?
Goodbye, Contessa.
I get very bored, darling.
Hmph.
Gyorgy, are you receiving?
Stirling's definitely here for the conclave, which means risky bids. He's always been a gambler.
Voice and GPS implant both loud and clear, Baboushka.
I have never liked that Scottish assassin.
Relax. I may be rusty, but I can still take care of myself.

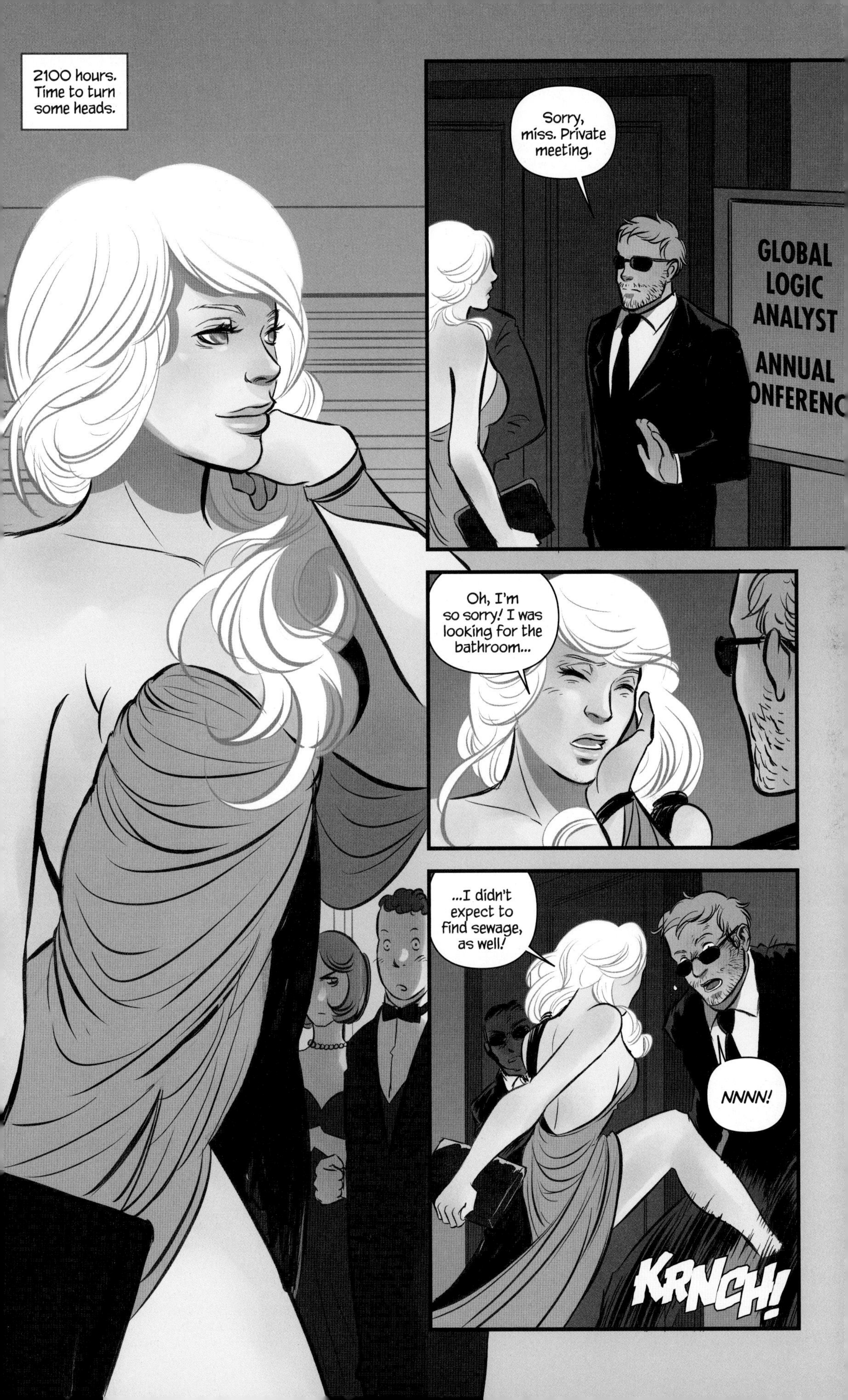
2100 hours. Time to turn some heads.
Sorry, miss. Private meeting.
GLOBAL LOGIC ANALYST ANNUAL ONFERENC
Oh, I'm so sorry! I was looking for the bathroom...
...I didn't expect to find sewage, as well!
NNNN!
KRNCH!

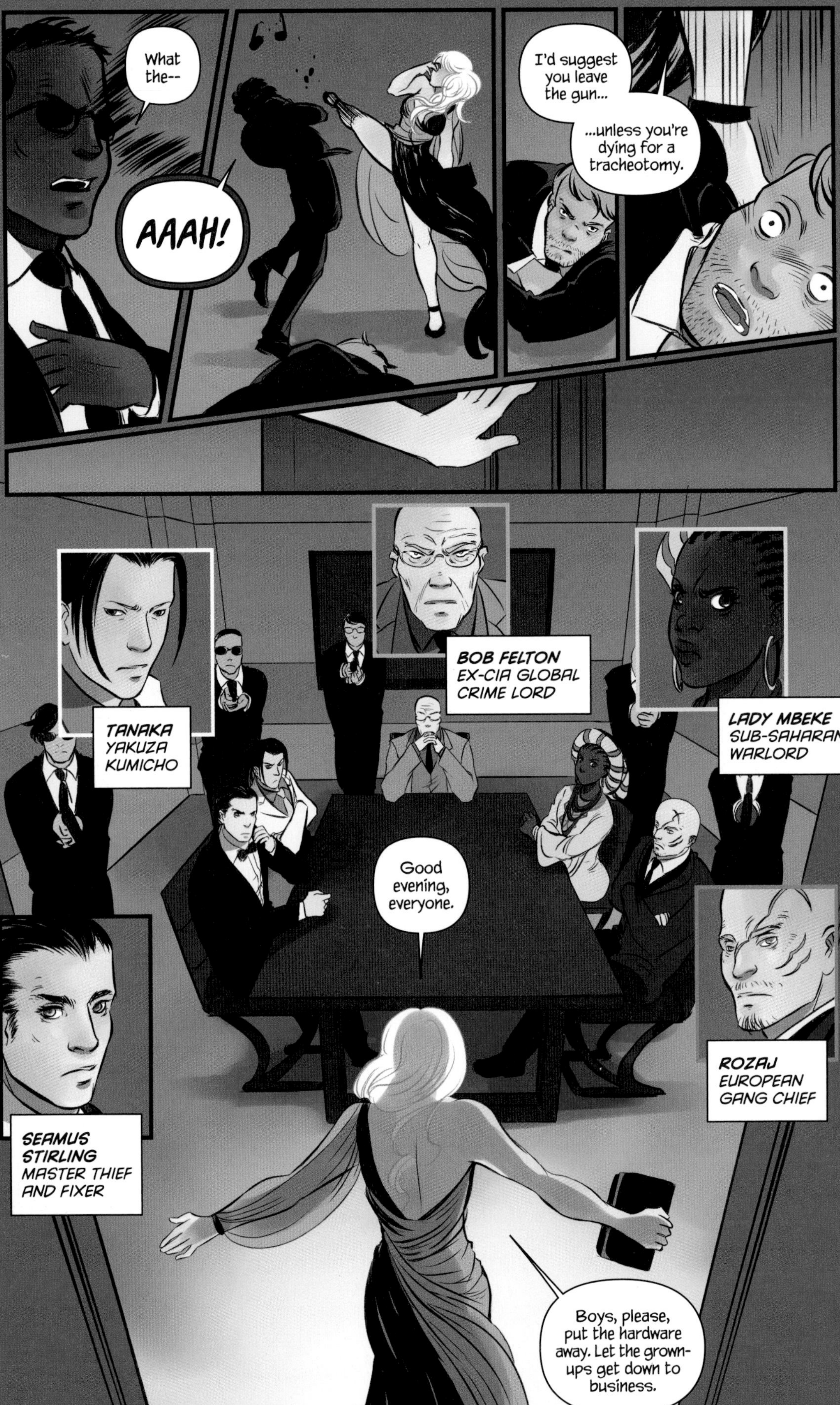
What the--
AAAH!
I'd suggest you leave the gun...
...unless you're dying for a tracheotomy.
BOB FELTON
EX-CIA GLOBAL CRIME LORD
TANAKA
YAKUZA KUMICHO
LADY MBEKE
SUB-SAHARAN WARLORD
Good evening, everyone.
SEAMUS STIRLING
MASTER THIEF AND FIXER
ROZAJ
EUROPEAN GANG CHIEF
Boys, please, put the hardware away. Let the grown-ups get down to business.

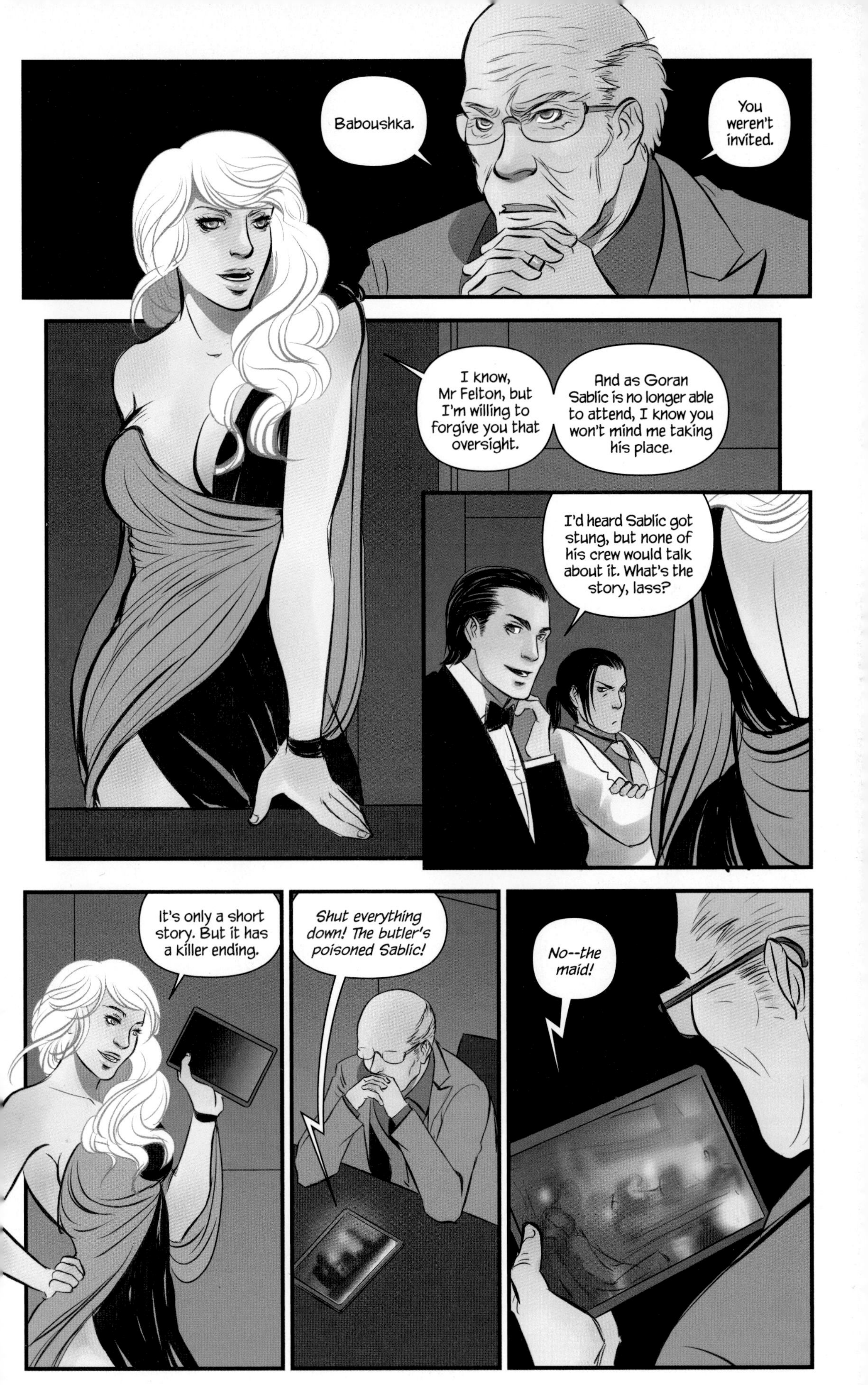
Baboushka.
You weren't invited.
I know, Mr Felton, but I'm willing to forgive you that oversight.
And as Goran Sablic is no longer able to attend, I know you won't mind me taking his place.
I'd heard Sablic got stung, but none of his crew would talk about it. What's the story, lass?
It's only a short story. But it has a killer ending.
Shut everything down! The butler's poisoned Sablic!
No--the maid!

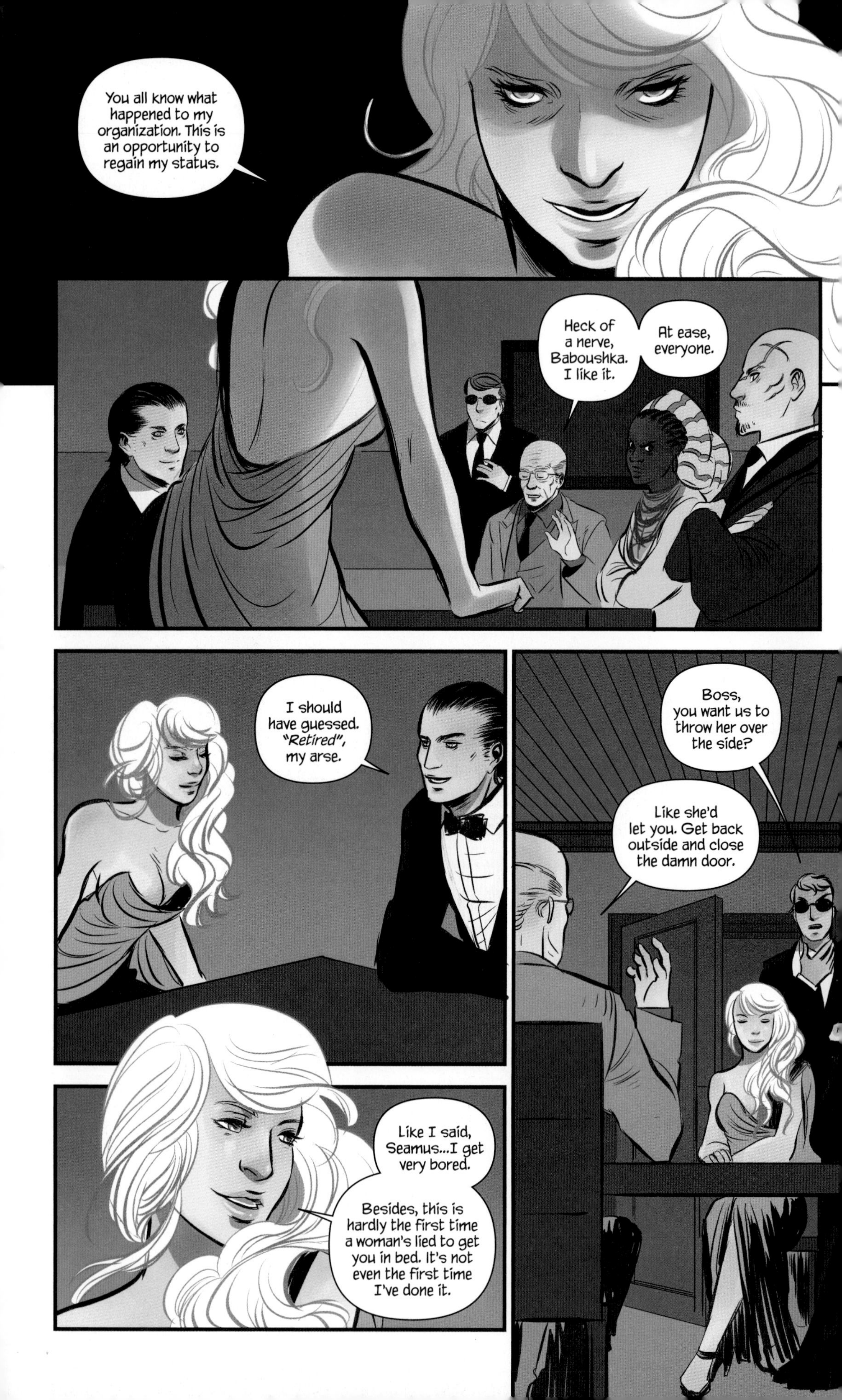
You all know what happened to my organization. This is an opportunity to regain my status.
Heck of a nerve, Baboushka. I like it.
At ease, everyone.
I should have guessed. "*Retired*", my arse.
Boss, you want us to throw her over the side?
Like she'd let you. Get back outside and close the damn door.
Like I said, Seamus...I get very bored.
Besides, this is hardly the first time a woman's lied to get you in bed. It's not even the first time I've done it.

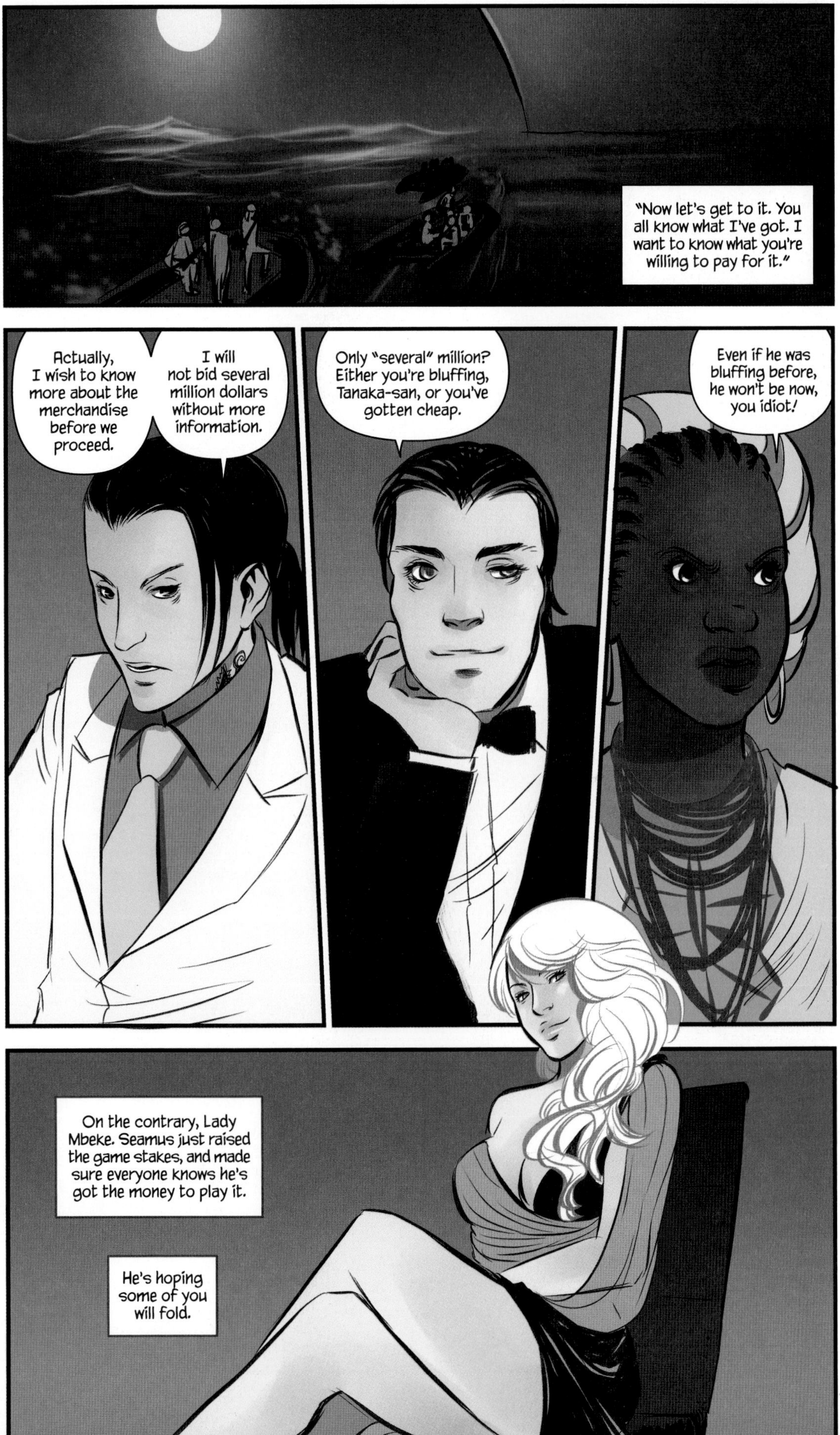
"Now let's get to it. You all know what I've got. I want to know what you're willing to pay for it."
Actually, I wish to know more about the merchandise before we proceed.
I will not bid several million dollars without more information.
Only "several" million? Either you're bluffing, Tanaka-san, or you've gotten cheap.
Even if he was bluffing before, he won't be now, you idiot!
On the contrary, Lady Mbeke. Seamus just raised the game stakes, and made sure everyone knows he's got the money to play it.
He's hoping some of you will fold.

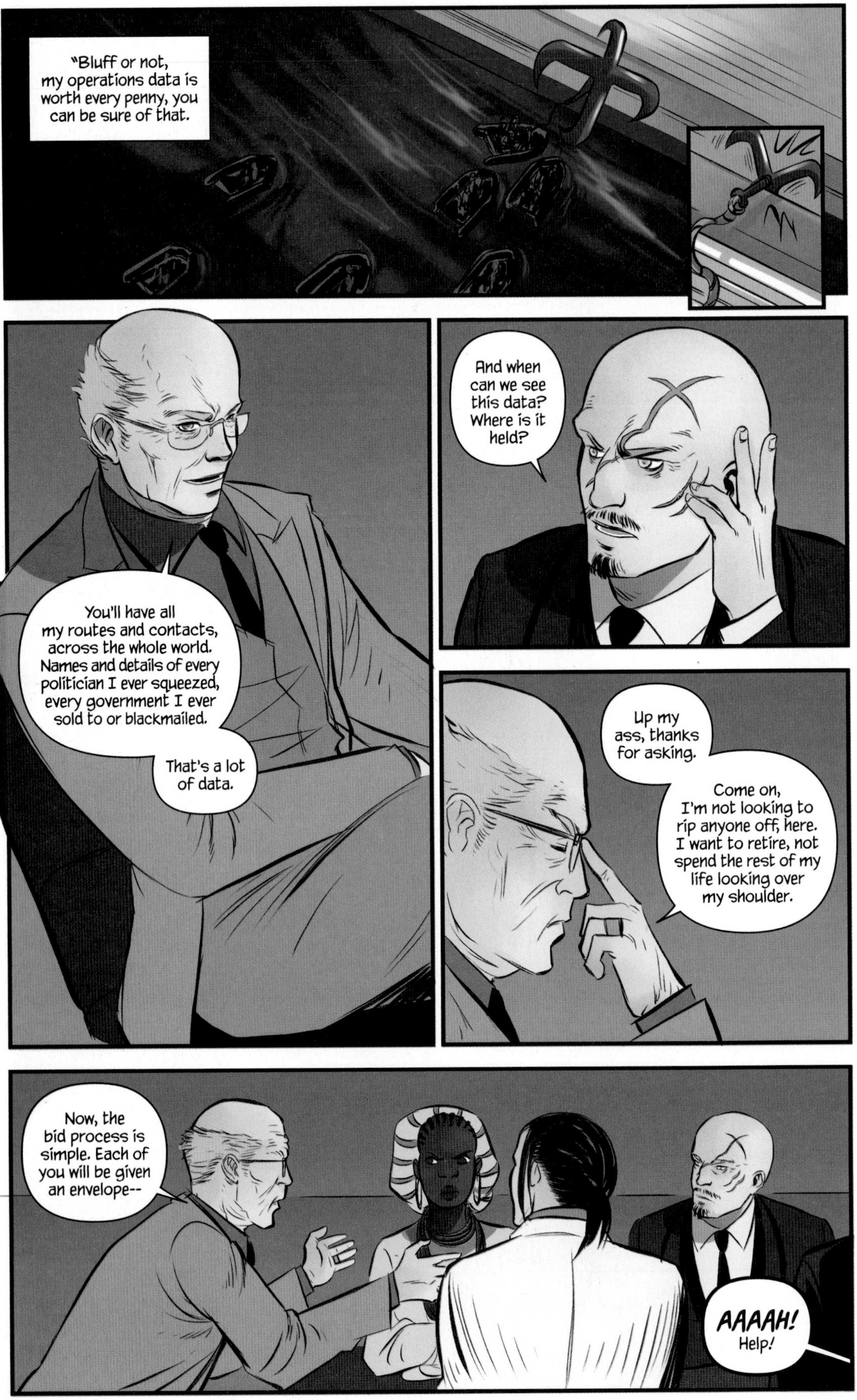
"Bluff or not, my operations data is worth every penny, you can be sure of that.
And when can we see this data? Where is it held?
You'll have all my routes and contacts, across the whole world. Names and details of every politician I ever squeezed, every government I ever sold to or blackmailed.
That's a lot of data.
Up my ass, thanks for asking.
Come on, I'm not looking to rip anyone off, here. I want to retire, not spend the rest of my life looking over my shoulder.
Now, the bid process is simple. Each of you will be given an envelope--
AAAAH! Help!

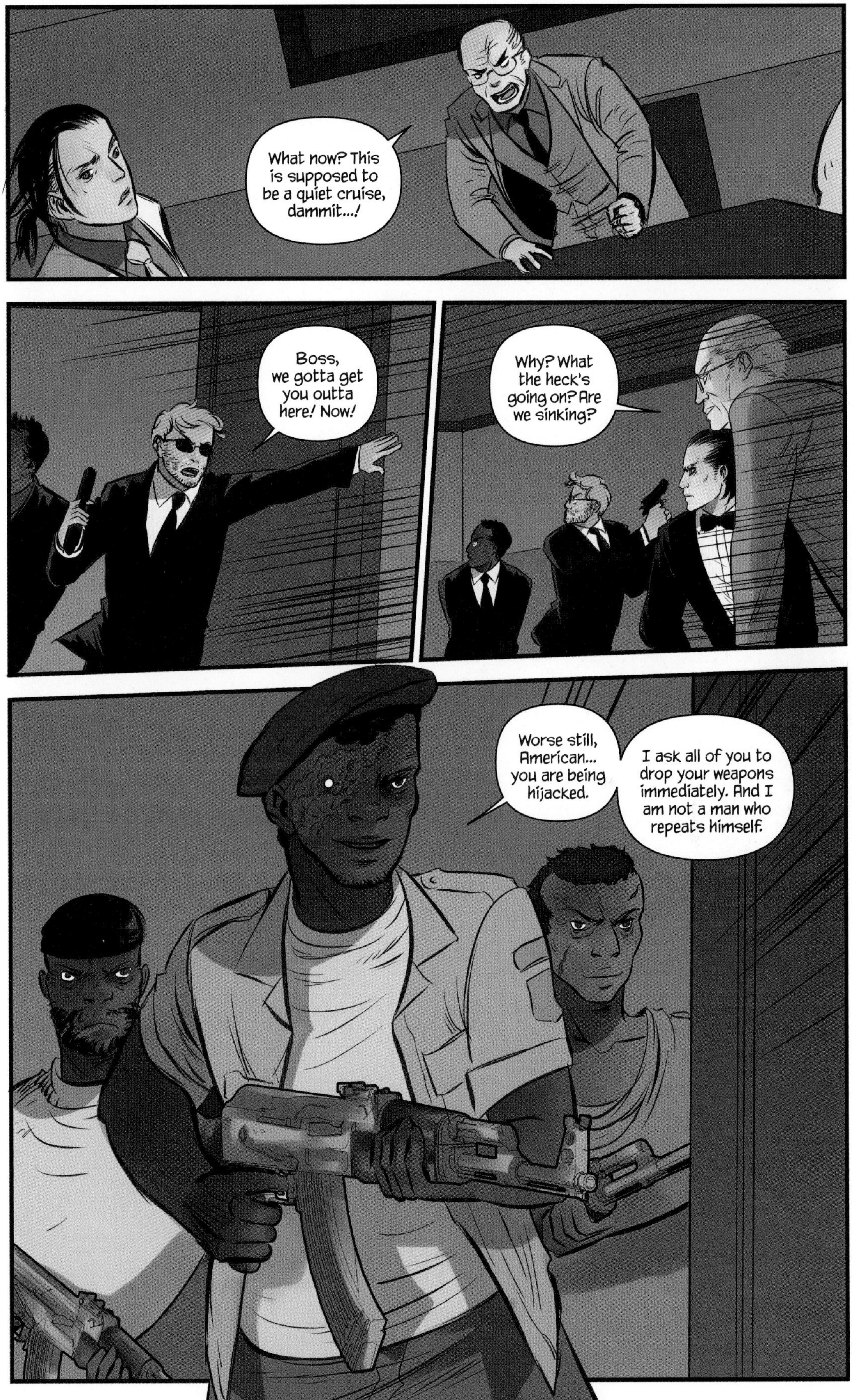
What now? This is supposed to be a quiet cruise, dammit...!
Boss, we gotta get you outta here! Now!
Why? What the heck's going on? Are we sinking?
Worse still, American... you are being hijacked.
I ask all of you to drop your weapons immediately. And I am not a man who repeats himself.

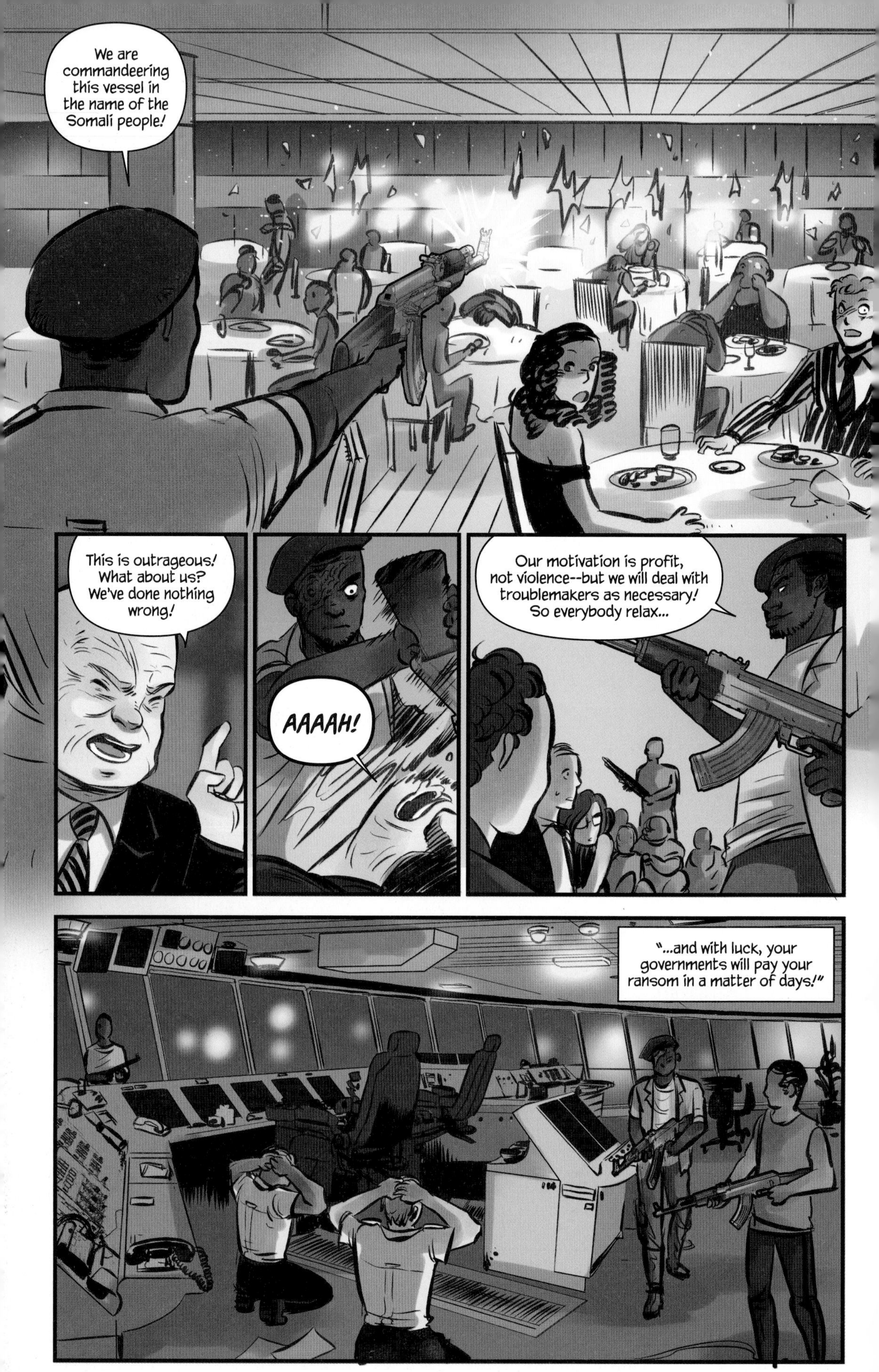
We are commandeering this vessel in the name of the Somali people!
This is outrageous! What about us? We've done nothing wrong!
AAAAH!
Our motivation is profit, not violence--but we will deal with troublemakers as necessary! So everybody relax...
"...and with luck, your governments will pay your ransom in a matter of days!"

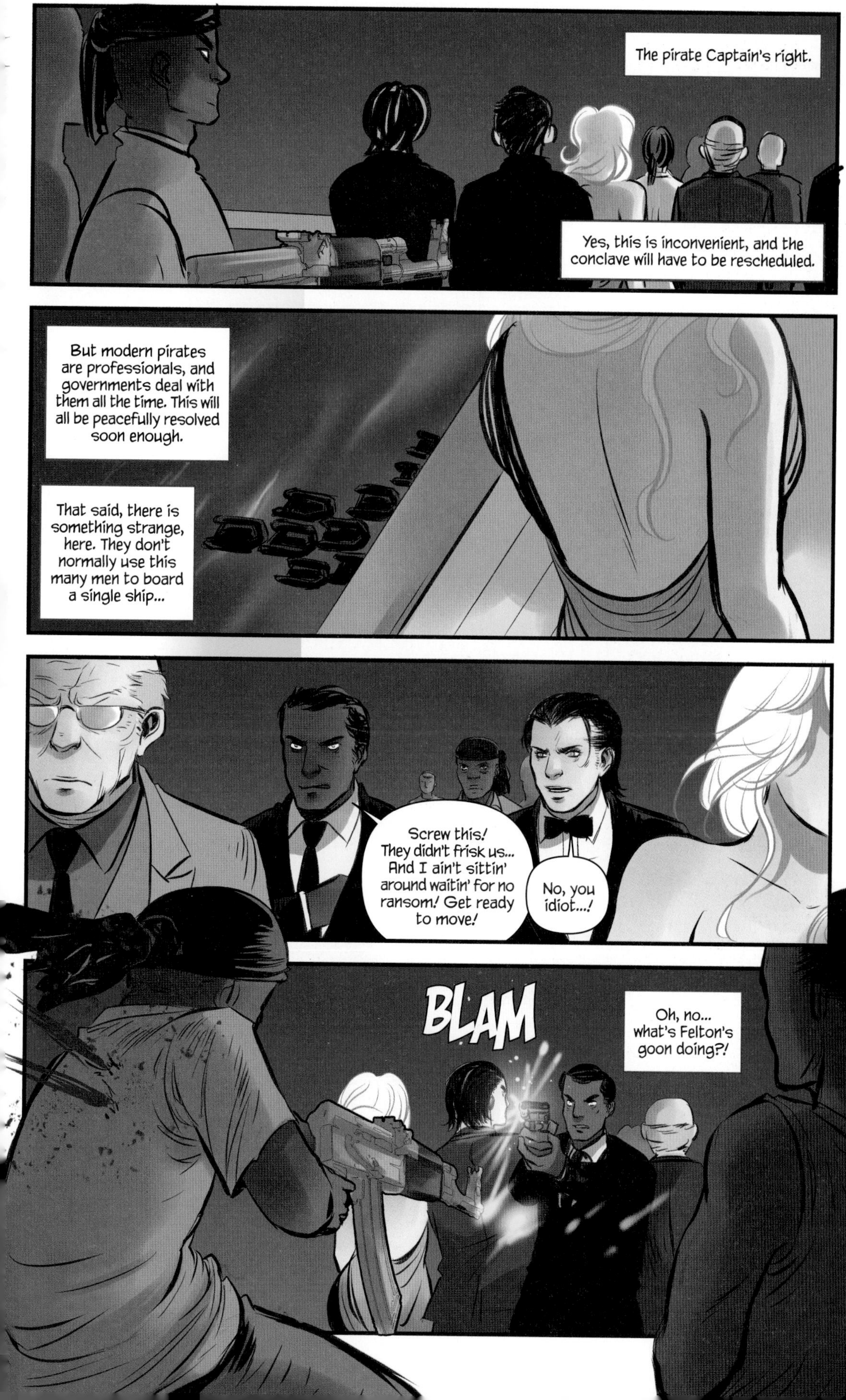

The pirate Captain's right.
Yes, this is inconvenient, and the conclave will have to be rescheduled.
But modern pirates are professionals, and governments deal with them all the time. This will all be peacefully resolved soon enough.
That said, there is something strange, here. They don't normally use this many men to board a single ship...
Screw this! They didn't frisk us... And I ain't sittin' around waitin' for no ransom! Get ready to move!
No, you idiot...!
BLAM
Oh, no... what's Felton's goon doing?!

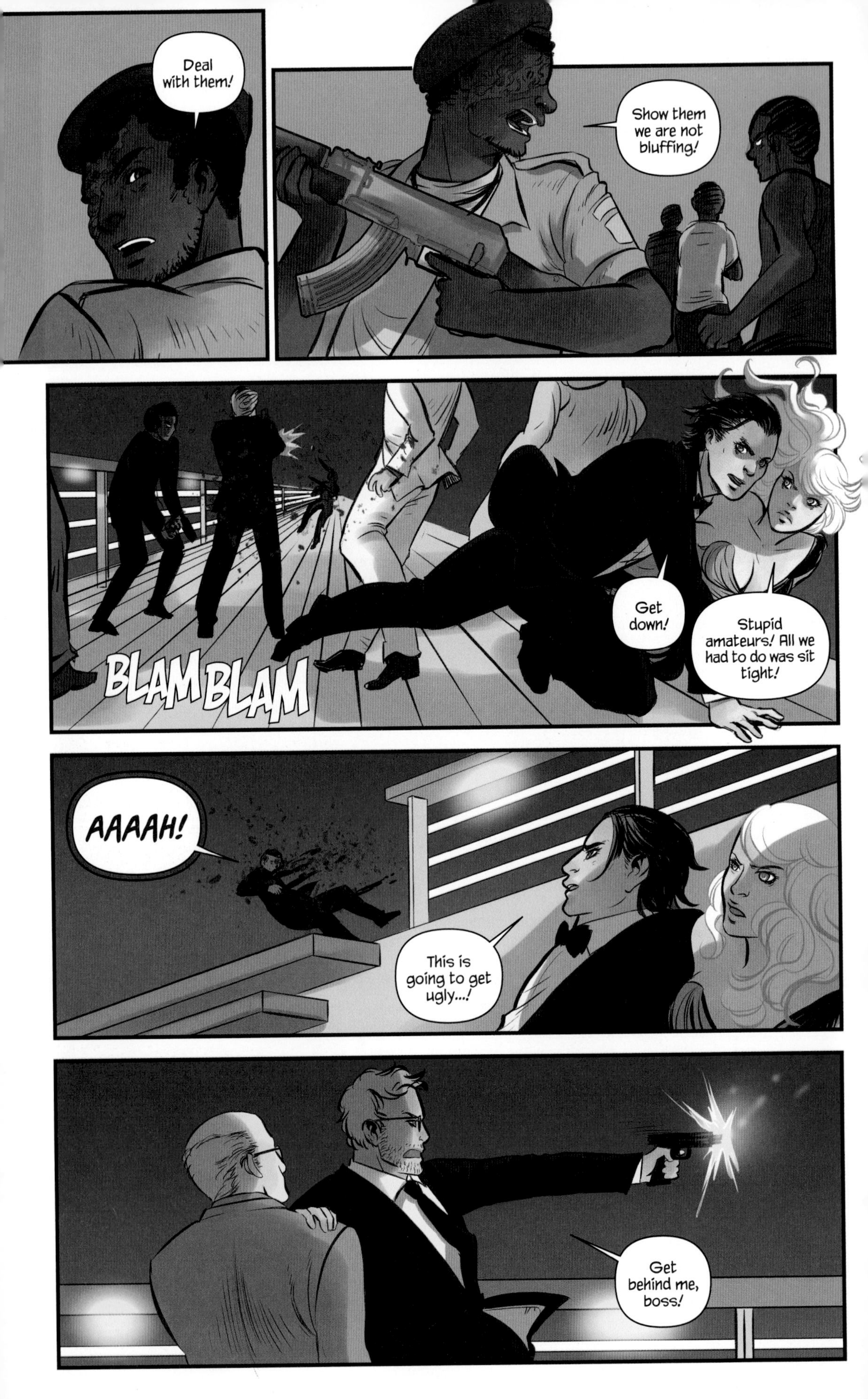
Deal with them!
Show them we are not bluffing!
BLAM BLAM
Get down!
Stupid amateurs! All we had to do was sit tight!
AAAAH!
This is going to get ugly...!
Get behind me, boss!

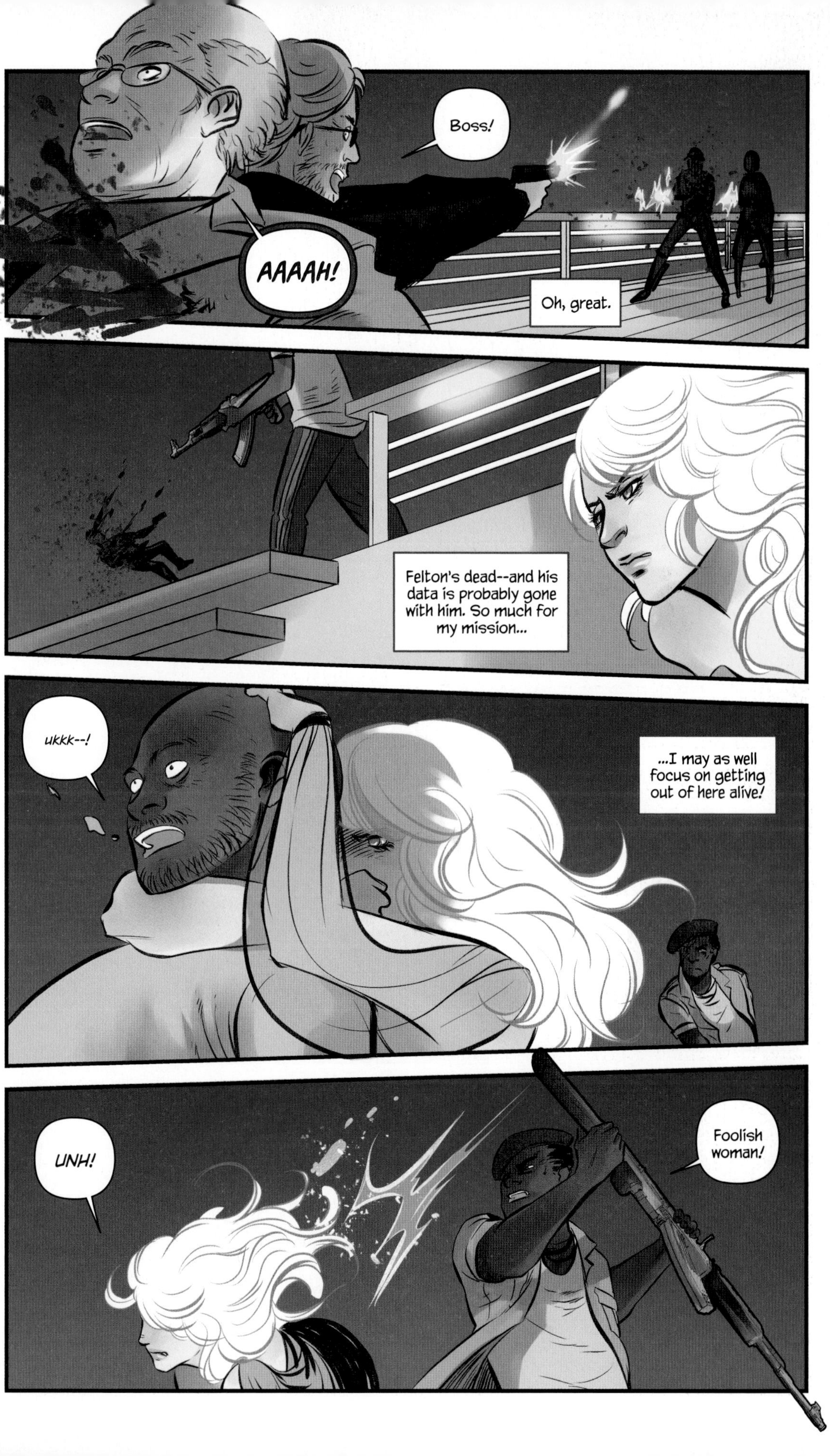
Boss!
AAAAH!
Oh, great.
Felton's dead--and his data is probably gone with him. So much for my mission...
ukkk--!
...I may as well focus on getting out of here alive!
UNH!
Foolish woman!

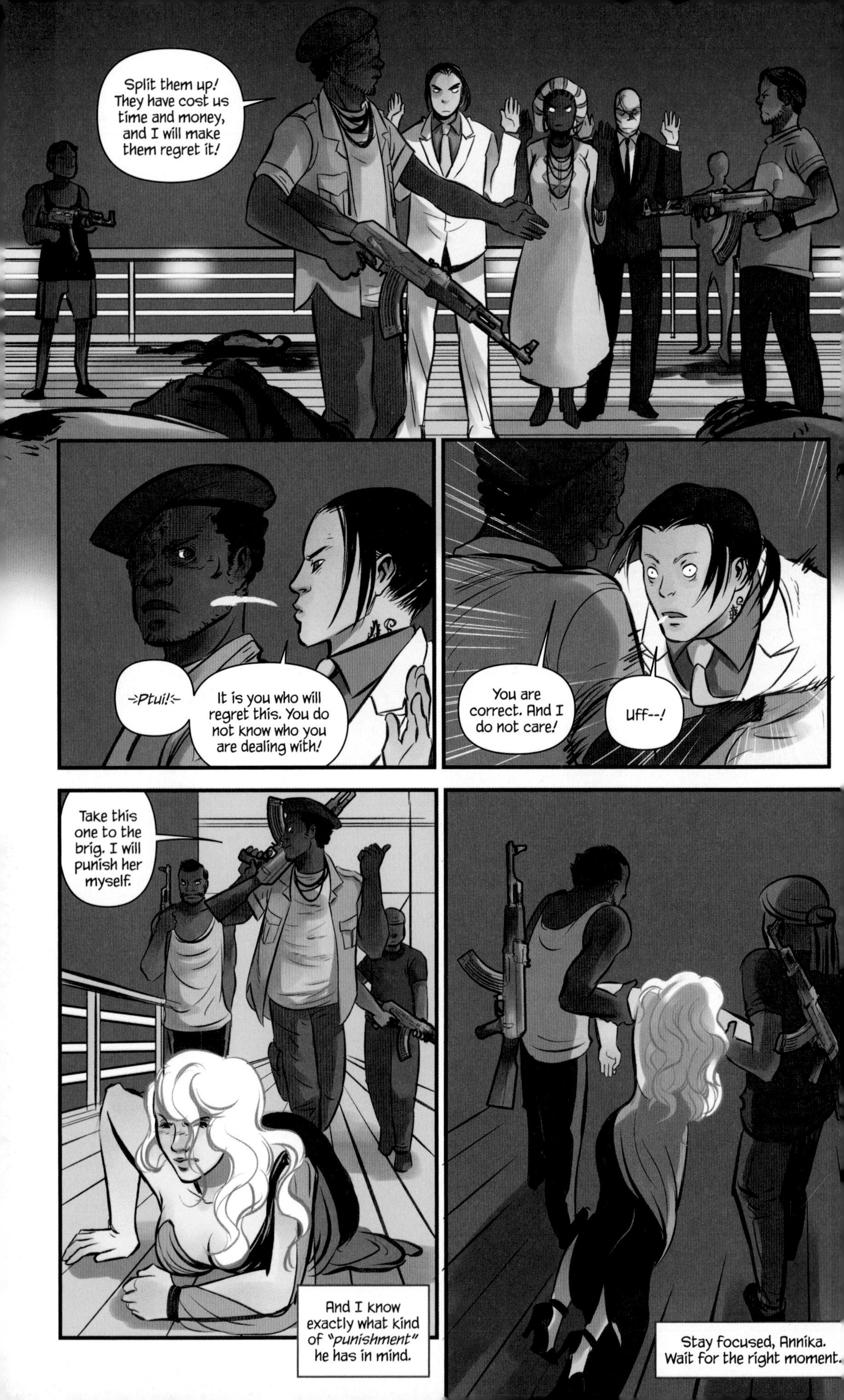
Split them up! They have cost us time and money, and I will make them regret it!
-Ptui!-
It is you who will regret this. You do not know who you are dealing with!
You are correct. And I do not care!
Uff--!
Take this one to the brig. I will punish her myself.
And I know exactly what kind of "punishment" he has in mind.
Stay focused, Annika. Wait for the right moment.

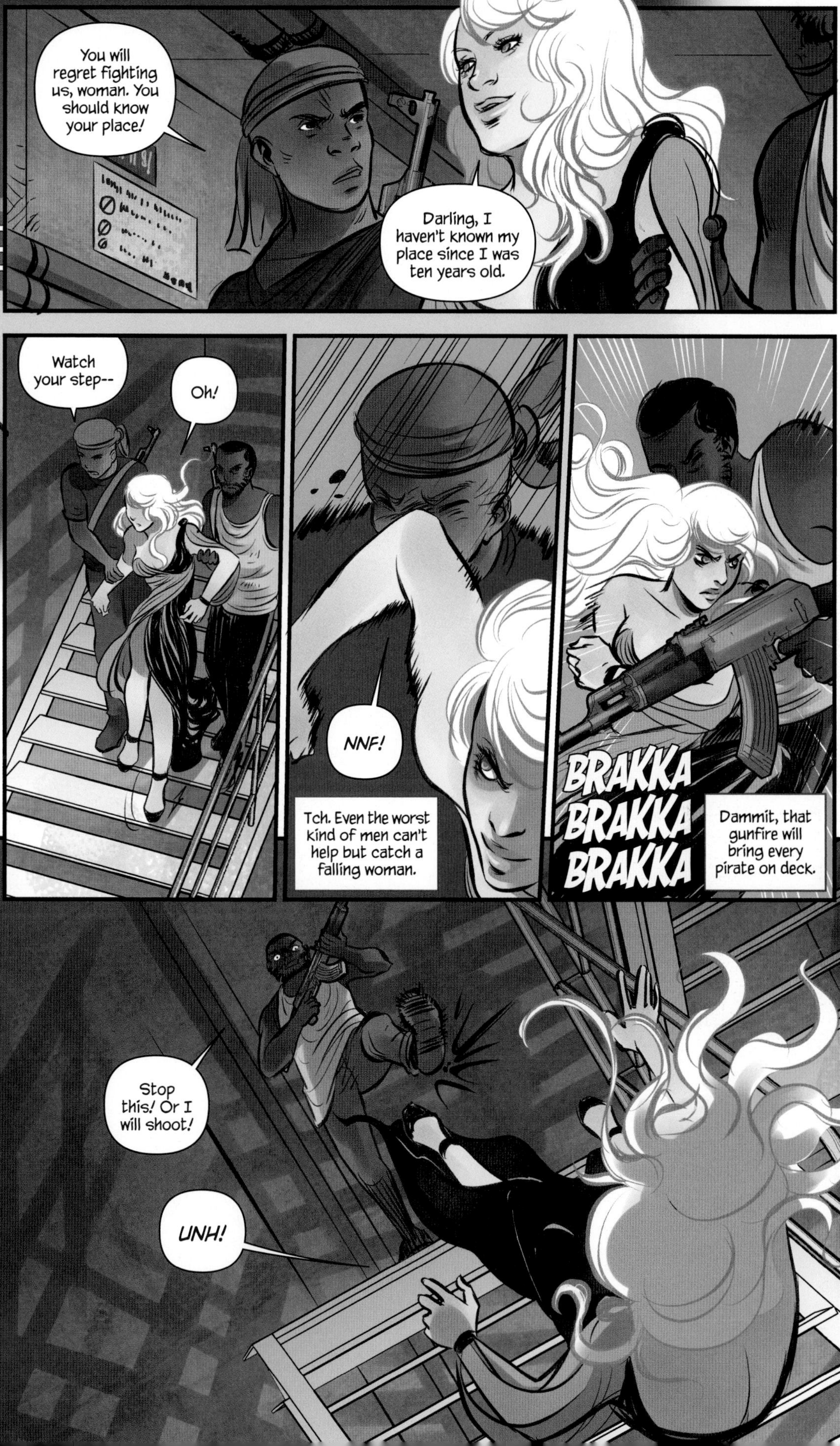
You will regret fighting us, woman. You should know your place!
Darling, I haven't known my place since I was ten years old.
Watch your step--
Oh!
NNF!
Tch. Even the worst kind of men can't help but catch a falling woman.
BRAKKA BRAKKA BRAKKA
Dammit, that gunfire will bring every pirate on deck.
Stop this! Or I will shoot!
UNH!

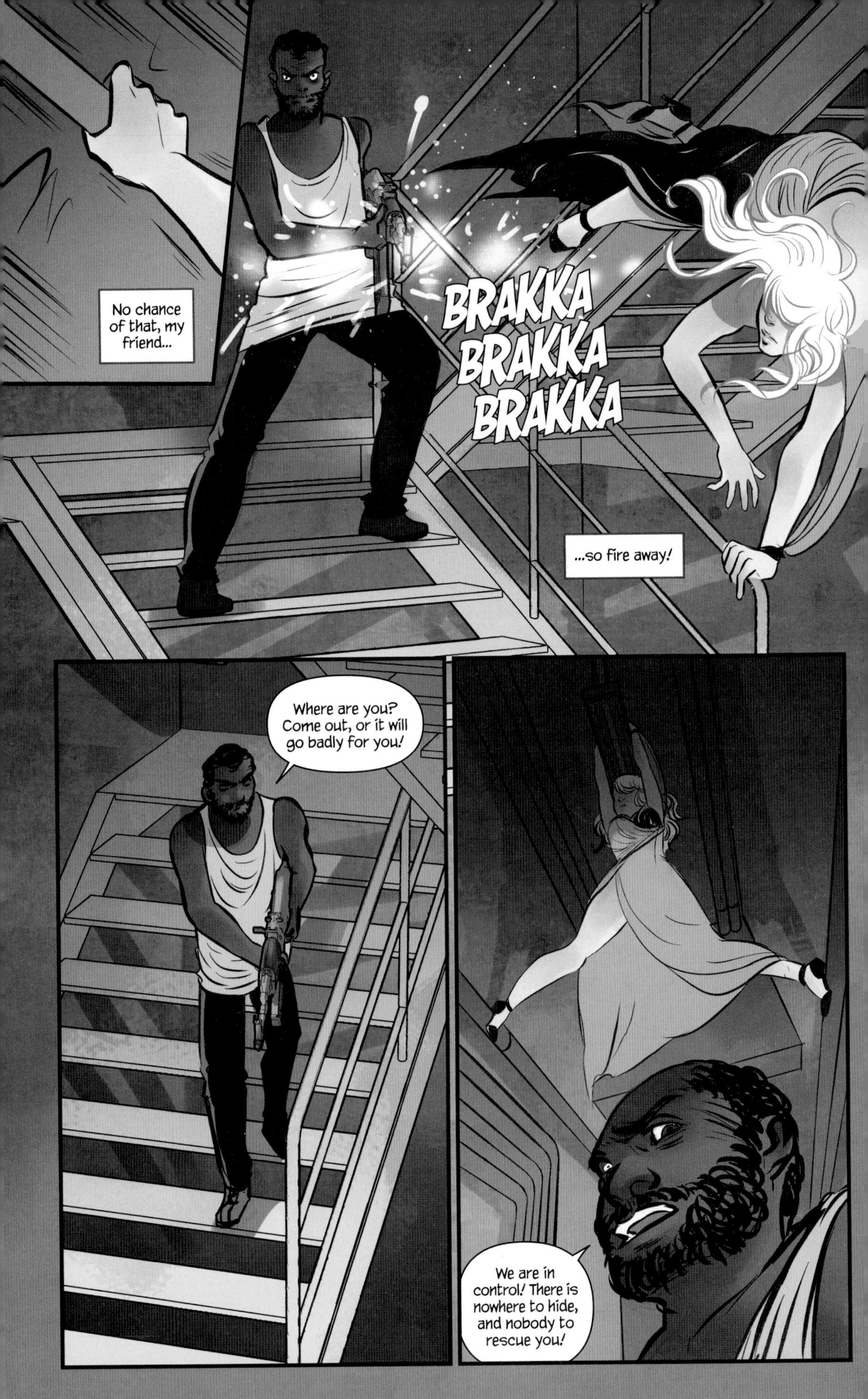
No chance of that, my friend...
BRAKKA BRAKKA BRAKKA
...so fire away!
Where are you? Come out, or it will go badly for you!
We are in control! There is nowhere to hide, and nobody to rescue you!

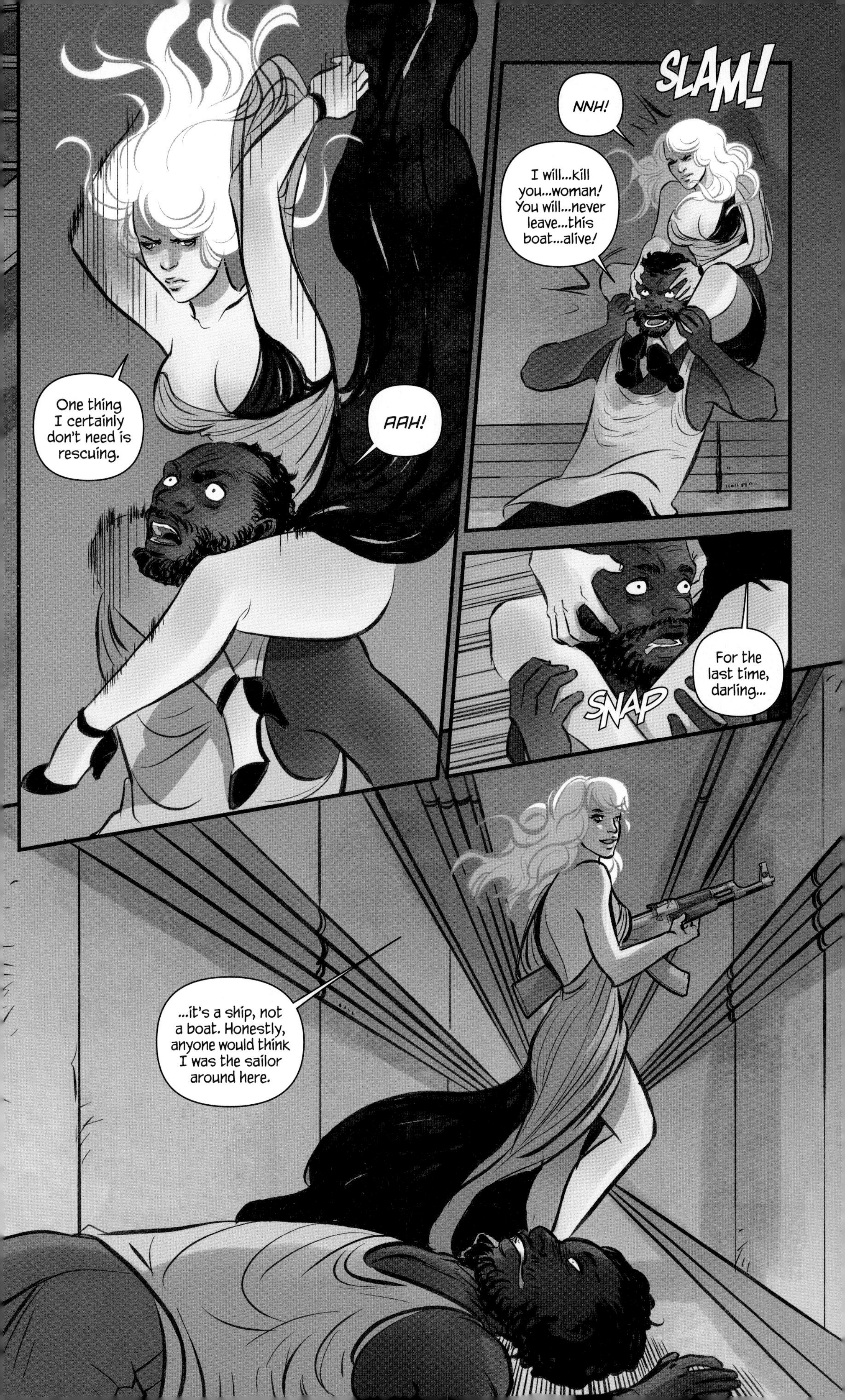
One thing I certainly don't need is rescuing.
AAH!
SLAM!
NNH!
I will...kill you...woman! You will...never leave...this boat...alive!
For the last time, darling...
SNAP
...it's a ship, not a boat. Honestly, anyone would think I was the sailor around here.

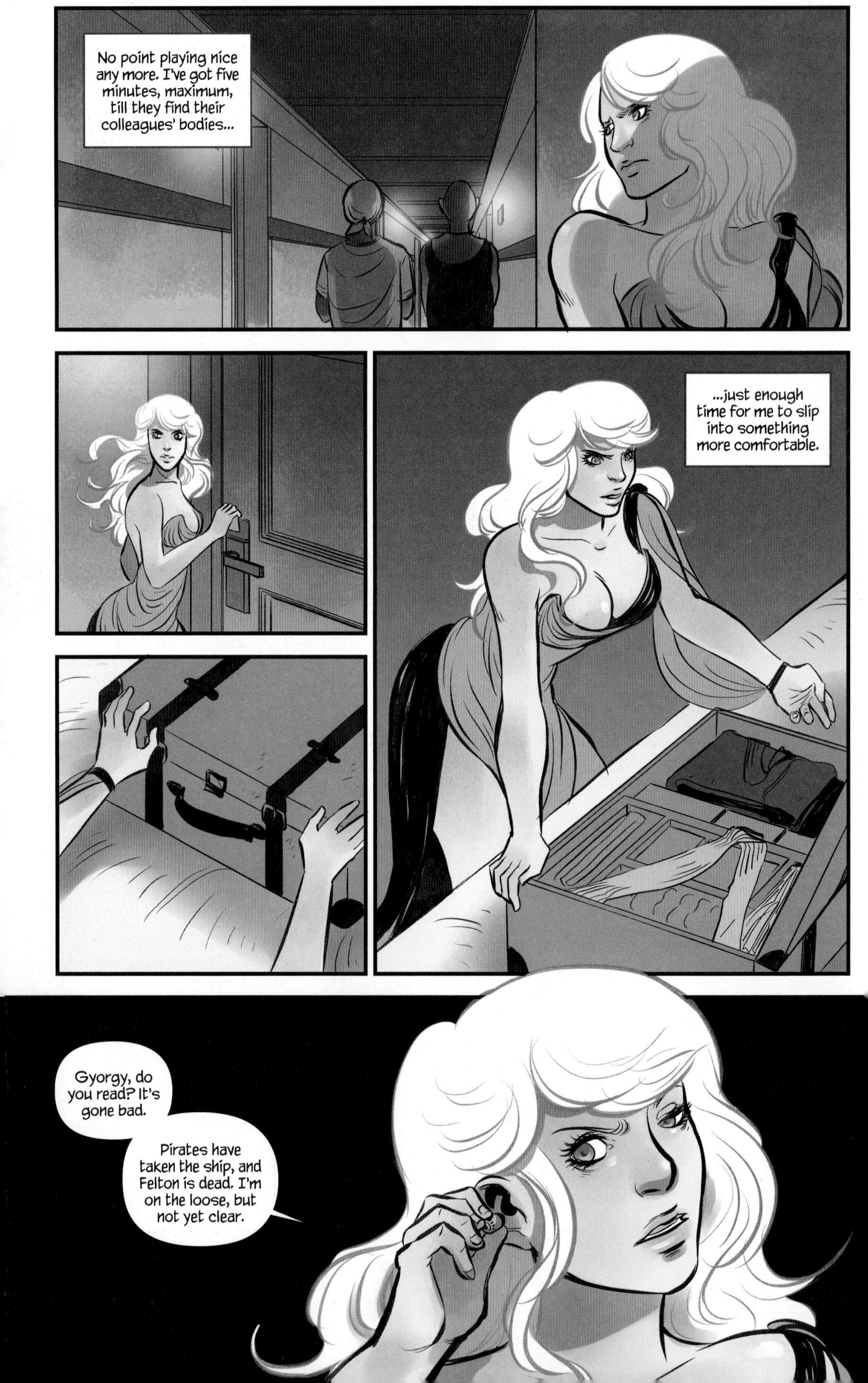
No point playing nice any more. I've got five minutes, maximum, till they find their colleagues' bodies...
...just enough time for me to slip into something more comfortable.
Gyorgy, do you read? It's gone bad.
Pirates have taken the ship, and Felton is dead. I'm on the loose, but not yet clear.

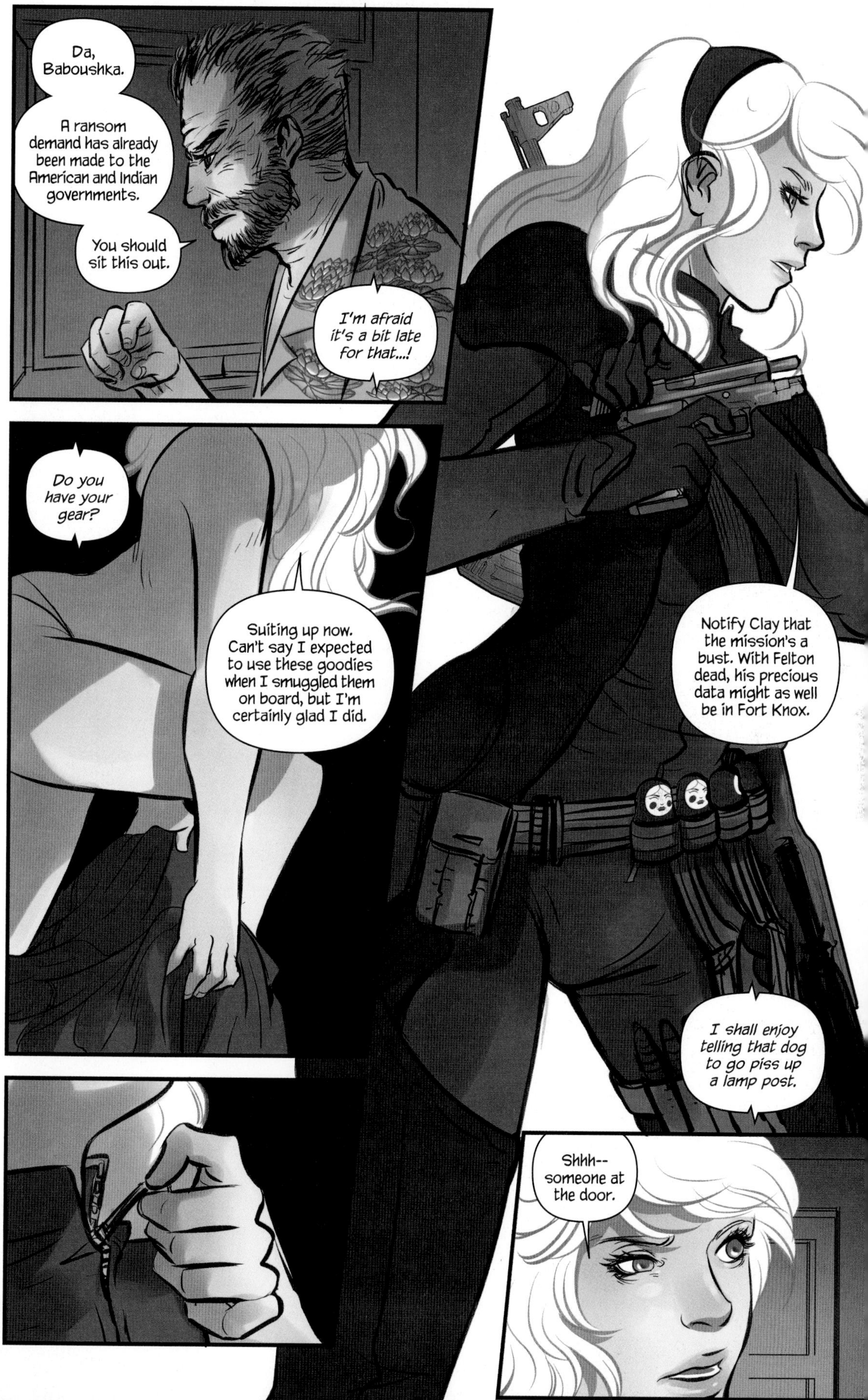
Da, Baboushka.
A ransom demand has already been made to the American and Indian governments.
You should sit this out.
I'm afraid it's a bit late for that...!
Do you have your gear?
Suiting up now. Can't say I expected to use these goodies when I smuggled them on board, but I'm certainly glad I did.
Notify Clay that the mission's a bust. With Felton dead, his precious data might as well be in Fort Knox.
I shall enjoy telling that dog to go piss up a lamp post.
Shhh-- someone at the door.

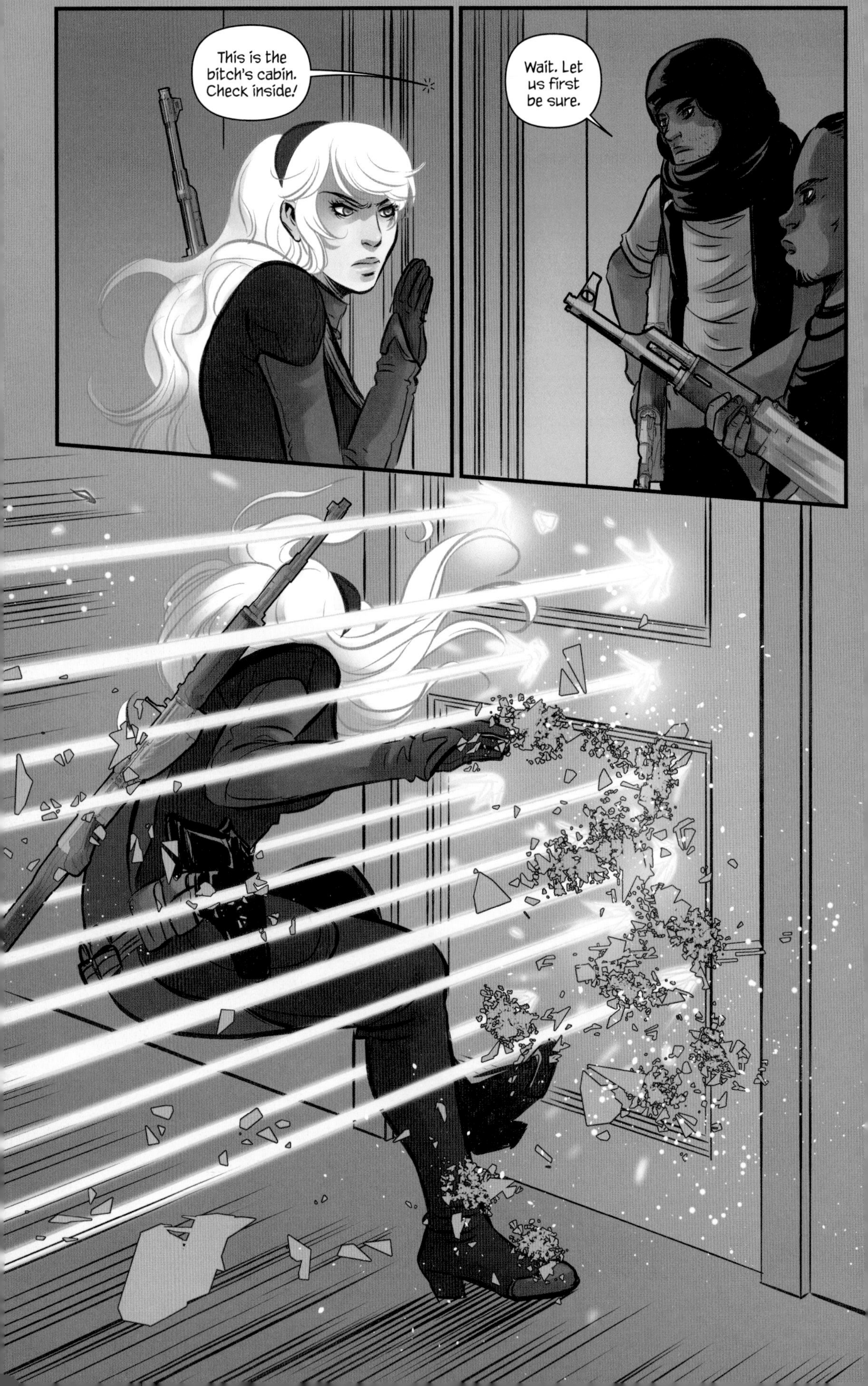
This is the bitch's cabin. Check inside!
Wait. Let us first be sure.

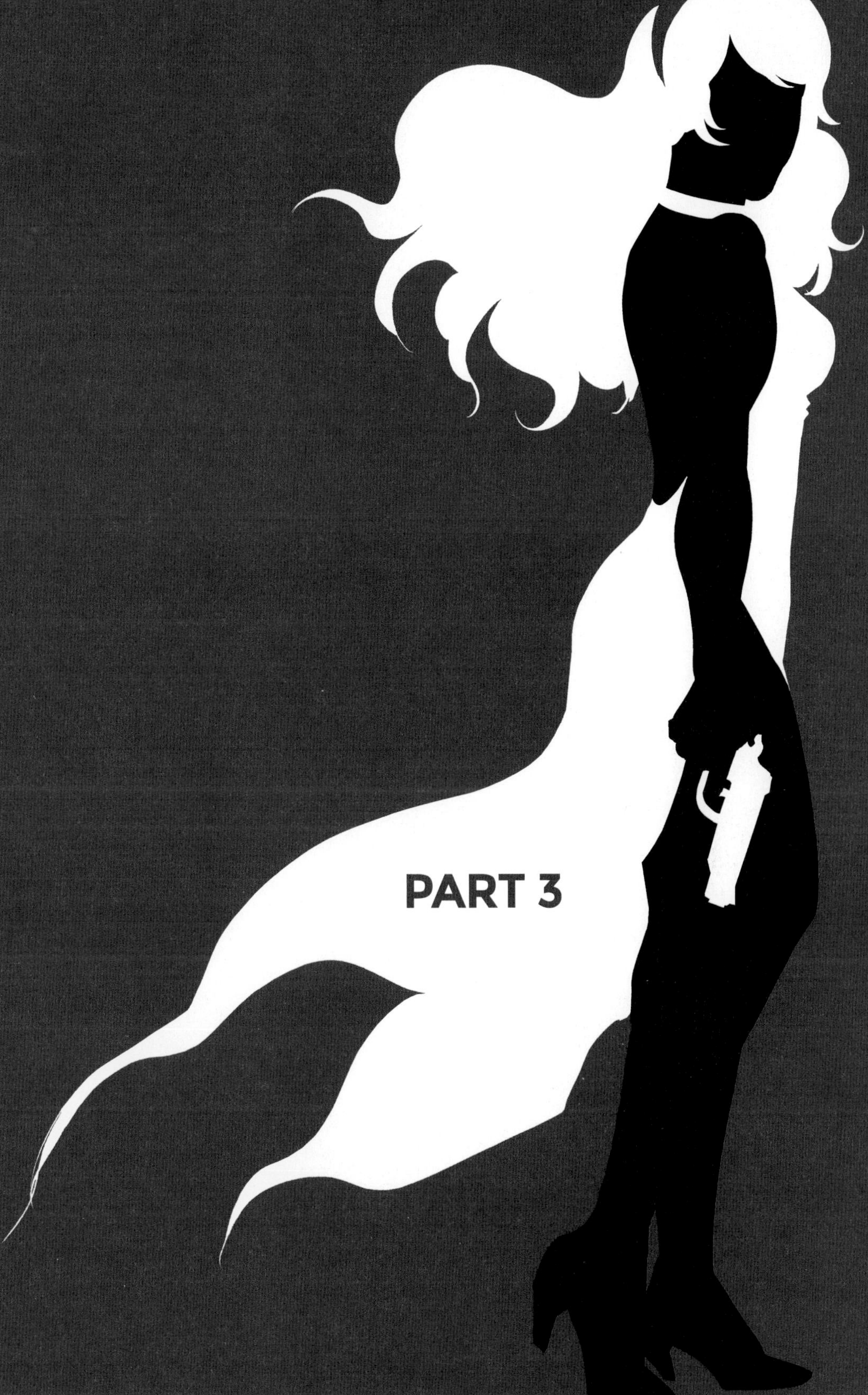

PART 3

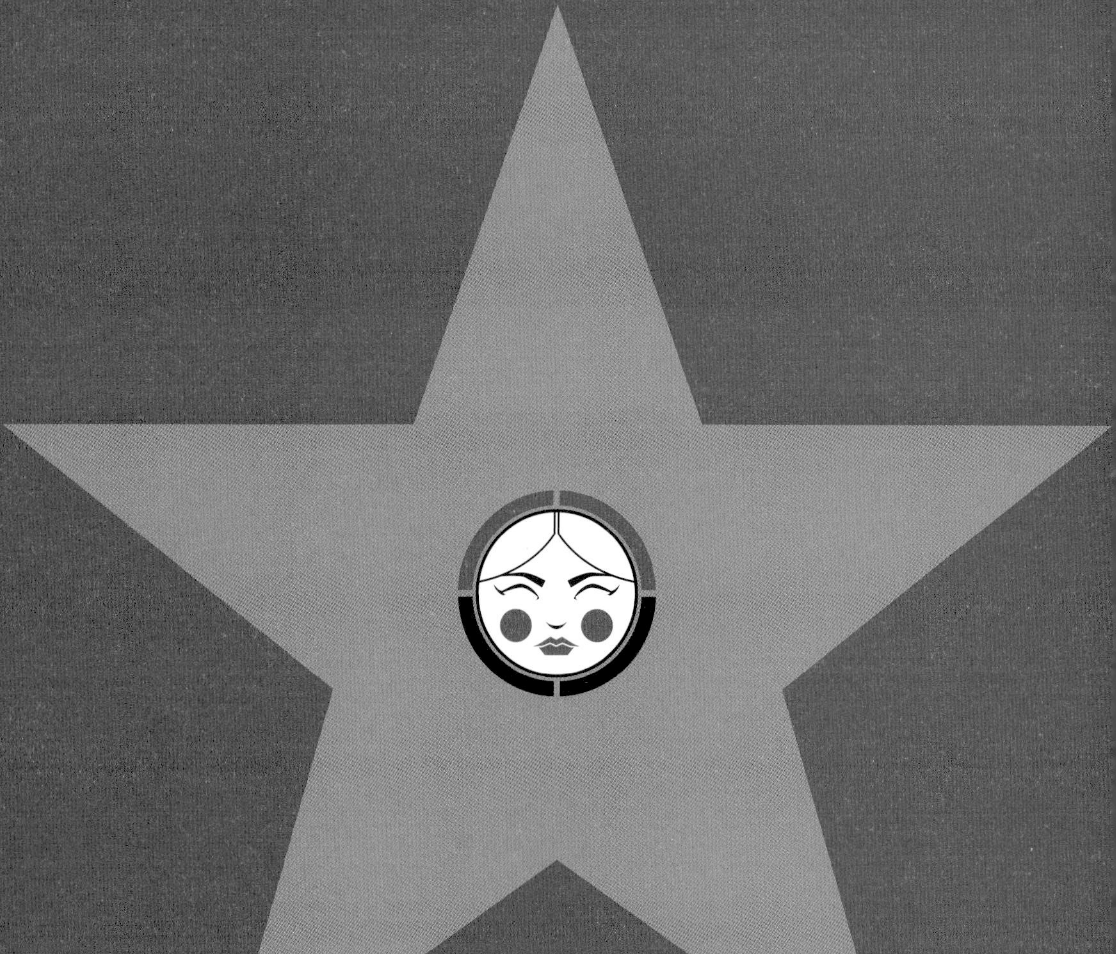

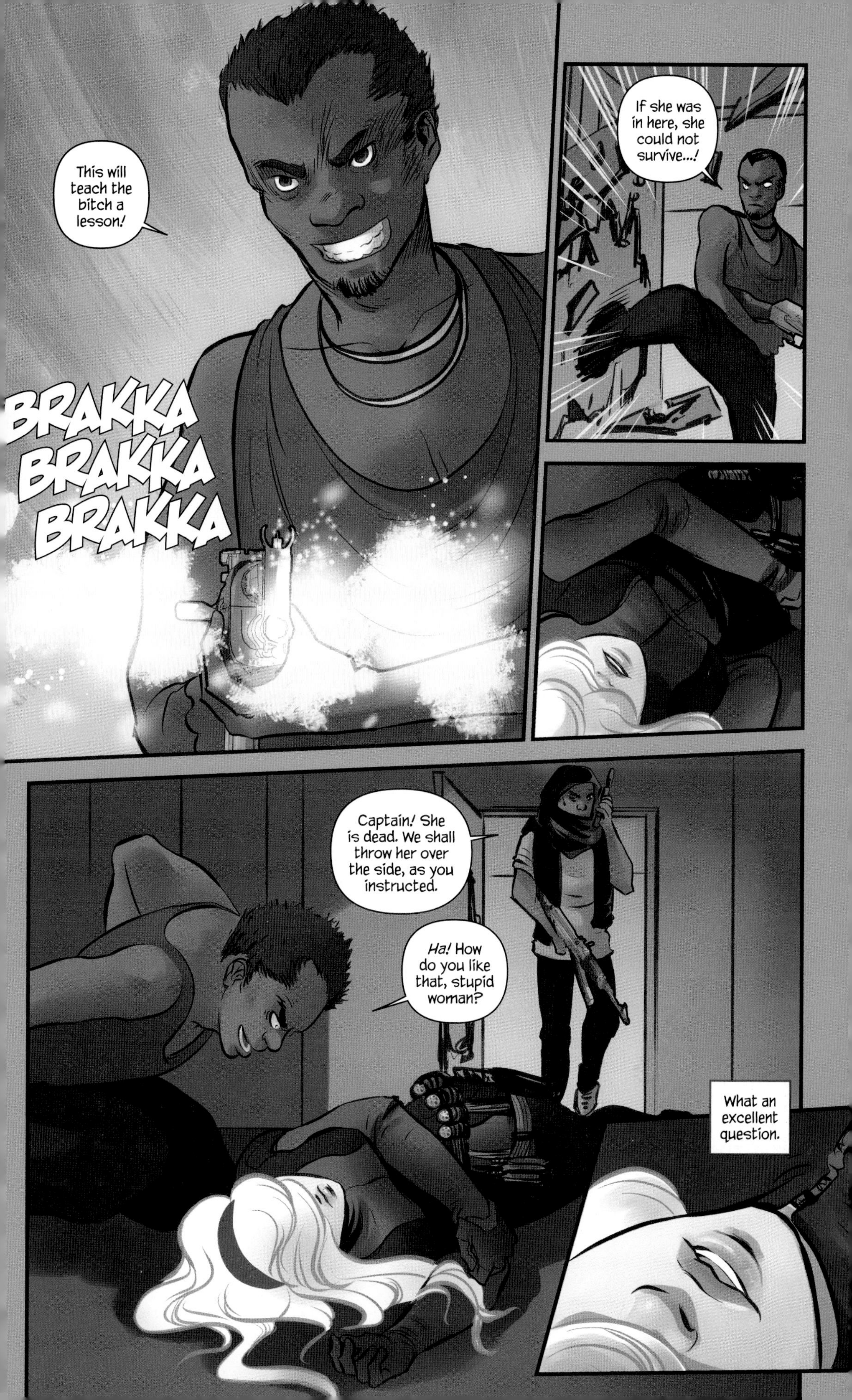
This will teach the bitch a lesson!
BRAKKA BRAKKA BRAKKA
If she was in here, she could not survive...!
Captain! She is dead. We shall throw her over the side, as you instructed.
Ha! How do you like that, stupid woman?
What an excellent question.

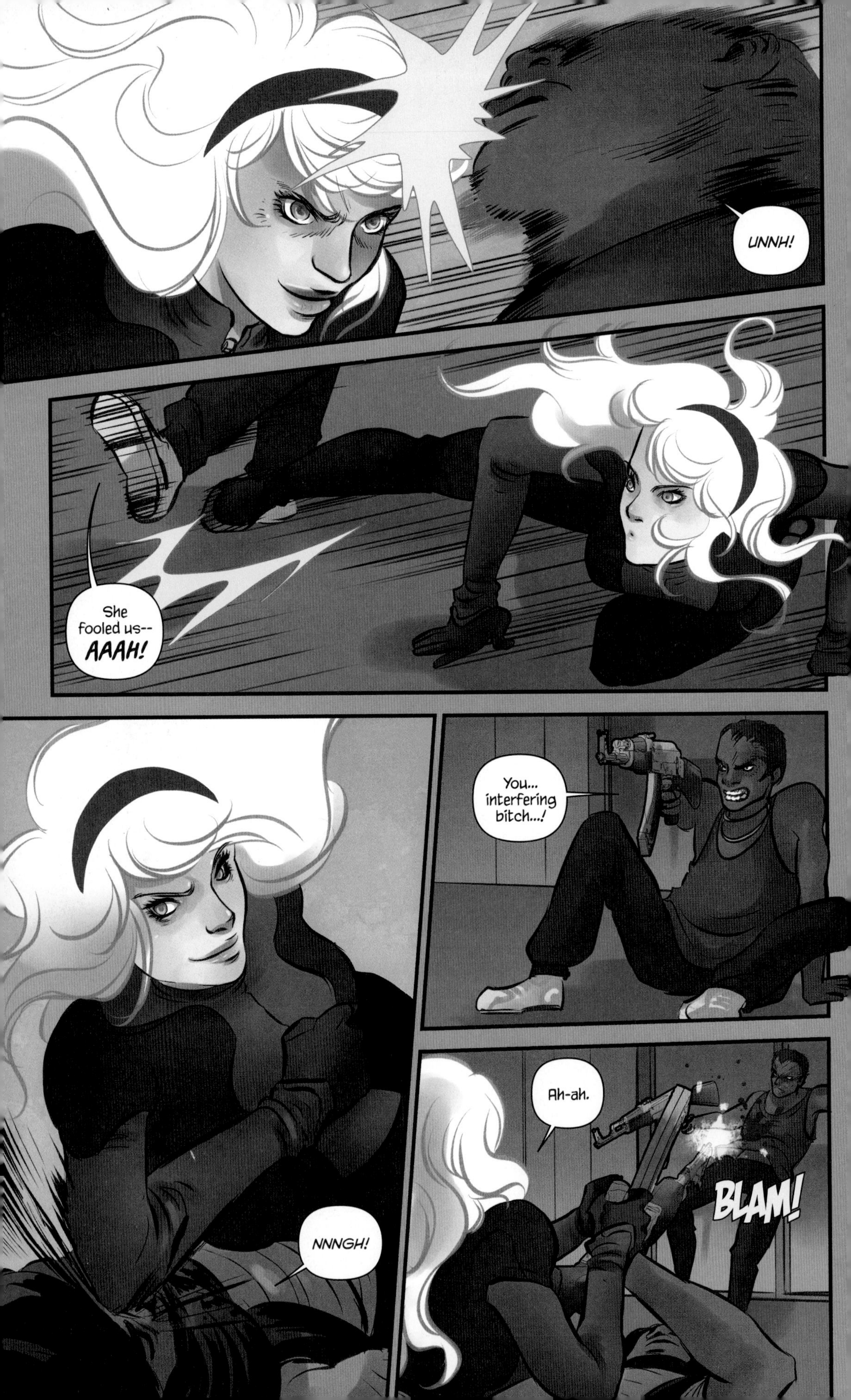
UNNH!
She fooled us-- AAAH!
You... interfering bitch...!
NNNGH!
Ah-ah.
BLAM!

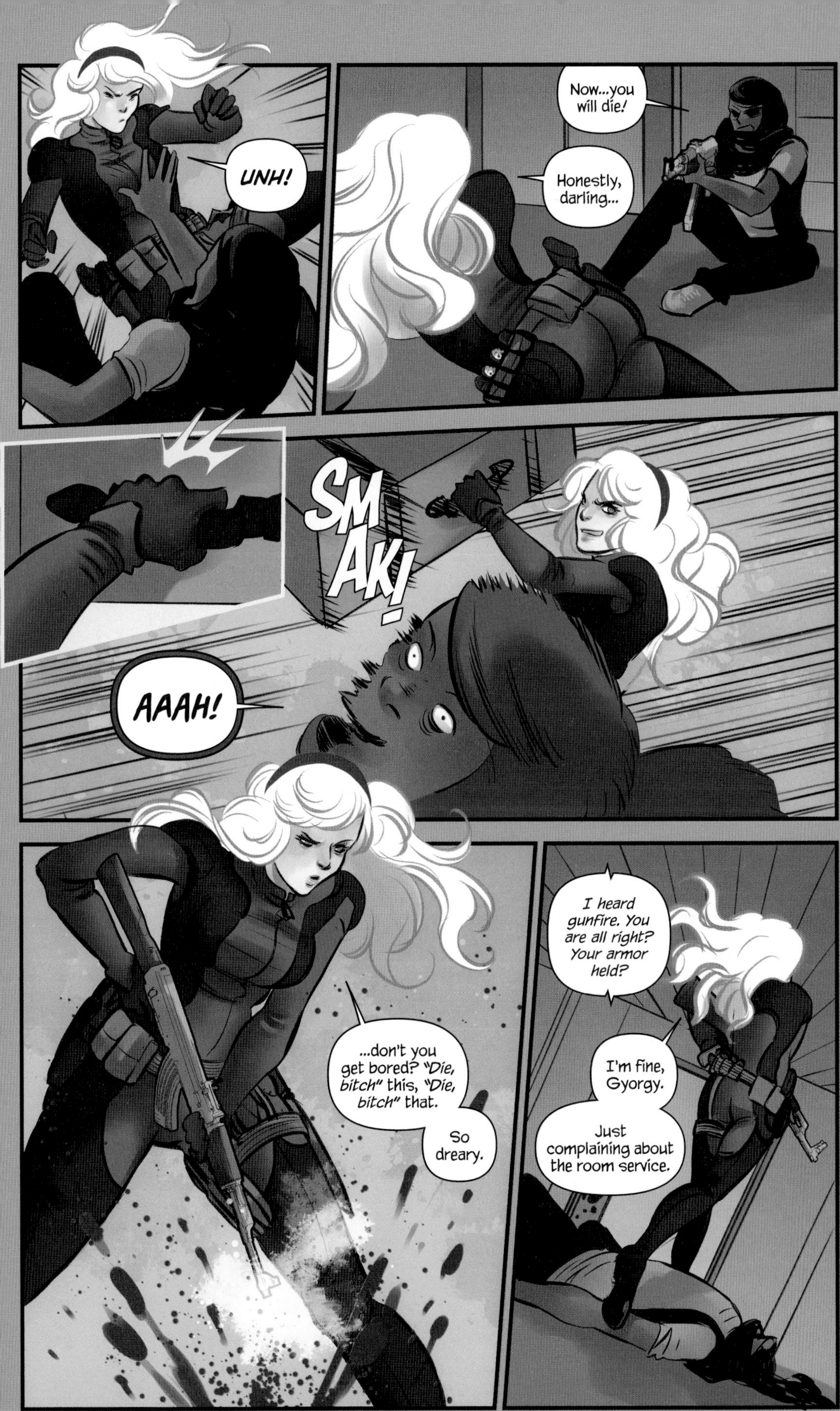
UNH!
Now...you will die!
Honestly, darling...
SMAK!
AAAH!
...don't you get bored? "Die, bitch" this, "Die, bitch" that.
So dreary.
I heard gunfire. You are all right? Your armor held?
I'm fine, Gyorgy.
Just complaining about the room service.

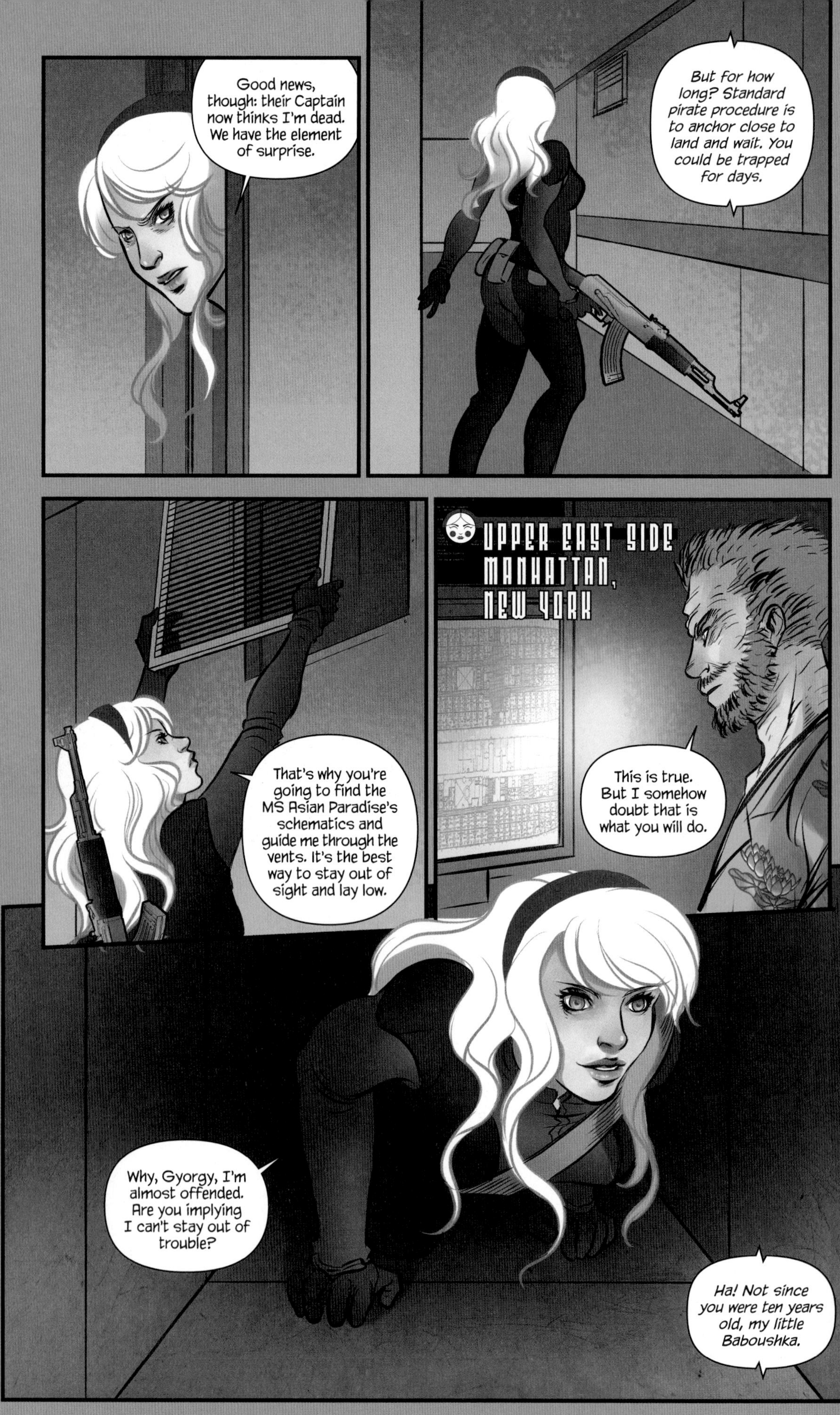
Good news, though: their Captain now thinks I'm dead. We have the element of surprise.
But for how long? Standard pirate procedure is to anchor close to land and wait. You could be trapped for days.
That's why you're going to find the MS Asian Paradise's schematics and guide me through the vents. It's the best way to stay out of sight and lay low.
UPPER EAST SIDE MANHATTAN, NEW YORK
This is true. But I somehow doubt that is what you will do.
Why, Gyorgy, I'm almost offended. Are you implying I can't stay out of trouble?
Ha! Not since you were ten years old, my little Baboushka.

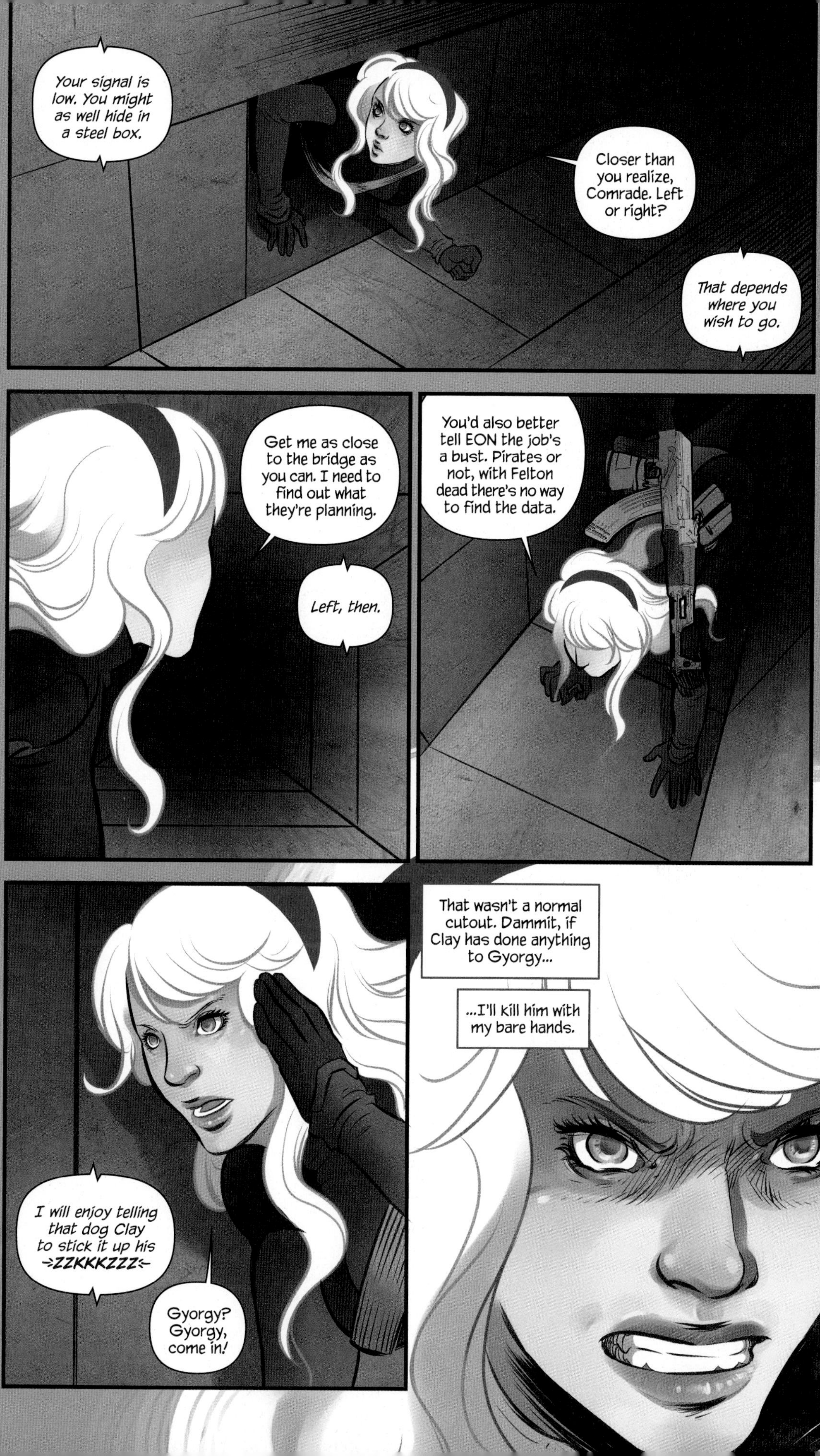
Your signal is low. You might as well hide in a steel box.
Closer than you realize, Comrade. Left or right?
That depends where you wish to go.
Get me as close to the bridge as you can. I need to find out what they're planning.
Left, then.
You'd also better tell EON the job's a bust. Pirates or not, with Felton dead there's no way to find the data.
I will enjoy telling that dog Clay to stick it up his -ZZKKKZZZ-
Gyorgy? Gyorgy, come in!
That wasn't a normal cutout. Dammit, if Clay has done anything to Gyorgy...
...I'll kill him with my bare hands.

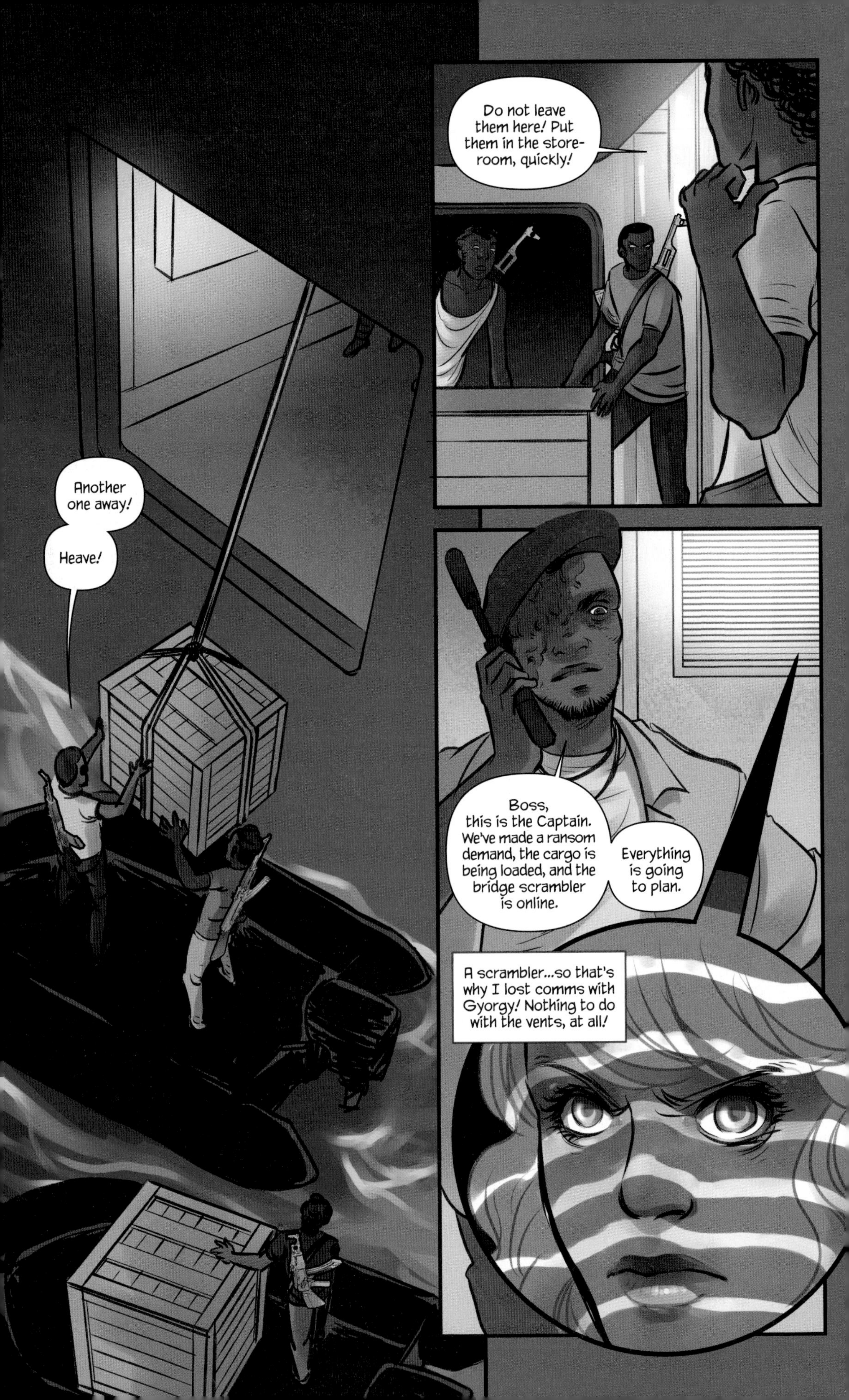
Another one away!
Heave!
Do not leave them here! Put them in the store-room, quickly!
Boss, this is the Captain. We've made a ransom demand, the cargo is being loaded, and the bridge scrambler is online.
Everything is going to plan.
A scrambler...so that's why I lost comms with Gyorgy! Nothing to do with the vents, at all!

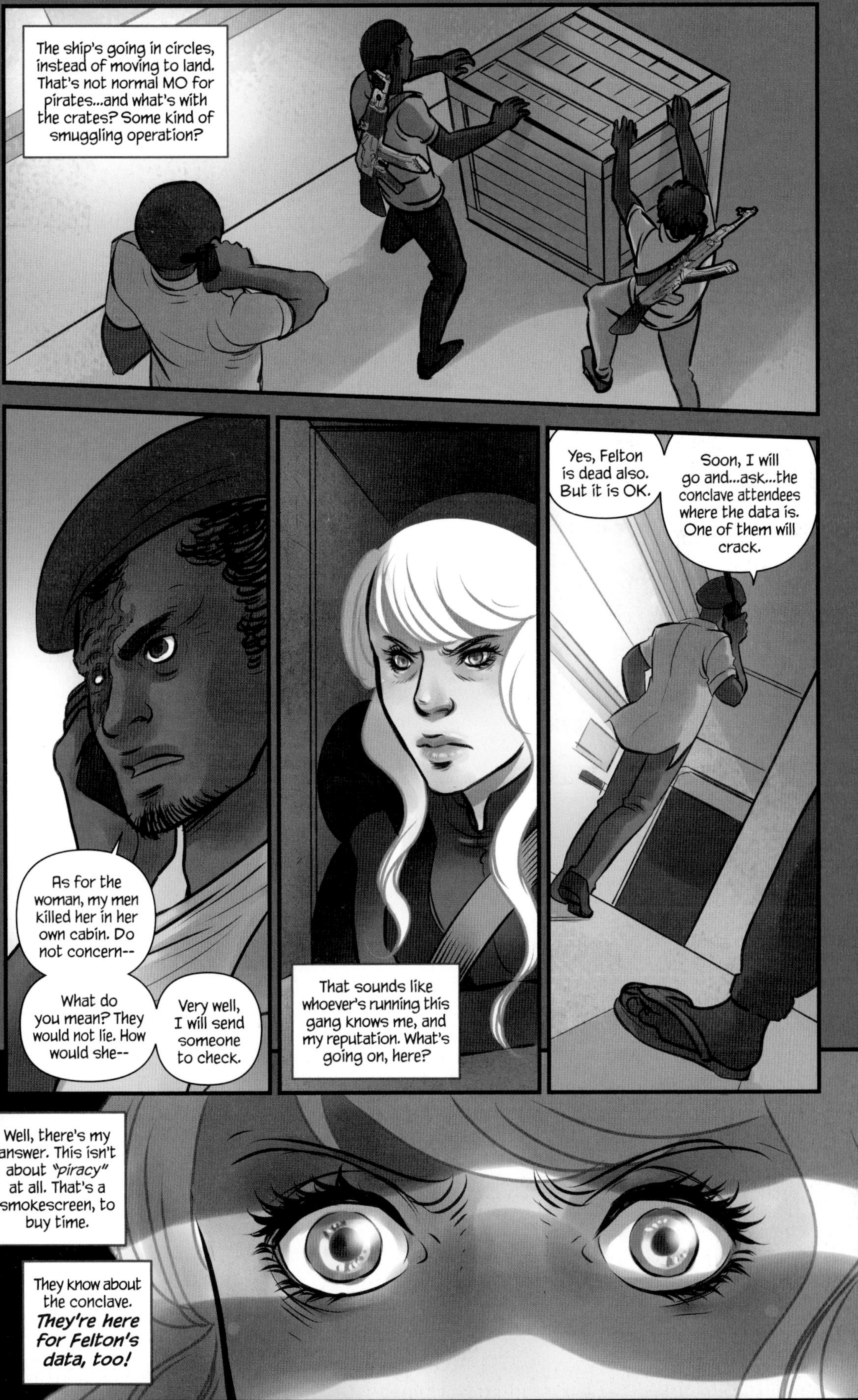
The ship's going in circles, instead of moving to land. That's not normal MO for pirates...and what's with the crates? Some kind of smuggling operation?
Yes, Felton is dead also. But it is OK.
Soon, I will go and...ask...the conclave attendees where the data is. One of them will crack.
As for the woman, my men killed her in her own cabin. Do not concern--
What do you mean? They would not lie. How would she--
Very well, I will send someone to check.
That sounds like whoever's running this gang knows me, and my reputation. What's going on, here?
Well, there's my answer. This isn't about *"piracy"* at all. That's a smokescreen, to buy time.
They know about the conclave. ***They're here for Felton's data, too!***

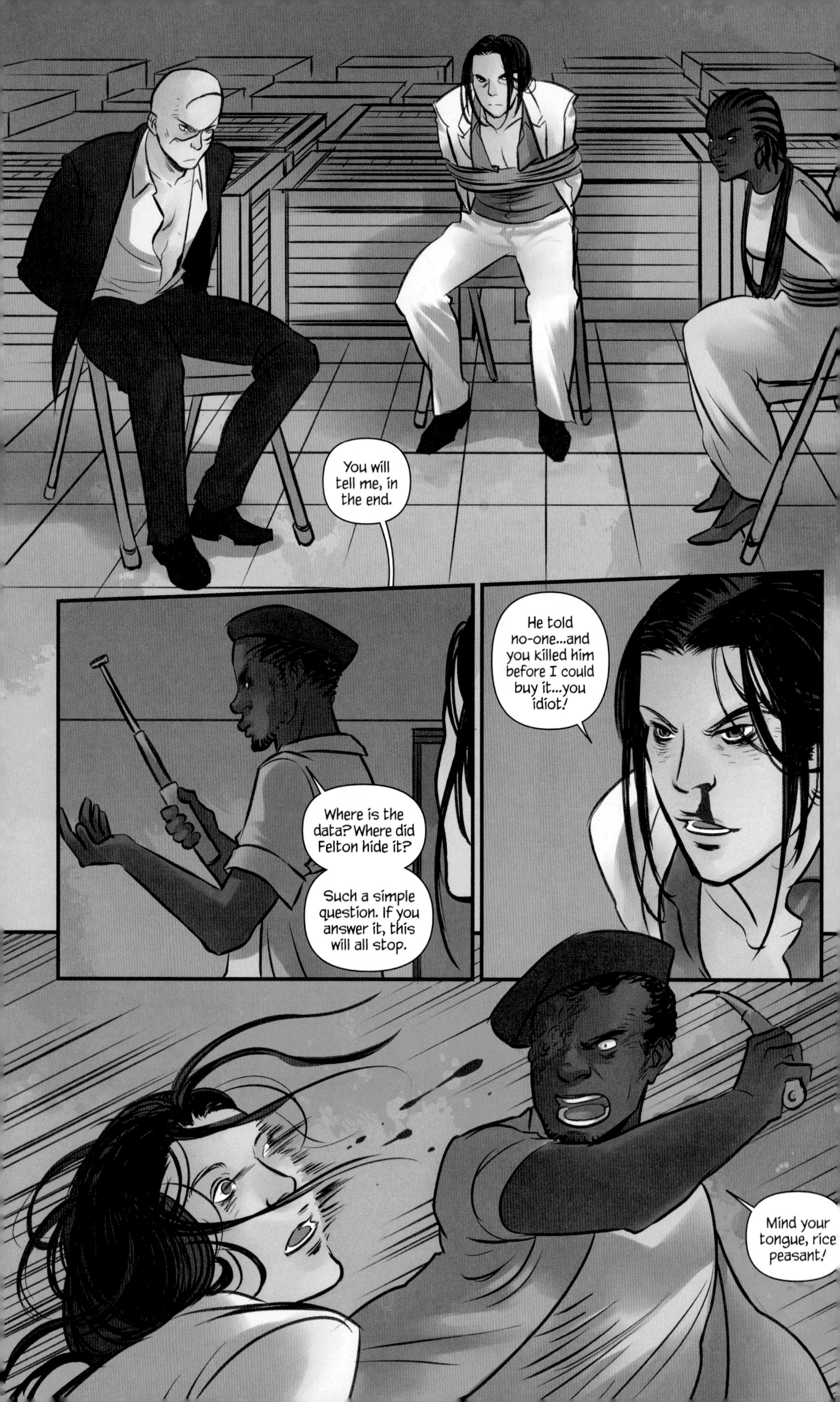
You will tell me, in the end.
Where is the data? Where did Felton hide it?
Such a simple question. If you answer it, this will all stop.
He told no-one...and you killed him before I could buy it...you idiot!
Mind your tongue, rice peasant!

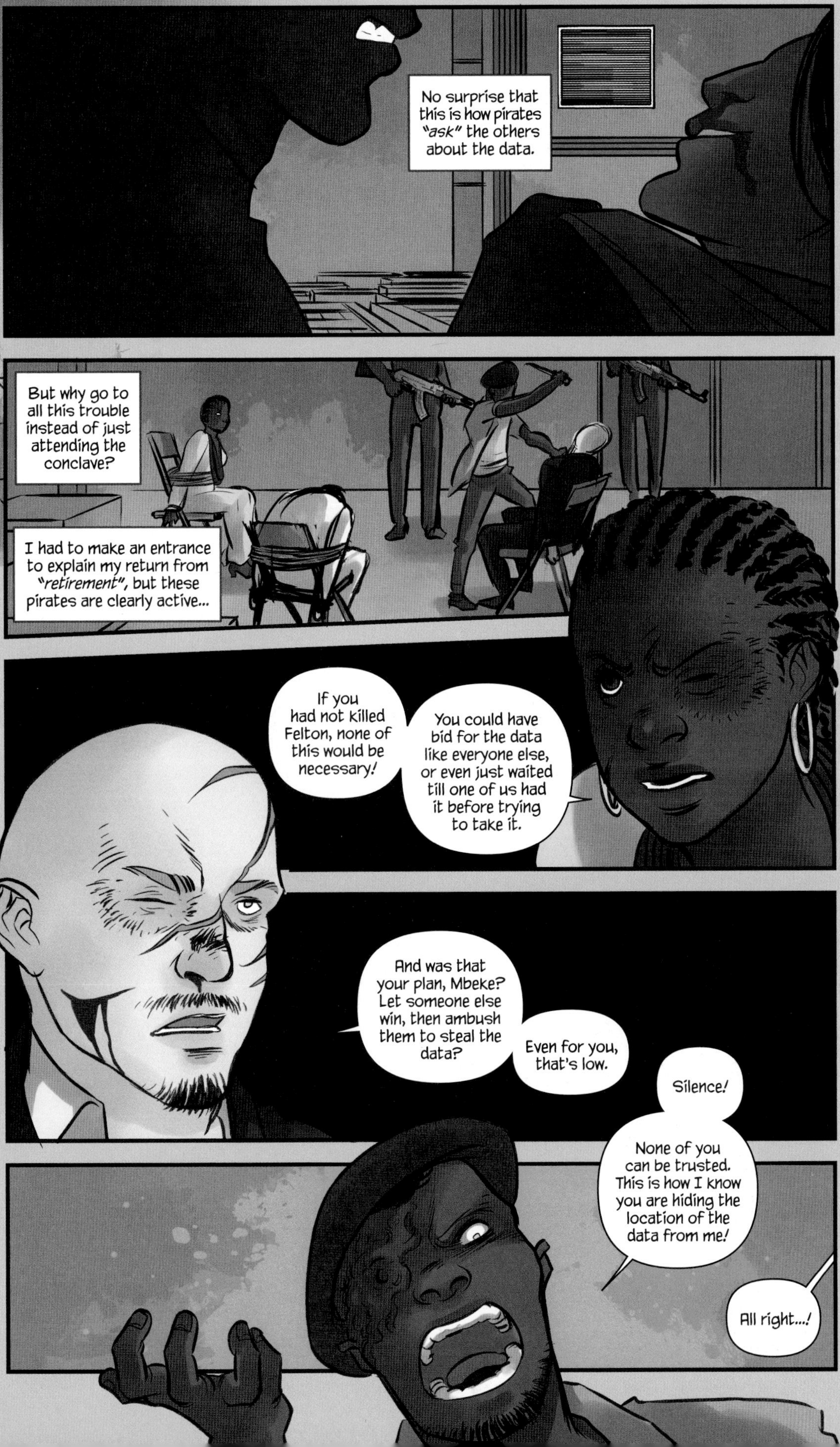
No surprise that this is how pirates "ask" the others about the data.
But why go to all this trouble instead of just attending the conclave?
I had to make an entrance to explain my return from "retirement", but these pirates are clearly active...
If you had not killed Felton, none of this would be necessary!
You could have bid for the data like everyone else, or even just waited till one of us had it before trying to take it.
And was that your plan, Mbeke? Let someone else win, then ambush them to steal the data?
Even for you, that's low.
Silence!
None of you can be trusted. This is how I know you are hiding the location of the data from me!
All right...!

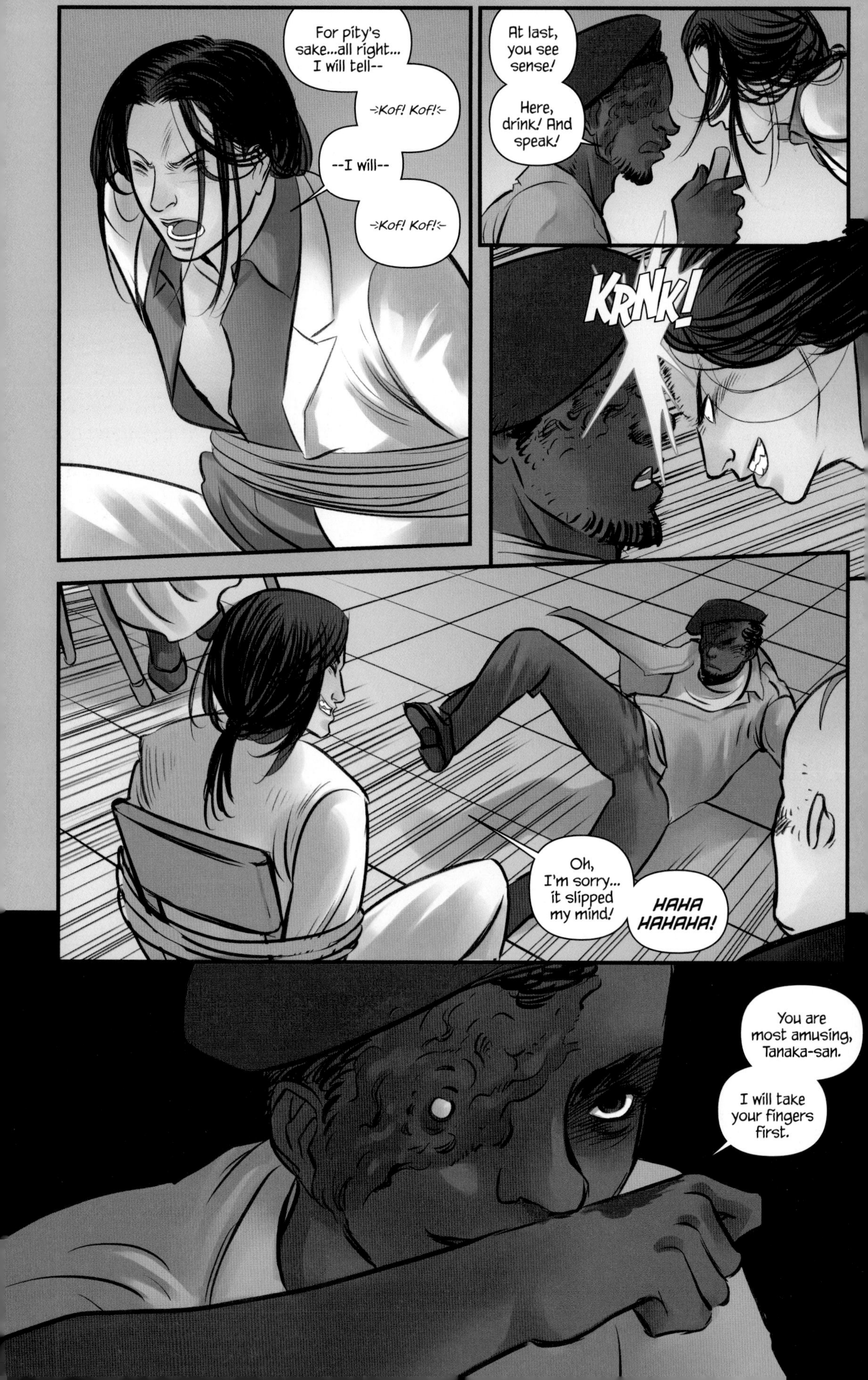
For pity's sake...all right... I will tell--
-Kof! Kof!-
--I will--
-Kof! Kof!-
At last, you see sense!
Here, drink! And speak!
KRNK!
Oh, I'm sorry... it slipped my mind!
HAHA HAHAHA!
You are most amusing, Tanaka-san.
I will take your fingers first.

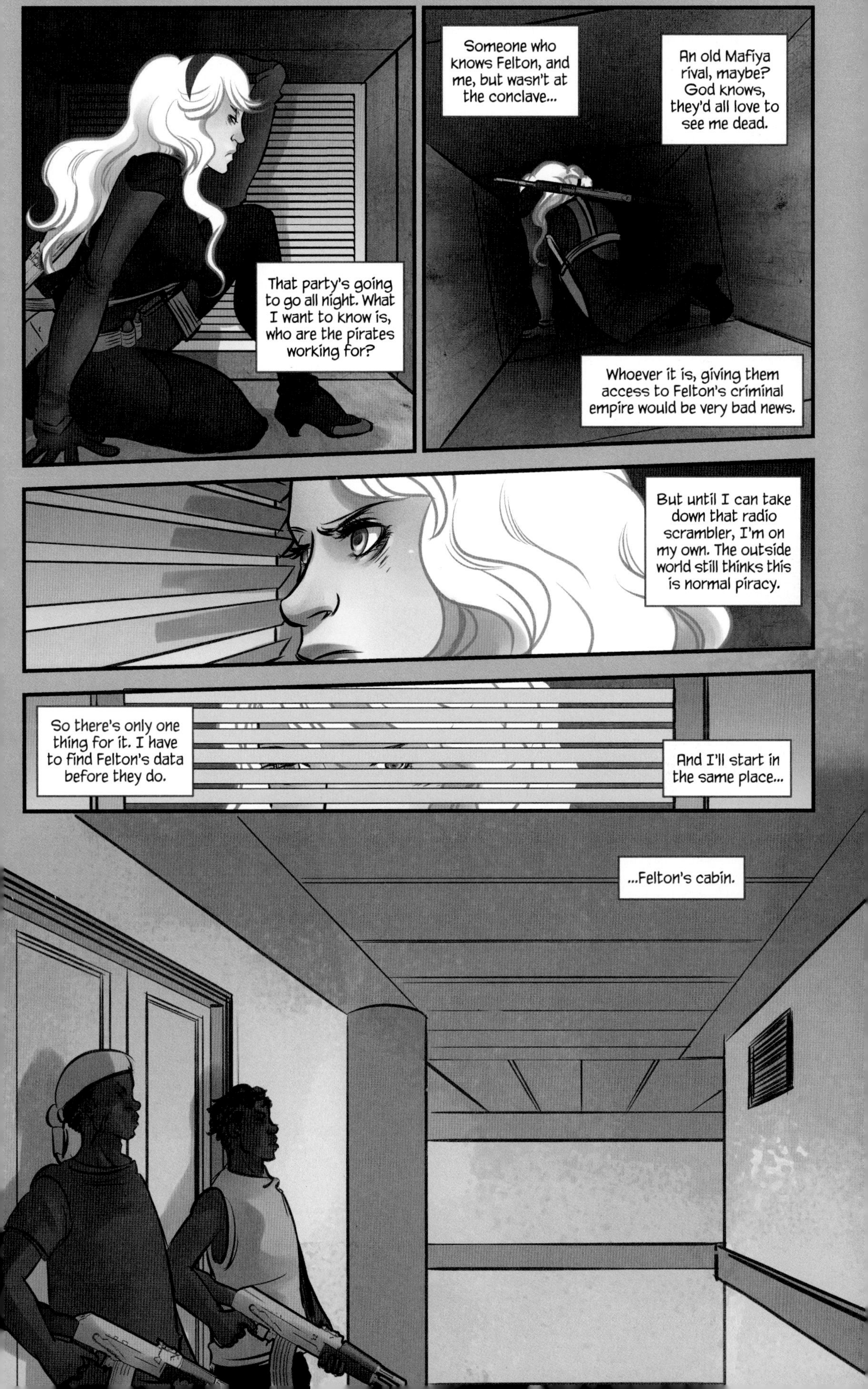

That party's going to go all night. What I want to know is, who are the pirates working for?
Someone who knows Felton, and me, but wasn't at the conclave...
An old Mafiya rival, maybe? God knows, they'd all love to see me dead.
Whoever it is, giving them access to Felton's criminal empire would be very bad news.
But until I can take down that radio scrambler, I'm on my own. The outside world still thinks this is normal piracy.
So there's only one thing for it. I have to find Felton's data before they do.
And I'll start in the same place...
...Felton's cabin.

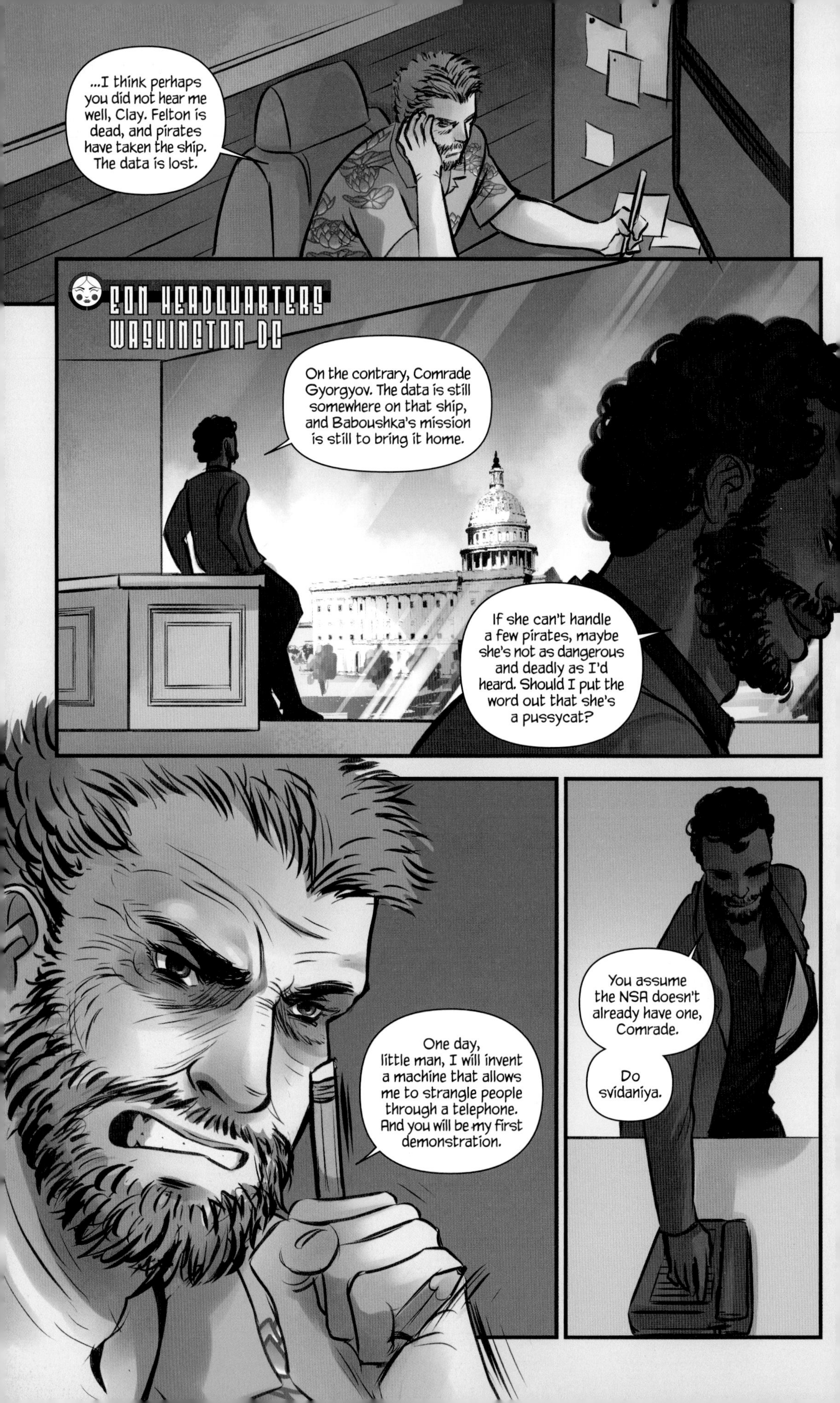
...I think perhaps you did not hear me well, Clay. Felton is dead, and pirates have taken the ship. The data is lost.
EON HEADQUARTERS WASHINGTON DC
On the contrary, Comrade Gyorgyov. The data is still somewhere on that ship, and Baboushka's mission is still to bring it home.
If she can't handle a few pirates, maybe she's not as dangerous and deadly as I'd heard. Should I put the word out that she's a pussycat?
One day, little man, I will invent a machine that allows me to strangle people through a telephone. And you will be my first demonstration.
You assume the NSA doesn't already have one, Comrade.
Do svidaniya.

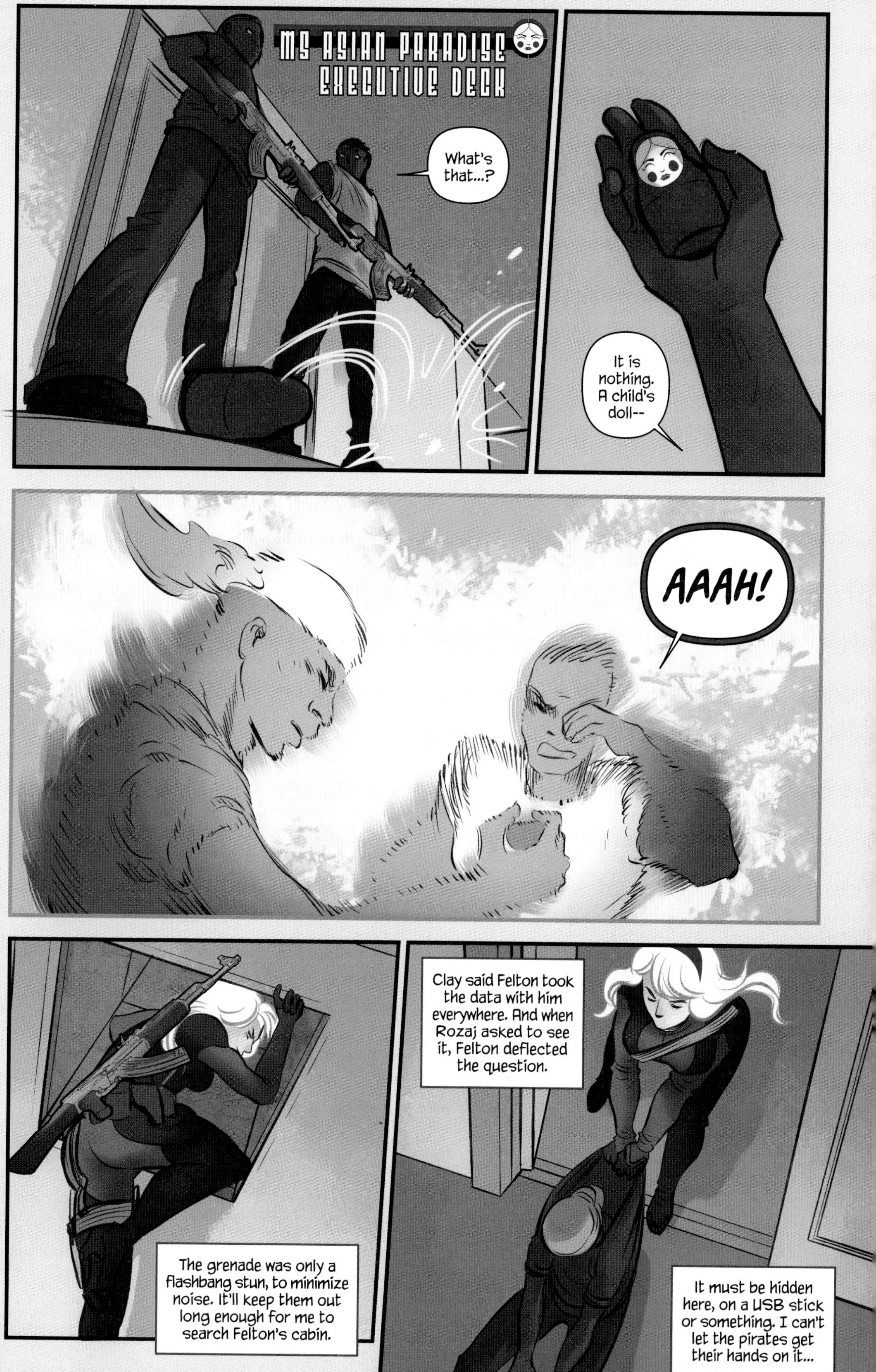
MS ASIAN PARADISE
EXECUTIVE DECK
What's that...?
It is nothing. A child's doll--
AAAH!
The grenade was only a flashbang stun, to minimize noise. It'll keep them out long enough for me to search Felton's cabin.
Clay said Felton took the data with him everywhere. And when Rozaj asked to see it, Felton deflected the question.
It must be hidden here, on a USB stick or something. I can't let the pirates get their hands on it...

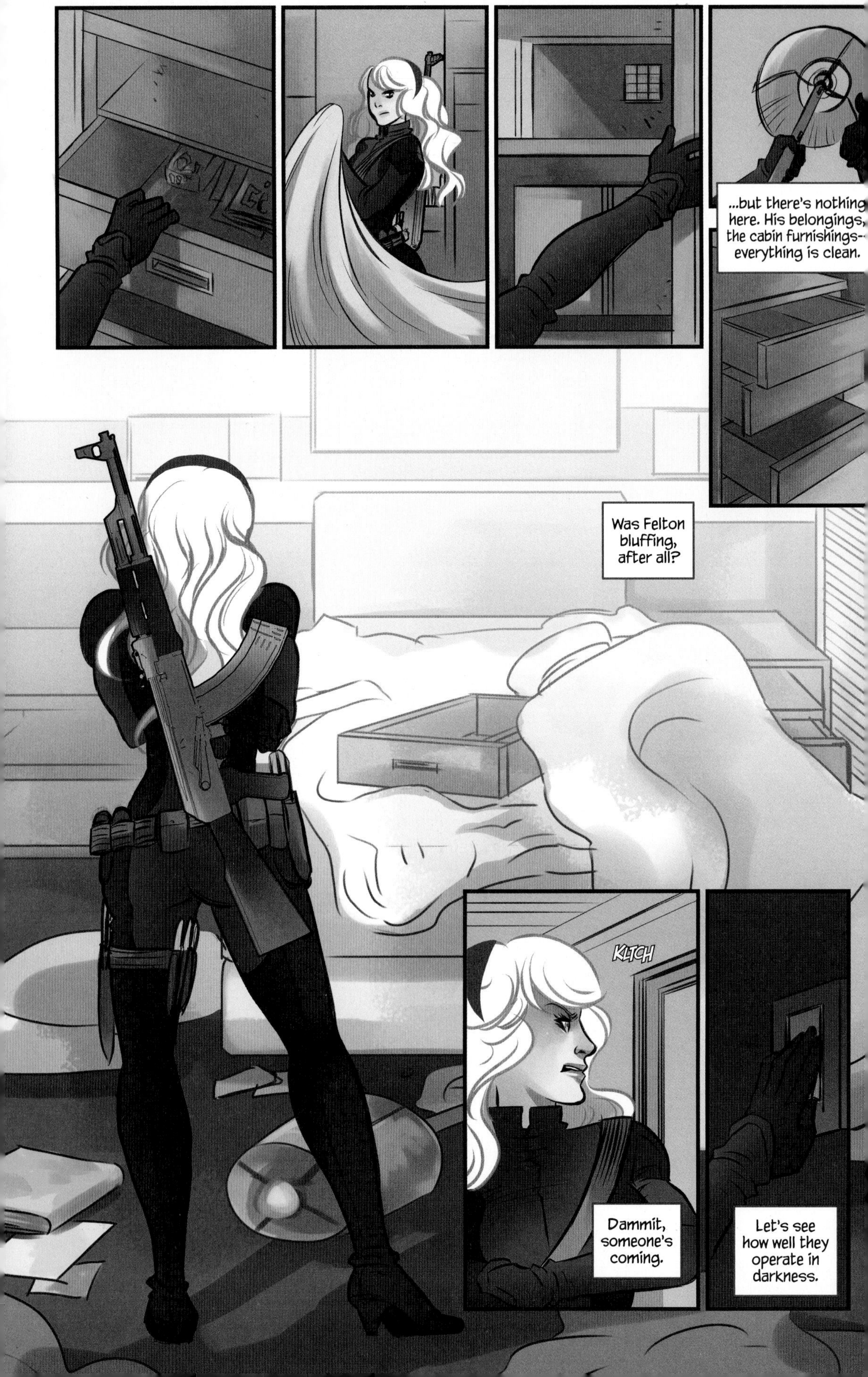
...but there's nothing here. His belongings, the cabin furnishings--everything is clean.
Was Felton bluffing, after all?
KLTCH
Dammit, someone's coming.
Let's see how well they operate in darkness.

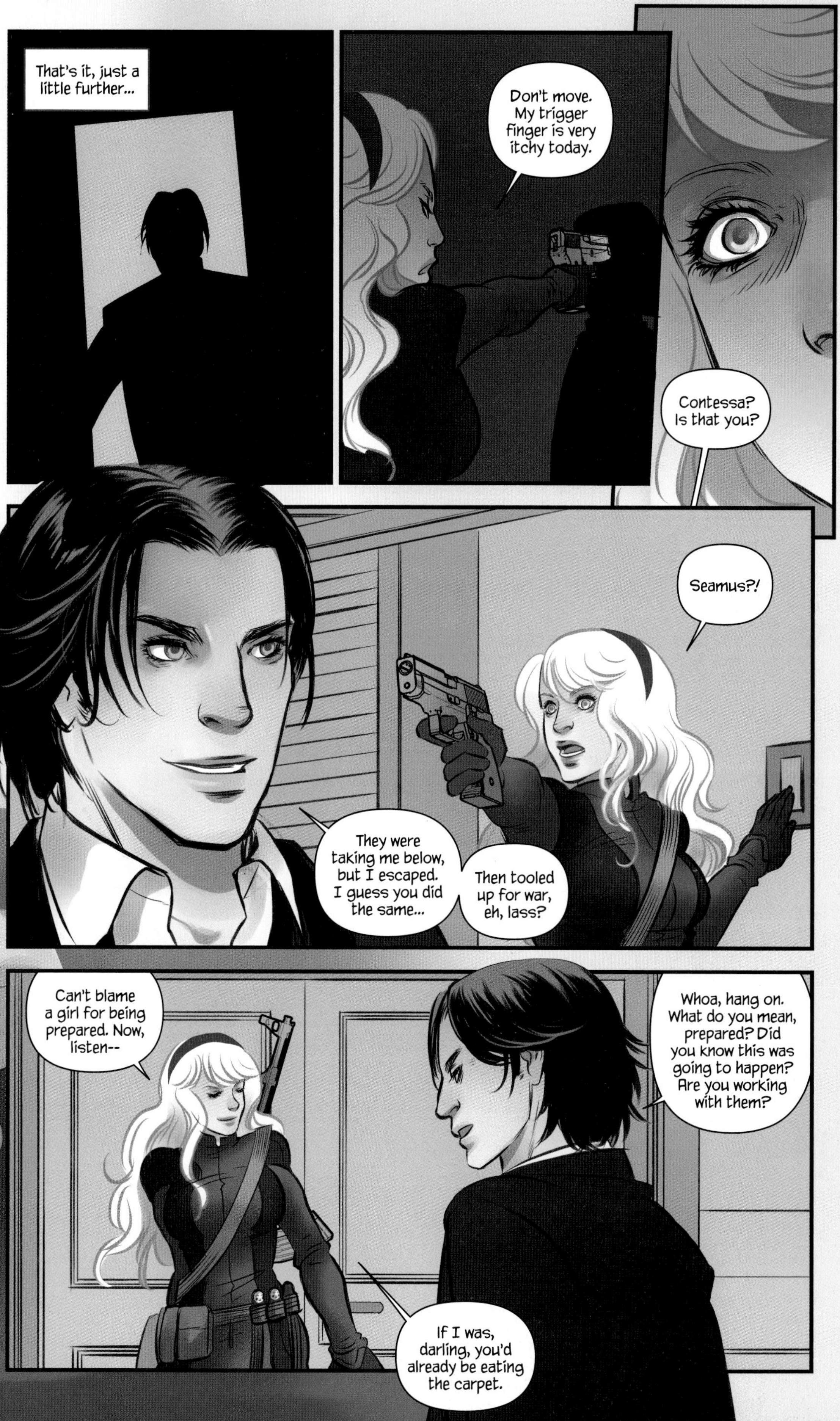
That's it, just a little further...
Don't move. My trigger finger is very itchy today.
Contessa? Is that you?
Seamus?!
They were taking me below, but I escaped. I guess you did the same...
Then tooled up for war, eh, lass?
Can't blame a girl for being prepared. Now, listen--
Whoa, hang on. What do you mean, prepared? Did you know this was going to happen? Are you working with them?
If I was, darling, you'd already be eating the carpet.

Dead, or just a nasty headache?

Let's hope we never have to find out. I'd hate to waste those lips.

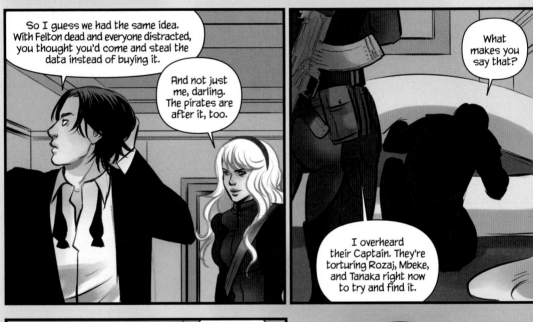

So I guess we had the same idea. With Felton dead and everyone distracted, you thought you'd come and steal the data instead of buying it.

And not just me, darling. The pirates are after it, too.

What makes you say that?

I overheard their Captain. They're torturing Rozaj, Mbeke, and Tanaka right now to try and find it.

You mean one of them knows where the data is?

Search me, but this whole piracy thing is a smokescreen. Whoever they're working for is after the data, like us.

And it won't be long before they realize it's not here.

And how do I know that's not because you already found it, before I arrived?

It wouldn't even be the first time you've lied to me today.

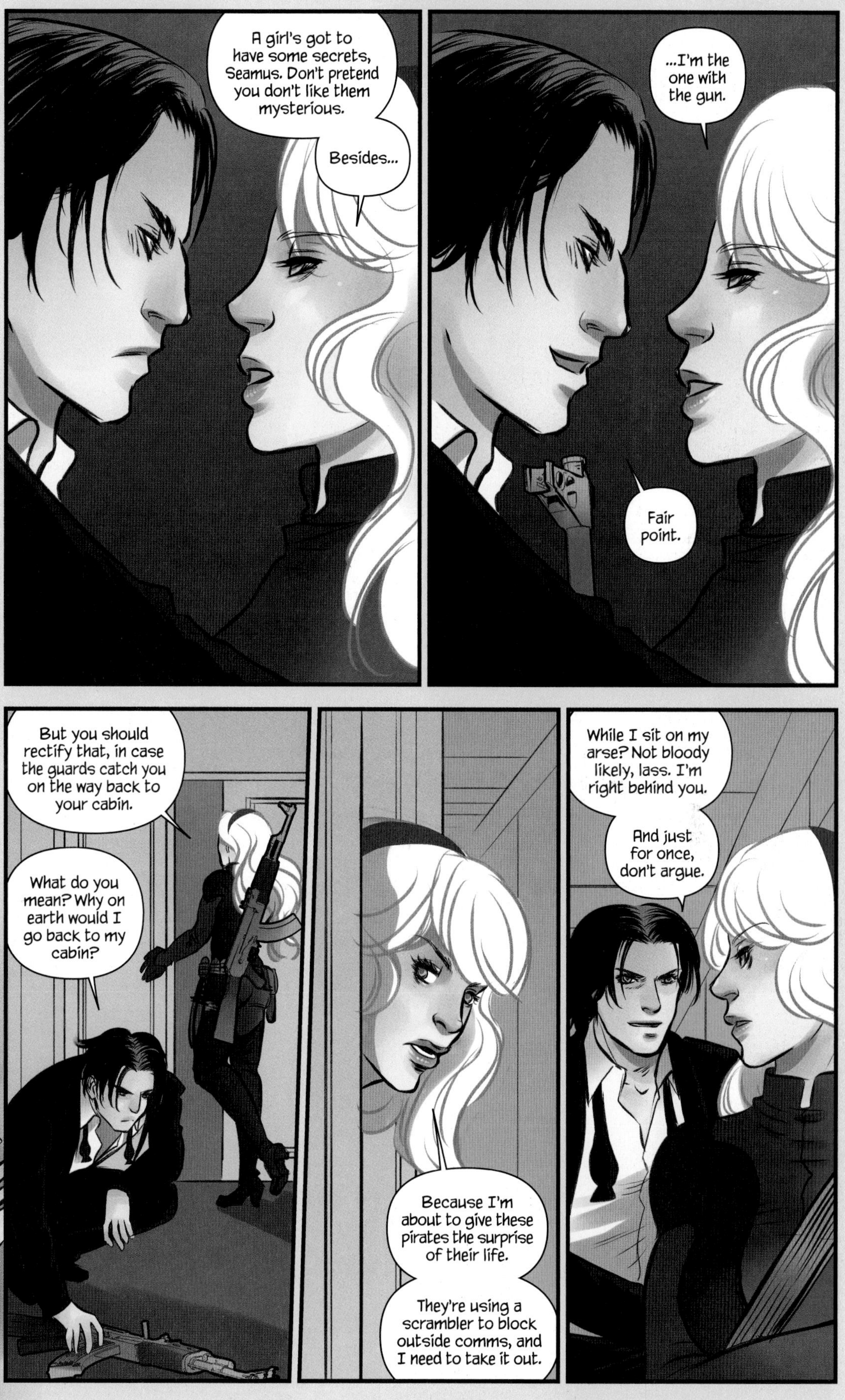
A girl's got to have some secrets, Seamus. Don't pretend you don't like them mysterious.
Besides...
...I'm the one with the gun.
Fair point.
But you should rectify that, in case the guards catch you on the way back to your cabin.
What do you mean? Why on earth would I go back to my cabin?
Because I'm about to give these pirates the surprise of their life.
They're using a scrambler to block outside comms, and I need to take it out.
While I sit on my arse? Not bloody likely, lass. I'm right behind you.
And just for once, don't argue.

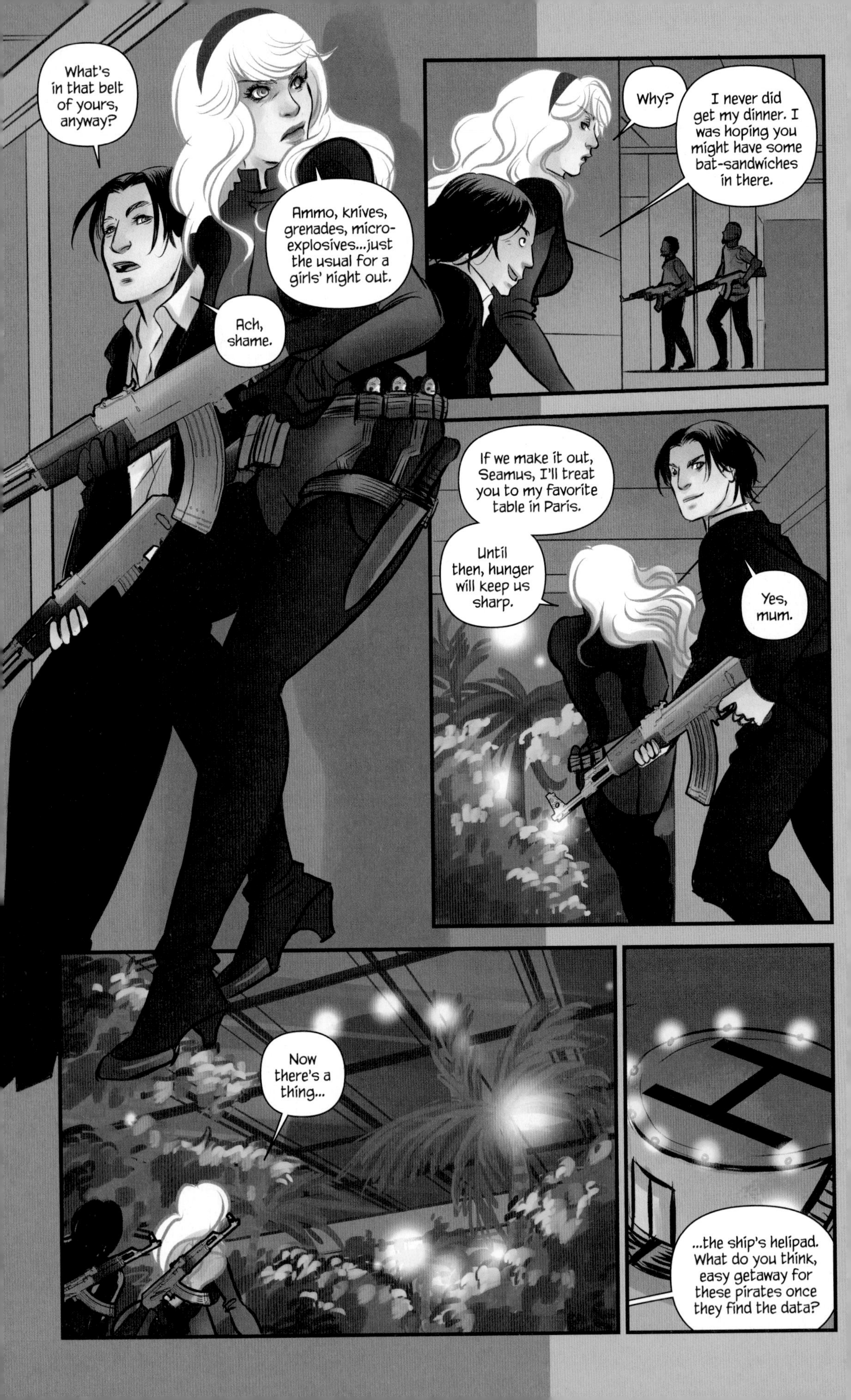
What's in that belt of yours, anyway?
Ammo, knives, grenades, micro-explosives...just the usual for a girls' night out.
Ach, shame.
Why?
I never did get my dinner. I was hoping you might have some bat-sandwiches in there.
If we make it out, Seamus, I'll treat you to my favorite table in Paris.
Until then, hunger will keep us sharp.
Yes, mum.
Now there's a thing...
...the ship's helipad. What do you think, easy getaway for these pirates once they find the data?

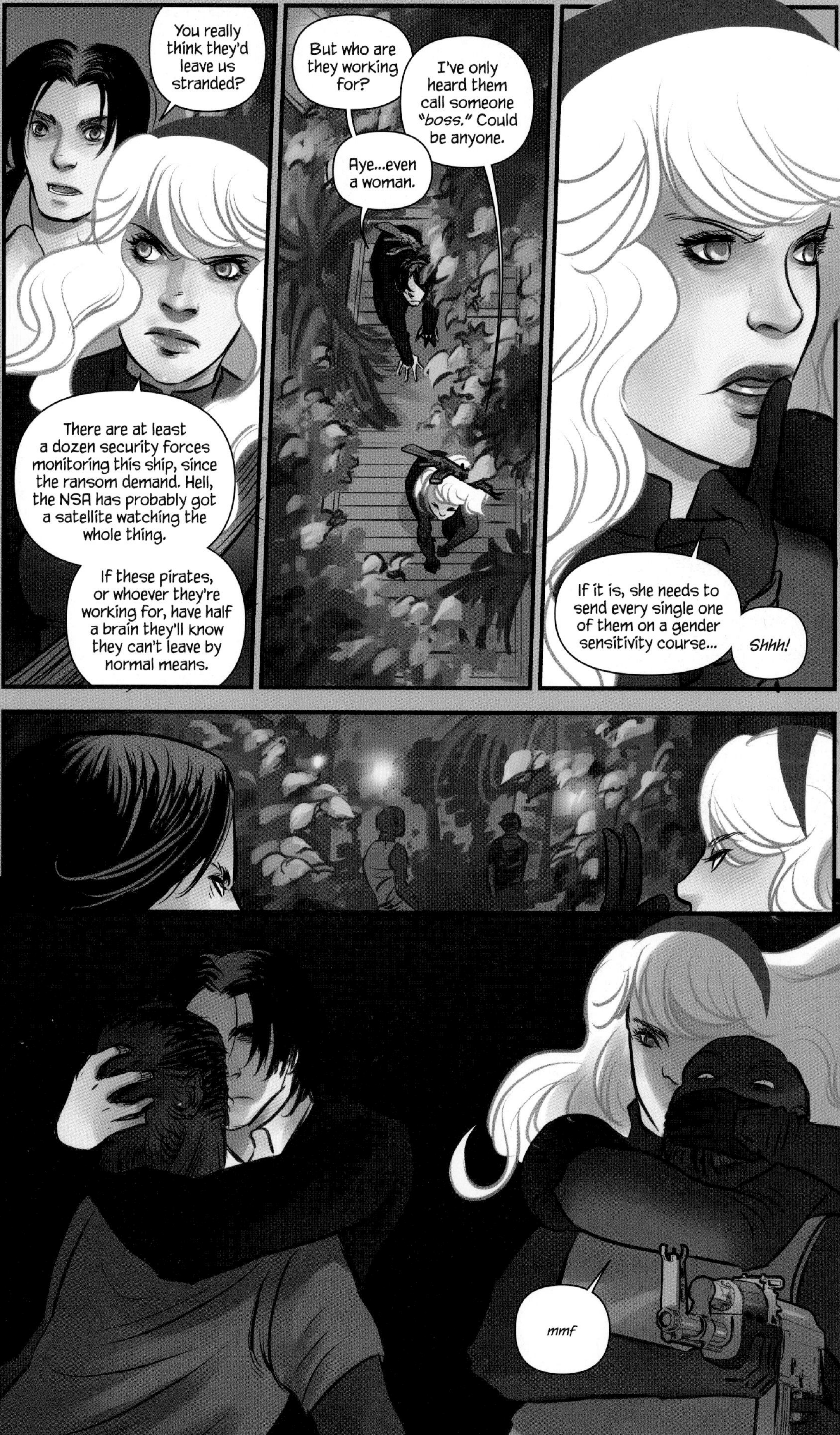
You really think they'd leave us stranded?
There are at least a dozen security forces monitoring this ship, since the ransom demand. Hell, the NSA has probably got a satellite watching the whole thing.
If these pirates, or whoever they're working for, have half a brain they'll know they can't leave by normal means.
But who are they working for?
I've only heard them call someone *"boss."* Could be anyone.
Aye...even a woman.
If it is, she needs to send every single one of them on a gender sensitivity course...
Shhh!
mmf

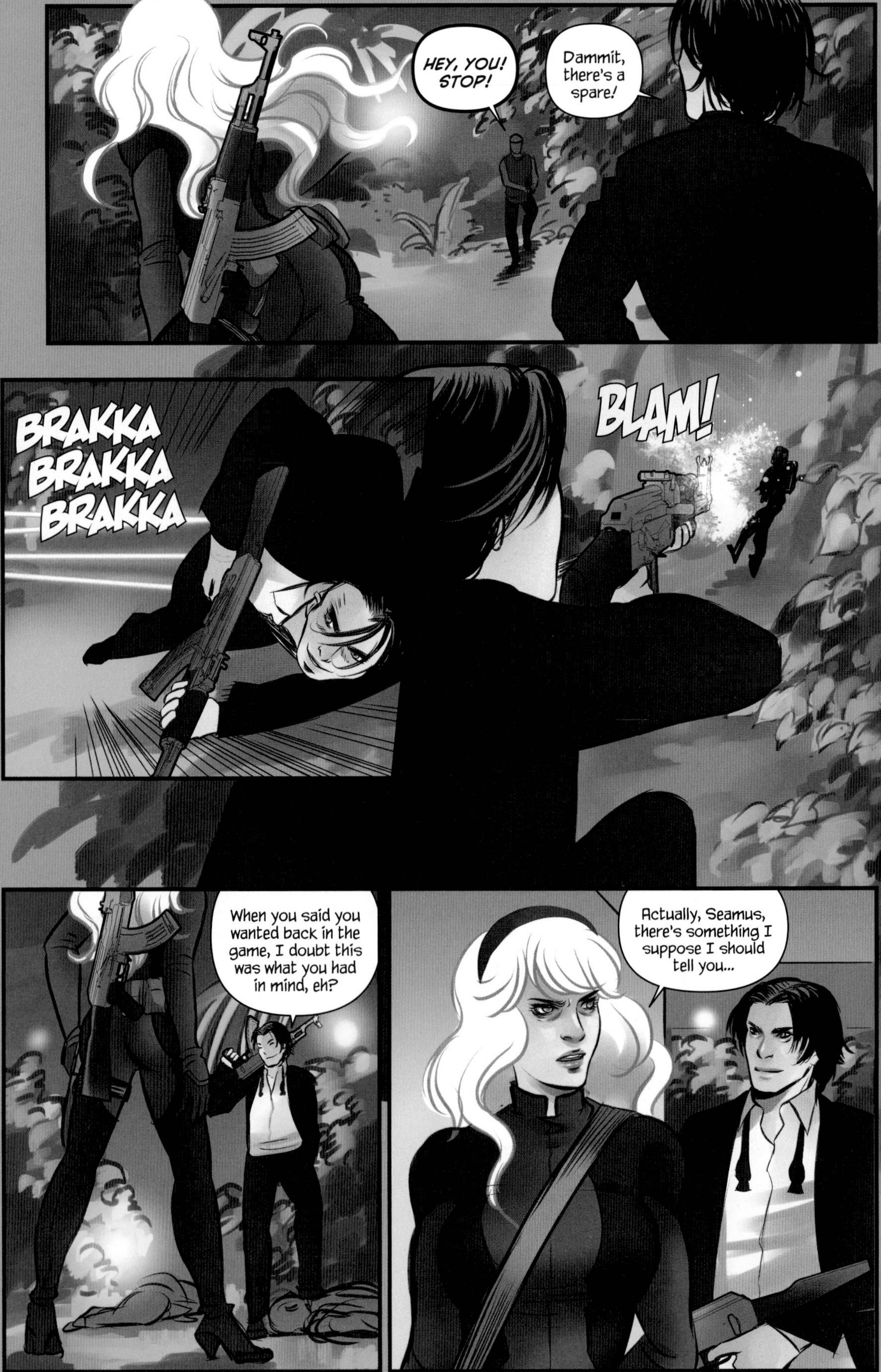
HEY, YOU! STOP!
Dammit, there's a spare!
BRAKKA BRAKKA BRAKKA
BLAM!
When you said you wanted back in the game, I doubt this was what you had in mind, eh?
Actually, Seamus, there's something I suppose I should tell you...

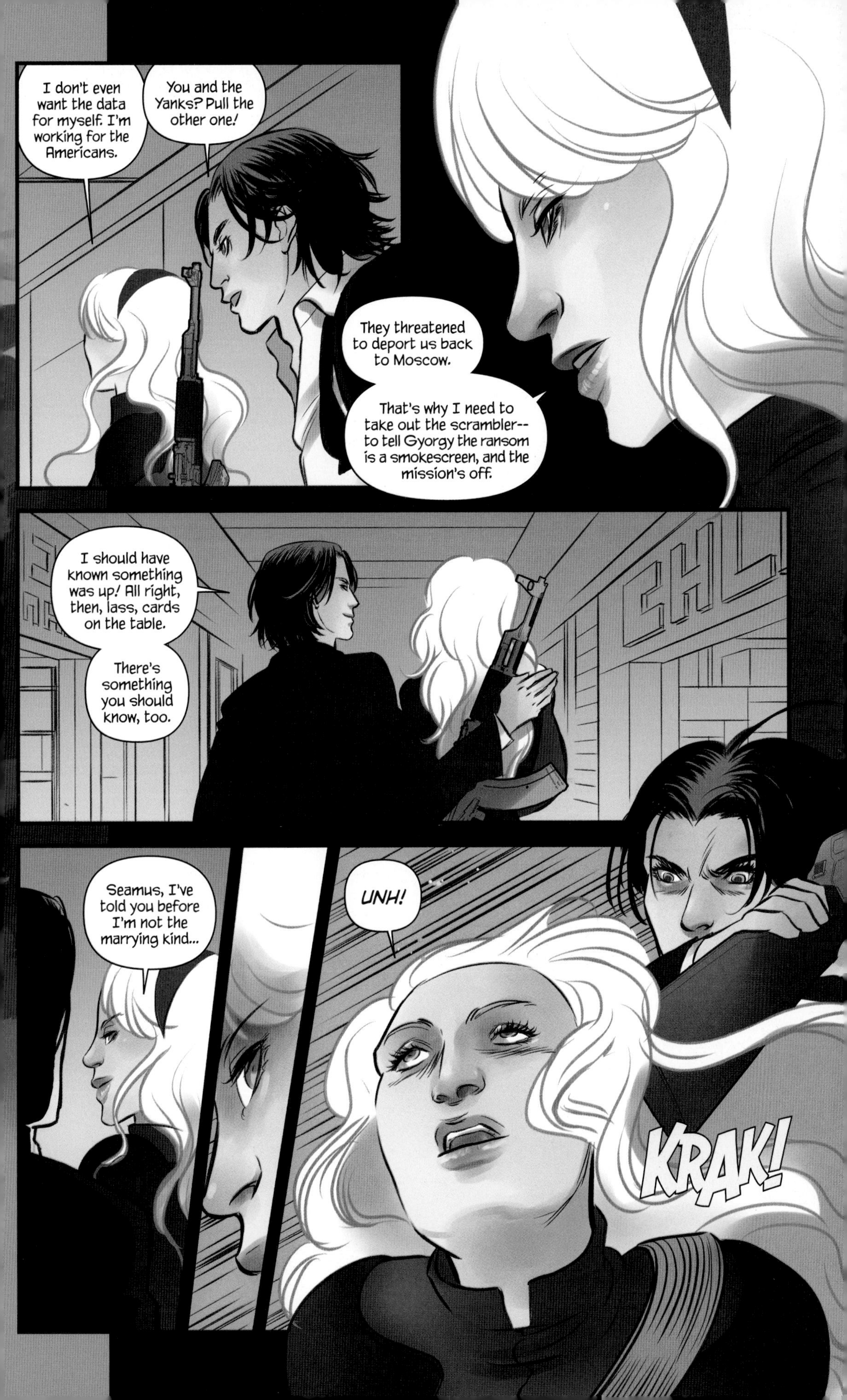
I don't even want the data for myself. I'm working for the Americans.
You and the Yanks? Pull the other one!
They threatened to deport us back to Moscow.
That's why I need to take out the scrambler-- to tell Gyorgy the ransom is a smokescreen, and the mission's off.
I should have known something was up! All right, then, lass, cards on the table.
There's something you should know, too.
Seamus, I've told you before I'm not the marrying kind...
UNH!
KRAK!

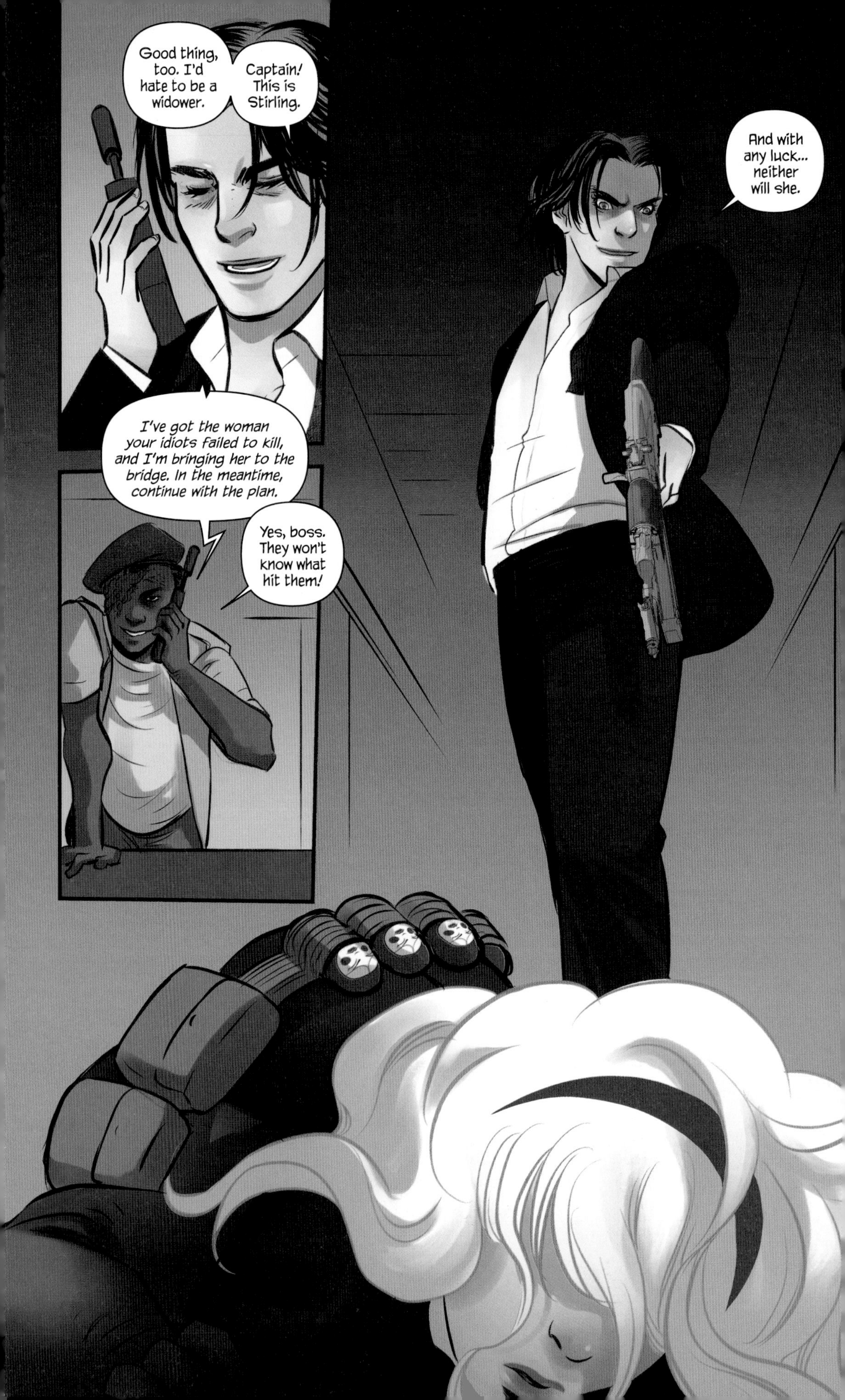
Good thing, too. I'd hate to be a widower.
Captain! This is Stirling.
And with any luck... neither will she.
I've got the woman your idiots failed to kill, and I'm bringing her to the bridge. In the meantime, continue with the plan.
Yes, boss. They won't know what hit them!

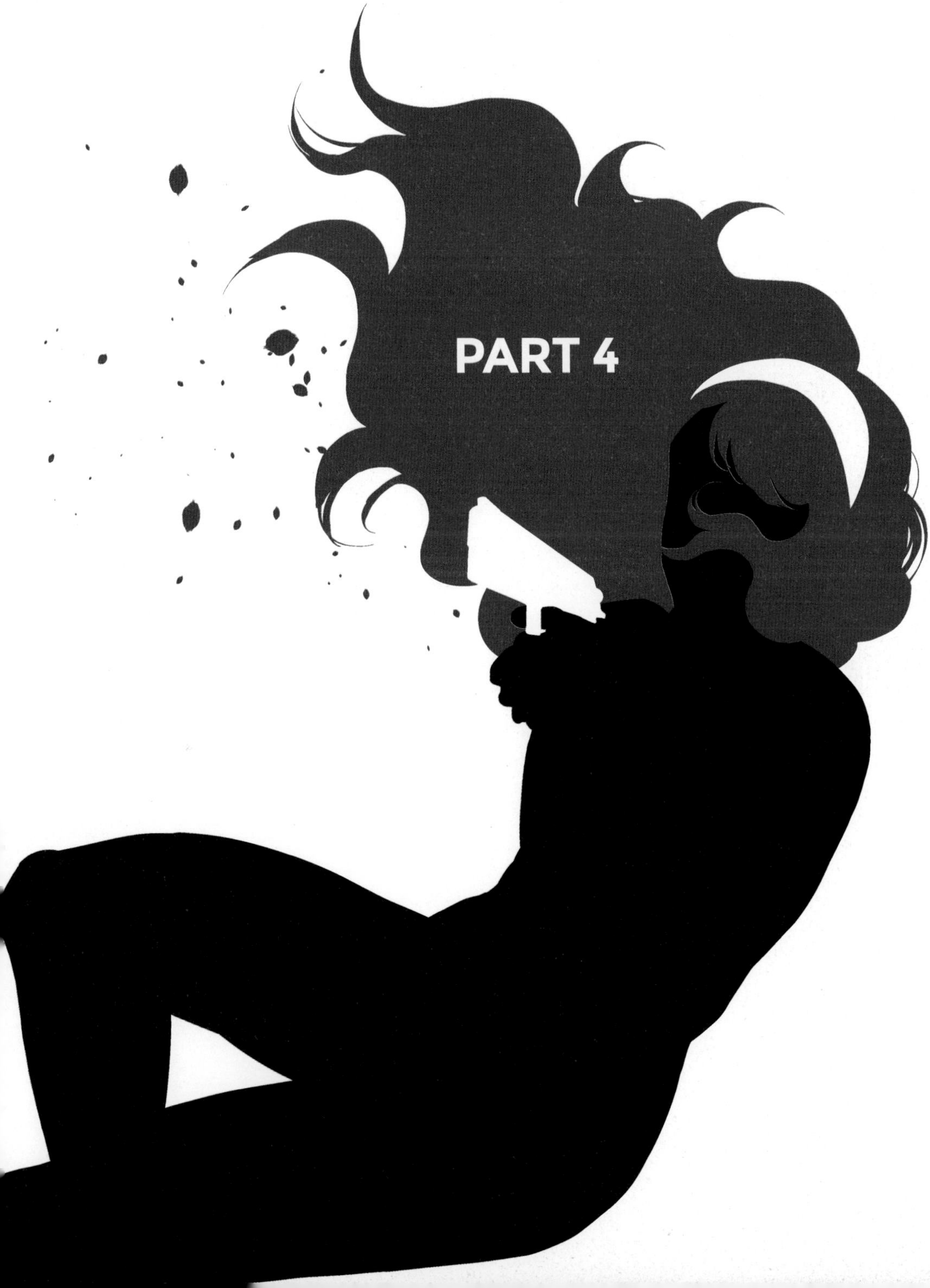
PART 4

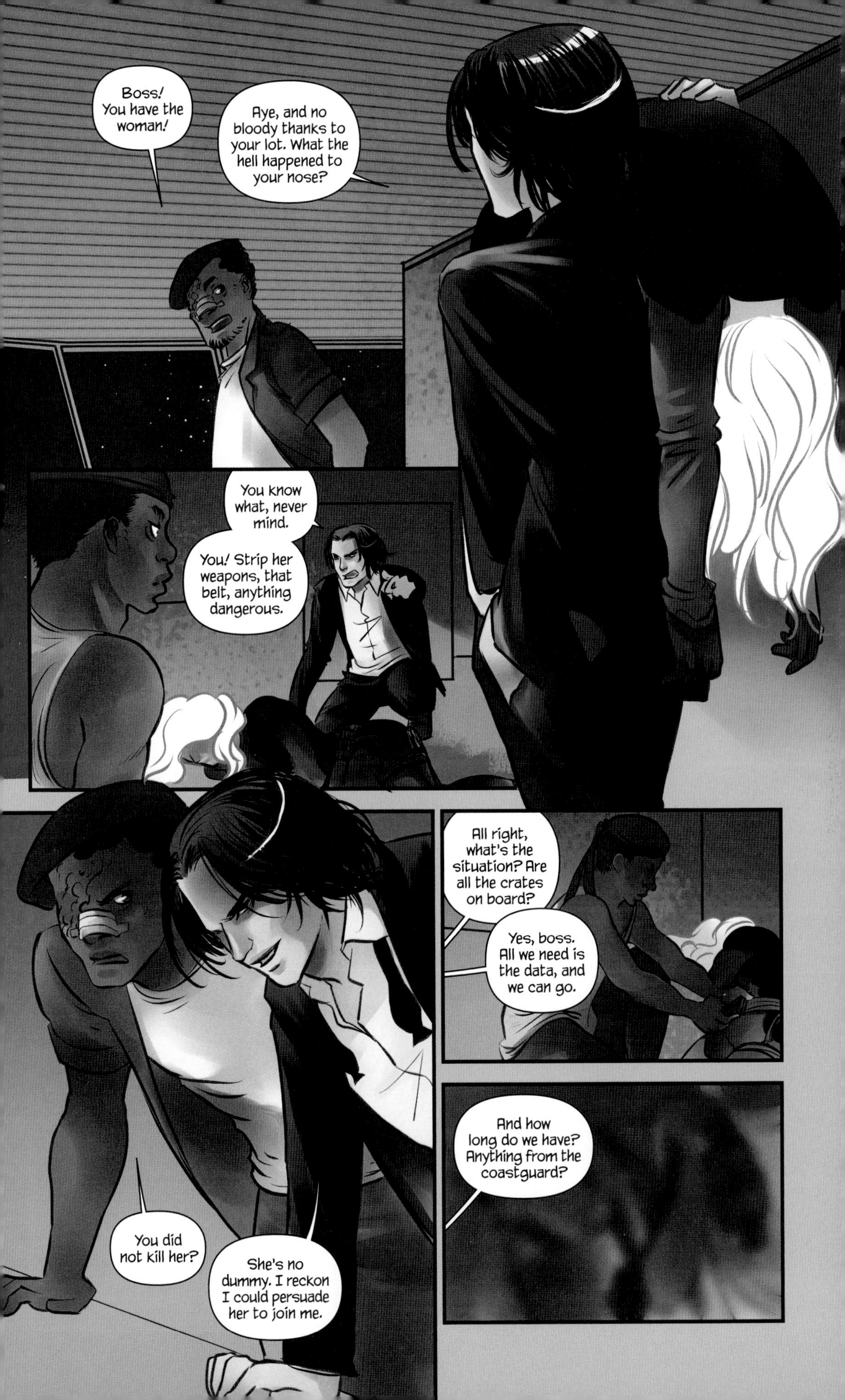
Boss! You have the woman!
Aye, and no bloody thanks to your lot. What the hell happened to your nose?
You know what, never mind.
You! Strip her weapons, that belt, anything dangerous.
You did not kill her?
She's no dummy. I reckon I could persuade her to join me.
All right, what's the situation? Are all the crates on board?
Yes, boss. All we need is the data, and we can go.
And how long do we have? Anything from the coastguard?

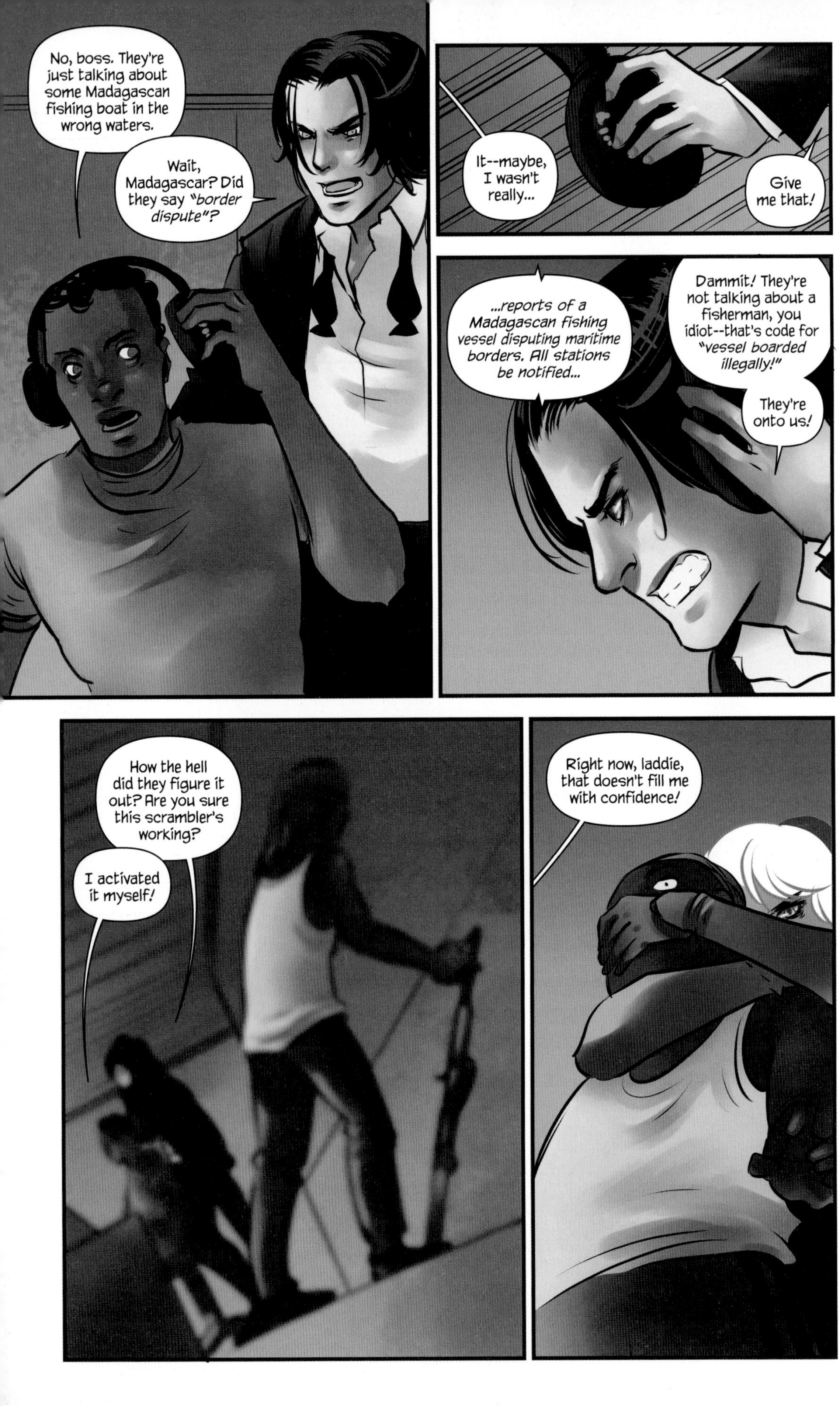
No, boss. They're just talking about some Madagascan fishing boat in the wrong waters.
Wait, Madagascar? Did they say "border dispute"?
It--maybe, I wasn't really...
Give me that!
...reports of a Madagascan fishing vessel disputing maritime borders. All stations be notified...
Dammit! They're not talking about a fisherman, you idiot--that's code for "vessel boarded illegally!"
They're onto us!
How the hell did they figure it out? Are you sure this scrambler's working?
I activated it myself!
Right now, laddie, that doesn't fill me with confidence!

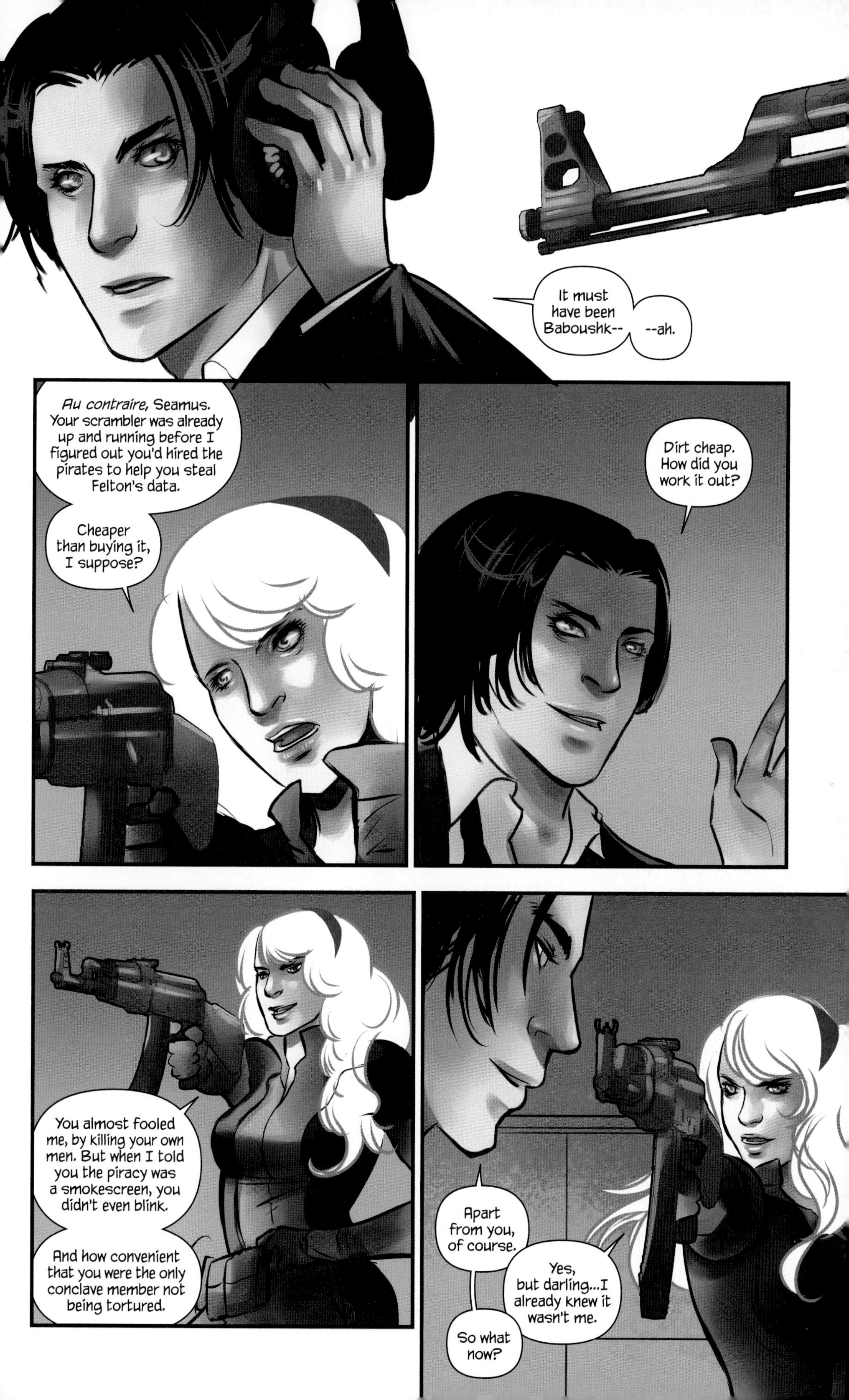
It must have been Baboushk--
--ah.
Au contraire, Seamus. Your scrambler was already up and running before I figured out you'd hired the pirates to help you steal Felton's data.
Cheaper than buying it, I suppose?
Dirt cheap. How did you work it out?
You almost fooled me, by killing your own men. But when I told you the piracy was a smokescreen, you didn't even blink.
And how convenient that you were the only conclave member not being tortured.
Apart from you, of course.
Yes, but darling...I already knew it wasn't me.
So what now?

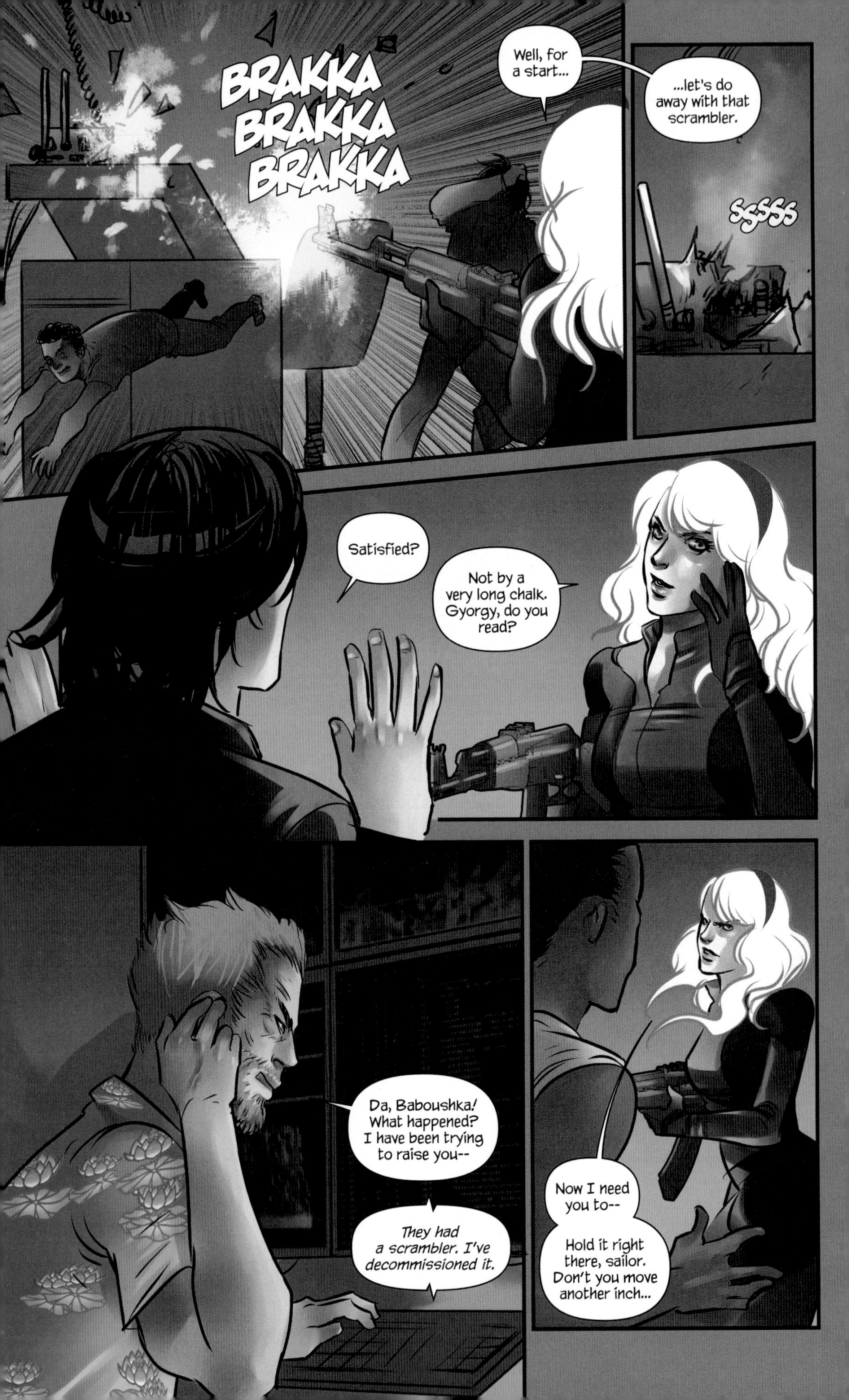
BRAKKA
BRAKKA
BRAKKA
Well, for a start...
...let's do away with that scrambler.
SSSSS
Satisfied?
Not by a very long chalk. Gyorgy, do you read?
Da, Baboushka! What happened? I have been trying to raise you--
They had a scrambler. I've decommissioned it.
Now I need you to--
Hold it right there, sailor. Don't you move another inch...

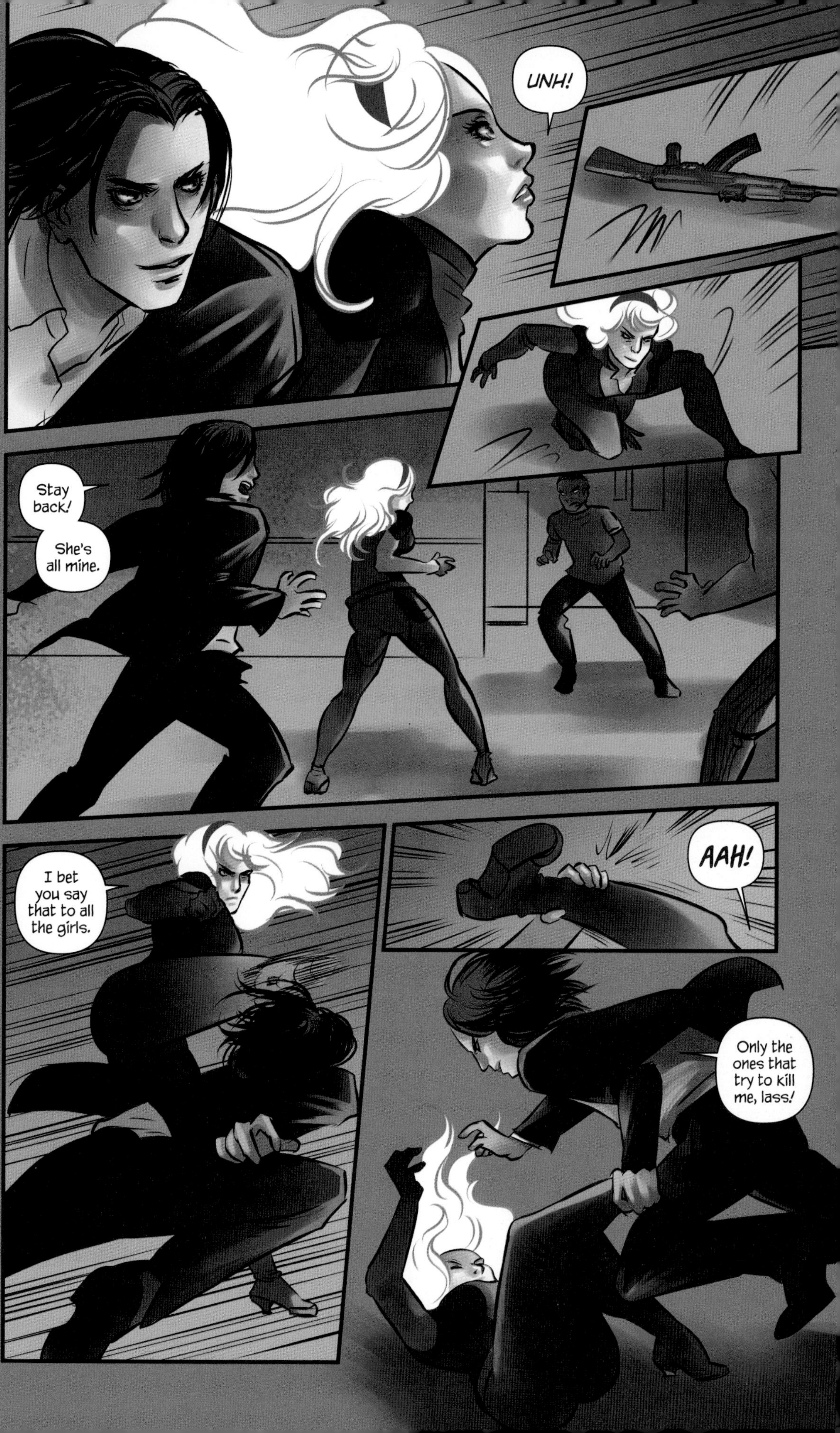
UNH!
Stay back!
She's all mine.
I bet you say that to all the girls.
AAH!
Only the ones that try to kill me, lass!

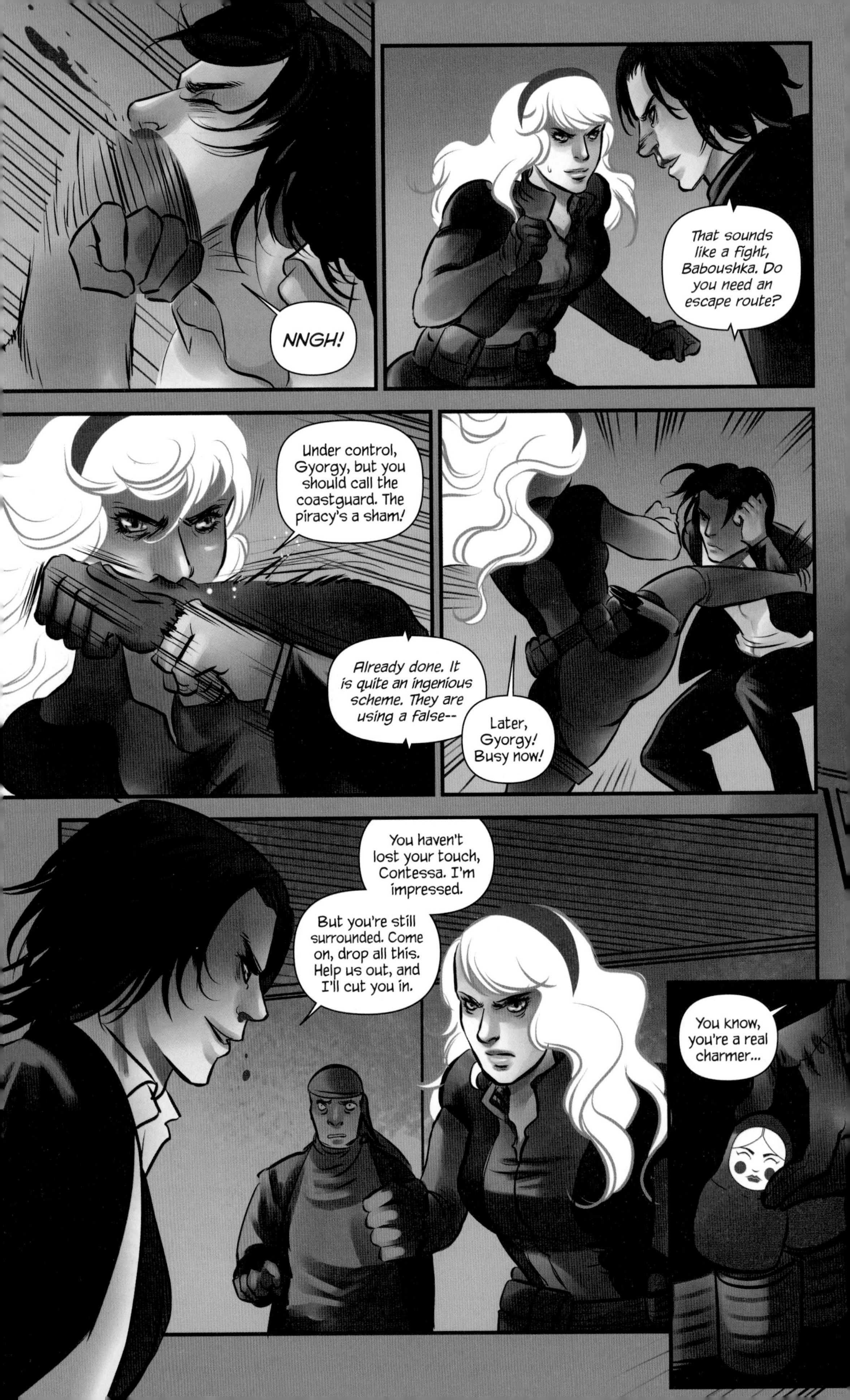
NNGH!
That sounds like a fight, Baboushka. Do you need an escape route?
Under control, Gyorgy, but you should call the coastguard. The piracy's a sham!
Already done. It is quite an ingenious scheme. They are using a false--
Later, Gyorgy! Busy now!
You haven't lost your touch, Contessa. I'm impressed.
But you're still surrounded. Come on, drop all this. Help us out, and I'll cut you in.
You know, you're a real charmer...

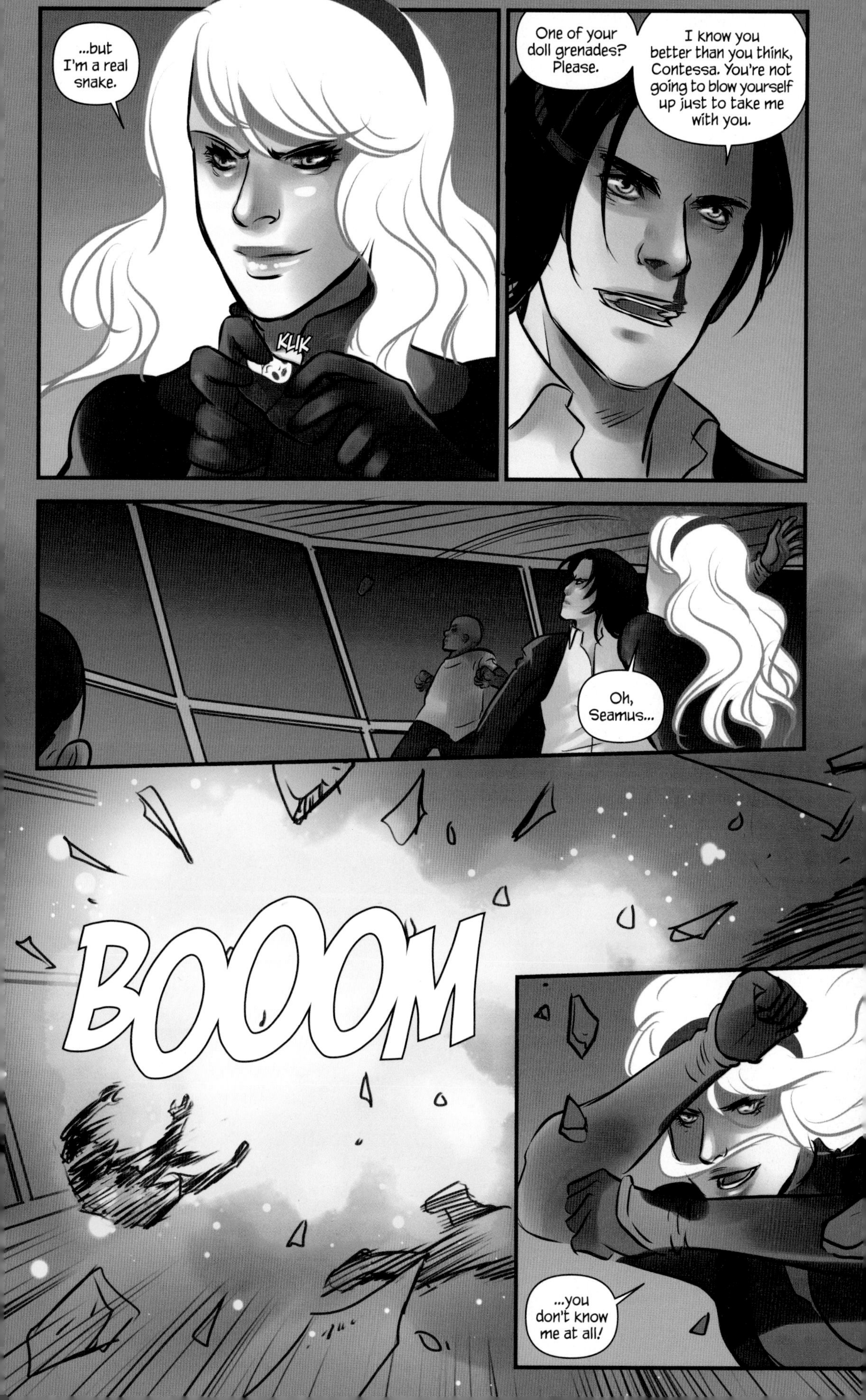
...but I'm a real snake.
KLIK
One of your doll grenades? Please.
I know you better than you think, Contessa. You're not going to blow yourself up just to take me with you.
Oh, Seamus...
BOOOM
...you don't know me at all!

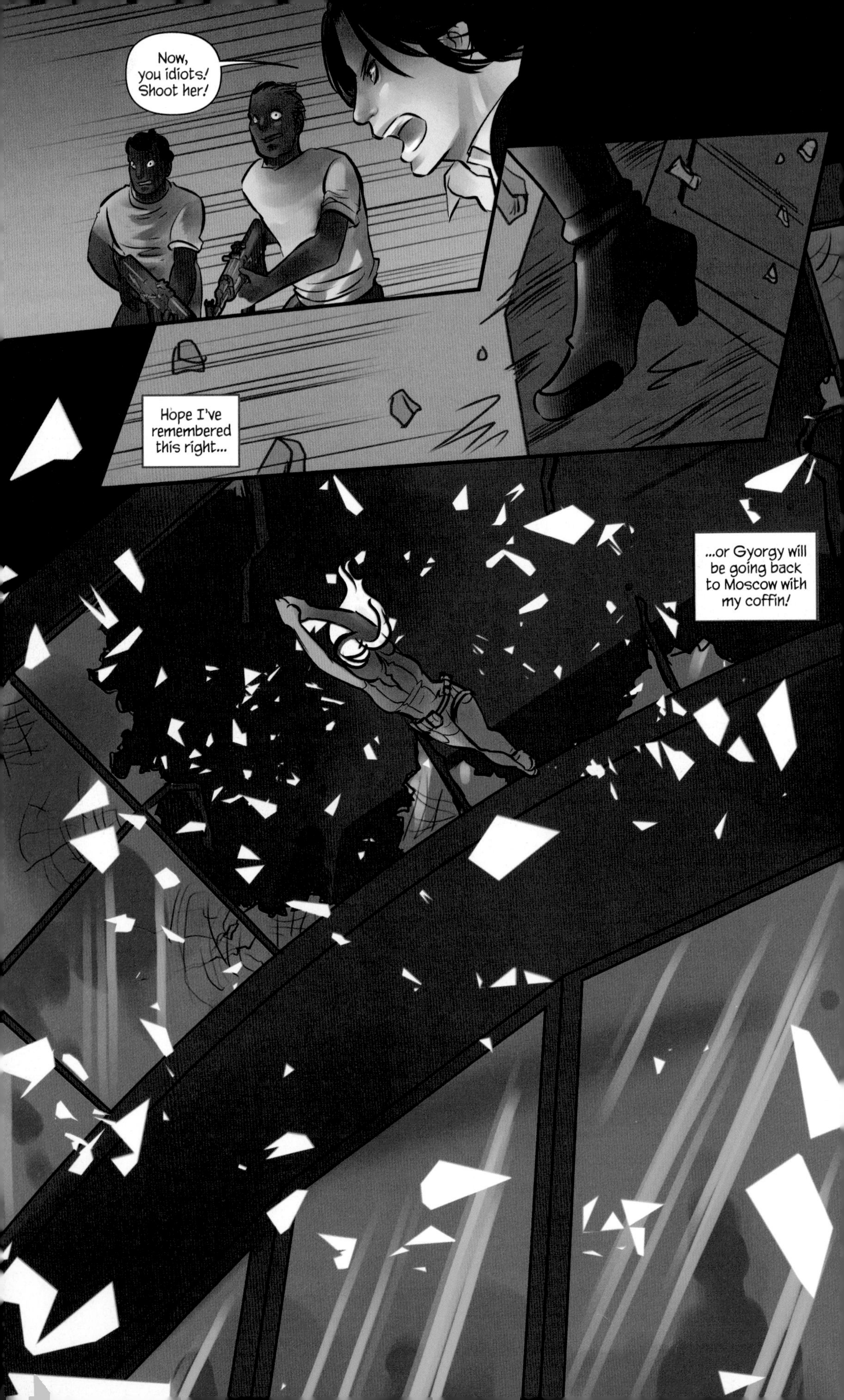
Now, you idiots! Shoot her!
Hope I've remembered this right...
...or Gyorgy will be going back to Moscow with my coffin!

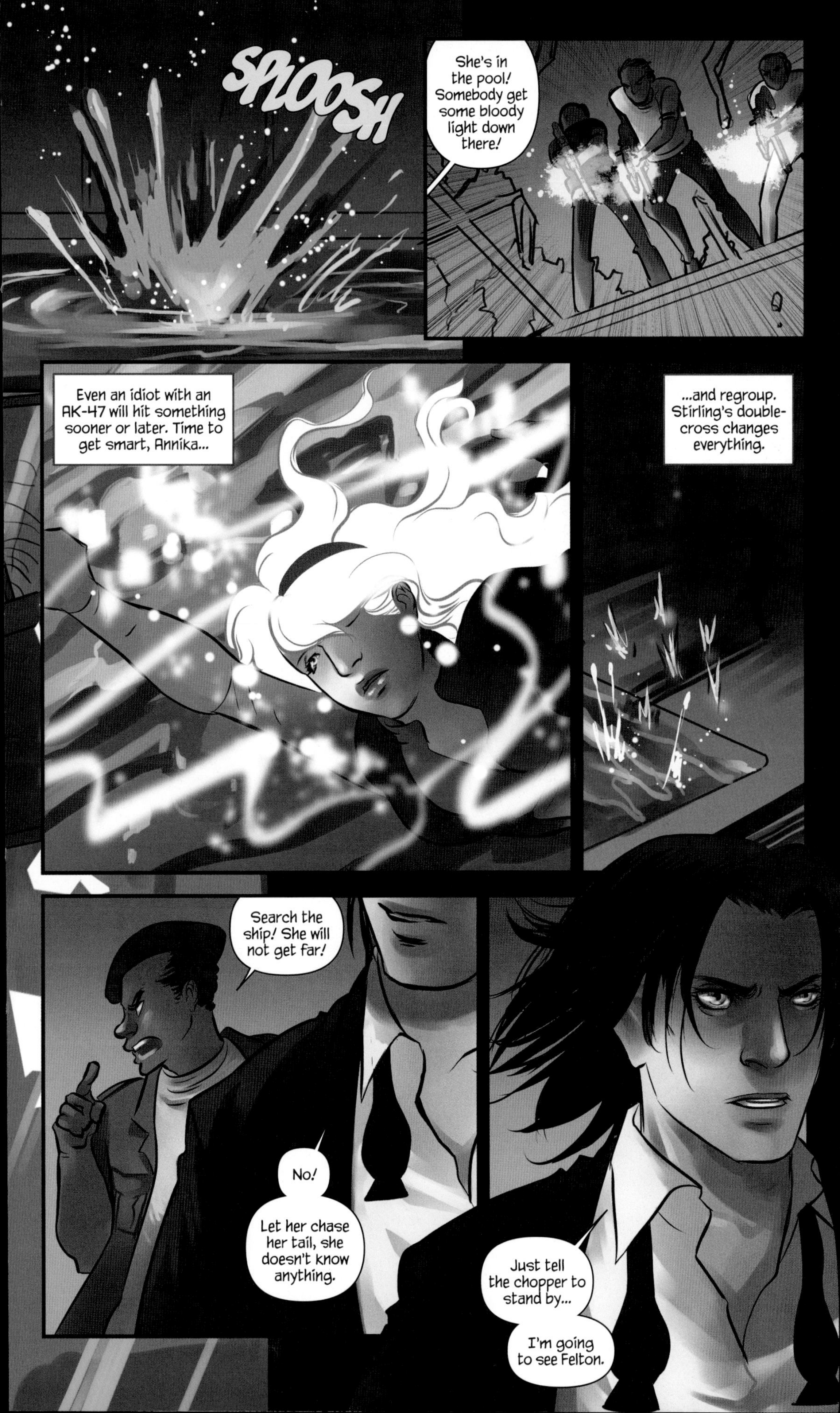
SPLOOSH
She's in the pool! Somebody get some bloody light down there!
Even an idiot with an AK-47 will hit something sooner or later. Time to get smart, Annika...
...and regroup. Stirling's double-cross changes everything.
Search the ship! She will not get far!
No!
Let her chase her tail, she doesn't know anything.
Just tell the chopper to stand by...
I'm going to see Felton.

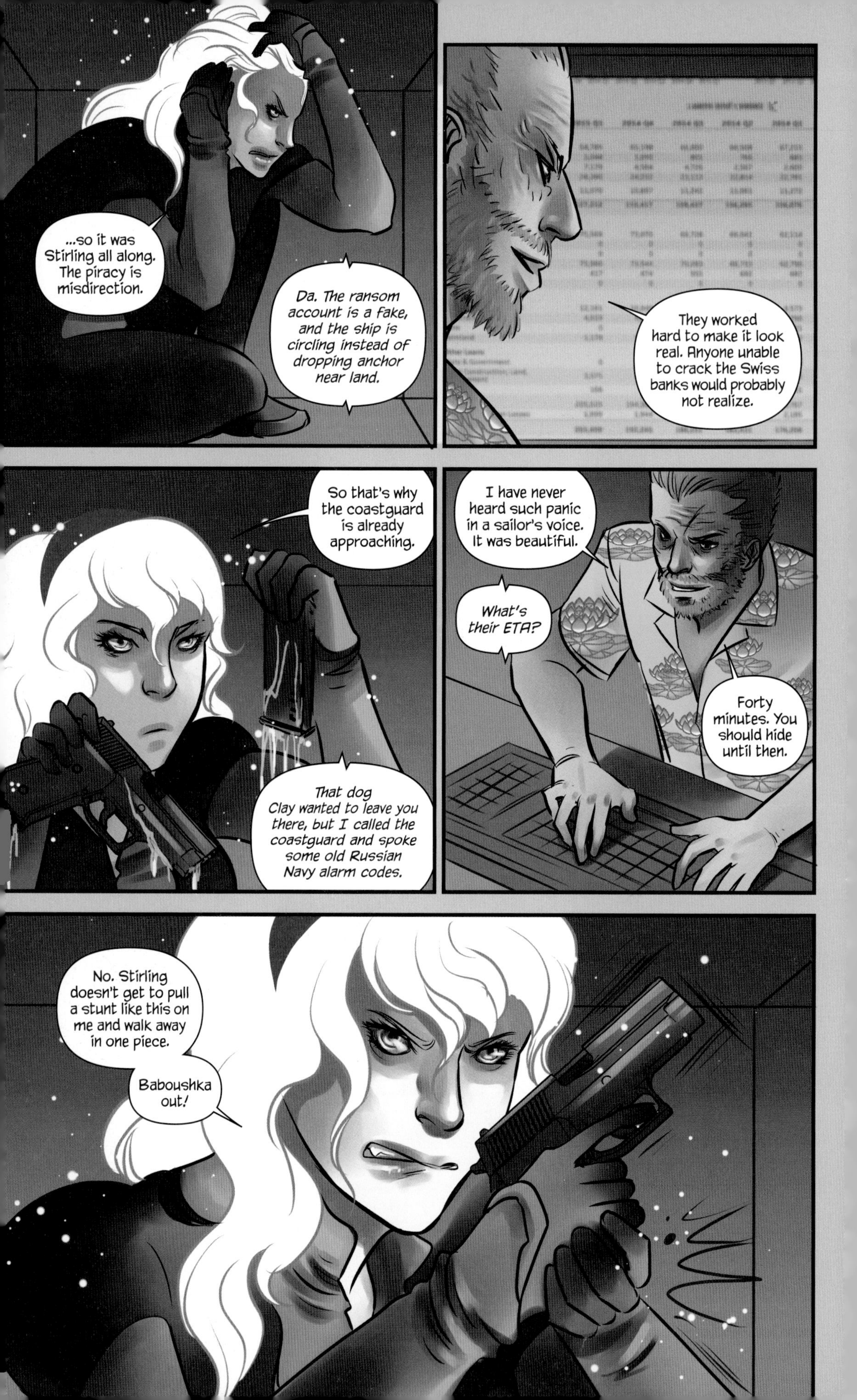
...so it was Stirling all along. The piracy is misdirection.
Da. The ransom account is a fake, and the ship is circling instead of dropping anchor near land.
They worked hard to make it look real. Anyone unable to crack the Swiss banks would probably not realize.
So that's why the coastguard is already approaching.
That dog Clay wanted to leave you there, but I called the coastguard and spoke some old Russian Navy alarm codes.
I have never heard such panic in a sailor's voice. It was beautiful.
What's their ETA?
Forty minutes. You should hide until then.
No. Stirling doesn't get to pull a stunt like this on me and walk away in one piece.
Baboushka out!

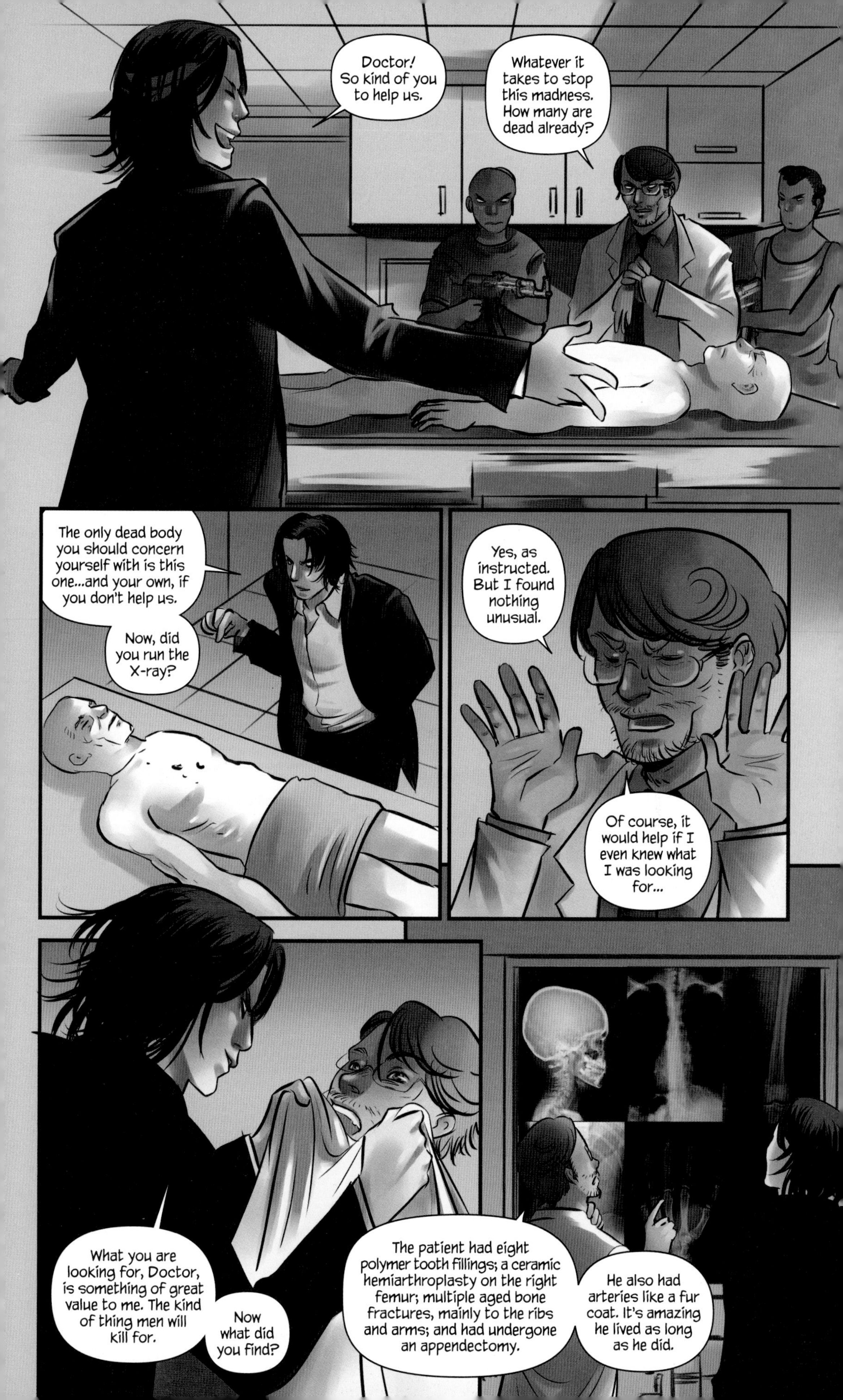

Doctor! So kind of you to help us.
Whatever it takes to stop this madness. How many are dead already?
The only dead body you should concern yourself with is this one...and your own, if you don't help us.
Now, did you run the X-ray?
Yes, as instructed. But I found nothing unusual.
Of course, it would help if I even knew what I was looking for...
What you are looking for, Doctor, is something of great value to me. The kind of thing men will kill for.
Now what did you find?
The patient had eight polymer tooth fillings; a ceramic hemiarthroplasty on the right femur; multiple aged bone fractures, mainly to the ribs and arms; and had undergone an appendectomy.
He also had arteries like a fur coat. It's amazing he lived as long as he did.

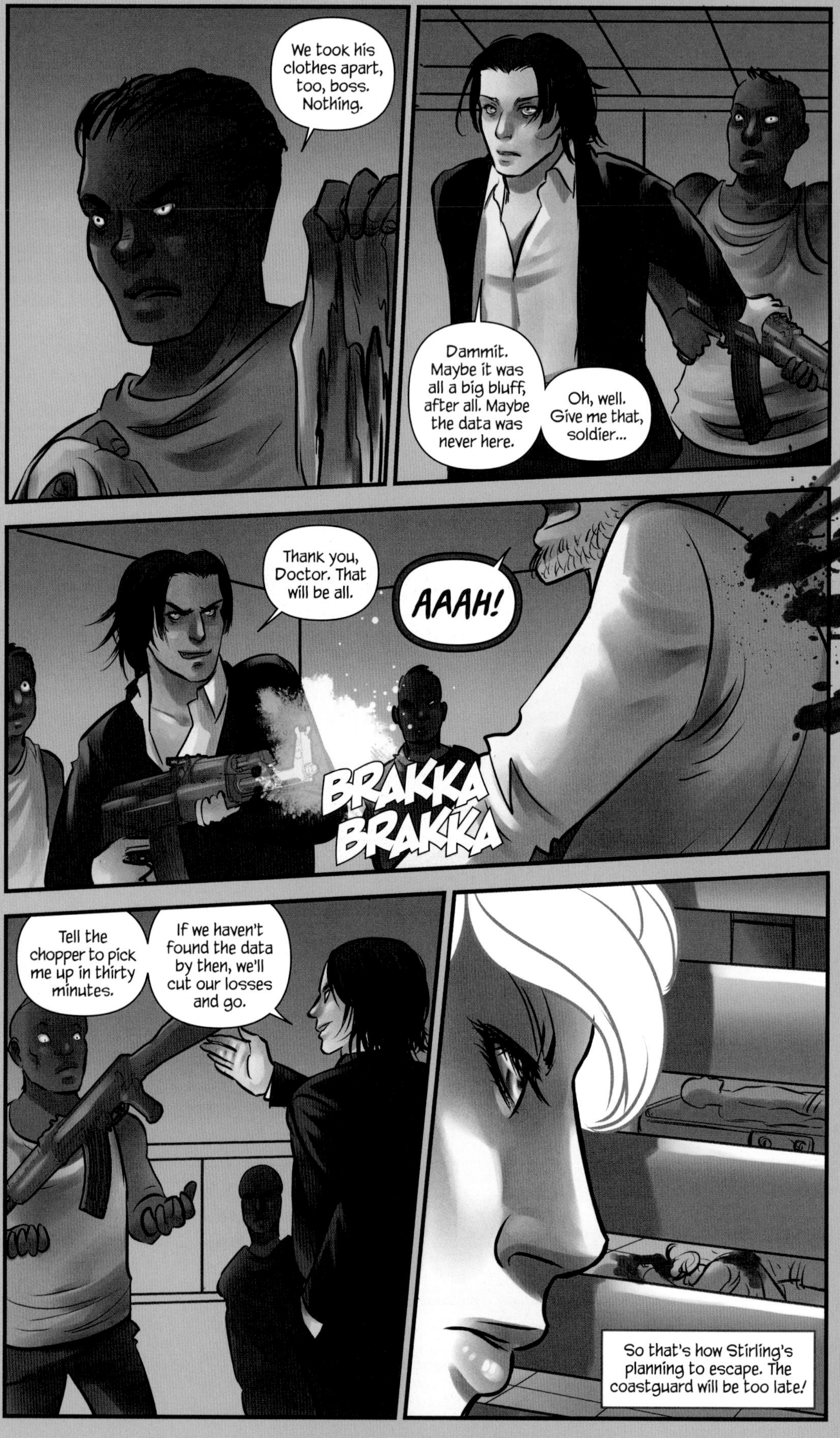

We took his clothes apart, too, boss. Nothing.
Dammit. Maybe it was all a big bluff, after all. Maybe the data was never here.
Oh, well. Give me that, soldier...
Thank you, Doctor. That will be all.
AAAH!
BRAKKA BRAKKA
Tell the chopper to pick me up in thirty minutes.
If we haven't found the data by then, we'll cut our losses and go.
So that's how Stirling's planning to escape. The coastguard will be too late!

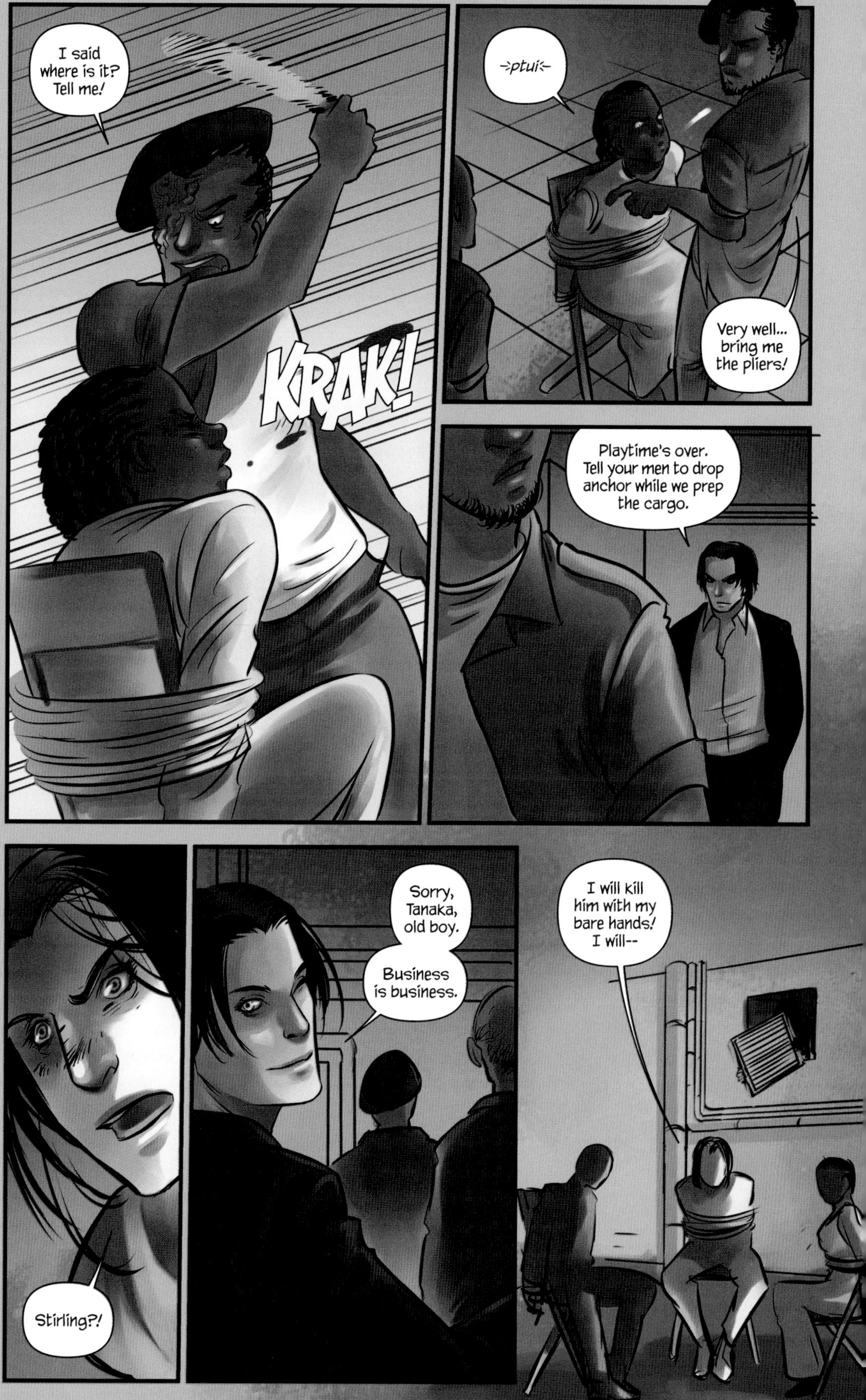
I said where is it? Tell me!
KRAK!
-ptui-
Very well... bring me the pliers!
Playtime's over. Tell your men to drop anchor while we prep the cargo.
Stirling?!
Sorry, Tanaka, old boy.
Business is business.
I will kill him with my bare hands! I will--

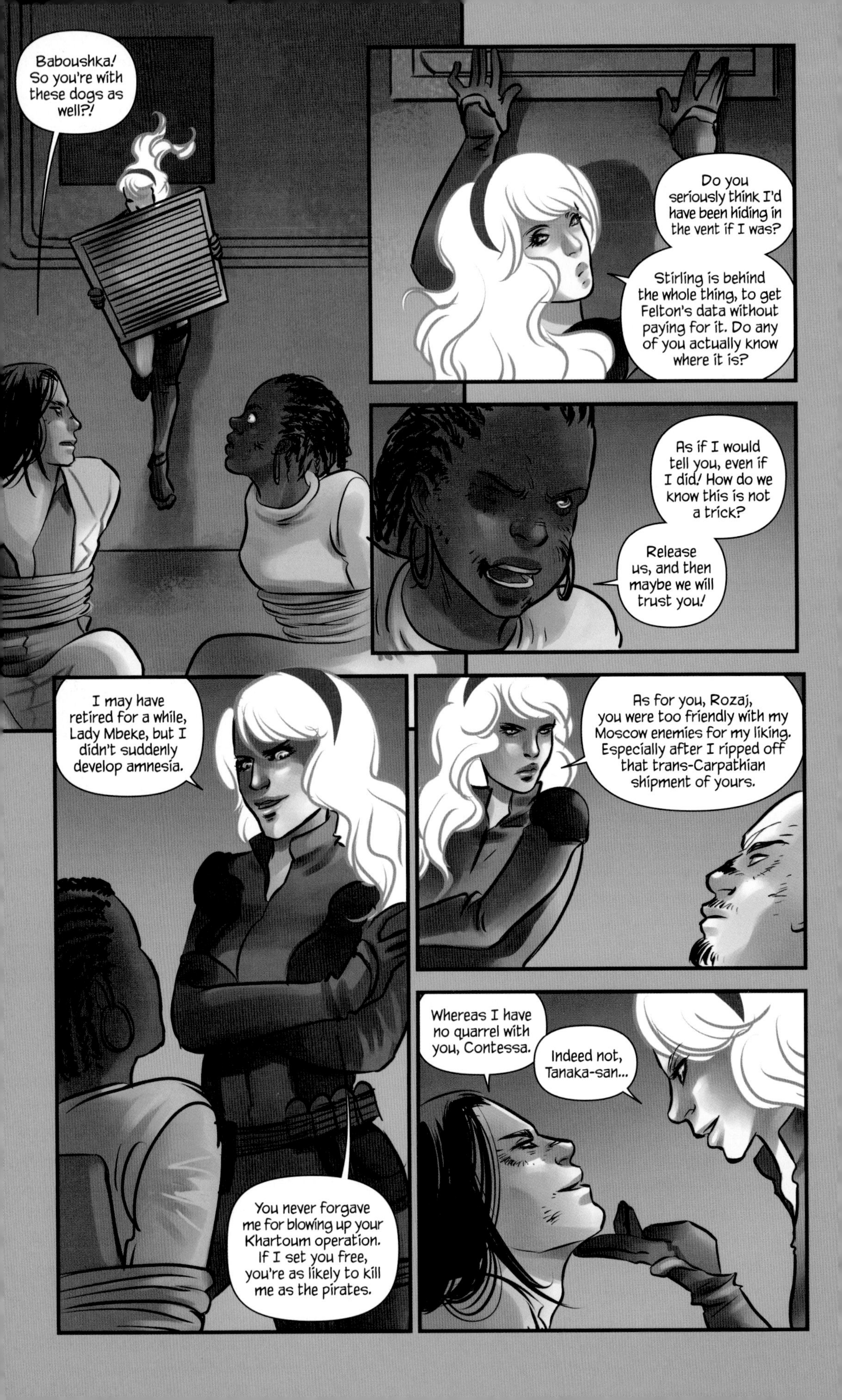

Baboushka! So you're with these dogs as well?!
Do you seriously think I'd have been hiding in the vent if I was?
Stirling is behind the whole thing, to get Felton's data without paying for it. Do any of you actually know where it is?
As if I would tell you, even if I did! How do we know this is not a trick?
Release us, and then maybe we will trust you!
I may have retired for a while, Lady Mbeke, but I didn't suddenly develop amnesia.
You never forgave me for blowing up your Khartoum operation. If I set you free, you're as likely to kill me as the pirates.
As for you, Rozaj, you were too friendly with my Moscow enemies for my liking. Especially after I ripped off that trans-Carpathian shipment of yours.
Whereas I have no quarrel with you, Contessa.
Indeed not, Tanaka-san...

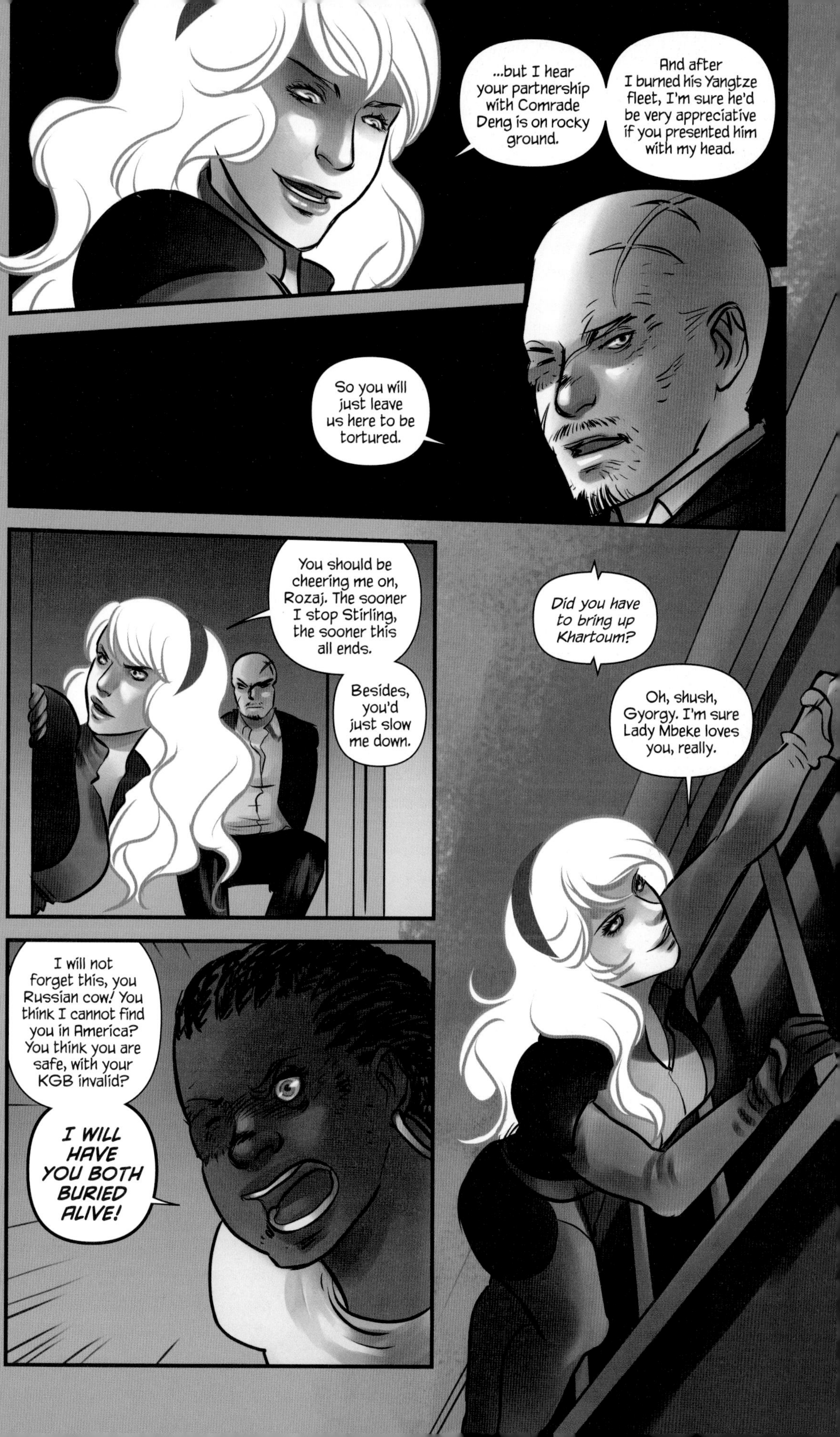
...but I hear your partnership with Comrade Deng is on rocky ground.
And after I burned his Yangtze fleet, I'm sure he'd be very appreciative if you presented him with my head.
So you will just leave us here to be tortured.
You should be cheering me on, Rozaj. The sooner I stop Stirling, the sooner this all ends.
Besides, you'd just slow me down.
Did you have to bring up Khartoum?
Oh, shush, Gyorgy. I'm sure Lady Mbeke loves you, really.
I will not forget this, you Russian cow! You think I cannot find you in America? You think you are safe, with your KGB invalid?
I WILL HAVE YOU BOTH BURIED ALIVE!

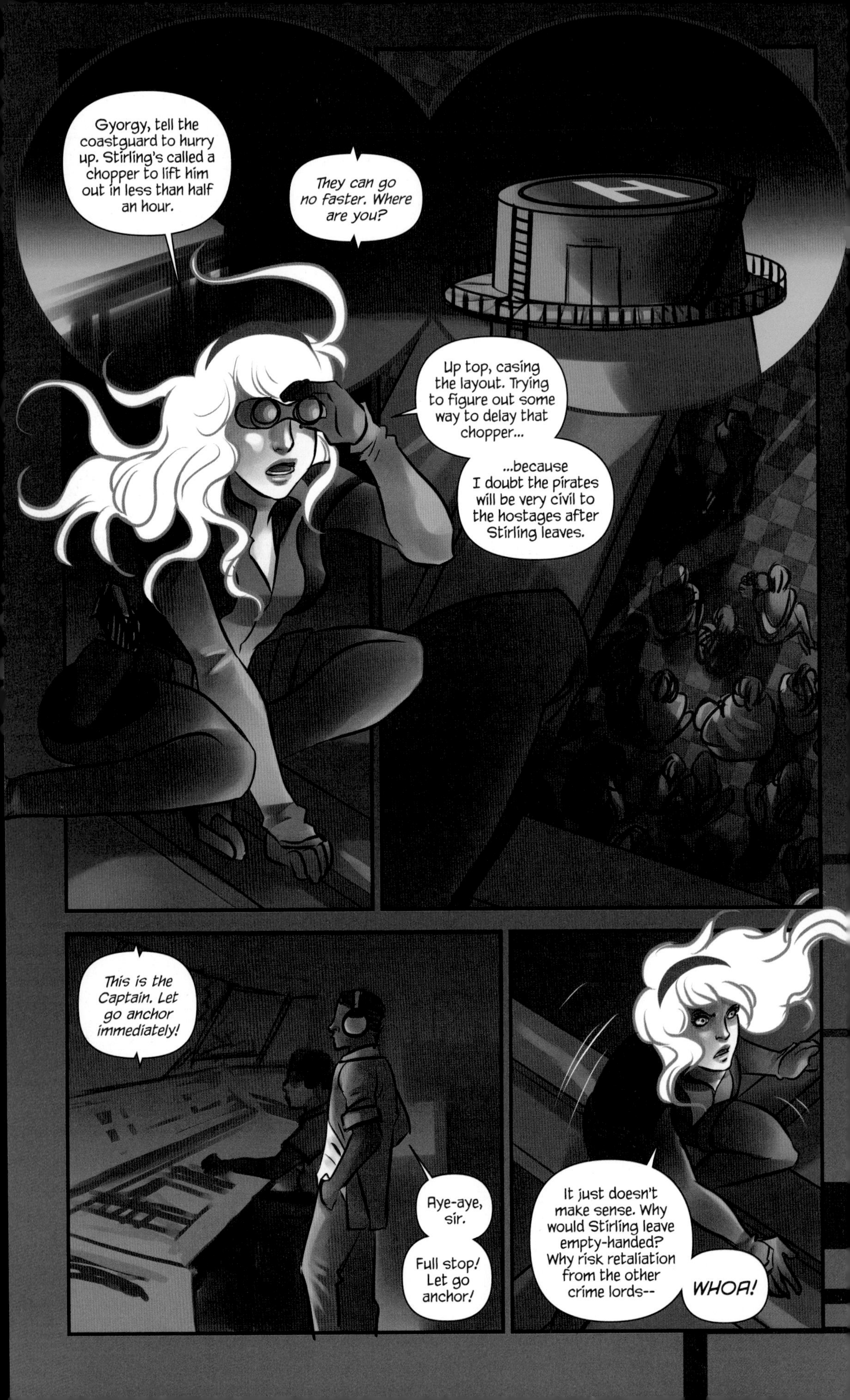
Gyorgy, tell the coastguard to hurry up. Stirling's called a chopper to lift him out in less than half an hour.
They can go no faster. Where are you?
Up top, casing the layout. Trying to figure out some way to delay that chopper...
...because I doubt the pirates will be very civil to the hostages after Stirling leaves.
This is the Captain. Let go anchor immediately!
Aye-aye, sir.
Full stop! Let go anchor!
It just doesn't make sense. Why would Stirling leave empty-handed? Why risk retaliation from the other crime lords--
WHOA!

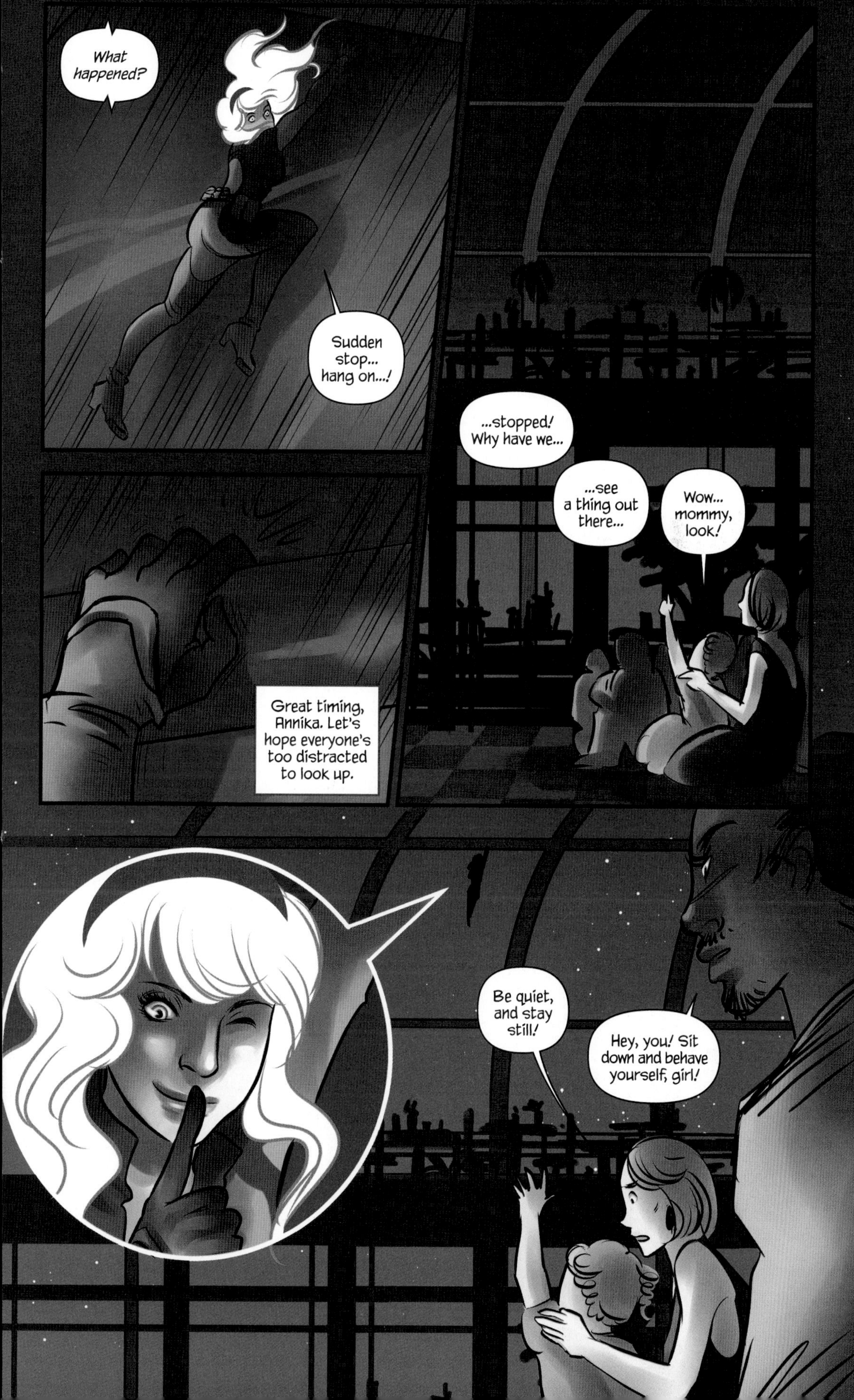
What happened?
Sudden stop... hang on...!
Great timing, Annika. Let's hope everyone's too distracted to look up.
...stopped! Why have we...
...see a thing out there...
Wow... mommy, look!
Be quiet, and stay still!
Hey, you! Sit down and behave yourself, girl!

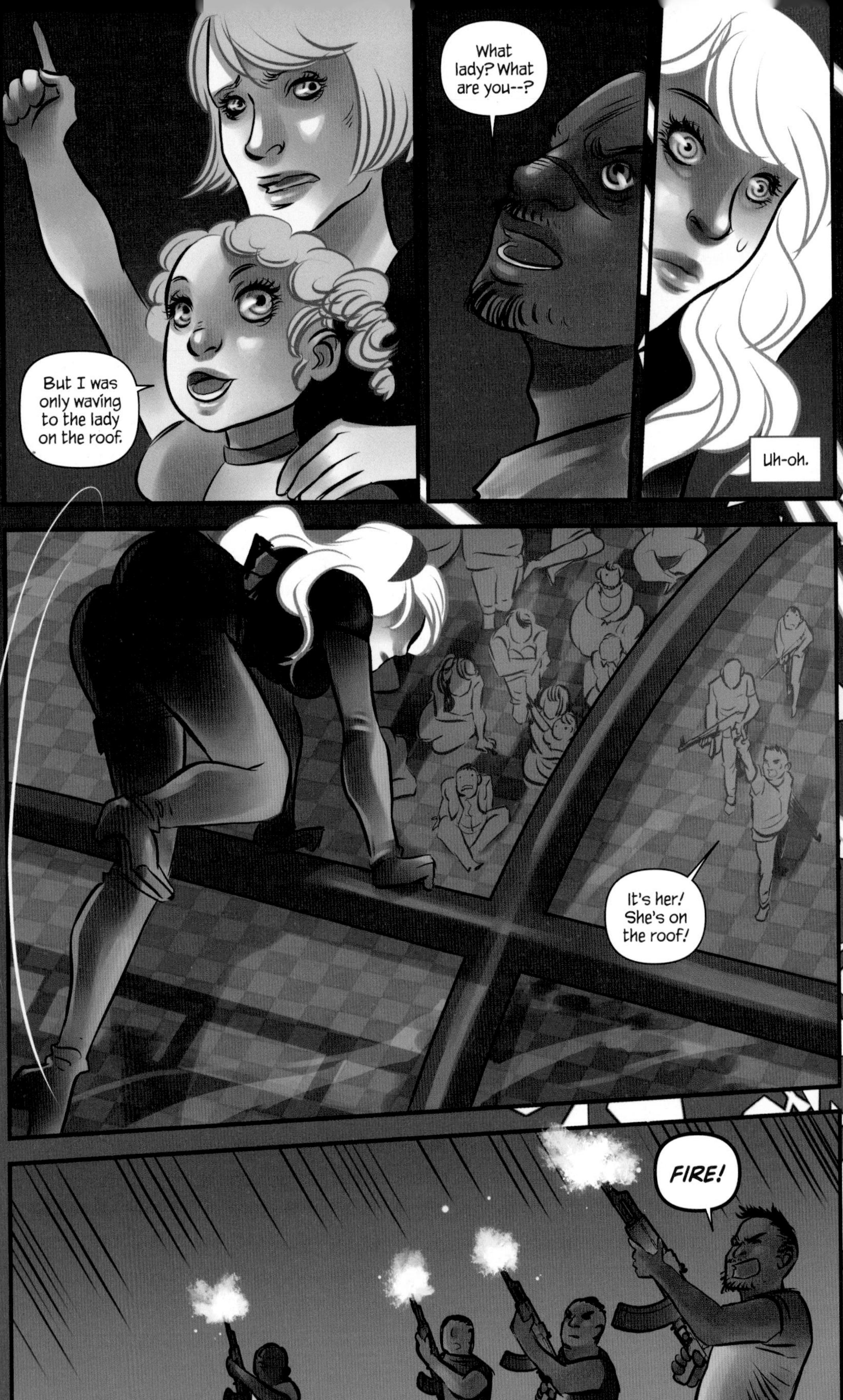

But I was only waving to the lady on the roof.
What lady? What are you--?
Uh-oh.
It's her! She's on the roof!
FIRE!

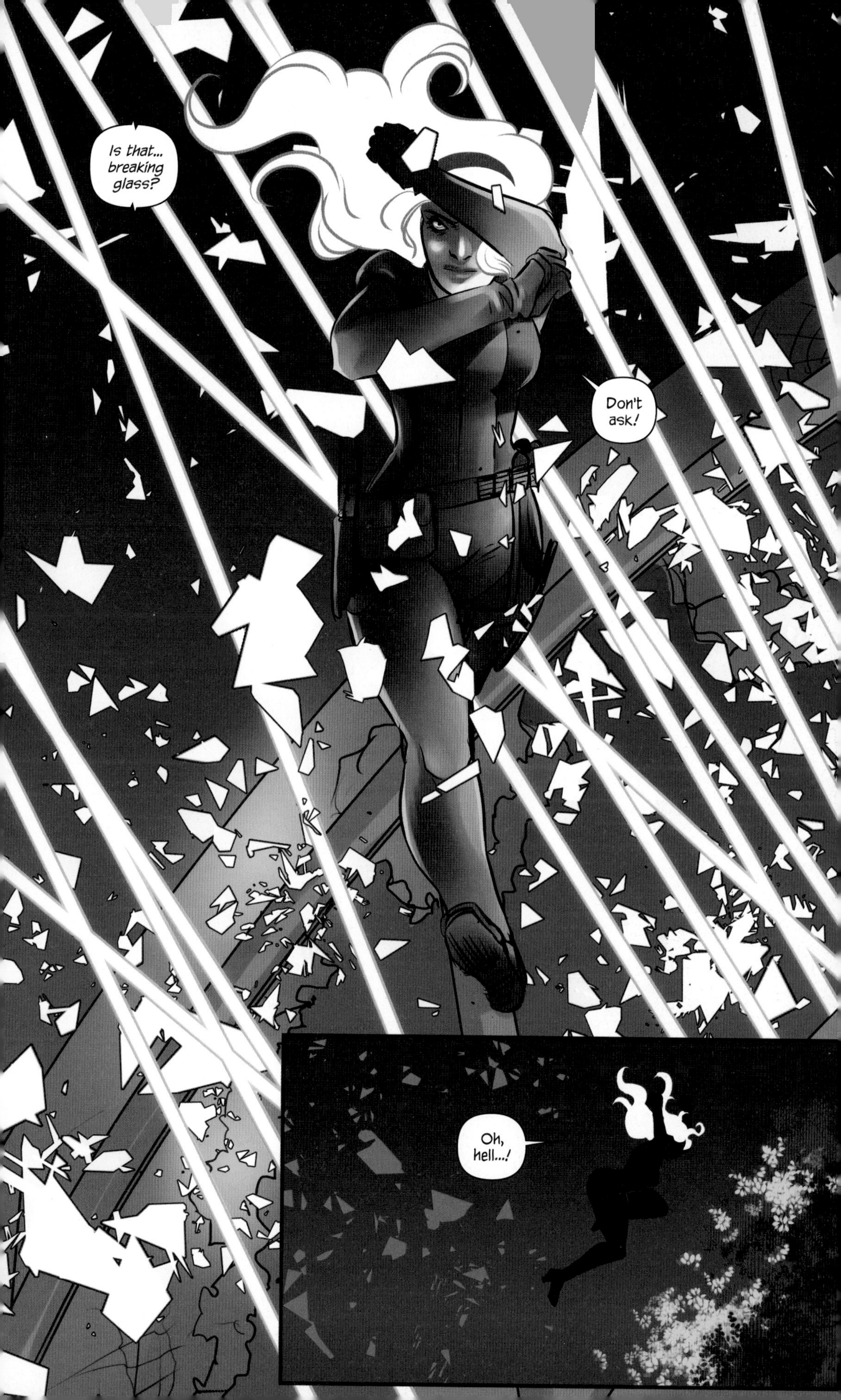
Is that... breaking glass?
Don't ask!
Oh, hell...!

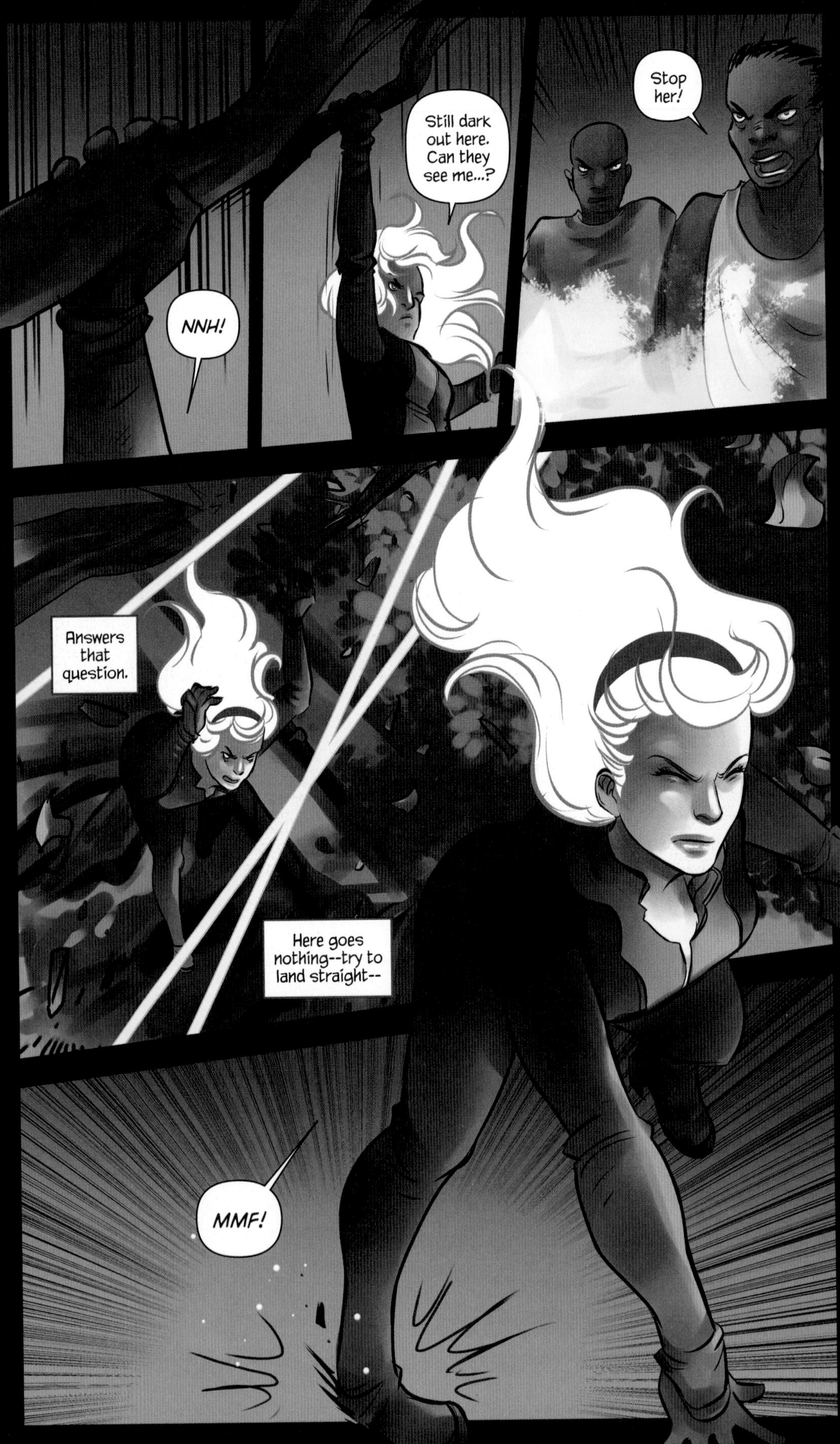
NNH!
Still dark out here. Can they see me...?
Stop her!
Answers that question.
Here goes nothing--try to land straight--
MMF!

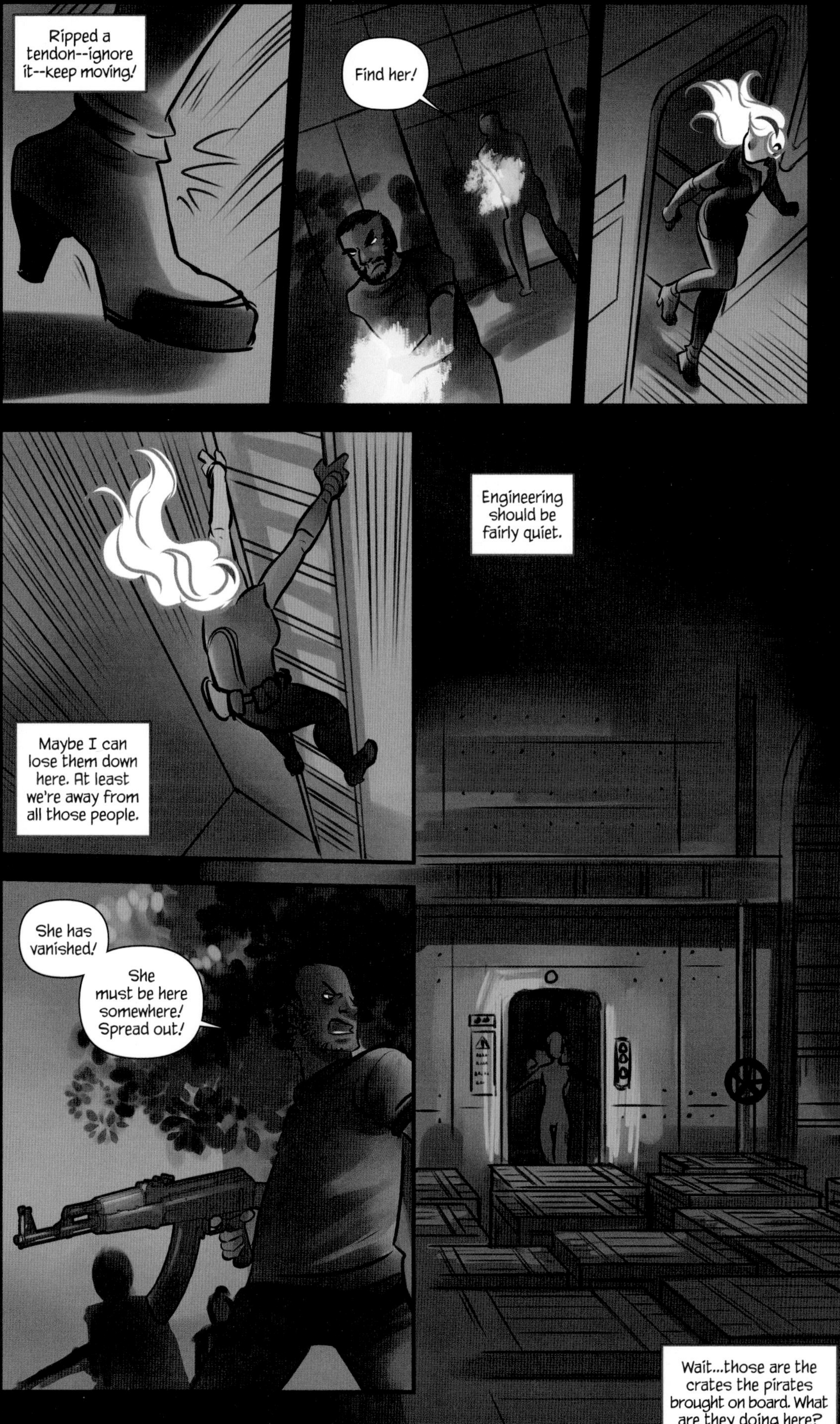
Ripped a tendon--ignore it--keep moving!
Find her!
Engineering should be fairly quiet.
Maybe I can lose them down here. At least we're away from all those people.
She has vanished!
She must be here somewhere! Spread out!
Wait...those are the crates the pirates brought on board. What are they doing here?

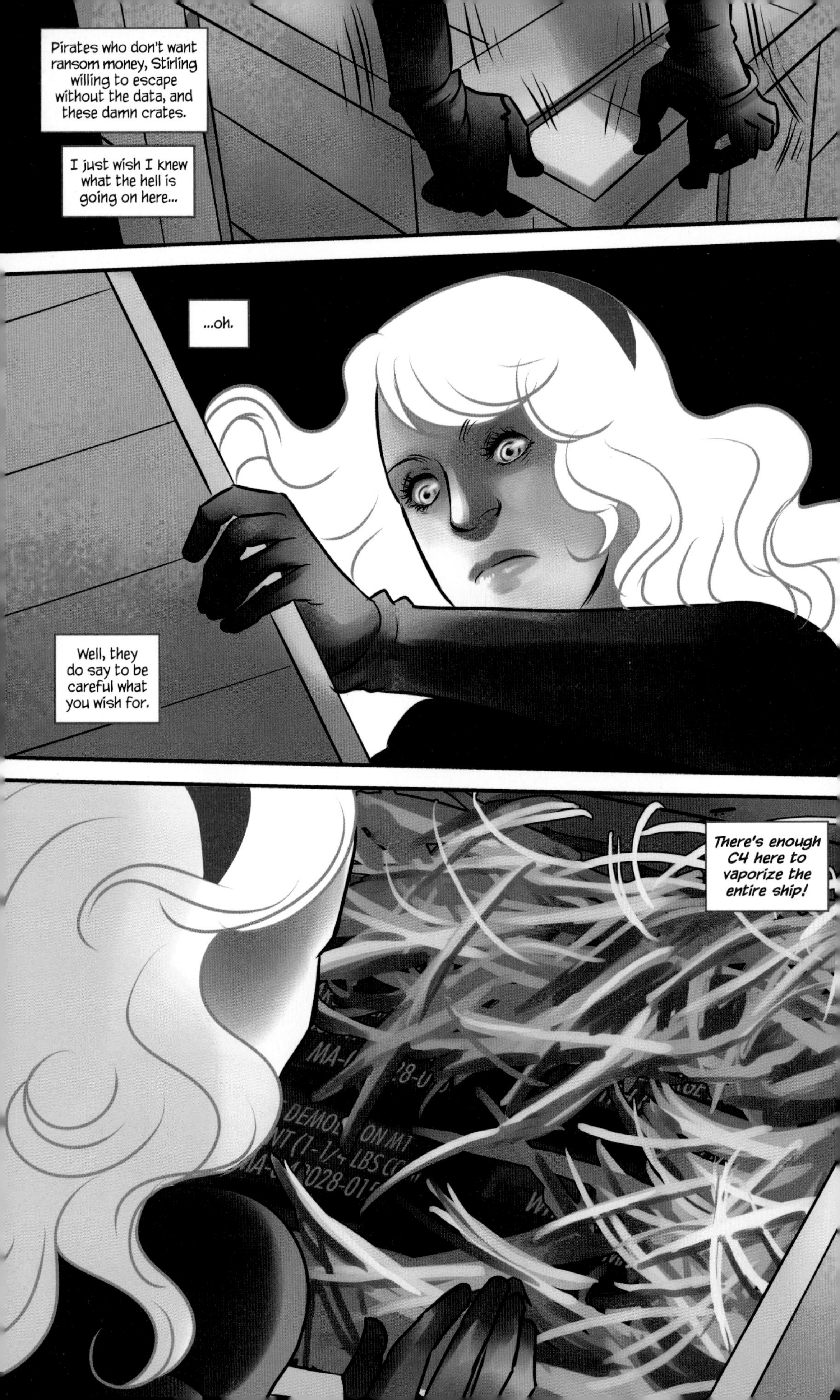
Pirates who don't want ransom money, Stirling willing to escape without the data, and these damn crates.
I just wish I knew what the hell is going on here...
...oh.
Well, they do say to be careful what you wish for.
There's enough C4 here to vaporize the entire ship!

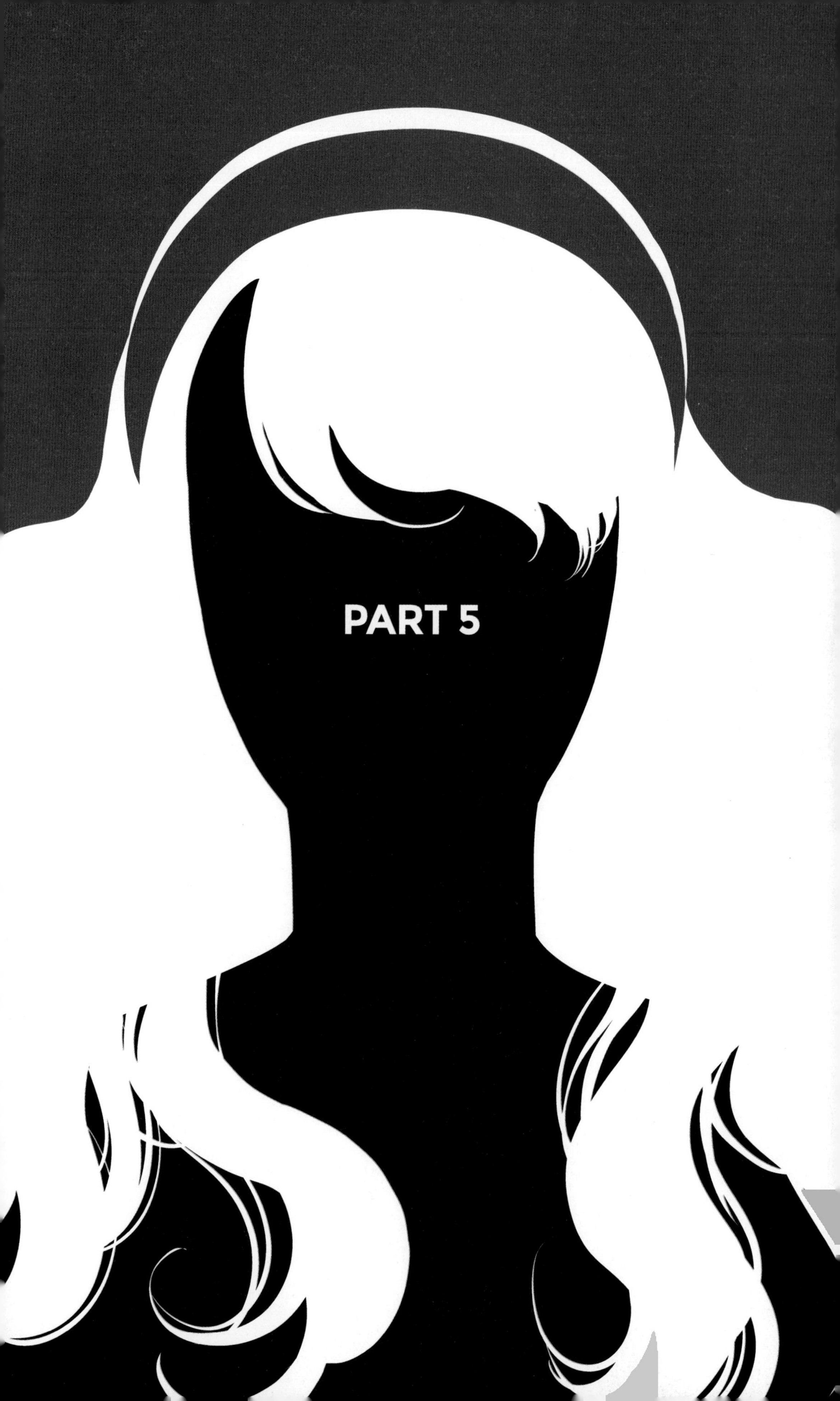
PART 5

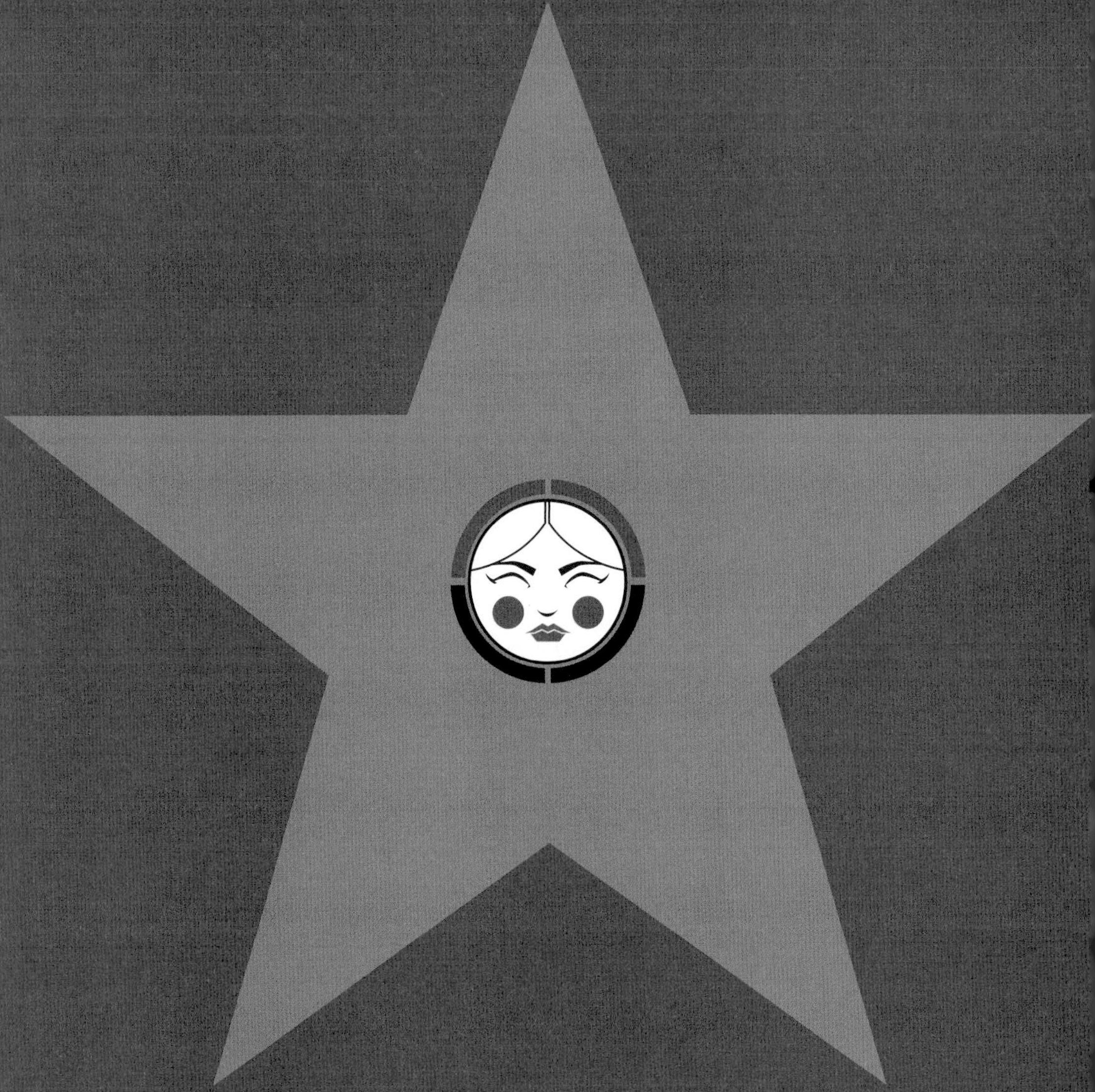

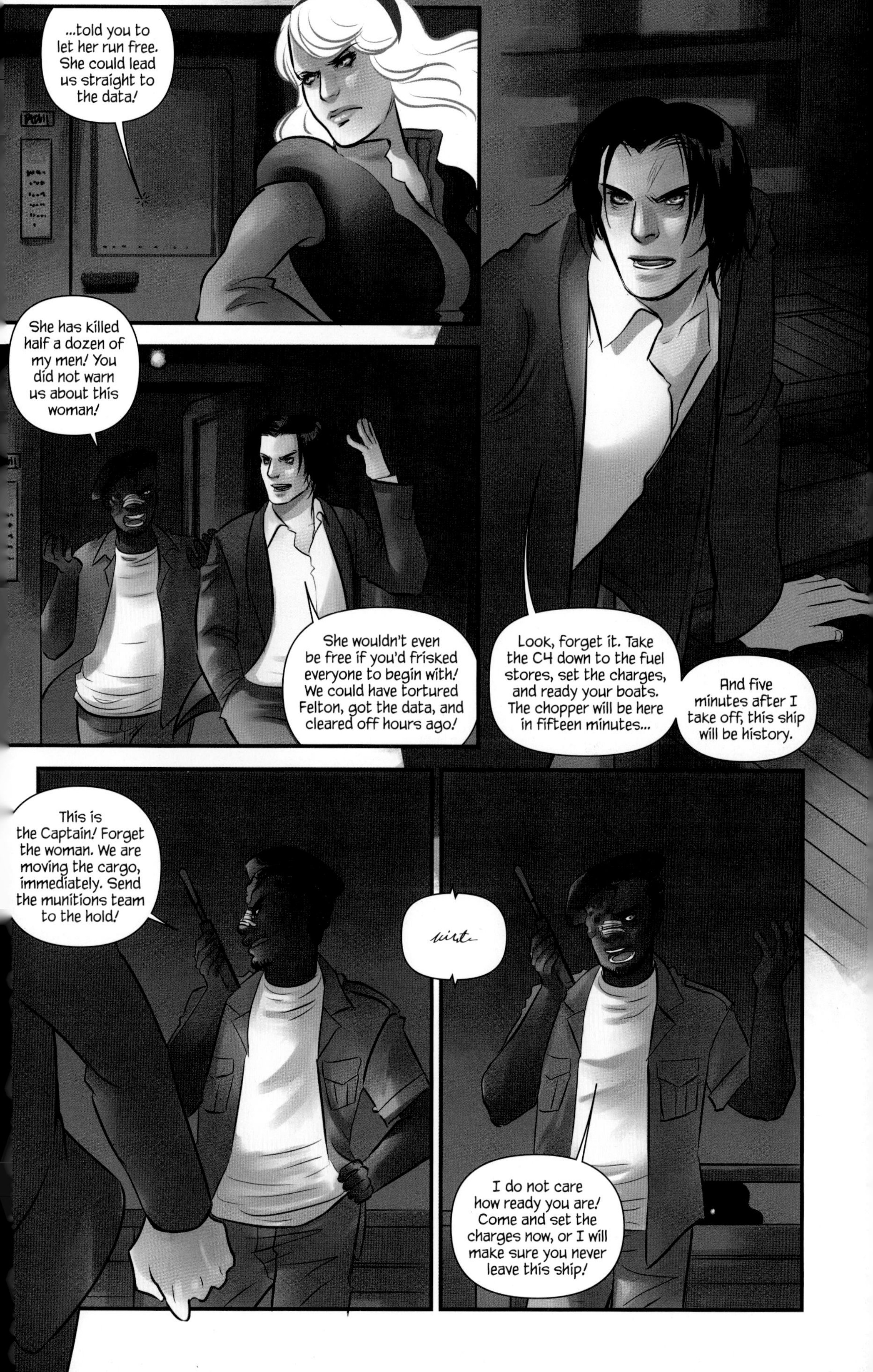
...told you to let her run free. She could lead us straight to the data!
She has killed half a dozen of my men! You did not warn us about this woman!
She wouldn't even be free if you'd frisked everyone to begin with! We could have tortured Felton, got the data, and cleared off hours ago!
Look, forget it. Take the C4 down to the fuel stores, set the charges, and ready your boats. The chopper will be here in fifteen minutes...
And five minutes after I take off, this ship will be history.
This is the Captain! Forget the woman. We are moving the cargo, immediately. Send the munitions team to the hold!
I do not care how ready you are! Come and set the charges now, or I will make sure you never leave this ship!

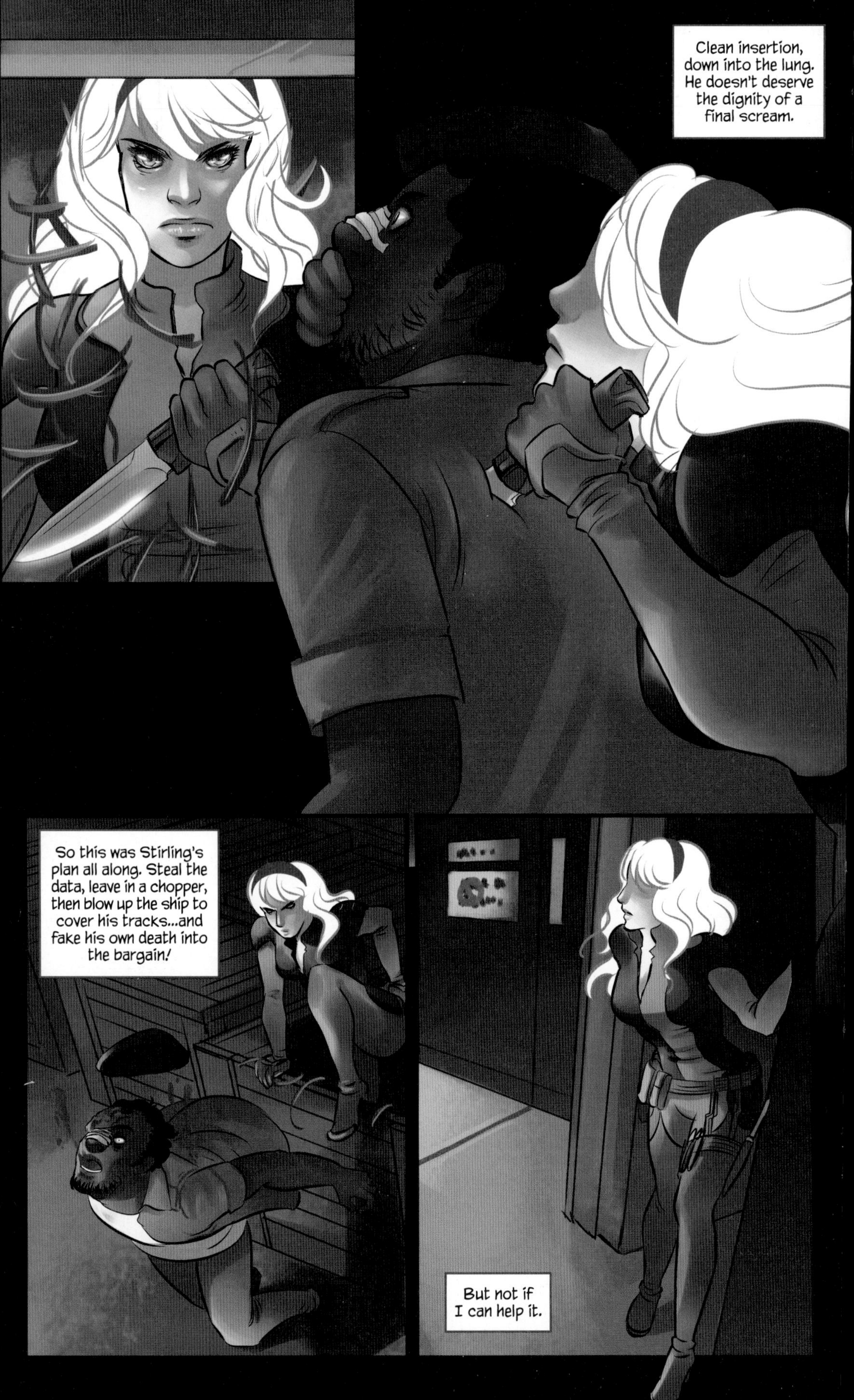
Clean insertion, down into the lung. He doesn't deserve the dignity of a final scream.
So this was Stirling's plan all along. Steal the data, leave in a chopper, then blow up the ship to cover his tracks...and fake his own death into the bargain!
But not if I can help it.

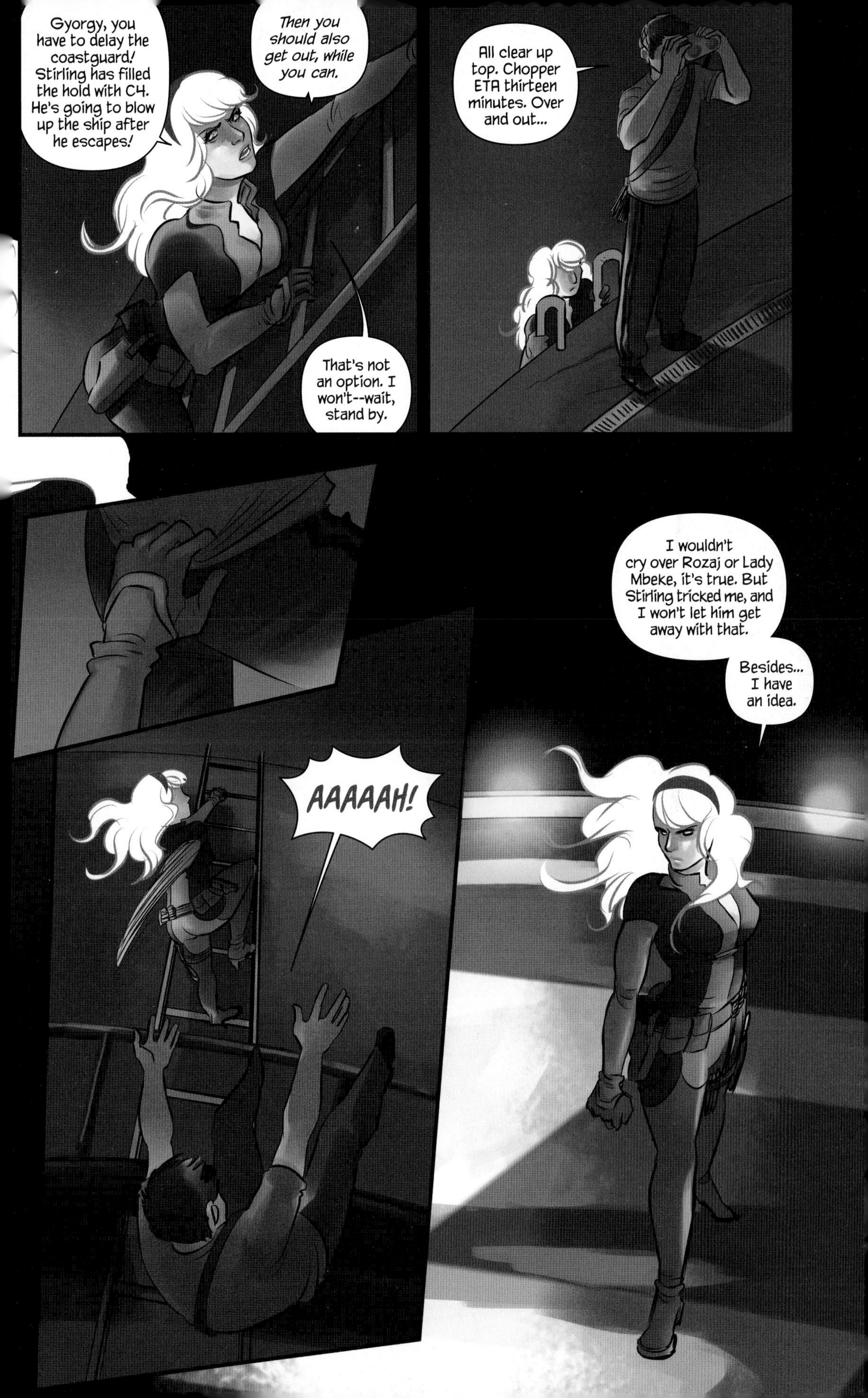
Gyorgy, you have to delay the coastguard! Stirling has filled the hold with C4. He's going to blow up the ship after he escapes!
Then you should also get out, while you can.
That's not an option. I won't--wait, stand by.
All clear up top. Chopper ETA thirteen minutes. Over and out...
AAAAAH!
I wouldn't cry over Rozaj or Lady Mbeke, it's true. But Stirling tricked me, and I won't let him get away with that.
Besides... I have an idea.

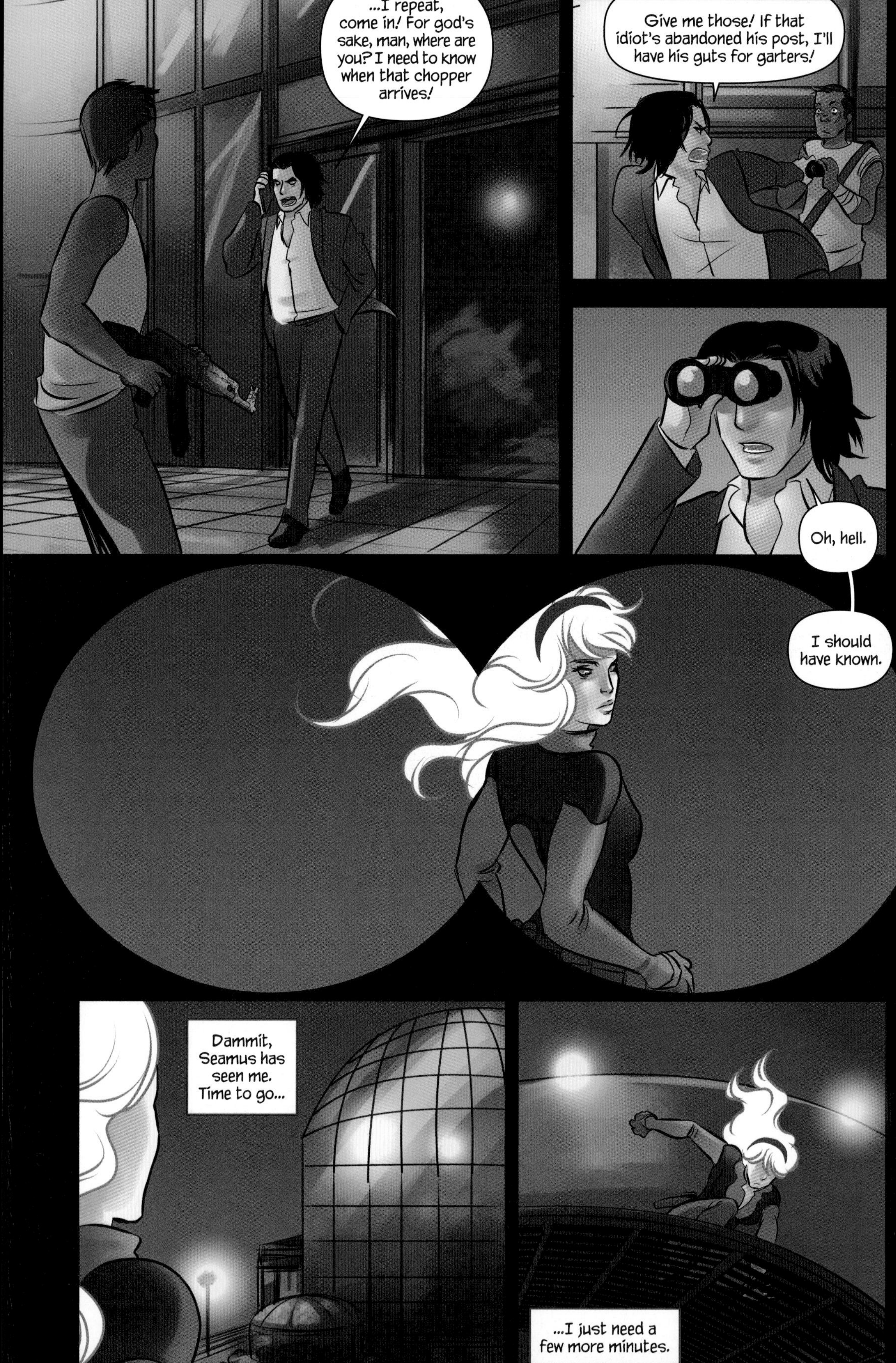
...I repeat, come in! For god's sake, man, where are you? I need to know when that chopper arrives!
Give me those! If that idiot's abandoned his post, I'll have his guts for garters!
Oh, hell.
I should have known.
Dammit, Seamus has seen me. Time to go...
...I just need a few more minutes.

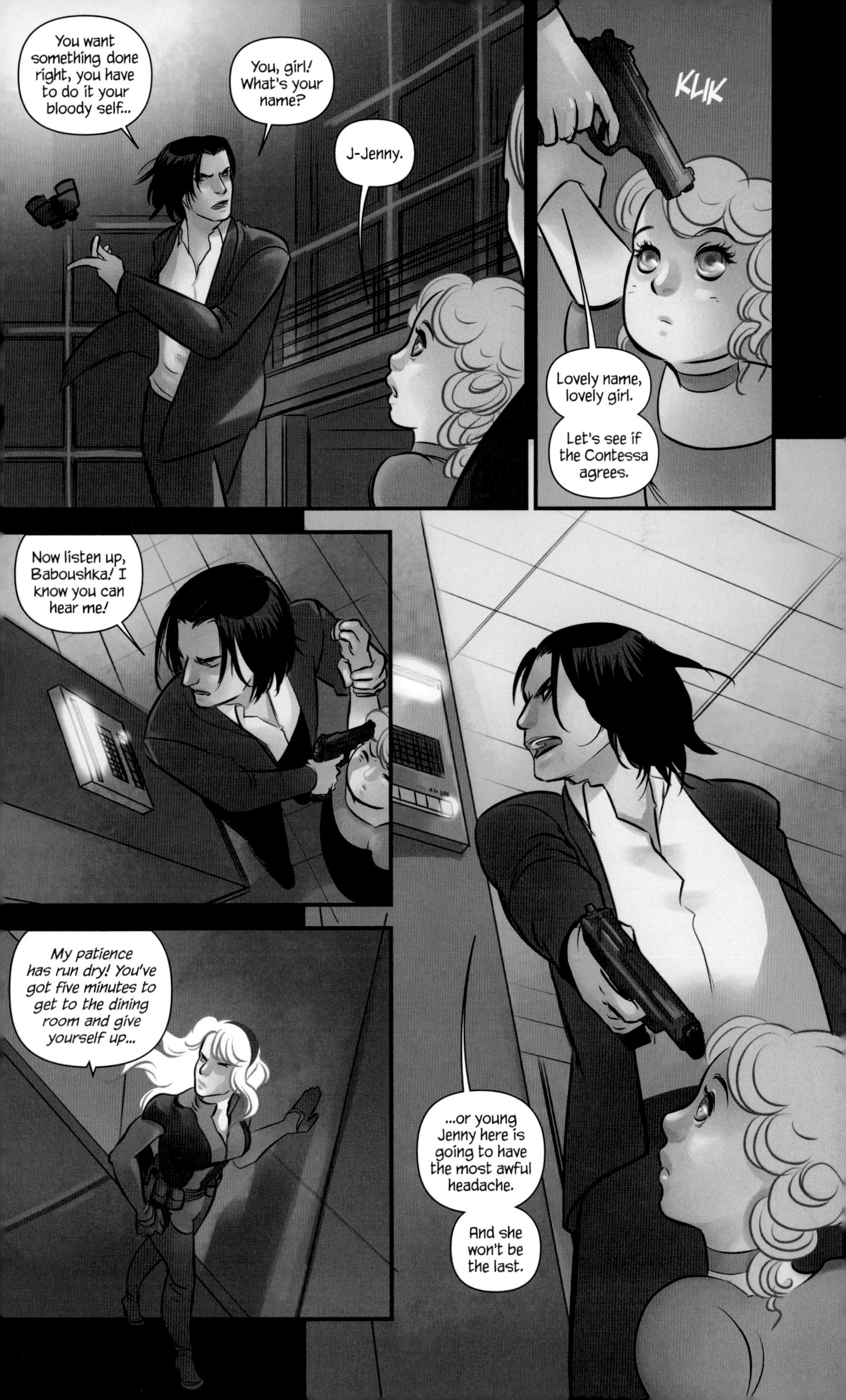

You want something done right, you have to do it your bloody self...
You, girl! What's your name?
J-Jenny.
KLIK
Lovely name, lovely girl.
Let's see if the Contessa agrees.
Now listen up, Baboushka! I know you can hear me!
My patience has run dry! You've got five minutes to get to the dining room and give yourself up...
...or young Jenny here is going to have the most awful headache.
And she won't be the last.

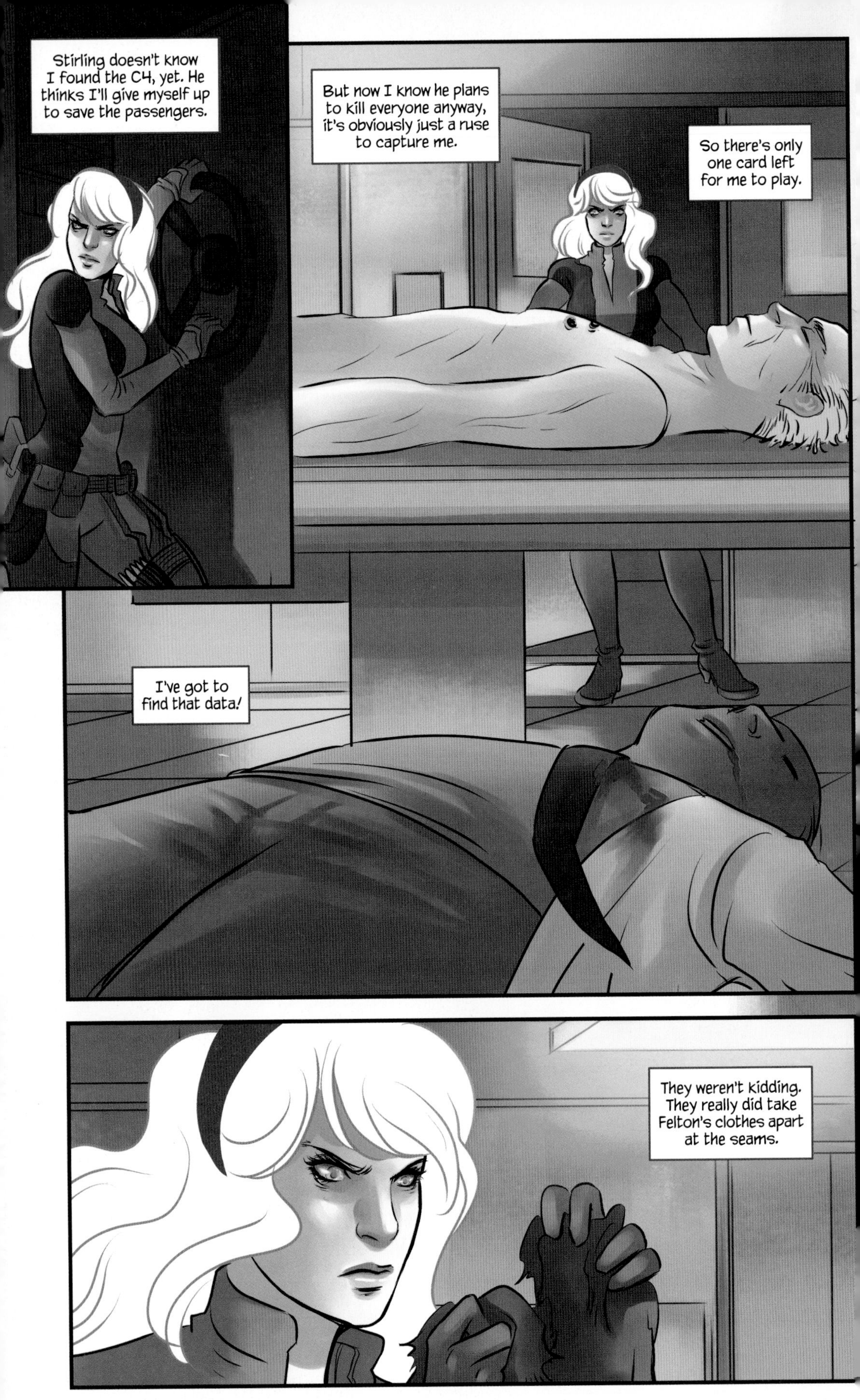
Stirling doesn't know I found the C4, yet. He thinks I'll give myself up to save the passengers.
But now I know he plans to kill everyone anyway, it's obviously just a ruse to capture me.
So there's only one card left for me to play.
I've got to find that data!
They weren't kidding. They really did take Felton's clothes apart at the seams.

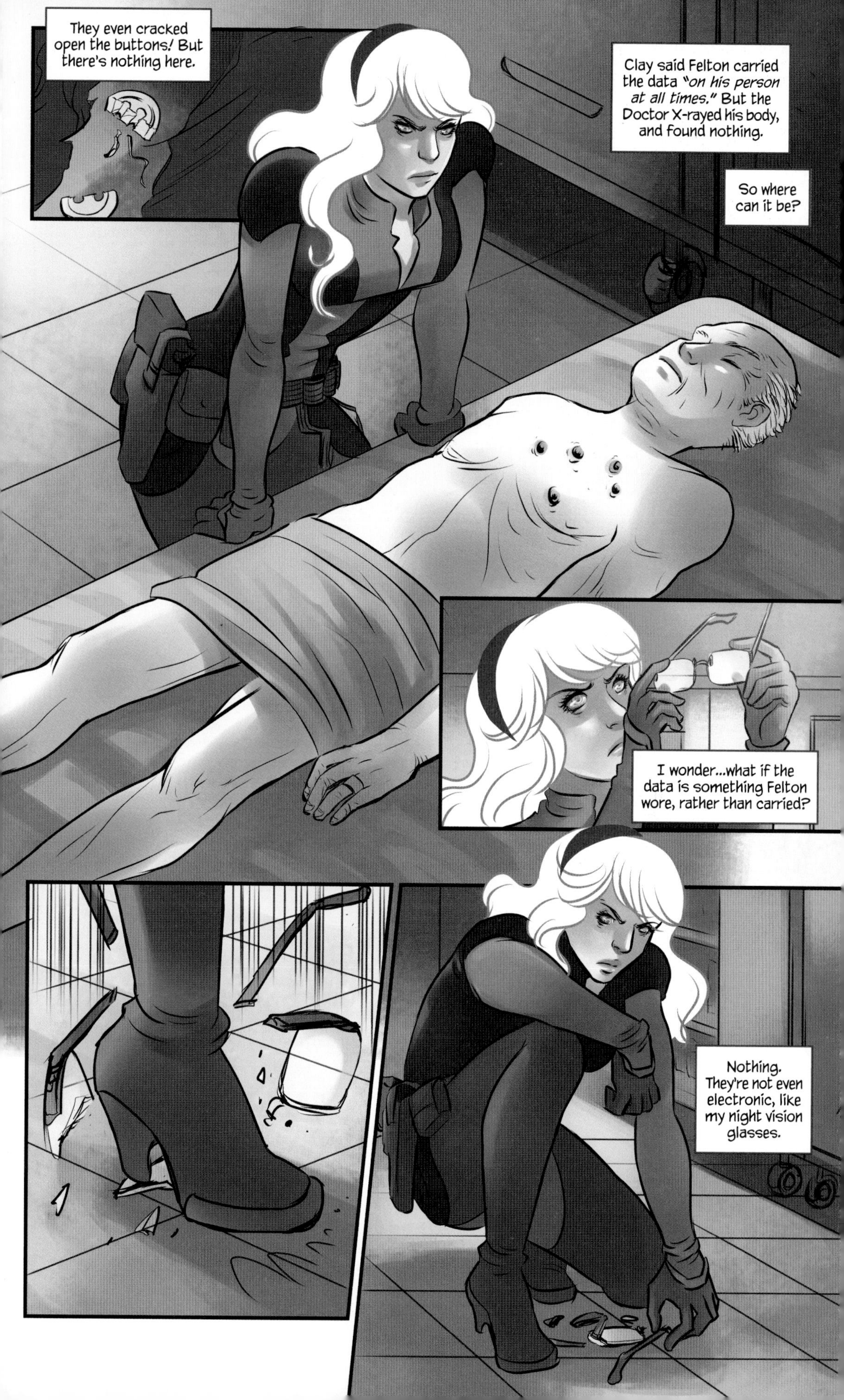
They even cracked open the buttons! But there's nothing here.
Clay said Felton carried the data *"on his person at all times."* But the Doctor X-rayed his body, and found nothing.
So where can it be?
I wonder...what if the data is something Felton wore, rather than carried?
Nothing. They're not even electronic, like my night vision glasses.

And he's not wearing anything else.

Except...

...his wedding ring!

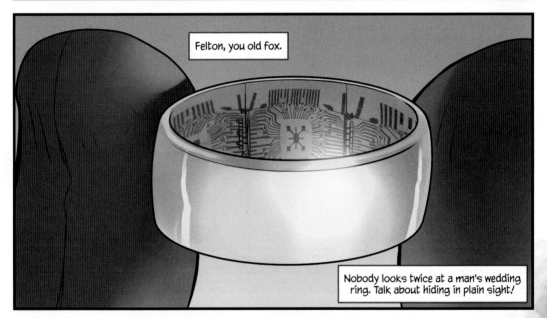

Felton, you old fox.

Nobody looks twice at a man's wedding ring. Talk about hiding in plain sight!

Two minutes, Contessa! You know I'm not the bluffing kind!

All right, Seamus. I'm ready.

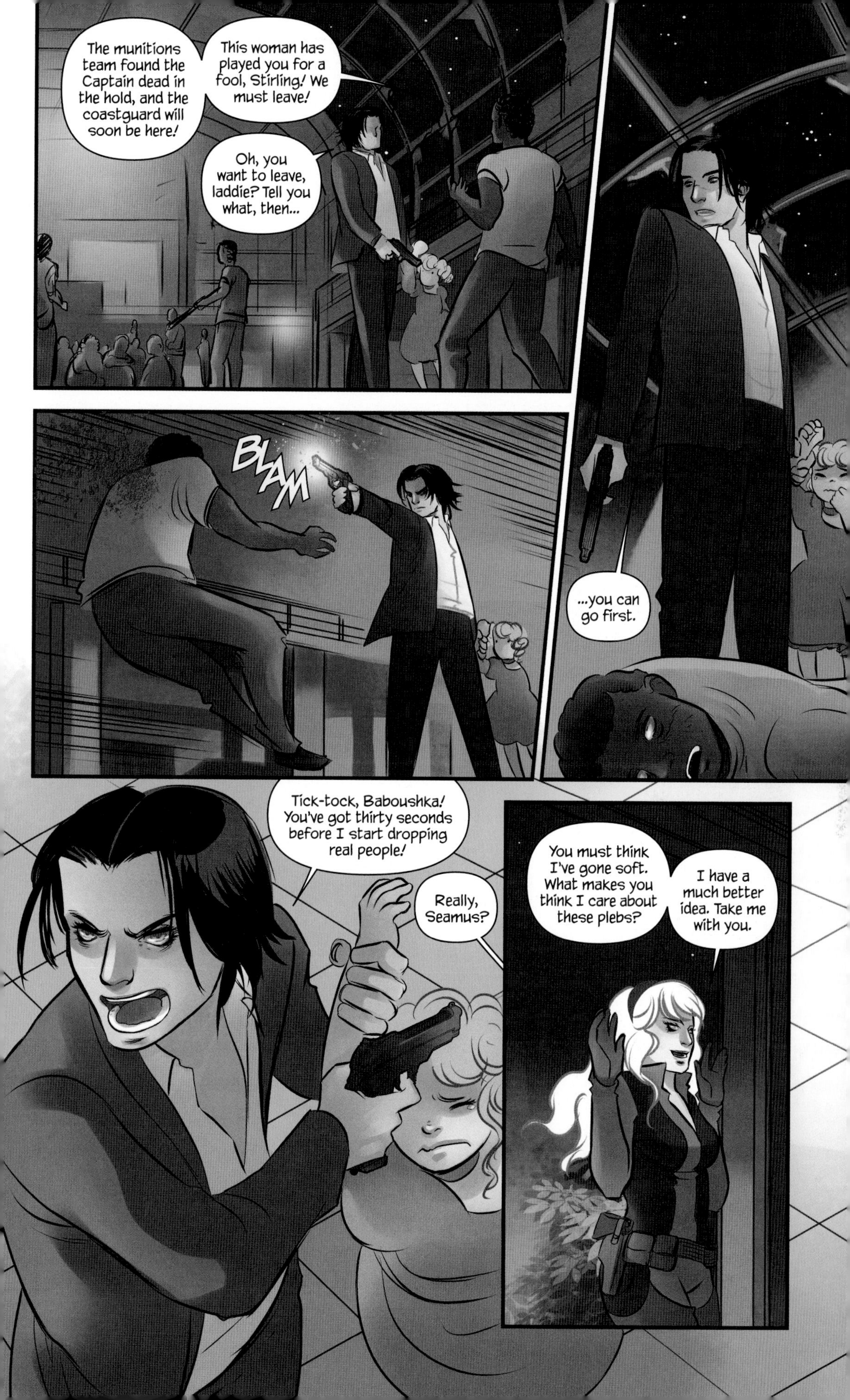
The munitions team found the Captain dead in the hold, and the coastguard will soon be here!
This woman has played you for a fool, Stirling! We must leave!
Oh, you want to leave, laddie? Tell you what, then...
BLAM
...you can go first.
Tick-tock, Baboushka! You've got thirty seconds before I start dropping real people!
Really, Seamus?
You must think I've gone soft. What makes you think I care about these plebs?
I have a much better idea. Take me with you.

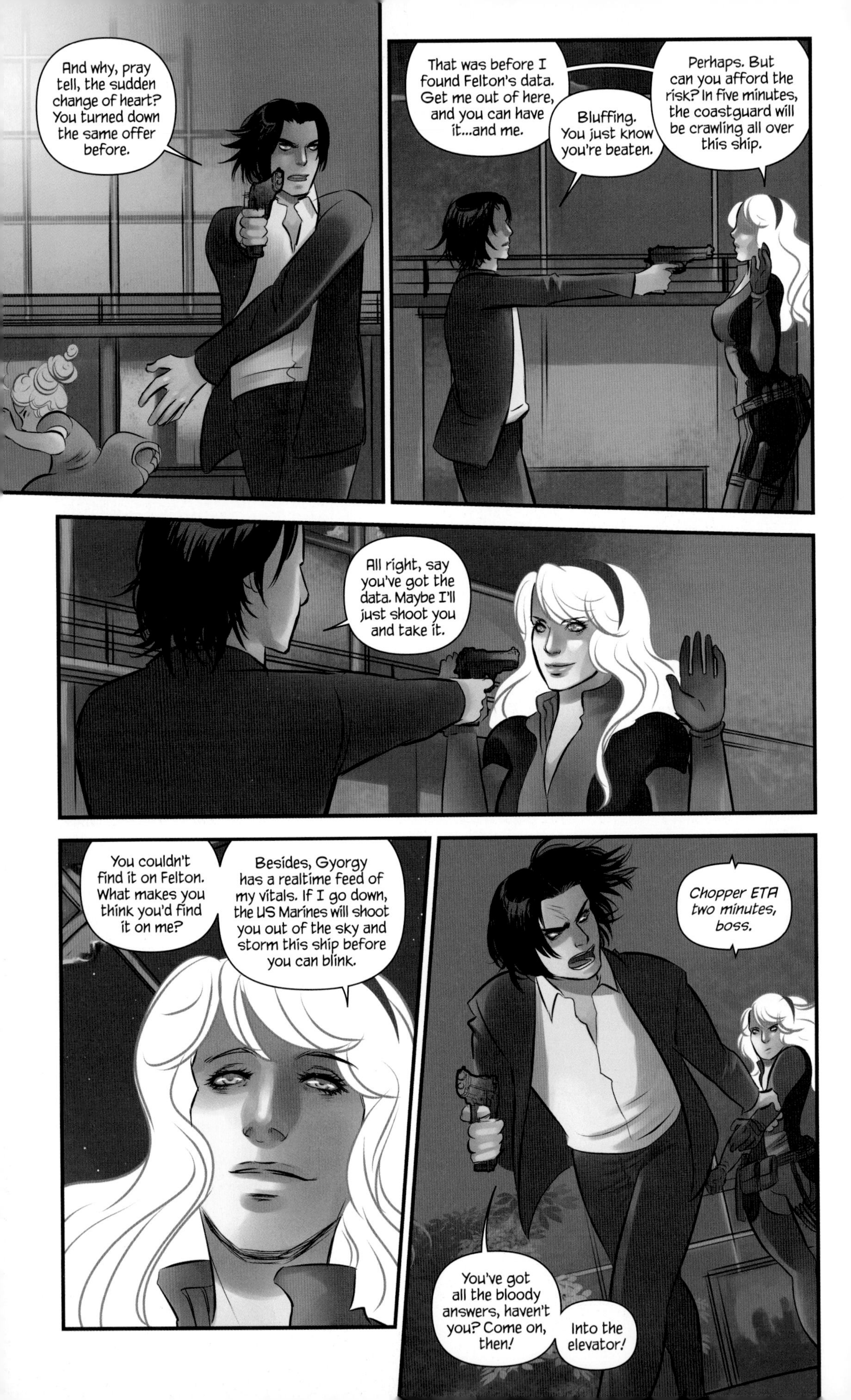
And why, pray tell, the sudden change of heart? You turned down the same offer before.
That was before I found Felton's data. Get me out of here, and you can have it...and me.
Bluffing. You just know you're beaten.
Perhaps. But can you afford the risk? In five minutes, the coastguard will be crawling all over this ship.
All right, say you've got the data. Maybe I'll just shoot you and take it.
You couldn't find it on Felton. What makes you think you'd find it on me?
Besides, Gyorgy has a realtime feed of my vitals. If I go down, the US Marines will shoot you out of the sky and storm this ship before you can blink.
Chopper ETA two minutes, boss.
You've got all the bloody answers, haven't you? Come on, then!
Into the elevator!

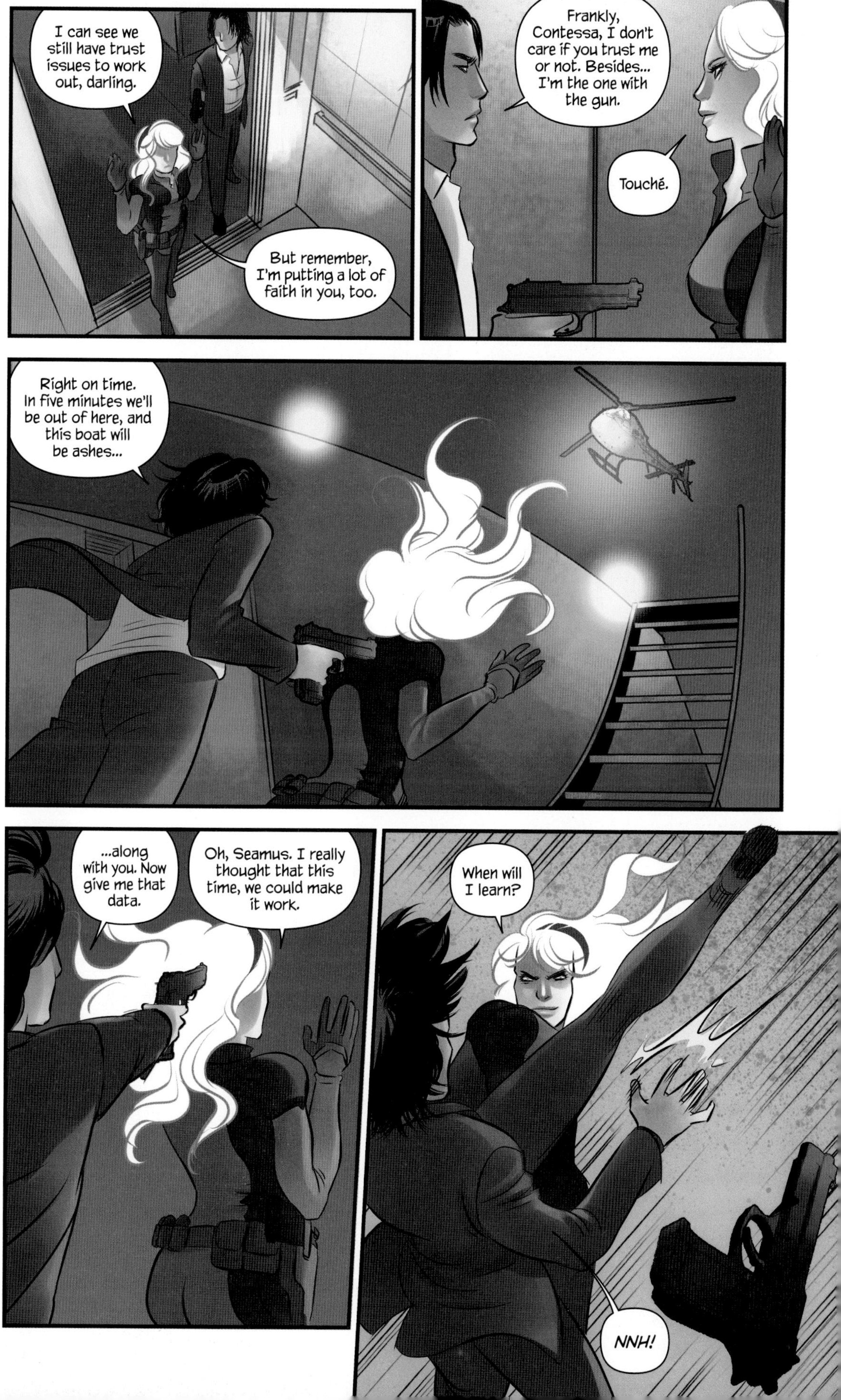
I can see we still have trust issues to work out, darling.
But remember, I'm putting a lot of faith in you, too.
Frankly, Contessa, I don't care if you trust me or not. Besides... I'm the one with the gun.
Touché.
Right on time. In five minutes we'll be out of here, and this boat will be ashes...
...along with you. Now give me that data.
Oh, Seamus. I really thought that this time, we could make it work.
When will I learn?
NNH!

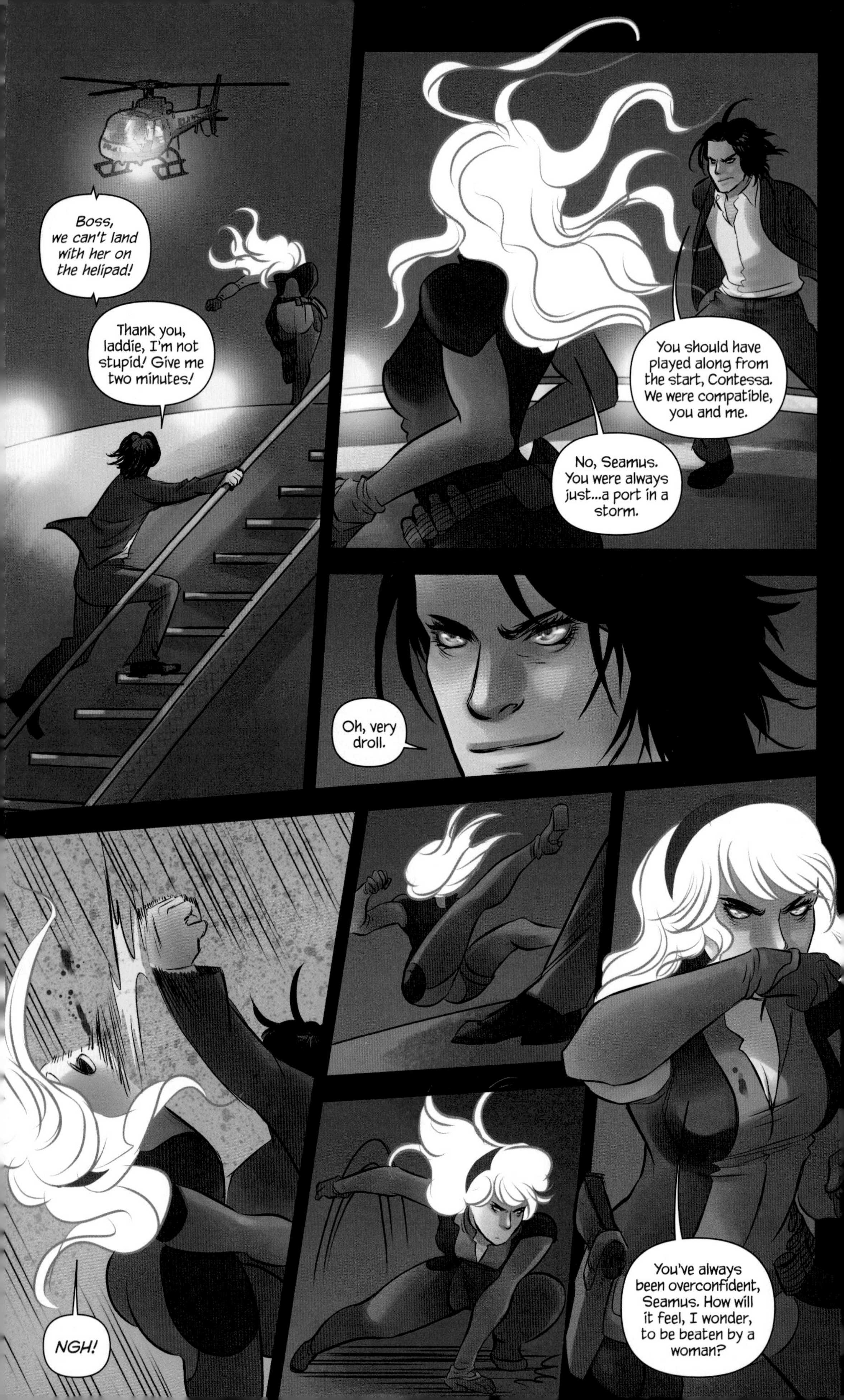
Boss, we can't land with her on the helipad!
Thank you, laddie, I'm not stupid! Give me two minutes!
You should have played along from the start, Contessa. We were compatible, you and me.
No, Seamus. You were always just...a port in a storm.
Oh, very droll.
NGH!
You've always been overconfident, Seamus. How will it feel, I wonder, to be beaten by a woman?

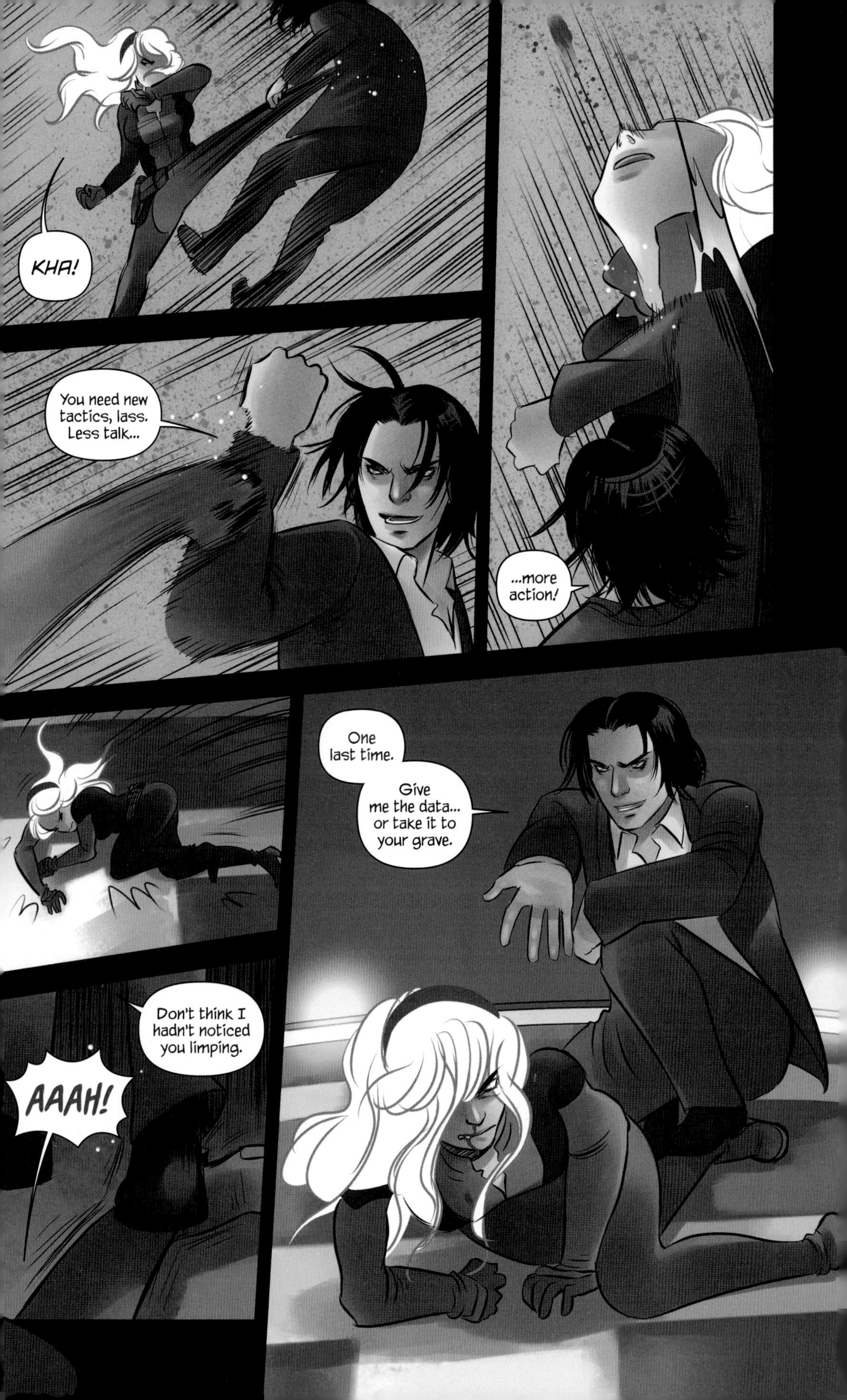
KHA!
You need new tactics, lass. Less talk...
...more action!
AAAH!
Don't think I hadn't noticed you limping.
One last time.
Give me the data... or take it to your grave.

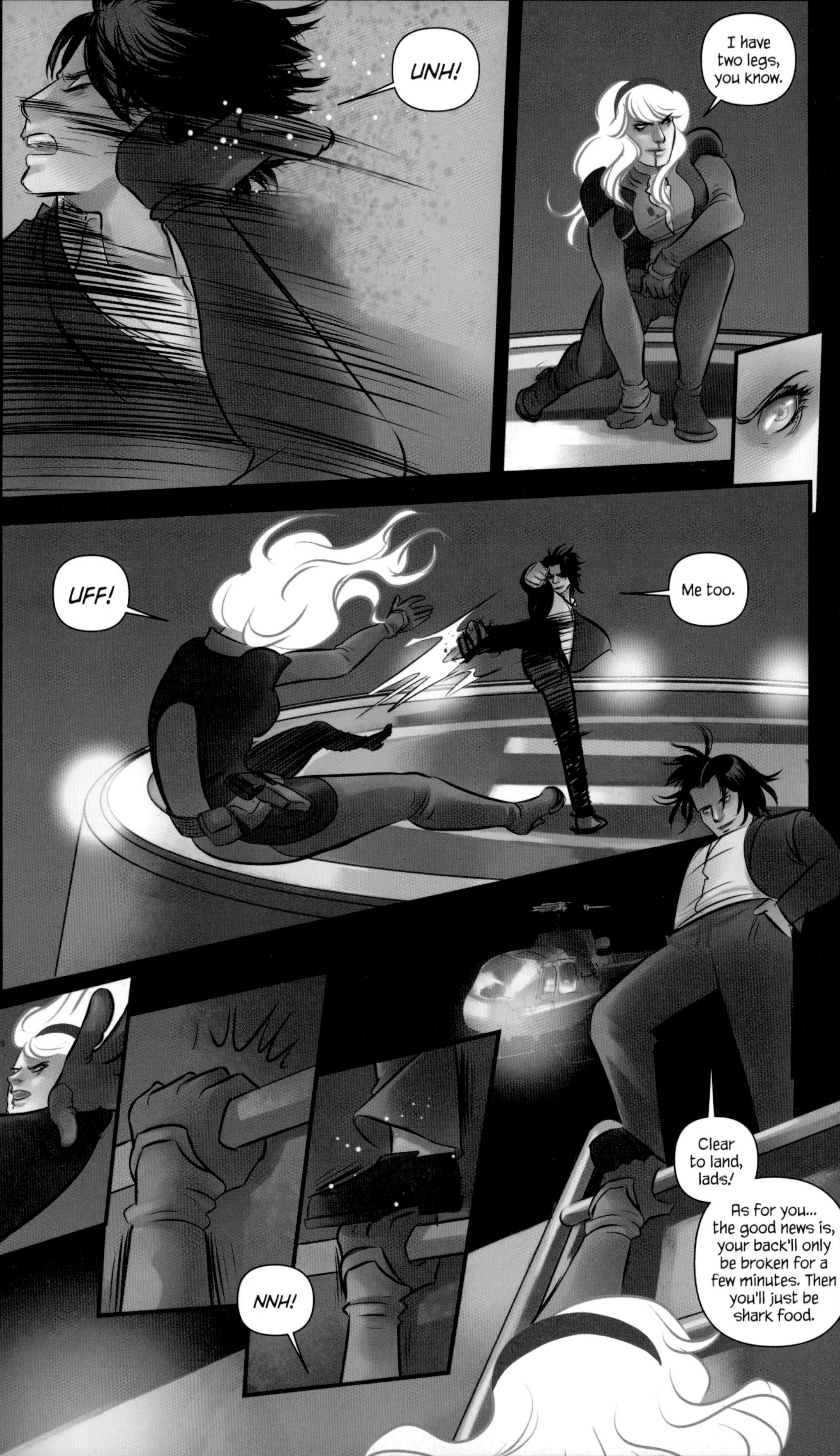
UNH!
I have two legs, you know.
UFF!
Me too.
Clear to land, lads!
As for you... the good news is, your back'll only be broken for a few minutes. Then you'll just be shark food.
NNH!

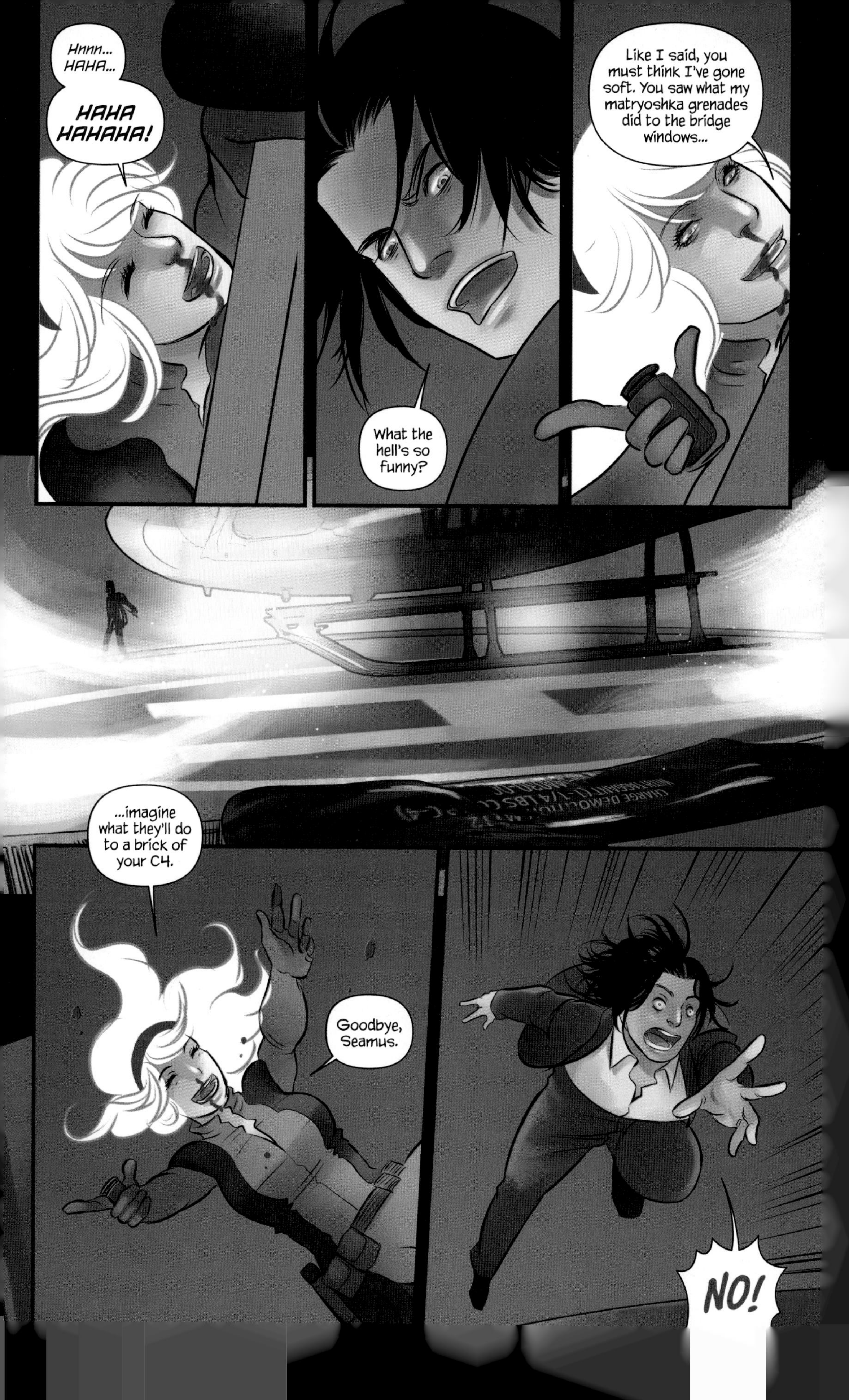
Hnnn... HAHA...
HAHA HAHAHA!
What the hell's so funny?
Like I said, you must think I've gone soft. You saw what my matryoshka grenades did to the bridge windows...
...imagine what they'll do to a brick of your C4.
Goodbye, Seamus.
NO!

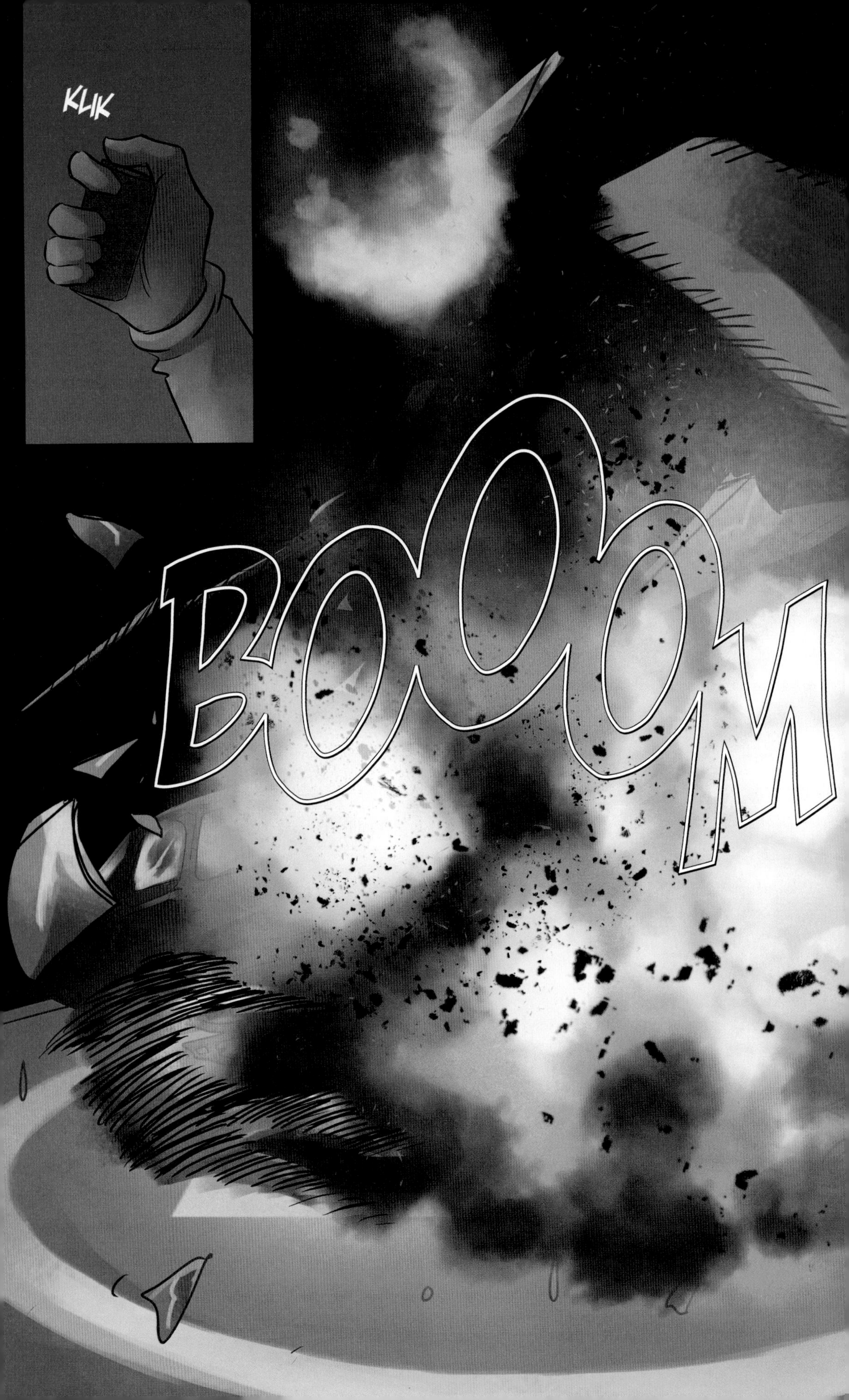
KLIK
BOOOM

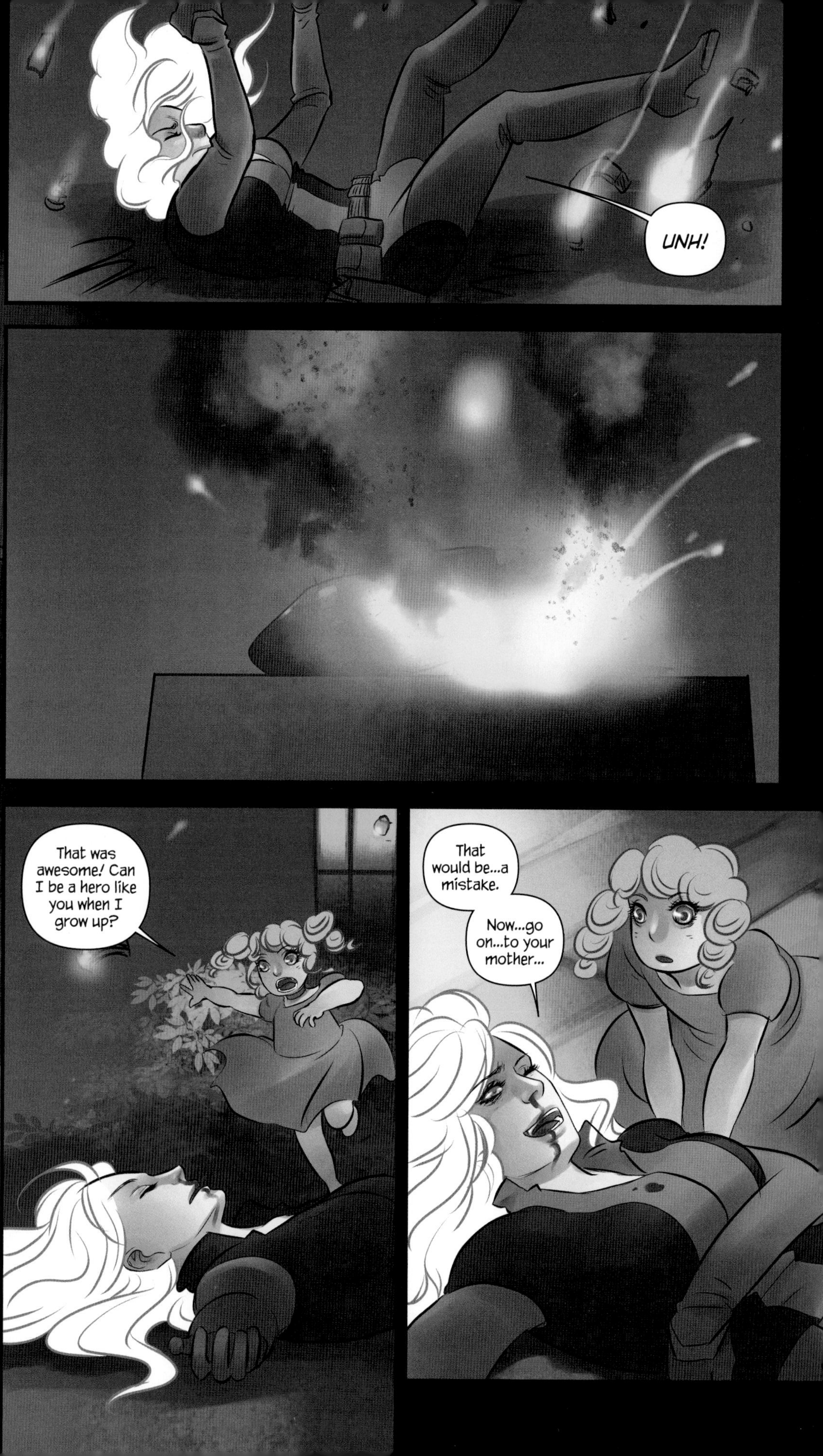
UNH!
That was awesome! Can I be a hero like you when I grow up?
That would be...a mistake.
Now...go on...to your mother...

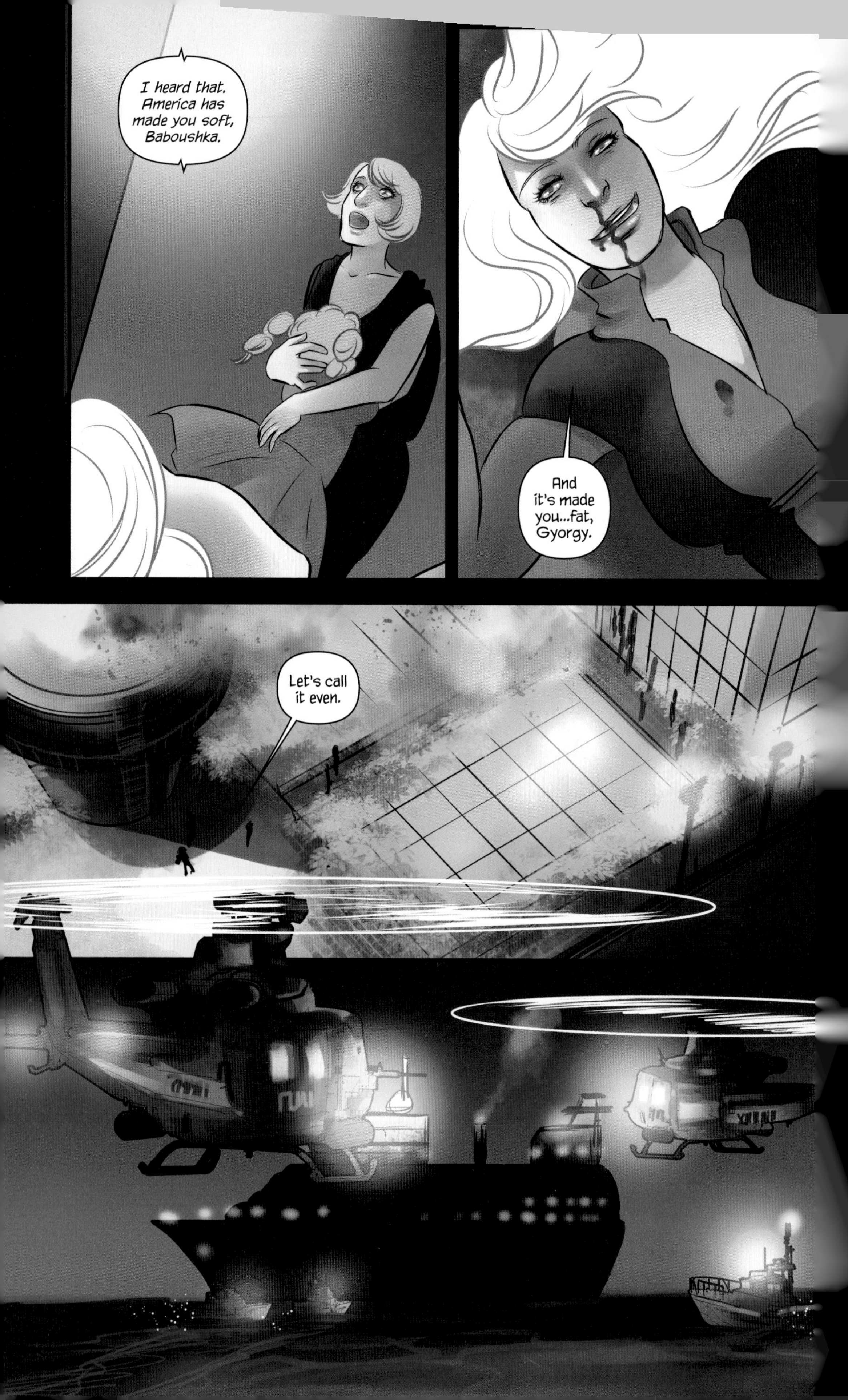
I heard that. America has made you soft, Baboushka.
And it's made you...fat, Gyorgy.
Let's call it even.

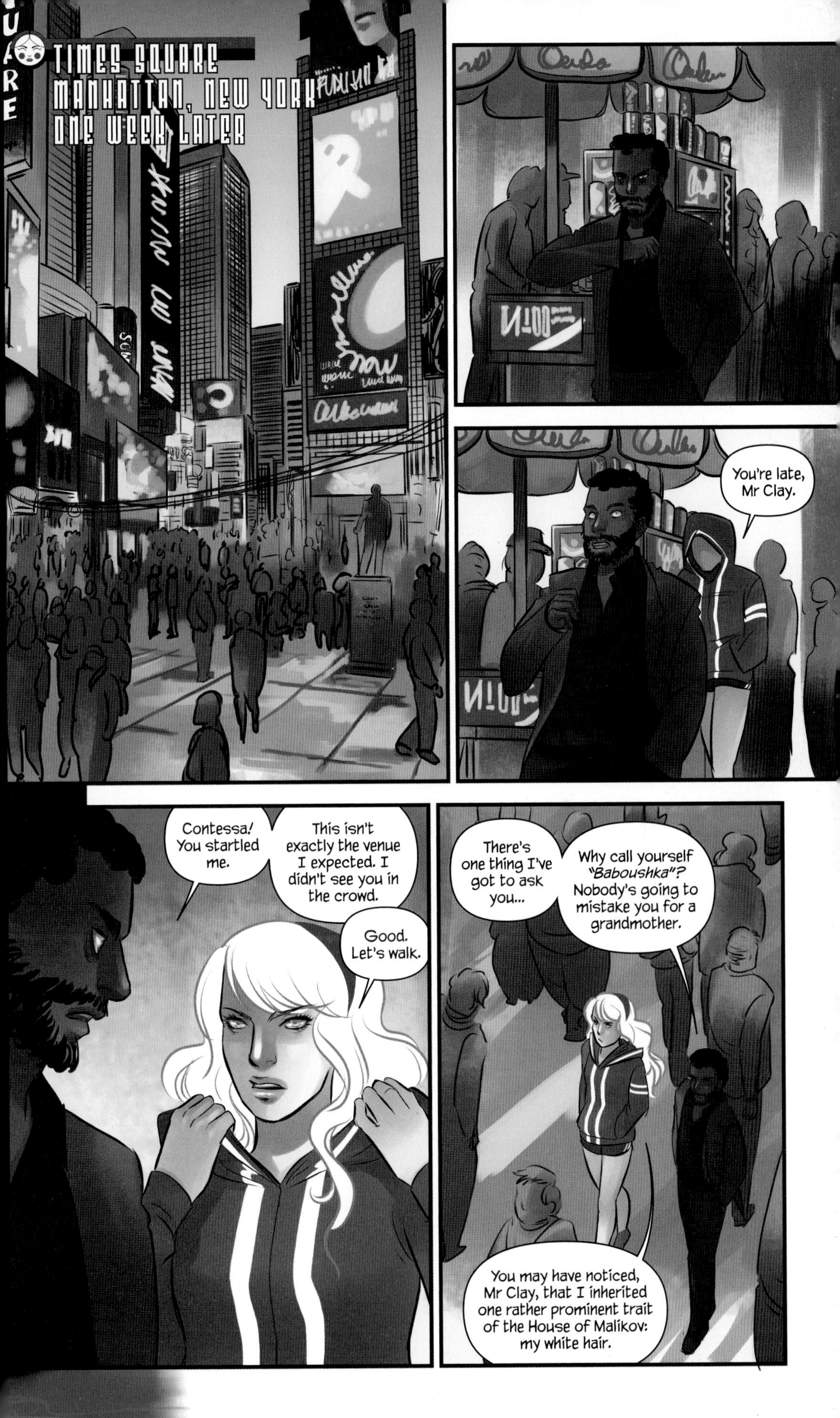
TIMES SQUARE
MANHATTAN, NEW YORK
ONE WEEK LATER
You're late, Mr Clay.
Contessa! You startled me.
This isn't exactly the venue I expected. I didn't see you in the crowd.
Good. Let's walk.
There's one thing I've got to ask you...
Why call yourself "*Baboushka*"? Nobody's going to mistake you for a grandmother.
You may have noticed, Mr Clay, that I inherited one rather prominent trait of the House of Malikov: my white hair.

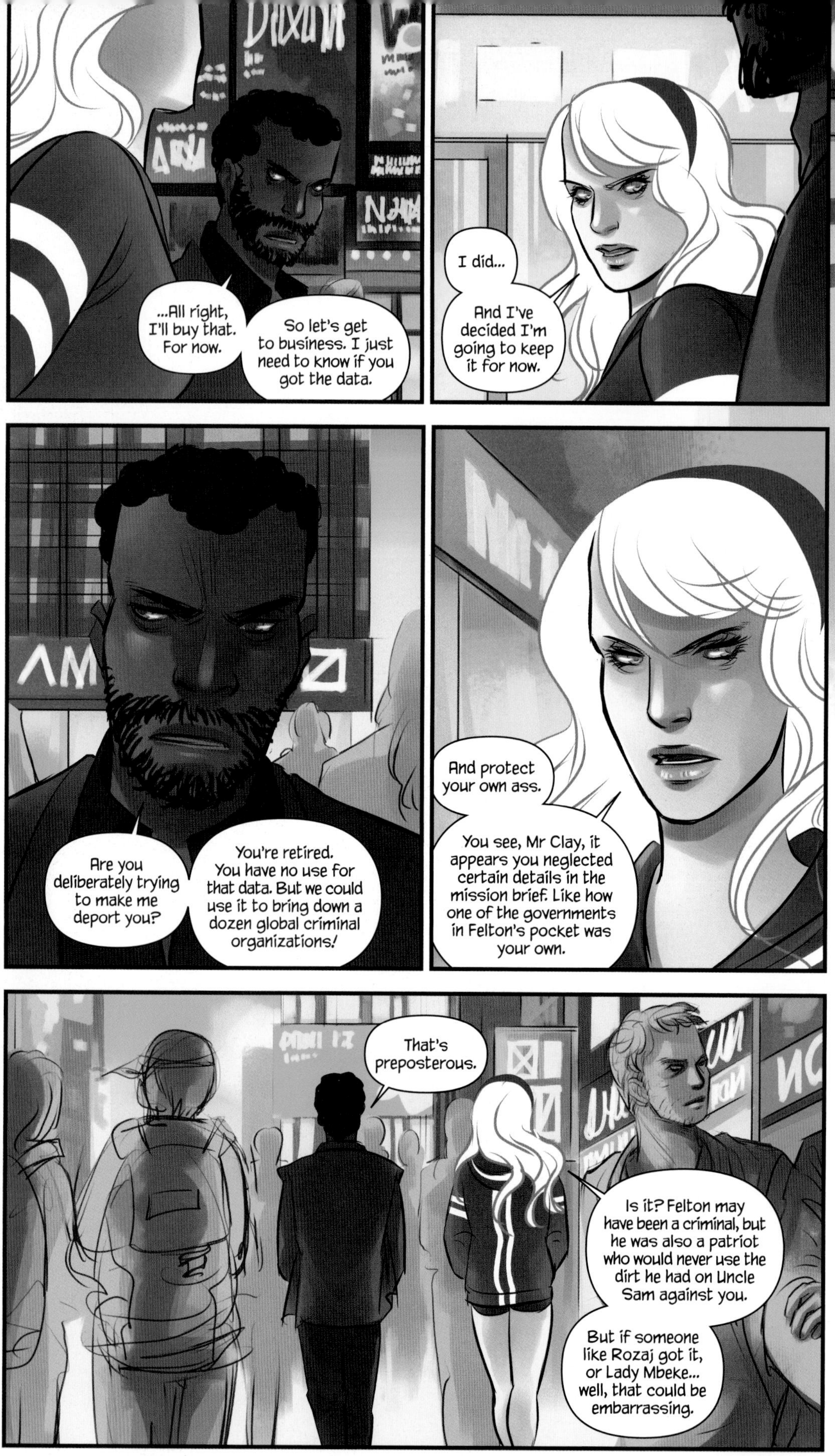

...All right, I'll buy that. For now.
So let's get to business. I just need to know if you got the data.
I did...
And I've decided I'm going to keep it for now.
Are you deliberately trying to make me deport you?
You're retired. You have no use for that data. But we could use it to bring down a dozen global criminal organizations!
And protect your own ass.
You see, Mr Clay, it appears you neglected certain details in the mission brief. Like how one of the governments in Felton's pocket was your own.
That's preposterous.
Is it? Felton may have been a criminal, but he was also a patriot who would never use the dirt he had on Uncle Sam against you.
But if someone like Rozaj got it, or Lady Mbeke... well, that could be embarrassing.

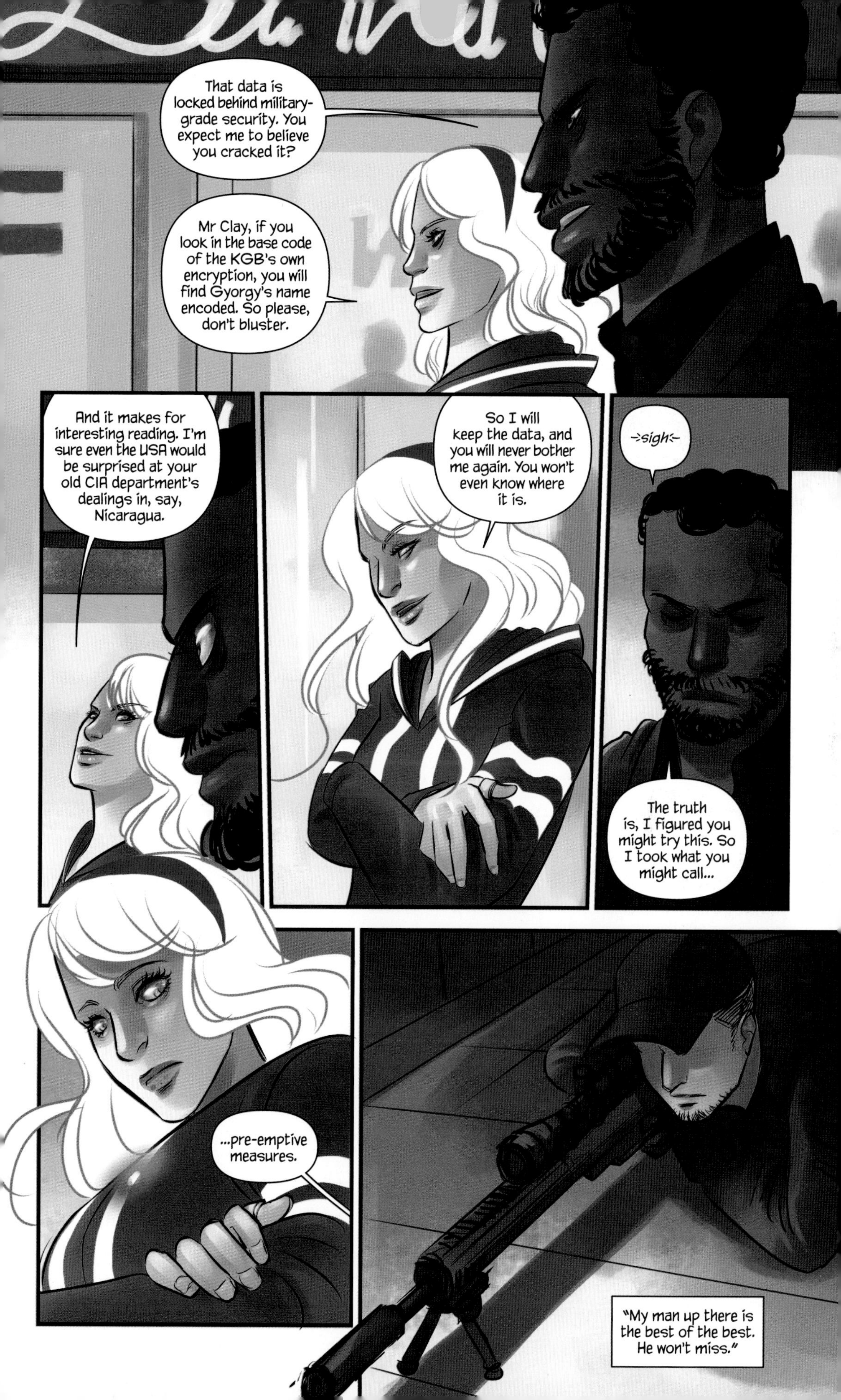

That data is locked behind military-grade security. You expect me to believe you cracked it?
Mr Clay, if you look in the base code of the KGB's own encryption, you will find Gyorgy's name encoded. So please, don't bluster.
And it makes for interesting reading. I'm sure even the USA would be surprised at your old CIA department's dealings in, say, Nicaragua.
So I will keep the data, and you will never bother me again. You won't even know where it is.
-sigh-
The truth is, I figured you might try this. So I took what you might call...
...pre-emptive measures.
"My man up there is the best of the best. He won't miss."

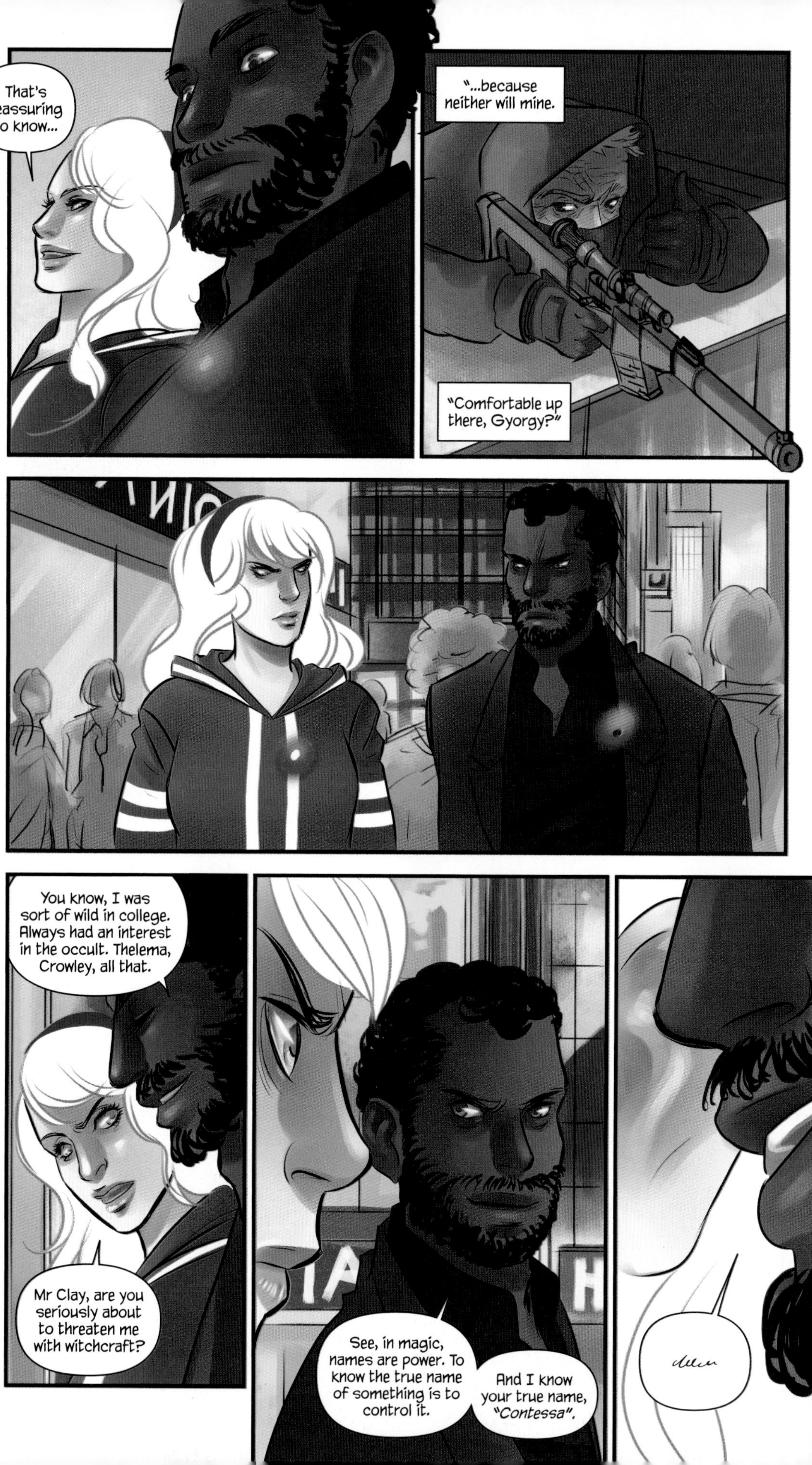
That's reassuring to know...
"...because neither will mine.
"Comfortable up there, Gyorgy?"
You know, I was sort of wild in college. Always had an interest in the occult. Thelema, Crowley, all that.
Mr Clay, are you seriously about to threaten me with witchcraft?
See, in magic, names are power. To know the true name of something is to control it.
And I know your true name, "Contessa".

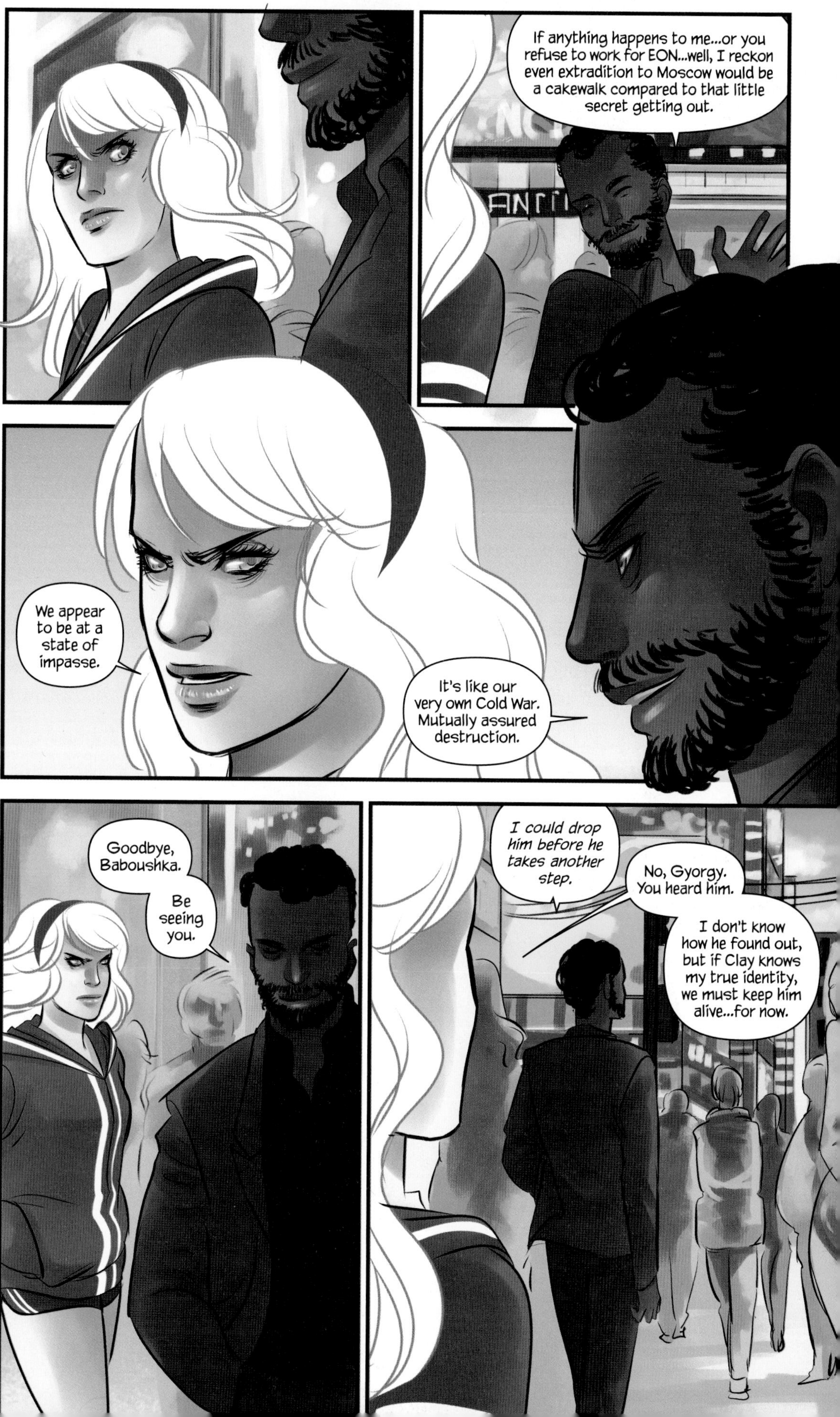
If anything happens to me...or you refuse to work for EON...well, I reckon even extradition to Moscow would be a cakewalk compared to that little secret getting out.
We appear to be at a state of impasse.
It's like our very own Cold War. Mutually assured destruction.
Goodbye, Baboushka.
Be seeing you.
I could drop him before he takes another step.
No, Gyorgy. You heard him.
I don't know how he found out, but if Clay knows my true identity, we must keep him alive...for now.

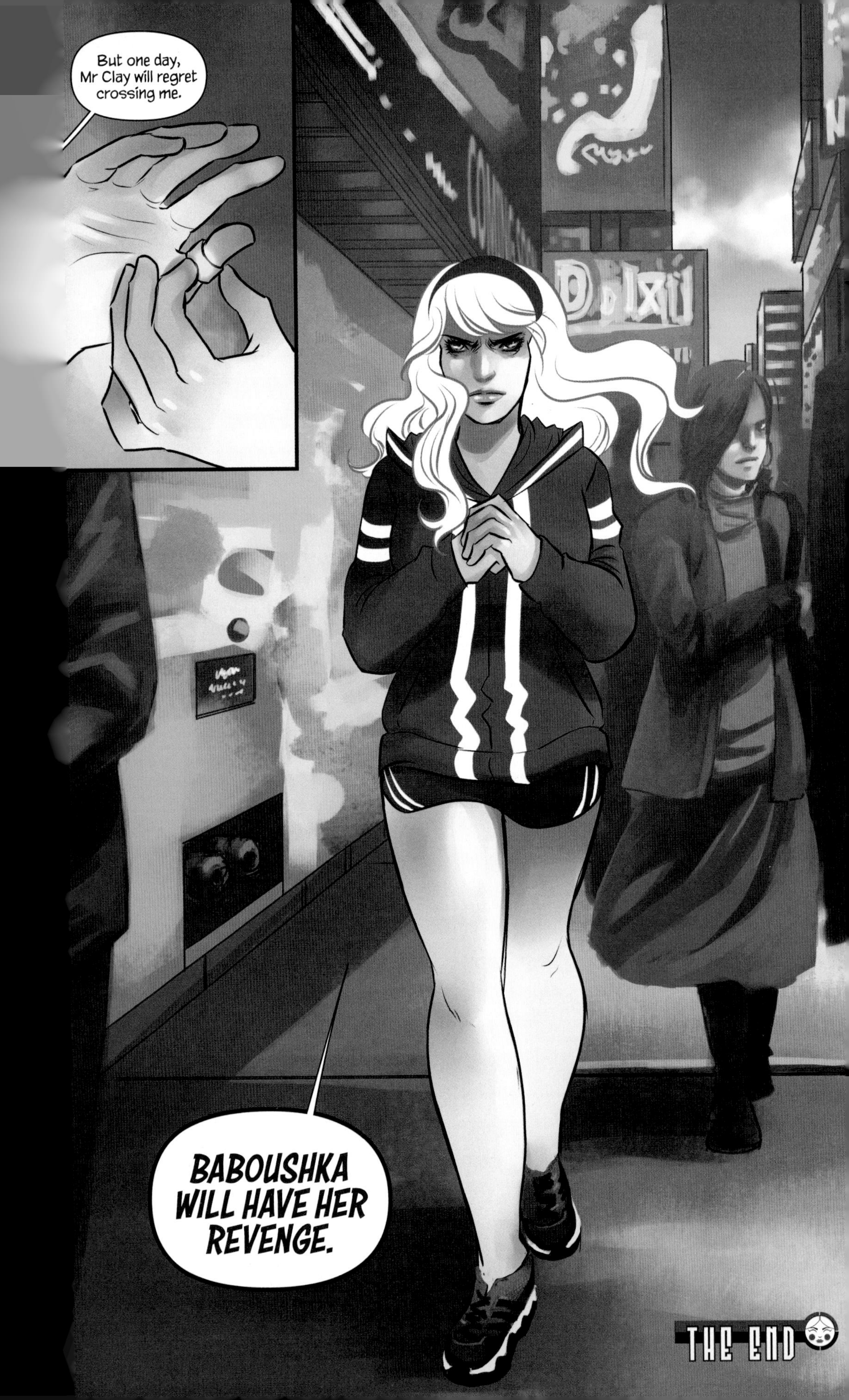
But one day, Mr Clay will regret crossing me.
BABOUSHKA WILL HAVE HER REVENGE.
THE END

CODENAME ★BABOUSHKA★

WILL RETURN

IN

"GHOST STATION ZERO"

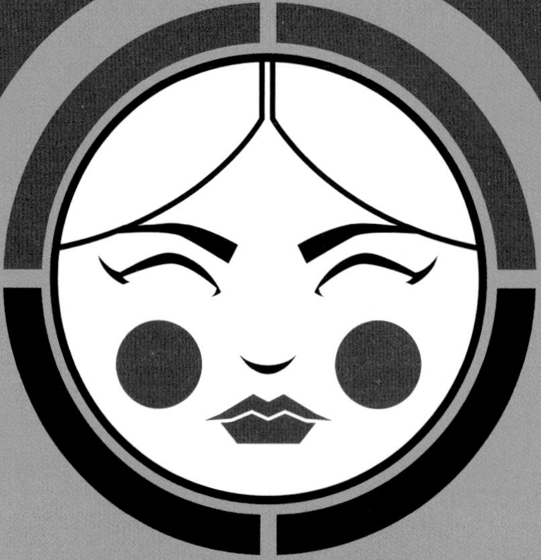

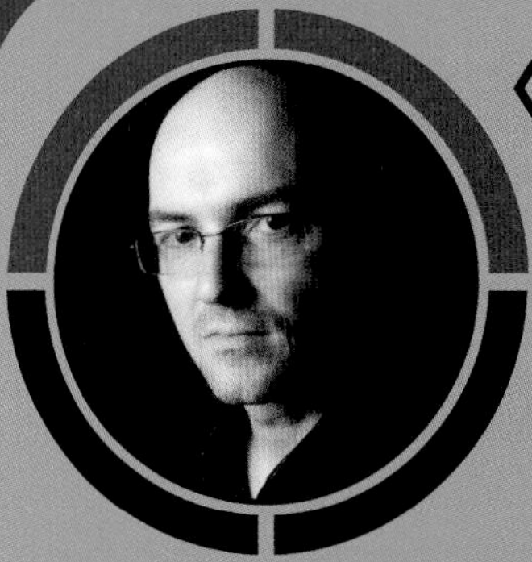

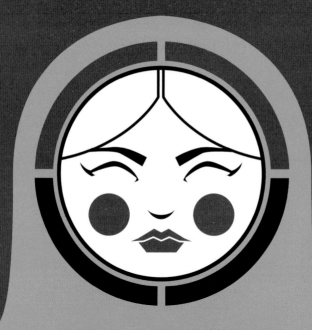

ANTONY JOHNSTON

is an award-winning, *New York Times* bestselling author of graphic novels, videogames, and books, whose work includes *The Fuse* (which Shari colors), *The Coldest City*, *Wasteland*, *Dead Space*, *Shadow of Mordor*, *ZombiU*, and more. He lives and works in England.

ANTONYJOHNSTON.COM / @ANTONYJOHNSTON

SHARI CHANKHAMMA

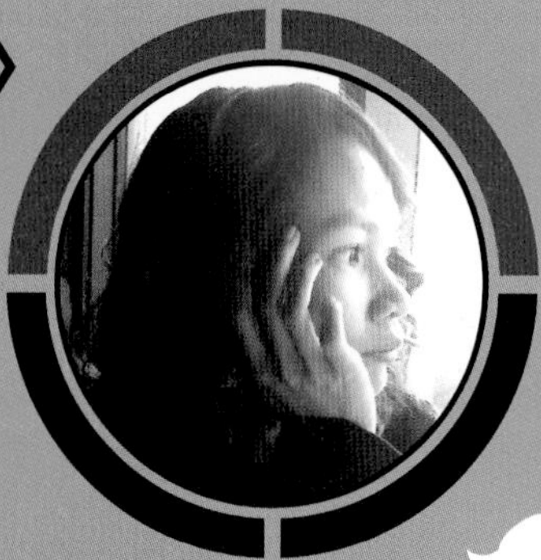

lives in Thailand and, as well as drawing *Codename Baboushka*, colors books like *The Fuse* (which Antony writes), *Sheltered*, and *Kill Shakespeare*. She also wrote and illustrated *The Sisters' Luck*, *The Clarence Principle*, *Pavlov's Dream*, and short stories in various anthologies.

SHARII.COM / @SHARIHES

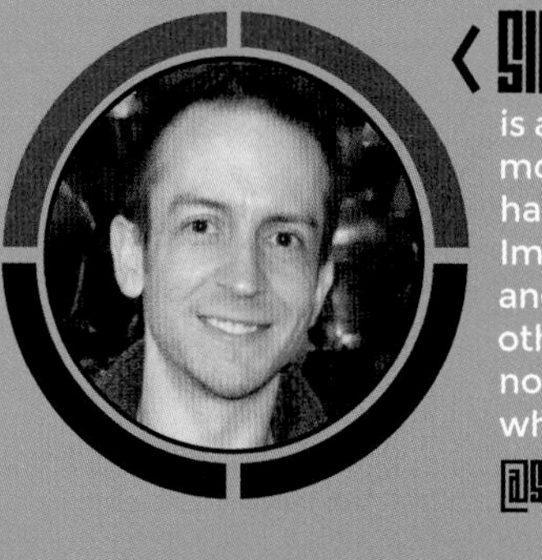

SIMON BOWLAND

is a comic book letterer of more than ten years, who has worked for Marvel, Image, 2000AD, Dynamite and Dark Horse, amongst others. He hails from the north-west of England, where he still lives today.

@SIMONBOWLAND

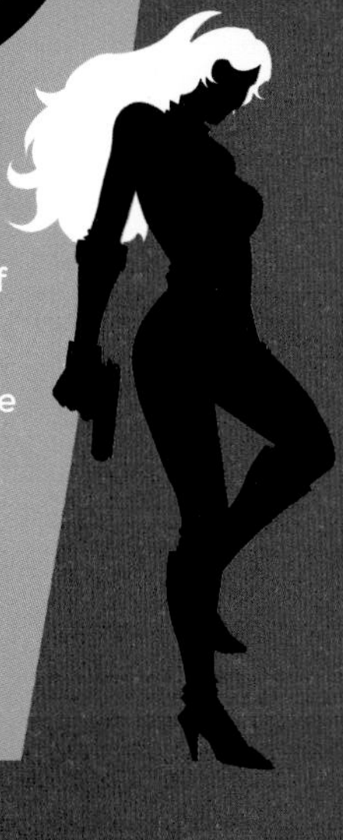

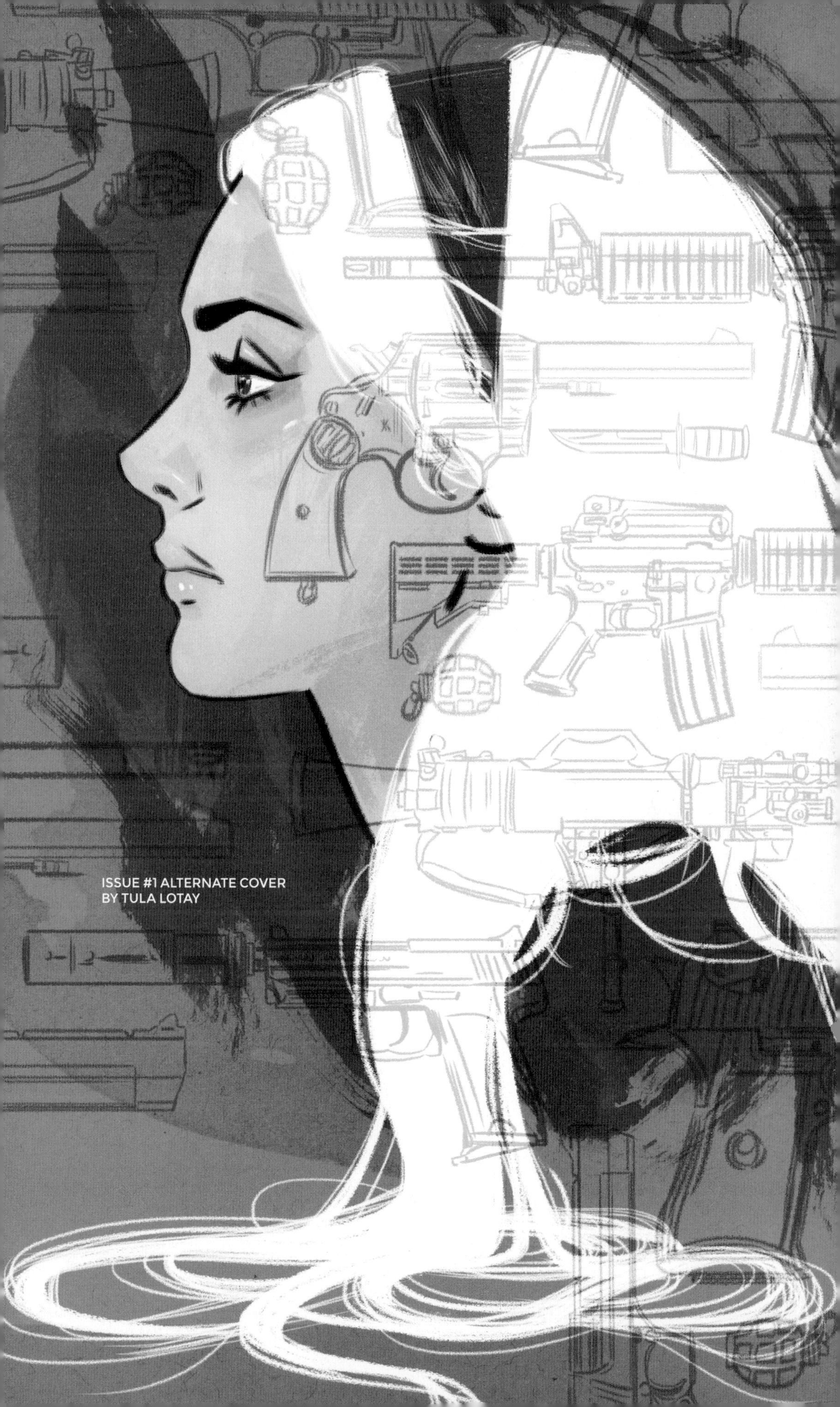

ISSUE #1 ALTERNATE COVER
BY TULA LOTAY

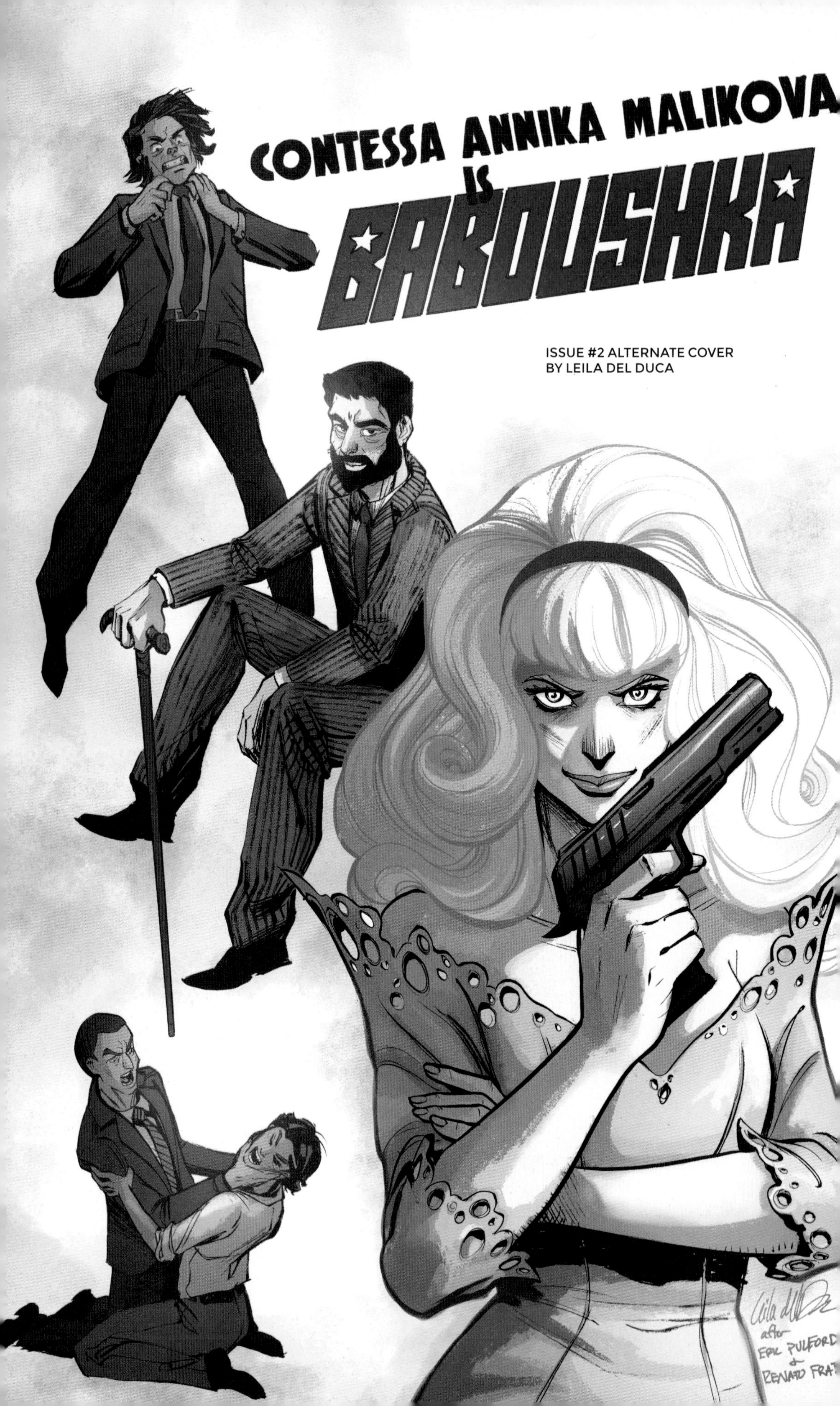
CONTESSA ANNIKA MALIKOVA
IS
BABOUSHKA

ISSUE #2 ALTERNATE COVER
BY LEILA DEL DUCA

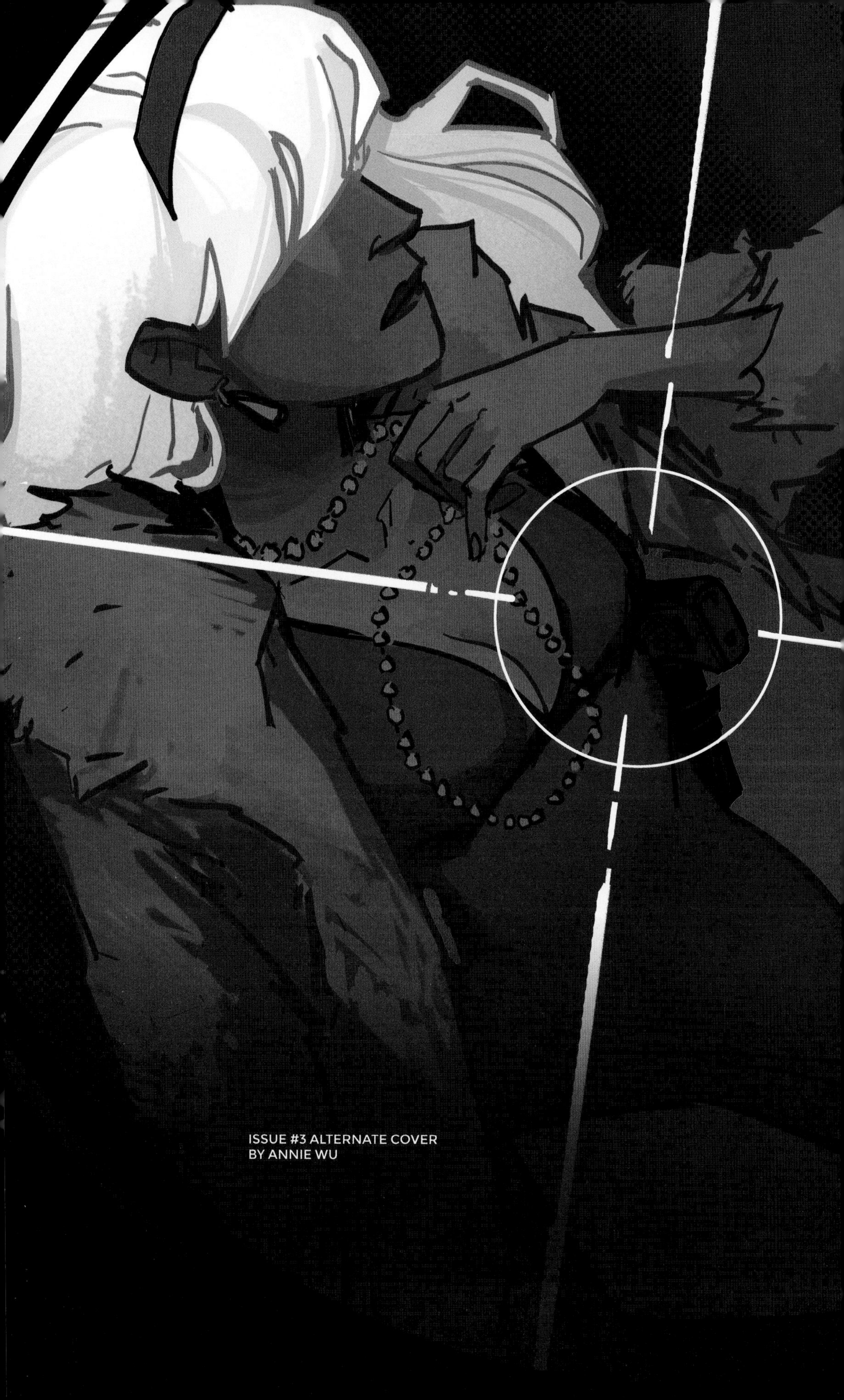
ISSUE #3 ALTERNATE COVER
BY ANNIE WU

ISSUE #4 ALTERNATE COVER
BY TESS FOWLER & TAMRA BONVILLAIN

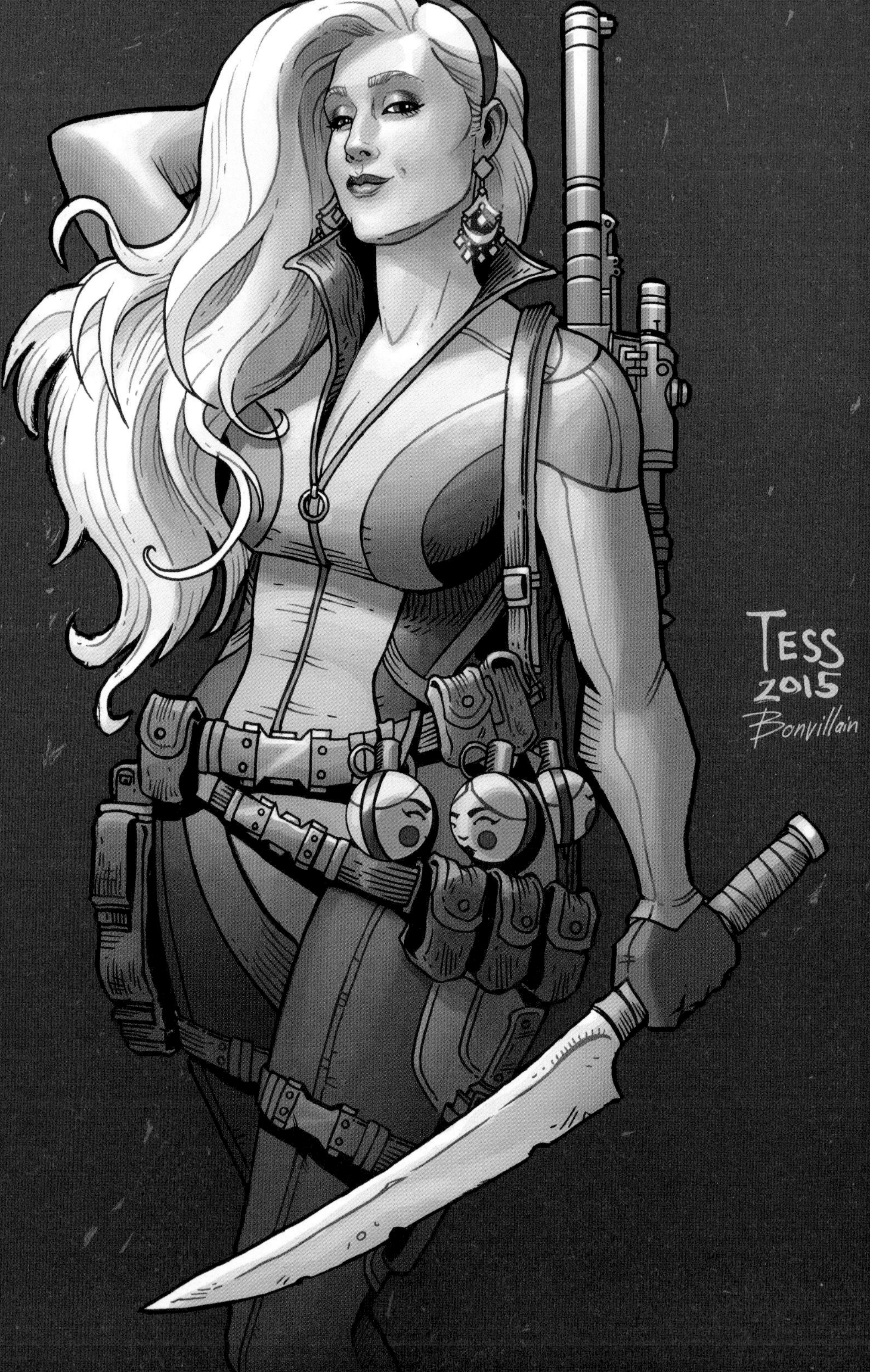
TESS
2015
Bonvillain

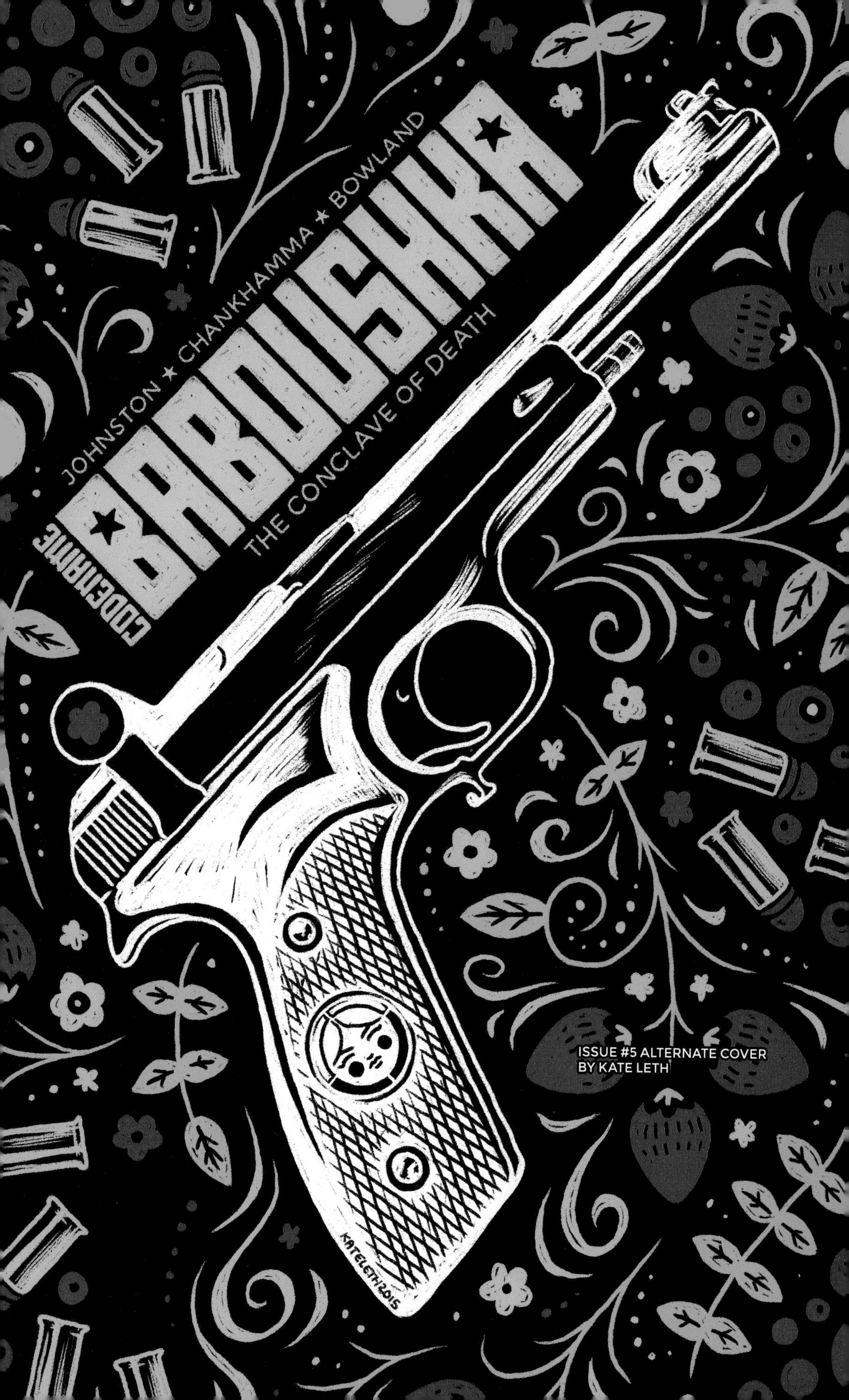
CODENAME
BABUSHKA
JOHNSTON ★ CHANKHAMMA ★ BOWLAND
THE CONCLAVE OF DEATH
KATELETH 2015

ISSUE #5 ALTERNATE COVER
BY KATE LETH

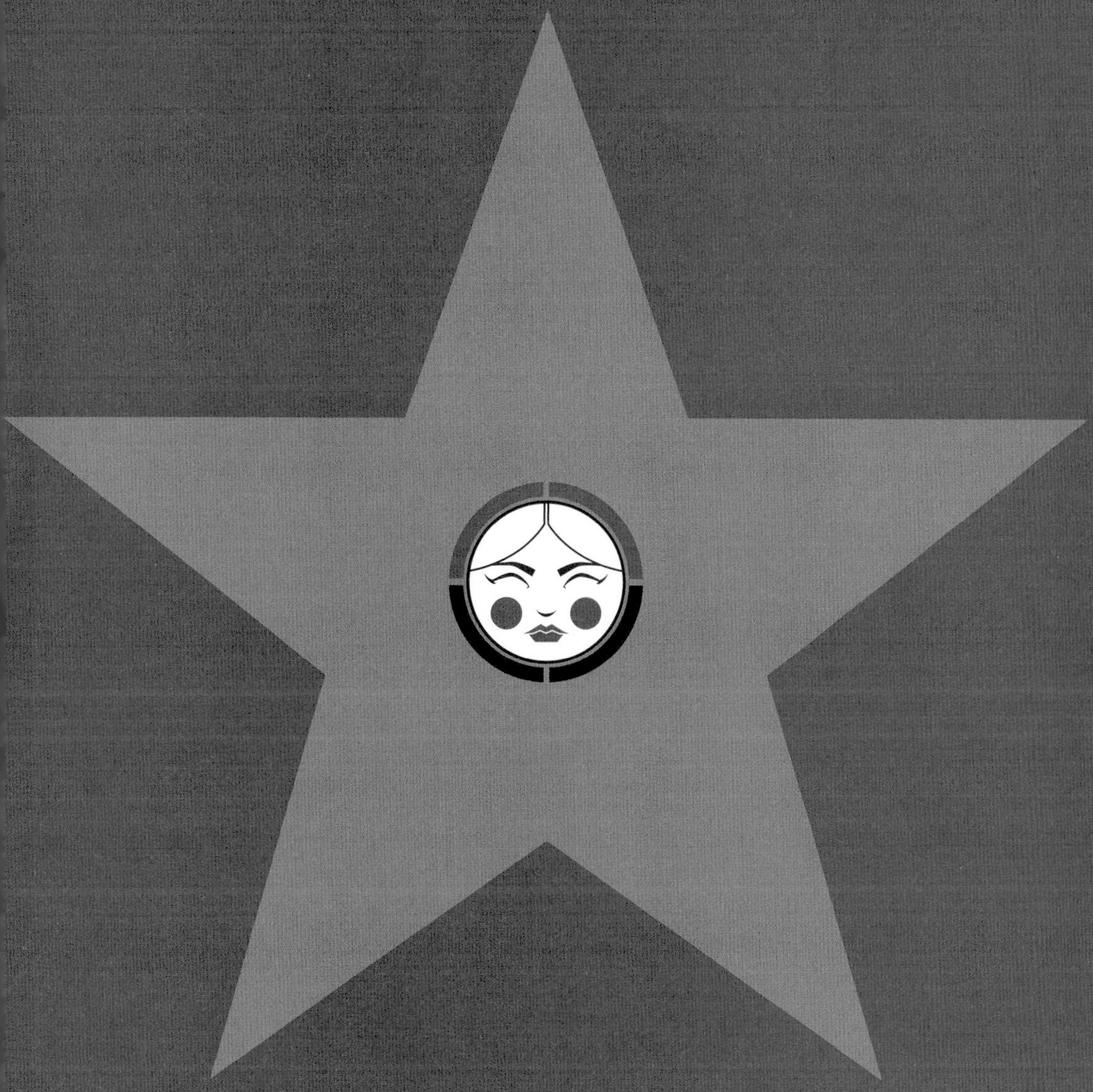

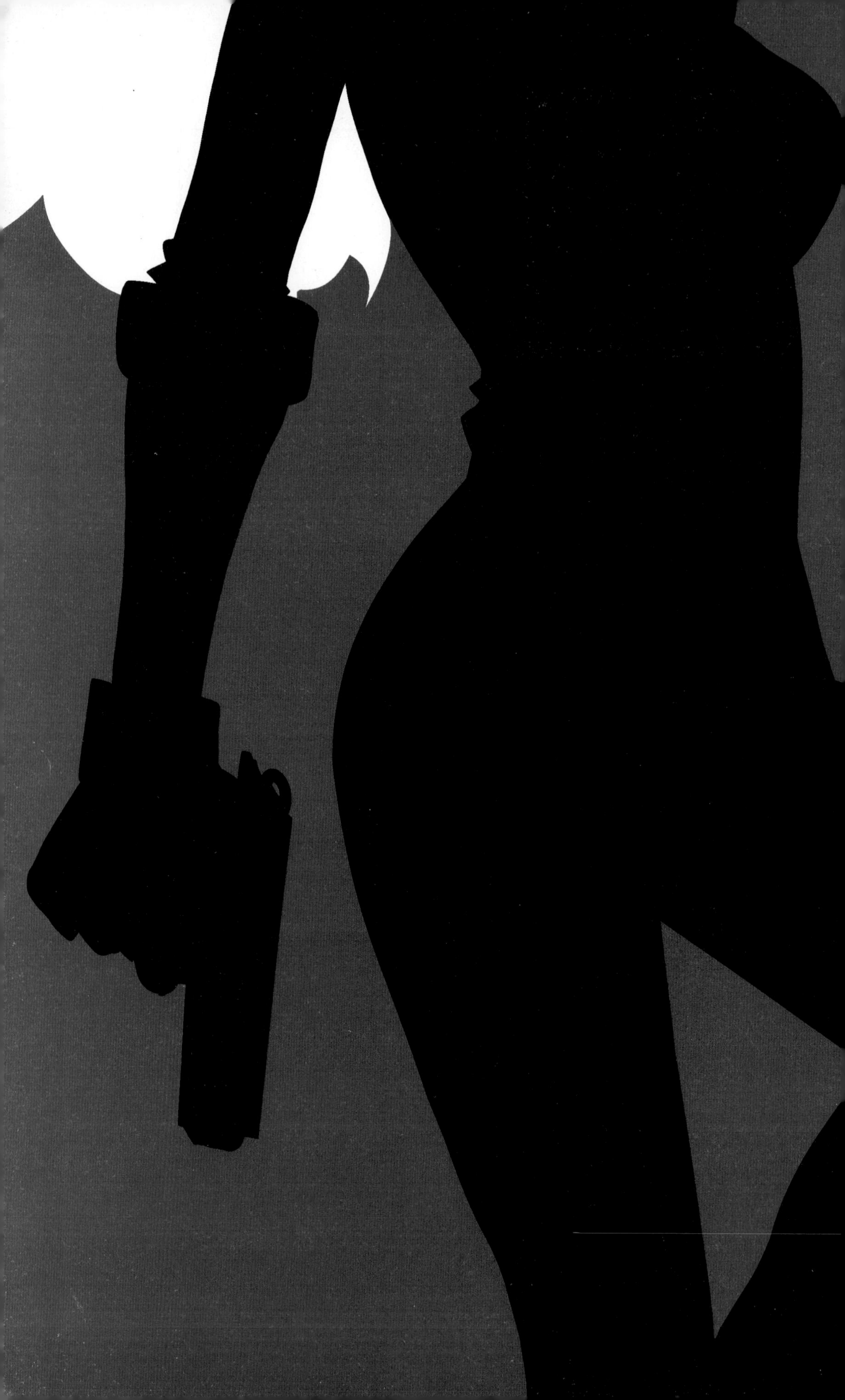